PRAISI
MATTHEW FI

PRAISE FOR *CONSTANCE*

An Amazon Best Book of the Month:
Science Fiction & Fantasy

"Maybe what we need most as this bewildering summer winds down is a diverting story about an interesting futuristic topic that injects no new anxiety into our nervous brains . . . [*Constance*] shines in its interstitial moments . . . In between the sleuthing and the schemes for world domination and the eluding of people with guns, we are invited to grapple with genuinely thoughtful questions about the philosophical, legal, and ethical implications of cloning and scientific innovation in general . . . The debates around cloning in *Constance* echo many of our contemporary preoccupations—skepticism of science, radical mistrust of those with opposing views, conspiracy theories."

—Sarah Lyall, critic, *The New York Times*

"Full of technological surprises and ethical dilemmas, this inventive thriller hums with the electric excitement of the best 1950s science fiction."

—Tom Nolan, critic, *The Wall Street Journal*

"In this timely thriller, tantalizing clues, complex motives, and shifting views of the truth flow around such issues as the relationship between money and power, the right to life, and the definition of self. FitzSimmons has upped his game with this one."

—*Publishers Weekly* (starred review)

"A super-brainy high-concept dystopian tale guaranteed to reward anyone who's in the mood."

—*Kirkus Reviews*

"A propulsive sci-fi thriller that questions the very nature of what makes us human."

—POPSUGAR

"What a book! Like all the best speculative fiction, FitzSimmons's compelling thriller *Constance* takes elements of real science and spins them up into a novel and terrifying premise."

—Blake Crouch, *New York Times* bestselling author of *Dark Matter* and *Recursion*

"*Constance* is a blistering, balletic read—silky-smooth world building that effortlessly grounds a wonderful, harrowing tale of mystery, suspense, identity, friendship, and redemption. This is, for all its twists, turns, and tricks, a novel that does what a novel should do: examine what makes us human after all. Genuinely one of the best books I have read in a long, long time."

—Greg Rucka, *New York Times* bestselling author and creator of *The Old Guard*

PRAISE FOR *ORIGAMI MAN*

"FitzSimmons brings Gibson Vaughn and an old enemy full circle in *Origami Man*—an intricately plotted, rapid-fire thriller guaranteed to hook you from page one. Easily the best Gibson Vaughn installment to date."

—Steven Konkoly, *Wall Street Journal* bestselling author

"Matthew FitzSimmons's rapid-fire novels are loaded with twisted plots, explosive action, and dialogue that crackles with wit and emotion. His bighearted characters keep me coming back, book after book. Grab this thriller with both hands because *Origami Man* is a total blast."

—Nick Petrie, bestselling author of *The Drifter*

PRAISE FOR *DEBRIS LINE*

"Matthew FitzSimmons writes the kinds of thrillers I love to read: smart, character driven, and brimming with creative action sequences. If you're not yet a fan of FitzSimmons's Gibson Vaughn series, strap in, because you soon will be. *Debris Line* is tense, twisty, and always ten steps ahead. Don't miss it."

—Chris Holm, Anthony Award–winning author of *The Killing Kind*

"Matt FitzSimmons continues his amazing literary feat of creating an ensemble cast of troubled heroes and shooting them through page-turning thrillers with his latest, *Debris Line*, continuing the fast-paced adventures of Gibson Vaughn and his crew as they battle to stay alive and find some measure of justice in this unforgiving world. The Gibson Vaughn series is on its way to being a classic franchise of thriller fiction, with a unique voice and an unusual approach that keep the stories as appealing as they are entertaining. Highly recommended."

—James Grady, author of *Six Days of the Condor*

"*Debris Line* . . . doesn't waste a word or miss a twist. It's always smart, always entertaining, and populated top to bottom with fascinating and unforgettable characters."

—Lou Berney, author of *November Road*

PRAISE FOR *COLD HARBOR*

"In FitzSimmons's action-packed third Gibson Vaughn thriller . . . fans of deep, dark government conspiracies will keep turning the pages to see how it all turns out."

—*Publishers Weekly*

"*Cold Harbor* interweaves two classic American tropes: the solitary prisoner imprisoned for who knows what and the American loner determined to rectify the injustices perpetrated on him. It's a page-turner that keeps the reader wondering—and looking forward to Gibson Vaughn number four."

—Criminal Element

"There are so many layers and twists to *Cold Harbor* . . . FitzSimmons masterfully fits together the myriad pieces of Gibson Vaughn's past like a high-quality Springbok puzzle."

—*Crimespree Magazine*

PRAISE FOR *POISONFEATHER*

"FitzSimmons's complicated hero leaps off the page with intensity and good intentions while a byzantine plot hums along, ensnaring characters into a tightening web of greed, betrayal, and violent death."

—*Publishers Weekly*

"[FitzSimmons] has knocked it out of the park, as they say. The characters' layers are being peeled back further and further, allowing readers to really root for the good guys! FitzSimmons has put together a great plot that doesn't let you rest for even a minute."

—*Suspense Magazine*

PRAISE FOR *THE SHORT DROP*

"FitzSimmons has come up with a doozy of a sociopath."

—*Washington Post*

"This live-wire debut begins with a promising lead in the long-ago disappearance of the vice president's daughter, then doubles down with tangled conspiracies, duplicitous politicians, and a disgraced hacker hankering for redemption . . . Hang on and enjoy the ride."

—*People*

"Writing with swift efficiency, FitzSimmons shows why the stakes are high, the heroes suitably tarnished, and the bad guys a pleasure to foil."

—*Kirkus Reviews*

"With a complex plot layered on top of unexpected emotional depth, *The Short Drop* is a wonderful surprise on every level . . . This is much more than a solid debut; it's proof that FitzSimmons has what it takes."

—Amazon.com, an Amazon Best Book of December 2015

"Beyond exceptional. Matthew FitzSimmons is the real deal."

—Andrew Peterson, author of the bestselling Nathan McBride series

"*The Short Drop* is an adrenaline-fueled thriller that has it all: political intrigue, murder, and suspense. Matthew FitzSimmons weaves a clever plot and deftly leads the reader on a rapid ride to an explosive end."

—Robert Dugoni, bestselling author of *My Sister's Grave*

CHANCE

OTHER TITLES BY MATTHEW FITZSIMMONS

CHANCE

MATTHEW FITZSIMMONS

Published by Thomas & Mercer, Seattle

www.apub.com

Amazon, the Amazon logo, and Thomas & Mercer are trademarks of Amazon.com, Inc., or its affiliates.

ISBN-13: 9781542009478 (hardcover)
ISBN-13: 9781542009485 (paperback)
ISBN-13: 9781542009461 (digital)

Cover design by Faceout Studio, Spencer Fuller
Cover image: © SVStudio / Shutterstock

Printed in the United States of America

First edition

For Robert Holifield

December 3, 2037

The dead lake was absolutely still beneath a cloudless midnight sky. A toxic velvet blanket draped languidly across the California desert. Moonlight didn't sparkle off its surface so much as suffocate in the gloomy waters. When it was very hot, which it always was nowadays, the lake vomited up hydrogen sulfide like a slow-decaying corpse, filling the air with the stench of a million rotting eggs. Locals claimed they couldn't even smell it anymore—the human brain working its magic trick of erasing the unpleasant so it could get on with the simple task of survival—but most families kept ventilators beside their children's beds for when the air became particularly unbreathable.

The Salton Sea was the stillborn bastard of an engineering mishap back at the dawn of the last century. In the quest for water for the voracious farms of the Imperial Valley, a canal had been dug to divert water from the then-mighty Colorado River. The canal ruptured like a diseased aorta, spilling hundreds of millions of gallons of water into an ancient lake bed and creating the largest lake in California.

In the 1950s, California did what it did best—rebranding mistake as opportunity—and the Salton Riviera was born. For a time the sea thrived, attracting millions of visitors. It even had its own yacht club. But by the 1970s, the Salton Sea had begun to die. The lake deoxygenated in the summers, and the shores became mass graveyards, buffets for seagulls that flocked inland to feast on the carcasses of asphyxiated fish. Vacationers went elsewhere and the resort towns were abandoned. In the decades since, the sea had devolved into a place devoid of life. It became, instead, an outpost of un-civilization, attracting a new breed looking to get away from it all. A patchwork tribe of artists and outcasts and the insane who could live beyond the rule of law, free by their own leave.

A gray van idled on the shore of the lake, headlights casting long shadows across the dried, cracked beachhead. It had no license plates or distinguishing features of any kind. Two men leaned against the grille, waiting in silence. Both had ski masks pushed back high on the tops of their heads, ready when the time came. Their birth certificates insisted they were brothers, but there was little family resemblance. One was a fair-skinned redhead with cauliflower ears and a nose permanently signaling for a right turn, while the other had dark, luxurious hair, a trait that reminded people of a young George Clooney. Something he enjoyed reminding his brother about at every opportunity. The redhead looked less like a movie star and more like a concrete barrier along a particularly treacherous span of highway. He was at least twice the size of his younger brother, a fact of life he reinforced through periodic beatdowns. His thick forearms rested on a rifle that hung from a tactical sling.

Two more men waited in the front seats of the van. The younger of the two was Chinese American and pecked away at an old laptop balanced precariously on the steering wheel. (There was no cell service by the sea: one of the reasons they'd chosen the location.) The other, a tall, willowy white man who was older than his three companions, dozed with his head against the window like a worker riding the bus home after a long shift. A black revolver rested on his knee. In back, a fifth man lay on his side, a hood drawn down over his face, wrists bound firmly together.

The big redhead looked up, listening intently. Was a vehicle approaching? It wasn't always easy to tell with electric engines, which could sound like anything but what they were. There it was again, a dull whisper from the desert. Certain now, he pulled the ski mask down over his face, elbowed his brother, and banged on the hood of the van to sound the alarm. The older man sat up, yawned once, swept his long black hair dramatically away from his face, and pulled on his ski mask.

"Get the drone up," he said with the authority of someone accustomed to having his instructions followed without question.

The man with the laptop toggled to a different screen and typed in a command. A small quadrotor drone lifted off silently from the roof of the van. It rose straight up two hundred feet and hovered there obediently. On the laptop, they had an infrared view of the beach. At the edge of the screen, a second car entered the frame. It wouldn't be long now.

"Keep an eye out for any uninvited guests," the leader said as he got out of the van.

"What's happening?" the man under the hood asked.

"Your father's here," the man with the laptop said. "Sit tight."

The approaching vehicle appeared over a low berm. It was a high-end sports car that wasn't built for the terrain and bumped slowly toward them, coming to a stop about thirty feet away. The two sets of headlights merged, creating a radiant corridor between the cars. The man in charge adjusted his ski mask and handed the revolver to the big redhead, who jammed it into his belt.

"Get out of the car," the leader yelled across the divide.

"I'll do whatever you say," the new arrival said. His skin had a handsome, healthy glow even though he hadn't slept in a week. His driver's license said he was fifty-five, but he looked easily ten years younger.

"I hope so, Mr. Harker. Chance is already dead because you thought you were smarter than us."

"That's not true. What you asked for wasn't easy."

"Do you have it?"

"I do," Harker said, holding up a black data drive. "Let me see Marley. Let me see my boy."

"First throw your LFD in the lake."

Harker took the device from behind his ear and heaved it into the air. It landed with a hollow splash somewhere offshore. Satisfied, the leader signaled the man with the rifle to fetch their prisoner. The big man did just that, dragging Marley Harker out carelessly and leading him to the front of the van. The leader yanked off the hood with the flair of a magician revealing an unexpected twist. The unexpected twist in this case was a white, twenty-year-old boy, handsome despite the dark bruising around his eyes that spoke to the conditions of his captivity. He blinked, his gaze caught in the wash of the headlights.

"Dad?" the kid called out.

"It's alright, Marley. I'm here."

The leader cut the family reunion short. "We need to see that it's all there. I'm sending your boy over. No hugging, no reunion. Just give him the drive. He'll bring it back to us. If everything is copacetic, he'll be right back to you and this will all be over."

The big man gave Marley Harker a shove in the right direction. Marley crossed from one car to the other. The redhead took a marksman's stance and sighted the rifle on the small of Marley's neck. When Marley reached his father, he held out his bound hands like a supplicant taking communion. Brett Harker placed the data drive in his palm.

"I'm sorry, Dad."

"Nothing to be sorry for. Just do what they say. I'll be right here. Mom and Chance are waiting at home."

"Hurry up," the leader called out.

Marley made the return trip. The leader took the thumb drive reverently. He handed it to his man still sitting behind the wheel, who plugged it into his laptop. The screen began to scroll with data.

"Well?" the leader said, impatient for the verdict.

"We're good. It's all there."

The four men shared a look that Moses might have recognized after his years in the wilderness.

"Well, that concludes our business, Mr. Harker. Marley, you can be on your way."

The kid gave the masked leader a last look for confirmation and started across the beach to his father. He made it less than halfway when the shot rang out across the lake.

CHAPTER ONE

Five Years Later

"So, who's ready to see me do something crazy?"

Chance had to shout to be heard over the thrum of the plane's engine and the roar of the wind buffeting his face. A spur-of-the-moment ad lib three years before that had become his official unofficial catchphrase. The one time he hadn't said it since, his viewers had nearly rioted. Had he known then that it would stick, he'd have come up with something that would make him sound less like a dystopian carnival barker. *Step right up, step right up, folks, and see the incredible, the stupendous, the death-defying Chance Harker!*

"So, here we are again. As promised, I've got something special for you all today. You've been requesting a say in what stunt I try next, so I selected three and ran a poll to let you, my heartless viewers, vote on your favorite. I think you all know what that means. It means it's time to give new meaning to *terminal velocity.*"

Across the cabin, the new cameraman flashed him a thumbs-up that the mics were working. Chance didn't know the guy's name. Crew turnover tended to be high, so he didn't see the point of remembering until they'd been with him at least a year. He was aware in some vague way that the new cameraman disliked him. They all did. In the last few years, Chance had developed a sixth sense for how people really felt about his work. It was an essential survival skill in his role as pariah and D-list provocateur.

Supposedly the new cameraman was some hotshot film student, which was why Chance was perched on this narrow dropdown bench by the open door of the little aircraft. This way the cameraman could film him in profile, the Mojave Desert far below serving as a majestic backdrop. It supposedly matched a shot from *Lawrence of Arabia*, which had appealed to Chance even though he'd never seen it. The film (not *movie, film*) was nearly four hours long, and who had that kind of time? Cinema had been his brother's thing, and Marley had always insisted that *Lawrence* was a stone-cold classic. Of course it didn't hurt any that Chance had been told he looked like a young Peter O'Toole—same blond hair, same angelic blue eyes. He thought the shot might lend him a bit of gravitas, but at fifteen thousand feet, the whole thing just felt pretentious. Plus, he really, really didn't like heights.

Over the past week, he and his team had made ten test jumps, rehearsing each step to give him the best shot at pulling this off. The fact that he'd succeeded in only four out of those ten attempts didn't overwhelm him with confidence. And, of course, he'd been wearing a parachute for the practice runs. Jumping out of an airplane was a slightly different proposition without one. Aware that there was a camera on him, he lifted his chin and sat forward, hoping it made him look thoughtful instead of scared. Out of habit, he fiddled with the band he wore on his right ring finger, twisting it counterclockwise. In poker, it would have been his tell that he was bluffing.

There'd been purpose behind all this once, back at the beginning. Back when he'd stopped being a person and had become "*the victim of a terrible crime.*" Or, to put it more accurately, the clone of the victim of a terrible crime. See, the thing was, normally, when two brothers were executed by vengeful kidnappers, the public at large was free to obsess over every lurid detail. Free to write its books, free to make its documentaries and movies and podcasts, free to turn a family's private tragedy into a shared public document. But what were the rules when the brothers didn't have the decency to stay dead and were instead revived in state-of-the-art clone wombs?

In Chance's experience, it didn't mean a damn thing. In the five years since his abduction, he'd rarely met anyone who didn't know the details of the Harker kidnapping. His trauma preceded him everywhere like a herald trumpeting his arrival. His life became a permanent car crash, with everyone slowing down to rubberneck and get a good long look at the freak.

He remembered his first day back at high school after the kidnapping. His parents had been dead set against the idea, arguing it was too soon. But he'd worn them down, pleading that he missed his friends and just wanted to feel normal. The moment he got out of the car outside the school, he'd known it was a mistake coming. His friends didn't feel like his friends anymore. They were just kids who knew the freak, aware of the social currency that gifted them. Everywhere he went that morning, the air changed with his arrival. At lunch, the cafeteria fell silent. A thousand eyes watching him, none actually seeing him. In the days after his revival, he hadn't felt anything but numb. Standing in the cafeteria doorway, he'd finally felt something. Fury.

Fine, if people were going to stare, he'd give them something to stare at. On his eighteenth birthday, after two years of troubling behavior (one of his father's many euphemisms for Chance), he'd climbed the retaining wall on the roof of the Ritz-Carlton. His goal had been to sprint around the edge eighteen times. That was a wildly optimistic number, because he completed only four laps before taking a wrong step, losing his balance, and plummeting fifty-four floors. One of his new friends recorded the whole thing.

After he'd been revived at Palingenesis, nothing had changed. If anything, he was treated like even more of a freak than before, but he felt better than at any time since the kidnapping. He'd been the victim in that story, a cautionary tale. But people weren't talking about the kidnapping anymore; they were talking about the video of what he'd done on the roof at the Ritz-Carlton. Somehow that made all the difference in the world. He wasn't a victim in this story. He wasn't even exactly a character in it. He'd become the author. And an author felt like a damn fine thing to be. If he was going to be known for dying, it would be on his terms.

Six months later he'd performed his first planned stunt—an homage to Harry Houdini's escape from a crate submerged in New York Harbor. Chance had tried something similar but in a pool. It was harder than it'd looked. He hadn't survived. Yet, abracadabra, here he was. It had freaked people out, much to his delight. For the first time since the kidnapping, people were talking about something he'd done, not something that had been done to him. That had felt powerful at the time. Lest anyone forget, he'd been pulling ever more dangerous stunts for three years now, a new one every six months. Today he turned twenty-one, and this would be his sixth. Six. It sounded absurd when he put it that way. He wasn't even sure why he was still doing it, other than that stopping would feel like a capitulation.

But that didn't change the fact that somewhere along the line his stunts had lost whatever power they'd once had. He couldn't say exactly when, or how, but he didn't feel like the author of this story anymore. It had slowly dawned on him that he'd become a character again. But what kind? No longer the victim, but he sure as hell wasn't the hero. So what did that make him, besides the fool?

He sure felt like a clown these days, shaking his fist impotently at an unjust and uncaring world. He didn't feel the same buzz after a stunt that he once did. Just a vague embarrassment and unease. Maybe that was why he'd granted unrestricted, behind-the-scenes access to the journalist. He thought she might rock his boat in a way he couldn't or wouldn't himself. Right this minute, she was sitting at the front of the plane, typing intently, as she had been continually for most of the past week, not counting the time she took off to pepper him with searingly uncomfortable questions. She was always there, lurking in the background, until he'd almost forgotten her presence and let his guard down.

It was intimidating and unnerving, but also exhilarating. He did his share of press, but only with reporters who let him dictate the terms and control what topics would be covered. But Imani Zari Highsmith wasn't just any reporter, and the only dictated terms were her own. She was a journalist, capital *J*, exclamation point, underline, underline, underline. Chance played the part of a buffoonish dilettante well, but he'd read every word she'd published. At thirty-four, she'd already won every major prize in her profession. She was a pulse-taking, voice-of-a-generation type who wrote important, long-form think pieces, casting light on pressing issues before most people recognized they were issues at all.

Over the last few years, Highsmith had written extensively on the issue of human cloning. Always a lightning-rod issue, it had become even more divisive in the past two years, following the Supreme Court's ruling on *Gaddis v. Virginia*. In a narrow five-to-four decision, the court recognized the legal standing of clones at the federal level. In the blink of an eye, all state-level anti-cloning laws had been wiped away, laying bare the country's seething anxiety and resentment surrounding clones. Highsmith had been chronicling America's newest culture war ever since.

She'd written the first major piece on Constance D'Arcy, the musician in Virginia who'd recently released a double album of songs written half before and half after she'd died and become a clone. Highsmith had used D'Arcy's music to make a larger point about the evolving social and political attitudes toward commercial human cloning. In so doing, she'd transformed D'Arcy from musical novelty act to cultural touchstone. D'Arcy was currently headlining a national tour that was selling out wherever it went, including traditionally anti-cloning states, although sometimes the protests were larger than the venues themselves.

At their first one-on-one interview, Chance had realized Highsmith might do more than rock his boat; she might capsize it entirely. She wasn't so much interested in him as in what he signified, and the crucial difference between the two. She was an anthropologist there to study an evolutionary curiosity, and Chance had naïvely invited her into his inner circle. She'd even learned to parachute so she could jump with him today, following him all the way down to the ground. How was that for commitment to craft?

Her piece was scheduled to come out in a few days. He didn't like to think about what damning conclusions she would draw. But he also couldn't wait to find out. There would be consequences; he knew that much. He'd lost faith in his ability to break the cycle he'd found himself trapped in. Knowing a thing was bad for you and doing something about it were two very different things. But things would have to change now, one way or another; things would have to change. Better or worse? He didn't care, as long as it was different.

A text message came in from Chelsea Klos, his agent slash manager. She'd been with him since shortly after his sprint around the Ritz-Carlton, but he still didn't know that he'd call her a friend. They'd always butted heads, but lately it had become an unrelenting game of chicken between them. When she saw what was in the Highsmith piece, it might be the last of her brittle straws. She was on the ground now with a second camera crew, and the drones that would pick up his free fall. If you included the camera rig he was wearing that would allow him to narrate his descent, there would be close to twenty cameras following him. Her message read that the plane was three minutes out.

How are you feeling? the text continued. Ready to do this?

No, he really wasn't. He felt nervous as hell and wanted to be anywhere but here. So why wasn't he? All he had to do was tell the pilot to turn around, but his mouth was dry as an old bone. If he twisted the ring any harder, he'd dislocate his finger.

Chelsea's message was still waiting for a reply. He typed, Born to do this. He thought that was pretty clever under the circumstances, but

Chelsea was all business on stunt days and wasn't paid enough to have a sense of humor.

What do you want me to tell you? she typed. If it goes wrong.

The deer has to be taken with one shot.

Got it. I'll see you on the ground.

If it did go wrong, he wouldn't remember that she'd said that—he wouldn't remember any of this—but he counted on her to help him through the transition. He depended on it.

Chance looked up at the cameraman and shifted into showman mode, adopting a welcoming smile. "Alright, boys and girls, I've just been alerted by my team on the ground that we're approaching the drop zone. It's 9:02 a.m. on April 14, 2042. We're currently cruising at eighty-five miles an hour above the Mojave Desert, where I'm told it's a cool eighty-three degrees on the ground. Beautiful, isn't it?" he said, gesturing toward the endless horizon. Fifteen thousand feet below, the desert shimmered like a lifeless, alien planet.

He smiled for the camera. It was a good smile, intimate with just a trace of cockiness. Years of practice had taught him exactly how to dial it up or dial it down as the situation dictated. He could smile his way through anything, and even he had trouble knowing what was going on behind it. That was half his problem. He'd become a sphinx even to himself.

Time to get on with it, sphinx, he told himself. He strapped on his helmet. It had a camera mount so that he could talk his audience through the experience of plummeting to earth without a parachute. His hands shook as he fumbled with the strap. *Just breathe,* he told himself, but his body wasn't fooled. It knew it was being forced to do something unwise, pumping out adrenaline in protest. He was pretty sure he shouldn't be able to hear his heart beating over the engines.

"Man, this first step is going to be a doozy, isn't it?" he said to no one and everyone. The cameraman gave him another thumbs-up that he was ready too. *Easy for you, pal.* Highsmith had stopped typing and was working her way back to the open door. Chance would go first, then the cameraman, then Highsmith. He took a series of short, fast breaths to psych himself up. This was it.

"Don't try this at home, kids."

He tossed his parachute out the door and watched it tumble away toward the earth.

Then he jumped after it.

Gravity took things from there.

CHAPTER TWO

Palingenesis made human cloning sound deceptively straightforward—if you die, we can bring you back exactly the same. From the moment it became public knowledge in 2032, the entire one percent began queuing up, eager to plunk down their eight-figure deposits. When you were living the enviably privileged existence of the modern billionaire, the last thing you wanted was it being cut short by anything as prosaic as death.

This was how it worked, according to the brochure . . .

For the low, low price of $25 million American, Palingenesis would speed-grow a clone of each new client. A process the company managed to make sound no more complicated than toasting a bagel. These inanimate clones were stored in one of Palingenesis's state-of-the-art "wombs," aging in parallel with the client. Monitored twenty-four seven, inanimate clones were fed and watered, and generally kept as near to mint condition as scientifically possible, ready in the case of a death event. How exactly a death event differed from death death, Chance still couldn't say. He'd had more of them than anyone in human history and could say without fear of contradiction that every one of them had felt like an event.

What happened next was the secret sauce in the process: A stored copy of the client's consciousness was downloaded into the inanimate clone. Then, after a few days' rest and recuperation in one of

Palingenesis's luxurious recovery suites, the newly cloned client could seamlessly integrate into their original's life. Palingenesis called it a revival, as if clients were rock bands getting back together for a nostalgic feel-good tour.

There was only one small problem with all that—the brochure was a lie. But clients didn't realize that until after they died, by which point it was much, much too late. Turned out that in practice, human cloning and toasting bagels had very little in common. What Palingenesis characterized as a simple consciousness download was in reality a primordial tug-of-war between body and mind. Only a sophisticated cocktail of pharmaceuticals prevented the brain from violently rejecting the implanted consciousness. Even then, the first day still felt like having your personality pulled out by the roots and jammed into a pot three sizes too small.

That was how Chance felt now. And having died so many times, he was a little frustrated not to be getting any better at it. This was his fifth revival. Fifth. Five deaths, five revivals. That was a lot of practice. So the moment he opened his eyes, it should have been obvious what had happened: he had jumped out of the plane after his parachute and not caught up to it in time.

Exactly as planned.

Moments after he'd hit the ground at 120 miles an hour, the biometric chip implanted in his neck had reported his death event back to Palingenesis, which swung into action, downloading the stored copy of his consciousness into his inanimate clone. And here he was—good as new?

Except his brain wasn't having any of that nonsense and clung tenaciously to the belief that this wasn't a revival at all, but only a refresh—the regular backing up of his consciousness to keep it up to date with all the latest memories and experiences. In the abstract, he knew better. If this were a refresh, then he'd be relaxing in a recovery suite cocooned in a terry cloth bathrobe. But he wasn't, was he? No, he was in a genuine hospital bed in a genuine hospital room, connected to a half dozen less-than-reassuring machines. He'd been in a room like this four times before and knew exactly what it meant. But knowing that you'd died and been revived as a clone and admitting it were two very different propositions.

A familiar, if not entirely welcome, face leaned into Chance's field of vision. Holifield, looking very much like a war widow with his brave eyes and tight-lipped, stoic, for-the-good-of-all smile. Holifield was what Palingenesis called a steward. One part registered nurse, one part therapist, and one part concierge, stewards were assigned to clients at the outset and advocated on behalf of their client after a revival. In those situations, stewards had to know more about their clients than the clients knew about themselves. Maybe that was why Chance resented Holifield the way he did.

"Welcome back, Chance," Holifield said. "This is your download, not your upload."

Thanks, genius.

Chance had come close to requesting a new steward multiple times. Palingenesis would have given him one, no questions asked. But the problem with that was a new steward meant there would then be two people in the world who had seen him this way. His stunts might be open to the public, but he hated that anyone had seen him flail his way through rebirth. As much as he hated Holifield, Chance knew he'd hate two Holifields even more.

Out of habit, he ran his thumb across his right ring finger.

It was missing. The ring was missing.

His stubborn stand against the truth finally broke. A great swell of panic overwhelmed him, tripping the machines, which beeped and screeched like back-alley snitches. This moment always felt like a dream. That he'd been through this four times before made no difference and did nothing to quell the awful lurching in the pit of his stomach, as if he were aboard a tiny sailboat atop a wave ten stories high, the bottom about to fall out of the world.

"Relax, Chance. Chance? Chance, relax. Chance," Holifield said, repeating his name over and over. Another thing that Palingenesis insisted on doing during revivals that irritated the hell out of him. It felt patronizing, like he was a child, but Palingenesis believed it reassured new clones of who they were. In a minute, Holifield would ask Chance to say his own name. It was a trap, though, because Chance wouldn't be able to yet. New clones struggled at first to say their own names or even use personal pronouns. It would take hours of practice before Chance would be able to spit out the word *me* without stammering. No one knew exactly why, but the experience was totally demoralizing, and Chance didn't feel much like being humiliated first thing. He tried to sit up, but his body barely responded. The mind-body connection was always tenuous early on and took time and physical therapy to reestablish.

"Chance, look at me," Holifield repeated, gently but firmly holding Chance down. "Look at me."

Grudgingly, Chance looked.

"You're okay, Chance. You're safe. Can you tell me who you are?"

There it was. Chance glared up at Holifield, or at least with what he hoped was a vague approximation of a glare. It was hard to be sure how much control he had of his expressions yet.

"No," Chance said, pleased with how clearly he was able to enunciate. Speech didn't always return this fast, and it felt like a victory over Holifield.

His steward didn't acknowledge the loss and only nodded a deeply understanding nod. It was an impressive display of the-customer-is-always-right restraint, although Chance wasn't handing out prizes.

"Let's just try and get through this, okay, Chance?" Holifield suggested.

"No," Chance repeated, aware of how much he sounded like a petulant child.

"It's important, Chance. You know that. Tell me your name."

Chance began to sob. It came out of nowhere, like a summer storm, hard and unrelenting. He couldn't have stopped if he tried. Every damn time. Palingenesis considered crying to be a healthy catharsis for new clones and always encouraged it. The worst part was that Holifield just stood there and let him cry himself out. No privacy, no dignity. When it was finally over, Holifield wiped Chance's face with a tissue he'd been holding for just such an eventuality.

"Can you tell me your name, Chance?" Holifield asked.

"Where is Chelsea?" Knowing if his manager was here would give him another foothold in the truth. Chelsea never came to his refreshes but was always on hand for his revivals.

"She's in the waiting room," Holifield admitted with all the enthusiasm of a defendant implicating himself in a crime. He didn't seem to appreciate that Chance had figured out a system that worked for him. No matter that Chance was now the most revived person in history. After five times, maybe, just maybe, he knew a little something about what worked and what didn't. But Palingenesis wasn't in the business of taking constructive criticism.

"Get her."

"Chance, we really need to finish our evaluation first before you see visitors."

"Just get her, Holifield."

His steward bristled and left the room. He returned with Chelsea, who pushed past him and hurried over to the bed, all concern and righteous irritation at having been held at bay.

"I don't know why they insist on this idiotic charade," she said loudly for the benefit of the entire room. Squeezing Chance's hand, she perched on the edge of the bed and fussed over him. "Are you ready?"

"Ready," Chance said, trying to squeeze back but unable to summon the strength.

"The deer has to be taken with one shot."

Before his final refresh, he always picked a line from an old movie, one his brother had loved and always tried to get him to watch. That way he would remember it afterward because it was part of his uploaded memories. So if Chelsea knew it, then what Holifield had been telling him must be true—Chance Harker had died, but Chance Harker was alive. This *was* his download, not his upload.

"Do you have it?" he asked.

Chelsea nodded and gave him the ring, a black tungsten carbide band with a sapphire-blue groove around the center. Chance turned it over in his fingers, a supreme effort of concentration and manual dexterity that caused beads of sweat to appear on his forehead like blisters. The ring had belonged to his brother, Marley, a gift from their parents to commemorate his high school graduation. Back when such things still mattered to anyone in the family. Engraved on the inside were the words To our son, 6/3/35.

After the kidnapping, Marley had had an even harder time adapting to being a clone than his brother. He'd been in agony; everyone saw it, but no one knew how to help him. After two months of increasingly disturbing behavior, the police found Marley's truck abandoned up past Malibu at El Matador, the same beach where the kidnappers had grabbed the brothers. On the dashboard was a note held in place by Marley's bloodied biometric tracking chip. The note read simply, "Please don't bring me back again." Down at the waterline, Marley's surfboard was found bobbing in the surf.

The funeral had been a small, private affair, although the media had been waiting for the family at the gates of Forest Lawn Memorial-Park. It was the last time Chance saw his parents together. The morning the police returned the original Chance's and Marley's personal effects from the kidnapping, their parents had been at a doomed mediation session with their respective lawyers. Chance had slipped the ring on, surprised that it fit so well. A tenuous connection to his brother. He expected his parents to want it back, but they never said a word. Over time the ring had become his totem and a reminder of everything he'd lost. With a feeling of relief, he slipped it back on his right ring finger and closed his fist. He had died, but he was still here.

Hallelujah.

"How did it go?" Chance said, working around to the question he needed to ask but didn't necessarily want answered.

"Amazing," Chelsea said, clearly happy to be moving on. She didn't like reminders that she didn't know absolutely everything there was to know about Chance Harker. "Our numbers were up across the board and outperformed all our projections. We racked up new subscribers and first-views. We absolutely killed in China. At this rate, we have to start attracting major sponsorship interest. Advertisers won't be able to resist these numbers, not to this demographic."

She went on and on, gushing about brand awareness and unique captures with the zeal of a storefront preacher on the eve of the Rapture. He nodded along but didn't care about the business side. Never had. Not even at the beginning, when the prospect of embarrassing his father had still felt like a noble calling. When she came to a point when she had no choice but to pause and take a breath, he cut in.

"No, how did *it* go?"

"Oh," she said, realizing awkwardly that she'd answered the wrong question. "You came close."

That wasn't descriptive enough. "Close like how?"

She hesitated but then went on. "You got one hand on the strap."

"Then what happened?"

"It got away from you."

He nodded. During the test jumps, he'd been pretty good at aiming for the parachute but tended to fumble the catch. "How was the end? Was it clean?"

"On impact," she confirmed.

That was a relief. He'd, miraculously or tragically, depending on your perspective, managed to survive his third stunt, taking an agonizing ninety minutes to die after being pulled from the wreckage. Jumping a motorcycle onto the roof of a moving train was harder than it looked. Since then, he'd been paranoid about it happening again. He wouldn't have thought falling out of an airplane could end any other way, but he'd found improbable stories of people surviving after their parachutes failed to open. *On impact* sounded like a much better way to go.

"And the video?" he asked.

"All queued up at the house waiting for you."

He found that reassuring, knowing that somewhere was a document of the lost time between his final refresh and his abrupt collision with the Mojave Desert. "Good. How much total time am I missing?"

Chelsea hesitated. "Six days, thirteen hours, and twenty-two minutes."

A cold, unpleasant sweat swept over his body. He could hear himself breathing too hard and too fast, like he'd just biked up a steep hill, only to find another steeper hill waiting for him. "Why so much?"

"You canceled your last refresh."

"Why the hell would I do that?" he demanded.

"I honestly don't know. You told me to mind my own business and focus on my job."

He had to admit that sounded like something he would say, even if he couldn't imagine a reason for saying it. The single hardest part of a revival, once a clone survived the immediate struggle of adapting to a new body, was the lag. *Lag* was Palingenesis's intentionally vague terminology for the gap in a clone's memories between their final refresh and their death event. Every clone experienced some degree of lag; it was only a matter of how much.

When a clone, already struggling with fears of being an imposter and a fraud, felt a gap in their memory, it felt like undeniable proof that they weren't who they claimed to be. And the more lag there was, the more intense the feelings of incompleteness. For that reason, Palingenesis strongly advised clients to refresh their memory uploads every thirty days at minimum. After ninety days without a refresh, the risks of a revival leading to a mental breakdown became so great that Palingenesis locked clients out of the system, denying access to their clones until they'd refreshed their uploaded consciousness.

The difficulty lay in the fact that waking from a refresh and being revived were indistinguishable from one another. Convincing a new clone that days, weeks, or even months had passed since their last refresh was a delicate process. The cognitive dissonance of accepting that they had died but were also still alive was traumatic. A clone was apt to reject the truth of their senses, sometimes violently, if the news wasn't framed carefully. It could make clones do crazy things, desperate things. To which Chance offered a heartfelt *amen*. He was the poster child for crazy, desperate clones.

Maybe that's why he'd never been able to move on or really grow up. He lived in a state of perpetually stunted and angry adolescence. In many ways, he was still that lonely little boy standing in the doorway of his high school cafeteria. But how was he supposed to imagine a future when the most important moments of his entire life would be beyond his reach? In the eighteen days between his last refresh and his first clone, he and his brother had been kidnapped and murdered. He didn't have memories of any of it, but when he'd been revived in a bed very much like this one, nothing was the same. His parents, once so much in love, were bitter, heartbroken shells of themselves, on their way to a notoriously vicious divorce. Chance had found himself on his own to make sense of those missing eighteen days and to accept the fact that he would never know what had happened to him. Not really. The only thing he had to be grateful for was that he wasn't his brother, whose two and a half months of lag, so close to Palingenesis's redline, had been crippling.

Watching Marley disintegrate had made Chance obsessive about his own refreshes. Once you'd been through a revival, the thought of waiting thirty days between refreshes was madness. It didn't matter that a refresh took five or six hours; sometimes he scheduled multiple appointments in a single week. And he always, always, kept a standing appointment the day before a stunt. The idea that he would cancel it and jump out of an airplane with nearly a week of lag was absurd.

At least his life was backed up to video, his fail-safe in the event of accidental death. He recorded everything and backed it all up to a private server at his house. There wasn't an inch of his home that wasn't wired with cameras. Same went for his car, and he wore a body camera for everything else. That way, after revival, he could watch everything he'd done, over and over, until it almost felt like an actual memory. He'd never had an entire missing week, though, not since the kidnapping anyway, and that troubled him.

Chelsea looked as if she had something else on her mind.

"What?" he asked, suddenly feeling bone tired. Fatigue was a common side effect of revival, but more and more it came from spending too much time around Chelsea. He suspected the feeling was mutual.

"The Highsmith article," she said.

"It's out already?"

"No, not yet, but my contact says it's going to be rough."

"How rough?" he asked, a faint, unfamiliar tremor of excitement shooting through him as if somewhere deep inside him, someone had found a dusty fuse box and flipped the breaker to see if it still worked.

"Her exact word was *bloodbath*. I told you we couldn't trust Highsmith." She'd argued that Highsmith wasn't some West Coast entertainment journo who knew how to play the game and could be controlled. Imani Highsmith was a snobby New York intellectual of the old school. A truth-to-power type who was more interested in being the voice of a generation than in making nice with her subjects. The last person on earth they should have granted access.

That was exactly why Chance had agreed to it.

He suppressed a grin. When he'd agreed to Highsmith's terms, he'd wondered if he'd chicken out when the time came to sit down with her one-on-one. Sounded like he'd really gone for it, though. But how much had he said? He wished he could remember what he'd told her.

"How did my sit-down interviews with her go?" he asked, his ability to string a sentence together starting to return. It was always uncomfortable asking about things he'd done like he was talking about someone else, but until he could watch the recordings of his missing time, he had no choice.

"You didn't seem concerned, so I assumed fine. Looks now like Highsmith sandbagged you," Chelsea said, the old insinuation implicit in her tone: that Chance was too naïve and unsophisticated to do much of anything without her there to keep him out of trouble. That attitude as much as anything was responsible for the tension between them. "I'm trying to get my hands on an advance copy now, but the magazine's got it on lockdown."

Holifield chose this moment to return, accompanied by the staff psychologist, a statically cheerful Canadian woman named Dr. Hughes.

"Sorry to interrupt, but we really need to get back to Chance's therapy," Holifield said.

That suited Chance fine. The sooner he got through it, the sooner he could get out of there. And there was only so much Chelsea Klos he could take after a revival.

"Anything else for now?" he asked Chelsea.

Chelsea glared at Holifield as if he were an indiscreet waiter who'd interrupted just as she was about to close a deal. "No, it can wait for now."

"See if you can get a copy, and we'll go from there," Chance said. Telling her what to do, even though she'd only just gotten through saying that was exactly what she was already doing, felt important.

After Chelsea was gone, Holifield and the psychologist fanned out on either side of the bed, and for a moment, Chance thought they were going to join hands and try to levitate him off the mattress. Instead, Dr. Hughes asked him a question he couldn't answer on any level.

"Chance, can you tell me who you are?"

CHAPTER THREE

Chance spent the next few days recuperating under the watchful super-vision of Holifield. His daily routine was divided between physical ther-apy, speech therapy, and traditional talk therapy. It was an exhausting and often frustrating process, but for the most part Chance kept his mouth shut and did everything they asked. If he put in the work now, by the time he was discharged he'd be almost as good as new. Pun intended. Once, after his fourth revival, he'd thrown a tantrum and refused to dance through Palingenesis's hoops. He'd spent the next few months regretting that decision as he played catch-up in his own body.

While he slept, Palingenesis saturated his tissues with drugs designed to accelerate the bonding process between his consciousness and his new body. Everything from state-of-the-art muscle-growth pro-teins to a forty-year-old antipsychotic that worked better than anything developed since. In the mornings, he woke up feeling like a sponge that had been left at the bottom of a wet sink. But never fear, Holifield was there, ready to wring him out ahead of another long day.

Palingenesis believed that the more a clone looked like their orig-inal, the easier the transition would be. To that end, his tattoos were re-inked using detailed photographs as a guide. He was grateful that he had only three small ones and hadn't gotten a new one since his second refresh. That was just an unnecessary amount of extra pain. A stylist tidied up the tangled mop of hair that had grown out of control in the womb. Plastic surgeons reproduced the scars and marks that he had picked up over his twenty-one years. Some clients declined, preferring a clean slate, but Palingenesis strongly encouraged accurate scarification. On this, Chance wholeheartedly agreed. He knew that if he looked in the mirror and didn't see the thin scar splitting his right eyebrow—the result of an epic skateboard fail in the eighth grade—the whispering doubts in his head would never quit. Finally, he spent time in a tanning booth that carefully, and at very mild and controlled levels, aged and toughened his skin. That way he wouldn't look like some kind of creepy five-foot-nine newborn when they released him into the wild, and also so that the relentless California sun wouldn't turn him into a rotisserie chicken in five minutes flat.

On his last morning, Chance was marched through a set of diagnostic tests to confirm he'd met Palingenesis's minimum competencies for release. He felt like a prized steer at auction being poked, prodded, and measured. Once he was cleared for discharge, Chance spent five hours refreshing his upload. Maybe it was overkill, but he was already staring at a week's worth of unexpected lag, and cameras weren't allowed inside Palingenesis. He had no record of anything since his revival. The last few days might have been nothing special, but if he had an accident on the way home, all these memories would be lost permanently. That would mean starting this all over from scratch. No way he could risk that.

Once the refresh was complete, Holifield moved Chance to a comfortable couch and left him for thirty minutes while his head cleared. He returned with Chance's street clothes. Chance took them eagerly. It would feel really good to wear anything that wasn't hospital scrubs.

"Alright, let's get you signed out," Holifield said, sounding very much like a kid who had thought Christmas morning would never arrive and had just caught sight of all the presents under the tree.

"You don't like me much, do you?" Chance said, pulling a Lakers T-shirt over his head.

Holifield gave that some thought, clearly looking for a diplomatic answer. "If you're at all unhappy with my work—"

"I'm not unhappy with your work, Holifield." That was true. Holifield was very good at his job, and Chance had come to realize that it wasn't Holifield he hated so much as Palingenesis itself. But Holifield was his steward, and thus to Chance, the avatar for the company. Maybe it wasn't deserved, but Holifield bore the brunt of Chance's resentment.

"Then why do you ask?" Holifield said.

"Just curious is all. I know you don't approve of what I do."

"I don't," Holifield agreed. "How long have we known each other now? Eight years?"

"Since I first got a clone."

Holifield nodded at the memory. "Your whole family came in together for orientation. You were, what? Thirteen. You were a nice kid, you know that? A little spoiled, which was probably unavoidable and not really your fault. You were one of my first clients. I'd read your file a dozen times. Straight-A student. A little introverted but really sweet. You asked a million questions about how everything worked. Not because you were scared, but because you were genuinely curious. I asked what you were going to be when you grew up; do you remember what you said?"

"A climate engineer." The environment had been an obsession after touring a carbon-reclamation plant in elementary school. Growing up in California and watching the unfolding devastation, and the near-total collapse of San Diego to the south, nothing else seemed to matter. By the age of fifteen, he'd been taking college-level math and science.

"What happened to that Chance Harker?"

"Someone shot him in the head and dumped his body in a creek bed."

Holifield nodded mildly, accustomed to Chance's aggressive hostility around the subject of his kidnapping. "Well, I miss that kid. My guess is I'm not alone in that."

Chance finished tying his shoes. "Can we go now?"

"You asked," Holifield reminded him. "I just don't feel great being complicit in what you do. It's not really what I signed up for."

"I'm just taking things to their logical conclusion, Holifield. You really think there's a difference between one revival and five? It's all the same lie."

Something approximating an unguarded emotion passed over Holifield's face, but consummate professional that he was, his benignly neutral steward expression quickly won out. "Of course." And with that, he escorted Chance out front and passed him off to a receptionist with discharge forms for Chance to sign.

"I'll see you soon," Holifield said, handing him the meds Chance would take for the next few weeks.

Not one minute later, a lawyer materialized to take Holifield's place, as if he and Holifield were wrestlers tag teaming a shaky opponent. Typically, Palingenesis sent someone from legal to lecture him while Chance was convalescing, so he'd begun to hope maybe they had finally given up the charade. No such luck, apparently.

"Mr. Harker, my name is Javier Paloma." He was new—young, shiny, eager to legal it up. He wore a suit but not an expensive one. Chance guessed he was only a few years out of UCLA or maybe Berkeley.

"A word?" the lawyer asked.

"What happened to the old guy?"

"He got promoted. I'm the new guy. A word?"

Chance told him to go for it but kept scrolling through the forms and initialing where indicated. He didn't begrudge the guy for doing his job, but he was eager to get out of there and had heard Palingenesis's concerns enough times that his undivided attention was no longer required.

"I've been asked to stress that Palingenesis does not approve of your misuse of its resources. The technology was never intended to be used this way."

"What way's that? If I die, you nice people bring me back. Isn't that exactly the intention?"

"Yes, but not like this. Do you know the previous record for revivals?" the lawyer asked. Chance did: it was three. "Three. And that was a soldier, back in the early days."

Chance knew all about him. His name was Joe Fine, from South Bend, Indiana. Winner of the Medal of Honor, two Silver Stars, and a fistful of Purple Hearts, Fine had been one of the first American soldiers placed in a new program to give key special forces personnel a second chance. Fine's first death had been in August of '29. Because the program was heavily classified, he hadn't been permitted to tell his family. When the *Washington Post* broke the story that a company called Palingenesis had been cloning US soldiers for the Pentagon back in '32, it had created a firestorm of scandal.

At the time, Joe Fine had been killed and revived three times in the line of duty. When his name appeared on a leaked list of cloned servicepeople, his father had shot him dead on the porch of his childhood home. Tragically, Fine had recently retired from active duty and so was out of the cloning program by then, so there wasn't a fourth clone waiting for him. There was also no funeral. It had taken another nine years before Joe Fine's remains were interred at Arlington National Cemetery. He was the first, and to date only, clone to be granted that honor. Meanwhile, Palingenesis had swiftly taken cloning to the private sector, marketing it to the obscenely wealthy.

"This is your fifth revival in five years," the lawyer said.

"So? I'm a trailblazer." He thought that might actually be true. While Palingenesis dutifully went through the motions of chastising him for misusing its technology, Chance suspected the company was privately delighted. He was a lab rat, and a volunteer one at that. His five revivals had generated mountains of data that would have been impossible to come by without him.

The lawyer frowned, indicating that this was not at all his point and that he would appreciate it if Chance stopped being obtuse. Obtuse . . . that was the way Chance saw this guy talking.

"What are you so worried about?" Chance asked. "That it might not be safe to upload a human consciousness this many times?"

"What I'm saying is this is *not* the intended usage," the lawyer reiterated.

"The terms of my family's life insurance policy are pretty unambiguous. It provides us with as many clone backups as we need." That was true, but Chance also knew that Palingenesis had rewritten the terms of this policy in light of him. He felt perversely proud of that fact.

"Yes, your father's policy covers dependents until their twenty-third birthday. But—"

Chance interrupted. "So look on the bright side: you've only got to worry about me for two more years." His father had served as Palingenesis's chief marketing officer, where he also authored most of Palingenesis's bullshit sales pitch and soothing terms of art. One of the perks had been a platinum cloning package that covered the entire family. When Brett Harker resigned in the wake of the kidnapping, the company had gifted him the package as a thank-you. Chance was intent on making them regret their generosity.

The lawyer took a stab at getting on the front foot. "It could be argued that you are violating the morals-clause policy."

"The morals clause? I'm not doing anything illegal."

"You're broadcasting your suicide and enriching yourself."

"I'm not committing suicide," Chance said hotly. He'd heard this argument before and wasn't buying it. "My stunts are extremely high risk. No one's denying that, but so is BASE jumping and free-climbing. People take unnecessary risks every day."

"You jumped out of an airplane without a parachute."

"I had a parachute. It just didn't happen to be on at the time," Chance said, and then graced him with his most charming smile. When he saw it wasn't having the intended effect, he shifted gears. "Look, I'm no different than Joseph Kittinger, or Johnny Knoxville, or Evel Knievel."

"Not even Evel Knievel took these kinds of risks. The only reason you do is because you have clones."

"Well, lucky, lucky me," Chance snarled, realizing his hands had balled up into fists.

"Children may be watching," the lawyer said.

"My servers have age checks baked in. So if kids are watching, take it up with their parents. Look . . . what's your name again?" he asked, although he knew perfectly well what the lawyer's name was.

"Javier Paloma."

"Look, Javier, you're new around here, right?"

"I don't know what that has to do with anything."

"What it's got to do with is that they send one of you down here to lecture me every time. Maybe it's a hazing ritual for the new guy, I don't know. But you all tell me the same thing every time. I've heard it all. So unless you're here to rescind my family's policy, can we skip to the end, where I acknowledge I've been duly chastised?"

Javier sighed with the frustration of someone who'd been warned a task would be aggravating but hadn't realized what an asshole he'd be dealing with.

"So, are you?" Chance asked.

The lawyer shook his head that he was not.

"Cool. Then consider me chastised," Chance said, and then slapped him on the shoulder. "But think positive: maybe I'll pull off the next stunt, and you won't have to see me again for a while."

CHAPTER FOUR

Chelsea was waiting in the garage with his car. She'd driven it from the house so Chance could leave Palingenesis like a rock star. Her words. It was a two-door 2041 Aston Martin DB11. Cherry red. The electric engine went from zero to one hundred in 5.6 seconds. He'd gotten it last year at Chelsea's insistence. The vanity plates with his name had been her suggestion as well. It was undeniably gorgeous, part of the glamorous lifestyle that she strove to project to the outside world. All in service to his almighty brand, with the end goal of landing a whale—a major sponsor that would legitimize him in the eyes of the world. He found it all more than a little embarrassing, especially the car, which he drove as little as possible.

The truth was, his public-facing life was an elaborate shell game of staged events and carefully choreographed encounters. The paparazzi photographs were carefully curated, and all the videos edited to the point of defamation. He wasn't actually pals with Brandon Giggs or Chris Jackson, both of whom had threatened to sue if Chelsea didn't stop planting stories about their supposed escapades in Las Vegas. Chance had never even been. And despite what Javier Paloma might think, Chance was closer to enriching uranium than himself. The Aston Martin was a lease, and he was two payments behind.

His dirty little secret was that despite his millions and millions of views, he was far too divisive for anyone legitimate to touch. It wasn't the twenties anymore. As was so often the case, the children of the YouTube and TikTok generation had shown no interest in the social media obsessions of their parents. Perhaps they resented having their childhoods put online without their consent or the pendulum had swung inevitably the other way, but times and tastes had changed. Online interconnectivity had given way to privacy and human interaction. The breakup of the social media giants had made it much harder for internet provocateurs like Chance to monetize controversy. He was a dinosaur: a fact that Chelsea lamented with growing regularity while insisting that back in the day, Chance would have been a massive star.

Instead, he eked out a living on the fringe, relying on a motley assortment of renegade companies that courted controversy. None of these companies were exactly offering "enrichment" dollars to sponsor him, and it took some creative accounting to keep their dinghy afloat. But whenever the subject of his tenuous finances came up, Chelsea assured him that it would all pay off. "Fortune favors the bold" was one of her favorite expressions. Chance didn't see how driving an expensive car would sway reluctant sponsors into taking a risk on an adrenaline junkie who'd combined the X Games with an actual death wish, but Chelsea believed. Oh, how she believed.

"How'd it go in there? Did they give you any crap?" she asked as Chance slid behind the wheel.

"Their lawyer called me immoral."

"Again?"

"It was a new guy," he said.

"Do I need to bust some heads?" Chelsea loved to talk about busting heads. If she'd kicked as much ass and taken as many names as she threatened, she'd be on death row. It was all part of her momma-bear persona that had helped convince him three years ago to let her manage his career. At the time, it had felt good to have someone unconditionally in his corner.

"No, it's fine. I just want to go home." *Need* was closer to the truth. All the recordings made in the week leading up to the jump were stored at the house. He was always anxious to watch them, but the mystery of what the Highsmith article might say or not say was making him a little crazy. Hopefully the recordings would give him a preview of exactly how many of the beans he'd spilled.

Chelsea passed him his LFD, which he slipped behind his ear. Light-field devices had been systematically eating the lunch and market share of smartphones for the past five years, at least with the under-twenty-five set. A lot of Gen Z and other legacy generations found LFDs too complicated. Poor Chelsea was a stubborn millennial who clung resolutely to her smartphone, and no matter how much crap he gave her, she refused to upgrade. There just seemed to be a point in life when some people lost the ability to adapt to change. The new felt threatening instead of exhilarating.

Personally, Chance couldn't imagine going back to something so clunky. Holding something in his hand all day just felt like a waste of a perfectly good hand. But then he was probably a bit biased, seeing as he was a living, breathing technological change that society was struggling to accept. He tried not to take it too personally, though. He couldn't prove it, but he imagined that back when they'd invented the wheel, someone had complained about how not dragging their belongings through the dirt would spoil the children.

He powered on the LFD, and a floating screen (the magical light field) appeared inches from his eyes. At the welcome screen, the LFD confirmed his biometrics and logged him in. He gave the LFD permission to interface with the Aston Martin.

"Home?" the car queried as its high-performance electric engine started silently.

"Home," Chance confirmed, wishing he were already there.

The car shifted into gear and steered itself out of the garage and into the sunshine. Off to their right, crowded in front of the main entrance to Palingenesis, protesters chanted about the evils of human cloning. After last year's landmark Supreme Court decision in support of clones' civil rights, Chance had naïvely thought the protests would fade away. Instead, the ruling had only galvanized opposition to cloning. Every time he came for an appointment, there were more demonstrators than the time before. And he knew that anti-clone groups like Children of Adam had a particular obsession with him.

The protesters recognized his car and surged toward it, screaming their nasty little chants.

"No birth, no soul!"

"God doesn't love you!"

It only got uglier from there. Chance wondered, not for the first time, if a bright-red sports car with his name on the license plate was really such a good idea.

As the car accelerated away, Chance fished around in the back seat for his body camera. Strictly speaking, it was unnecessary—cameras already recorded the interior of the Aston Martin and uploaded the footage to his private server—but as soon as he slipped on the camera rig, he felt himself relax, knowing that whatever happened, it wouldn't be lost.

"So, exciting news," Chelsea said, pivoting in her seat to face him. "Our numbers from the last event have really turned heads over on Avenue of the Stars. I have multiple requests to set meetings. It feels like our moment."

"That's great," Chance said, mostly because Chelsea only communicated in superlatives and became depressed if her enthusiasm wasn't reciprocated. How many meetings had they had with the big talent agencies in the last three years? Meetings were the currency by which those people justified their existence. If agents didn't keep their calendars packed, they would probably fade away like exorcised spirits.

"So as soon as you're feeling up to it—"

"Do you have my cigarettes?" he asked.

"I stopped on the way, but they were sold out."

"Why are you always waiting until the last minute?" Chance asked, knowing no good would come of picking a fight with her but unwilling or unable to let it lie.

"It's been so busy since your jump. There's just so much interest in you right now," Chelsea said, steering him back toward what she considered good news. Handling him. He hated that. She was always handling him, treating him like a child to be mollified. Looking back, it had always been that way between them, but maybe that was what he'd needed back then. He'd only just turned eighteen when she'd first offered to represent him. She might not have understood his anger, but at least she hadn't minimized it. That had meant something at the time.

Now? Now he was twenty-one, and her abiding condescension was all he could hear. He knew that she didn't care about him any more than anyone else did, so long as his anger kept him up on the ledge, ready to do another stupid thing. In between, she took care of him and kept studying ways to monetize his trauma.

"You know how I hate having my routine messed with."

"It won't happen again," she said, just the wrong side of an apology.

He rerouted the car to Smokey Joe's, his regular tobacconist on Sunset. Lying to himself that he was only checking his messages, Chance scanned down the list of missed calls and texts, hoping that Maggie had reached out. After what he'd said to her, it would have taken a miracle. They hadn't spoken in over six months, not since before his last stunt, but it still managed to hurt.

"In other news, still no word about what's in the Highsmith article," Chelsea said, moving on as though the debacle of the cigarettes were already a historical footnote.

"Fine," he said, hoping to cut this short. The last thing he wanted right now was another one of Chelsea's breathless updates on all the things she didn't know. The last few days it had been all she talked about. She wasn't a person accustomed to being in the dark, and getting the article before anyone else had become a holy crusade. Thankfully, the car pulled over and announced they had arrived, cutting short the discussion. Chance got out without a word and went into the shop, leaving Chelsea alone.

Two years earlier, Smokey Joe's had been a small, nameless bodega. It had closed down for a month and reopened as a tobacconist. Chance couldn't pinpoint the moment that analog cigarettes had become hip again, but the old-school brands were definitely having a renaissance. He took it as a sign that people felt there was less to live for, so why deny themselves? The shop was popular with young Hollywood because the proprietor, a middle-aged Greek man named Kostas Kouris, was part of the small subset of Los Angelenos who had mastered the art of respecting a celebrity's privacy. It was also possible he didn't realize that some of his customers were famous, or he simply didn't care.

Chance browsed the aisles, mostly to give himself time to cool down. The shop stocked a lot of exotic brands, but he smoked only Camel unfiltered. Twenty-two dollars a pack once you added up all the state and federal taxes. He'd picked Camels as his brand for two reasons: his great-grandfather had smoked them way back in the day, and they were terrible for him. One of the perks of getting a new set of lungs was not worrying too much about cancer. Kostas rang him up without a word, a book of crossword puzzles tented on his belly.

Back out on the street, Chance stood in the shade of the awning as he tapped the pack against his wrist. He wanted Chelsea to look up and see he was making her wait, but she was engrossed with work again. After opening the pack with the practiced flourish that was really the only part of smoking he enjoyed, he lit his first cigarette in his new body.

He'd picked up a lot of bad habits that first year after the kidnapping, but this was the only one he'd worked to keep. Did he have a smoking habit, or was he just in the habit of smoking? That depended on whether you believed addiction existed in the body or the mind. This body had never experienced nicotine, but that didn't stop his mind from wanting it, a weird bit of existential continuity. He took one defiant puff, although who or what he was defying was an enduring mystery. He tried to hold the smoke down, but these were virgin lungs, and he spluttered it up like a backfiring truck, one hand on the brick wall so he wouldn't fall over.

A white teenage boy in a turquoise porkpie hat sauntered past, smiling a wiseass smile. "Got to learn how to hold your smoke, brah."

Chance looked up, still coughing, and gave a thumbs-up to the good advice. He dropped the cigarette and stubbed it out with his toe. From experience, he knew that more than a few puffs so soon would make him sick. Also, he didn't feel like making any more of a fool of himself in public. No such luck, though; the kid did a theatrical double take and circled back. Chance couldn't decide if the kid was rich and slumming it, trying to look colorfully street, or just another runaway on the hustle. It wasn't always easy to tell on Sunset.

"You're that guy," the kid said. Maybe seventeen if he stood up straight, he wore an unbuttoned gaberdine vest, no shirt beneath. His rib cage stood out in stark relief beneath his tan skin. Not dirty, but not exactly clean either, his ragged jeans were more hole than denim. Behind his ear was an LFD that was maybe six generations old, held together by electrical tape and sweat. Chance figured the kid flopped somewhere around here, sleeping during the day and venturing out only at dusk. There was no shortage of abandoned buildings to choose from.

No one wanted to believe that what had happened in San Diego could happen here, but it wasn't that complicated if you followed the water. San Diego bought its water from Los Angeles, and so was the first major domino to fall. Los Angeles, in turn, bought its water from the Imperial Valley, which was running dry. The city had pinned its hopes on desalinization, but the technology was still years away from making up the shortfall.

Los Angeles County had grown steadily for 170 years. That had ended in 2017. At first a trickle, but over the past decade the trickle had become a relentless migration. People headed east in search of affordable water. Entire neighborhoods had been decimated. Neighborhoods on the edge of Los Angeles County had become ghost towns.

Mostly it had been the middle classes with enough resources to begin again somewhere else. That left only the wealthy and the poor— the two sides of LA's tarnished coin. One that barely registered that anything had changed, and the other trapped in a dying city that was the only home they had ever known.

"Come on, you're that guy," the kid said again.

"Isn't everyone?" Chance said warily. Two kinds of people recognized him on the street: fans and people who were decidedly not fans. It could get dicey, and he gauged the distance to the Aston Martin in case he had to run for it. Fortunately, the kid seemed more excited than angry.

"No, the one who does those crazy stunts."

"Isn't everyone?" he repeated, aware instinctively from the look in the kid's eyes that he was being recorded and to say something vague and mysterious. Something on brand. If he'd learned one thing from growing up in Los Angeles, it was to always know your part, memorize your lines, and never, ever break character. Give the people what they wanted or suffer the consequences.

"Yeah, I knew that was you. Saw you jump out of that airplane. You're straight crazy, brah. That was so badass. What was it like?"

"Wish I could tell you."

Anger flashed across the kid's face as he tried to work out if he was being disrespected. Then Chance saw a glimmer of recognition light up his face as the kid found the answer to the riddle. "Right, right, 'cause you don't remember, 'cause you died. That's hella deep, man."

"There's really nothing deep about it."

"I knew this girl. Portland Sally. She OD'd. Wasn't even no funeral. City cremated her and lost her ashes."

"I'm sorry."

"I miss her. She was stand-up, you know? Made me laugh when I was down," the kid said with distant eyes.

Whatever kind of moment they were having must have ended, because a grin appeared on the kid's face. "Mind if I get a selfie? My boys'll freak."

Chance waved him over and stood there blankly while the kid posed next to him, flashing a peace sign for reasons unknown. Maybe it wasn't even a peace sign to him anymore. Things had a way of being stripped of their context and repurposed. Chance looked past the camera as if he'd just caught sight of an old friend, or the devil on his trail. Another trademark.

"Thanks. Can I bum a cigarette?"

Chance handed him the pack and told him to keep it. Pleased, the kid held out his fist. Chance tapped it and watched him wander away down Sunset toward Hollywood, uneasy at the thought that this kid might represent his core demographic. He got back in the car, switched it to manual, and tested the steering wheel lightly. He suddenly felt like finding out if the car was really as fast as advertised.

"What are you doing?" Chelsea asked.

"Driving home."

"No. Please, Chance."

It irritated him how alarmed Chelsea sounded, like he'd suggested they rob a bank. "What's the big deal?"

"Your coordination is still coming back. It's too soon."

"I'm good," Chance said, wiggling all ten fingers in the air to demonstrate. "Anyway, it's less than a mile. What's the worst that could happen?"

Chelsea placed a cautioning hand on the steering wheel. "Put the car back in auto, Chance." She spoke his name like she was reading it off a label for the first time. "You have clones. I don't."

He felt his jaw working silently. As if he had too many words in his mouth and needed to spit a few out before he'd be able to speak. "Let go of the wheel."

Chelsea acquiesced, hand coming away slowly, palm open, as if demonstrating she wasn't armed. Chance toggled the car back to auto.

"Happy now?" he asked.

"Chance . . ."

"Take me home," he told the car.

It really was only a few minutes away, but one mile felt like a lifetime.

CHAPTER FIVE

Chance lived in a historically hip enclave in the Hollywood Hills known as the Bird Streets. It had earned the name for obvious reasons: Oriole Lane, Robin Drive, Mockingbird Place. The tradition had begun more than a century earlier in the roaring twenties and continued for the next forty years. Chance's street, Blue Jay Way, had been christened in 1964 and inspired the George Harrison song. Some people thought it was the other way around; Chance enjoyed correcting them.

The house felt like his refuge from the world. A sanctuary. Like any hopeful boy growing up in Los Angeles, a view of the city at night, glittering below like a Technicolor ocean, had been his brass ring, the pinnacle of human achievement. It took something drab and made it beautiful. What was more LA than that? Staring out at the city from the back of the house, he came as close as he ever did to peace of mind.

The Bird Streets had always attracted an A-list of actors, producers, and other celebrities. Next door to Chance was a twelve-thousand-square-foot behemoth that had sold for $42 million the year before. The owner, a twenty-six-year-old point guard, had been traded to the Bulls before he could move in but had yet to put the house back on the market. Built in 1966, the house where Chance lived was a comparatively modest twenty-seven hundred square feet. A charming midcentury modern on an eighteen-thousand-square-foot lot with killer views.

Or what real estate agents charitably called a *development opportunity*. Less charitably, a teardown. Rudely, an eyesore.

Chelsea led people to think Chance owned it—an address in the Bird Streets came with a history of cool that she coveted for him—but the house belonged to his mother. It had been his father's first house in Los Angeles, a reward to himself when his start-up took off. Whenever Brett Harker told stories about the house on Blue Jay Way, which was often, the affection and nostalgia in his voice were unmistakable. The parties. The big names who dropped by to hang out by the pool. It represented a golden moment in his father's youth, the beginning of his self-mythologizing.

He'd met Emelia Hobbes, Chance's mother, at one of his own parties. The most beautiful human he'd ever seen. She'd crashed with a girlfriend, her maid of honor a year later. After Marley was born, they'd needed more space and bought a house closer to the ocean. But his father could never bring himself to sell the house on Blue Jay Way. He liked to say it was where everything good in his life had begun.

No doubt that was why his mother had pried it away from him in the ugly divorce that followed the kidnapping. Once she had the deed in hand, developers lined up to buy. One overly aggressive woman had even knocked on the door and offered fifteen million on the spot. Chance had passed the offer on to his mother, who'd laughed into her vodka soda. She would never sell. She meant for the house to slide into ruin and referred to it as Satis House West. His mother had always had a sharp literary sense of humor that she wielded like a wry scalpel. Perhaps to remind the world, her husband included, that she was far more than just a retired cover girl. Unlike Miss Havisham, though, his mother was wise enough not to live in the house while it fell down around her.

That dubious honor was left to Chance, who knew that being allowed to stay at the house had nothing to do with maternal affection. He was just another cog in her never-ending campaign to torture her ex-husband from beyond the marriage. Nearly everything about Chance appalled his father at this point. His only goal as a parent had been to not raise aimless, spoiled delinquents. So his son living at the house on Blue Jay Way, nearly rent-free, made his father apoplectic. Not that Chance was complaining; he was happy to be the lump in his dad's oatmeal. He and his mother didn't have much in common anymore, but their shared resentment of Brett Harker was an unbreakable bond.

The Aston Martin pulled into the driveway beside Chelsea's car. Even before it rolled to a stop, Chance said, "I'll talk to you in a few days."

Chelsea collected her things on her lap, taking her time as she gathered her thoughts. "We really do need to strategize how we're going to respond to the Highsmith article."

"We'll get to it," he said, opening his car door in case she needed a demonstration of how one worked. "I'll call you when I'm done."

"How long will that take?"

"How the hell should I know? I've never processed this much lag before." It came out as if it were her fault. He was a little intimidated at the prospect. Usually there was only the one day of recordings to sort through. The thought of so much missing time made him a little sick.

She nodded in agreement but said, "It's just that we'll be swamped with requests for comment. If we're not prepared and I have to stonewall those jackals, that becomes the narrative. You know how these things play out."

Chance gazed through the windshield at Chelsea's car wistfully, wishing she were in it. "Tell them I recently died and that these things take time."

Chelsea looked at him, evidently trying to tell if he was serious. "I don't know if that's a good—"

"We don't even know what's in the article, Chelsea. How're we supposed to brainstorm a response?"

"Well, what did you intend to say to her? What was your mindset before the refresh?" What Chelsea meant was that since this version of his consciousness predated Imani Highsmith's arrival in California, he might at least remember his intentions. He was, after all, the fossil record of *that* Chance's emotional state.

"I don't know. Nothing out of the ordinary," he answered, although that wasn't remotely true. He changed the subject. "Has anyone been inside?"

After he died, no one went into the house before Chance was discharged from Palingenesis. He always wanted to be the first. Needed to be, so he could wander through his home and know this was exactly how his predecessor had left things, reassuring himself that he remembered the house and where everything belonged. It was part of his ritual that helped him to feel normal again. Chelsea knew that but still wouldn't quit. "Well?"

"Of course not."

"Then I will talk to you in a few days, and we'll figure out the Highsmith thing." He thought he'd put some tone of voice on it, but she only stared at him with disappointed eyes. "What?"

Chelsea sighed wearily and finally opened her door. "Your groceries are in the trunk."

Chance watched her walk to her car and drive away. Maybe his frustration with her was that they'd been together too long. Like partners in a marriage that had lost its spark, they saw through the other's bullshit. It was hard when half the planet bought the enigmatic mirage of your public persona, but the person you spent the most time with knew you were nothing but a scared kid.

Chance popped the trunk and carried the groceries up the stairs to the house in three trips. A fresh crack snaked up the wall from the foundation to the roof like a map of the Amazon River. It would need to be patched and painted over. The house might be falling apart inside, but Chance liked to keep the front facade from becoming an eyesore. Maintain appearances. An obvious metaphor.

The front door recognized his biometric signature and unlocked automatically as he came up the walk, but it stuck when Chance tried the handle, and he had to put his shoulder into it to force the stubborn door to open. He added that to the list of things that needed fixing.

Inside was cool, quiet. He stood on the threshold listening to the gentle white noise of the climate-controlled house. In fifth grade, he'd been obsessed with ancient Egypt, the pyramids, the hieroglyphics, the art. For school, he'd been assigned a five-minute presentation and a one-page summary; he'd written fifteen pages and talked for the entire class. Maybe that's why coming home after a revival felt as if he were defiling a tomb. He wasn't really Chance Harker, and he didn't belong here.

A bad case of imposter syndrome was a pretty common hang-up for clones. He knew, fundamentally, that he was the same person as the previous Chance Harker. Hadn't the house recognized his biometrics? But, at the same time, he knew it wasn't as simple as matching DNA. For one thing, he didn't even have the same fingerprints. He was five clones removed from the first and original Chance Harker. A copy of a copy of a copy. A sinister, unfriendly voice in his head was always questioning what might have been lost.

Lights flickered on as he went back to the kitchen. The house connected to his LFD and gave him a status update: no intrusions, no alarms, but the AC filter needed changing. He left the groceries on the counter and took a walk through the house, checking every room. The crack out front had upset his fragile equilibrium. Lag made unexpected change very difficult to accept. If there was anything else different about the house, he needed to know.

Whole rooms were completely empty now, so it wasn't as hard to tell as it once had been. The living room's only occupant was an eight-foot ficus. He'd sold off most of the furniture to pay the bills that helped maintain the illusion that Chance Harker was living Chelsea's fabled rock-star life. His father had exquisite taste, fetching a good price on consignment. Chance counted on his mother honoring her vow that it would take a cold day in hell before she'd ever set foot back inside the house. If LA ever did experience a sudden cold snap, he couldn't decide whether she'd be furious or secretly delighted to find he'd ransacked the house.

He checked the library, but everything looked more or less the same. He called it a library, but the space was really one of the guest bedrooms. Over time, it had been reduced to a comfortable armchair, footstool, and lamp. And thousands of books. Some were on bookshelves, but most were piled like haphazard stalagmites on the floor. Theoretically he had a system but was lucky if he could keep his to-be-read pile separate from the titles he'd already finished.

Books didn't fit his dim, party-boy persona, but he spent most of his spare time reading, either here or by the pool. He hadn't exactly finished high school in a blaze of glory, but he'd been a very good student once upon a time. College felt beyond him, and reading had become his great consolation. Recently, he'd been working his way through books set in Los Angeles, hoping it might grant insight into his uneasy relationship with his hometown. Kerouac had called LA the loneliest American city, and Chance knew exactly what he meant. That was probably why he'd felt right at home with the fatalistic noir of James Ellroy, Raymond Chandler, and Walter Mosley. But it had been Christopher Isherwood's *A Single Man* and Viet Thanh Nguyen's *The Sympathizer*, novels about outsiders living secret lives, that had struck the strongest chord in him.

Once he was confident that everything in the library was how he remembered it, he went into the bedroom and ran a shower. A faint, unpleasant scent always clung to his skin after a revival. Cars had a new smell to them; why not clones? He stood under the blistering water and scrubbed himself until his skin was pink. He toweled off and put on deodorant and far too much cologne, but the damn smell was still there. He'd never worked up the nerve to ask Holifield if it was all in his head. He sighed. The idea of psychosomatic body odor wasn't remotely appealing.

He went back to the kitchen to take his pills. The groceries were still sitting on the counter like tourists waiting for their bus. While he put them away, he weighed the pros and cons of calling Maggie. He'd always thought he liked living by himself, but ever since their fight, it had started to feel intolerable. Without her, he was conscious all the time of how alone he really was. Still, he stopped himself from dialing her number. Pride was a son of a bitch, making him believe that she should be the one to call him, that being right was more important than being happy. He was starting to think his pride might be an idiot.

He fished a cold Coke from the back of the refrigerator and went out to the lanai. Water rationing made it illegal to fill a pool in Los Angeles County, but most of his neighbors ignored the regulation, including the ones who publicly supported the proposition. It was only a $4,000 fine, *if* they were cited, and enforcement in the Bird Streets was relatively lax. Chance had heard his neighbors call it the *pool tax* and knew they were more than happy to pay.

Chance dragged one of the loungers into a shady spot near the edge of his empty pool. He might not have become an environmental engineer, as he'd dreamed of as a child, but it was the one thing he was unwilling to be a hypocrite about. And anyway, he didn't have $4,000 to spare.

On the little table where he went to set his Coke was a book he didn't recognize. *City of Glass*, by Paul Auster, published in 1985. The back cover said it was the first volume of the New York trilogy. Chance had never heard of it. On the title page was a note in his handwriting, "Made me think of us." Curious, Chance got comfortable and began to read from the beginning.

He thought the book had a great first paragraph but didn't make it much past that. When he woke hours later, the book was tented on his chest and the glory of Los Angeles at night glittered up at him. His Coke was warm, but he drank it anyway. Then he gathered his things and went back inside the house. He had questions that needed answering.

CHAPTER SIX

If his life were a comic book, Chance reckoned he would've had a cave filled with bats hidden away under the house. But this was Southern California and basements were in short supply, much less subterranean lairs, so he made do with the other spare bedroom at the end of the hall.

He boiled water for tea by the light of the city and fished the key from its hiding place beneath the sink. The bedroom door took both a traditional key and a voice-print password, and it required a biometric check before the house would open it. He'd splurged on the upgraded security not because he was afraid anyone would rob him—nothing inside would have significance to anyone besides himself—but because he was afraid someone might snoop around and see just how crazy he really was.

The curtains were always drawn, and in the dark the space might be mistaken for a little-used sitting room, nothing but a hodgepodge of old, musty furniture. *Are you roommates with teenage boys?* wouldn't be an unreasonable question. Only someone from the family would recognize the couch as the one from the brothers' rec room. It had taken a beating over the years; the springs were shot, the middle sagged, and stuffing hung out of the arms in clumps, but it was still the most comfortable couch in the world if you knew just where to sit. The coffee table hadn't had things any easier—it had more rings than Saturn. (Coasters had been a tough sell at the Harkers'.) The area rug, the lamps that he circled the room switching on, the movie posters, the dartboard . . . it had all been reclaimed from his parents during the chaos of their divorce.

Chance pulled a frayed blanket from the back of the couch and wrapped it around his shoulders. His grandmother had knitted it for him as a baby present, and the blanket had sat for years untouched on the windowsill of his childhood bedroom. Now it might just be his most prized possession.

What would Holifield and Dr. Hughes make of it? Chance figured building a museum to his lost childhood might raise a red flag with the good people at Palingenesis. And if that didn't convince them to measure him for a straitjacket, then the suspect board that covered the entire back wall would almost certainly do the trick.

He'd gotten the idea from old cop shows, and his had everything: photographs pinned to the wall with thumbtacks; index cards with important-sounding questions scrawled in black marker; crimson string fanned out between thumbtacks like arteries.

In theory it was a visual timeline of the events surrounding the kidnapping, beginning with his final refresh and ending with the moment of his revival after the kidnappers executed him as a warning to his father not to haggle over the ransom demands. At the suspect board's center was a photograph of Chance and Marley, taken a few days before the kidnapping. The two brothers were smiling easy, carefree smiles that Chance barely recognized. Beneath, written directly onto the wall, was a simple question: WHO KILLED US?

At first glance, his suspect board all looked impressively thorough. The work of a driven man on the verge of the breakthrough that would change everything. (He found it helped if he said that last part in a serious tone of voice.) But up close, it was pretty obvious that his suspect board was missing one essential element: suspects. He knew everything there was to know about his own kidnapping, but if the police had hit a dead end, all the string in the world wasn't going to magically create leads where there were none. Truth was, he hadn't updated the board in years. He only left it there to remind himself how little anyone actually knew about the nine days that had ended his childhood.

Did he still sometimes stare at it for hours, hoping to spot something he'd missed? No, because that would have been psychologically unhealthy. Nor did he entertain elaborately cruel fantasies of what he would do if he ever tracked down his kidnappers and murderers. Although if he had to choose between revenge and simply knowing the truth, if he could only have one, he'd choose the truth every time. He'd let them all go free if they would just tell him what had really happened.

Lag was just that unbearable.

Chance didn't think that anyone who hadn't experienced it first-hand could really comprehend the brutal way that it affected clones. The way lag undermined their sense of self and made them question their reality. After five revivals, Chance had more experience with it than anyone, but he had never gotten over his first. One look at the chaos up on the wall confirmed that. He'd left a happy, stable childhood and been revived nine days later to a broken family spinning apart like a dying solar system.

Palingenesis had a theory about why Chance did what he did. Holifield called it *repetition compulsion*, the inability to break a cycle of unhealthy behavior. Apparently it happened in clones whose lag contained a particularly traumatic event—say, for instance, your kidnapping and murder. Unless the clone made peace with the fact they'd never know what had really happened, unhealthy behaviors could develop. Chance thought that was a little melodramatic. How was jumping out of an airplane without a parachute unhealthy?

Okay . . . point taken.

Taped to the wall next to his red-string art installation was an old page from a spiral-bound notebook. Chance had torn it out of one of his brother's movie journals where he wrote down observations and ideas. This page was a list of Marley's favorite movie stunts. Five had been crossed out. Chance took a pen and drew a line through number seventeen: *Point Break*, Johnny Utah / Keanu Reeves jumps from a plane without a parachute. Looking down the remaining list, he wondered what should come next. He wouldn't have time to get through them all before he turned twenty-three and was no longer covered by his father's policy.

That was a question for another day. In addition to his childhood museum, the room also housed the rack of servers that controlled all his cameras and cataloged the Mount Everest of footage they generated. A program took all the footage and shuffled it together using time stamps. Chance got settled on the couch with his tea. Before powering off his LFD, he locked down the house and armed the alarm system. He would be in airplane mode now until it was done. The front doorbell wouldn't even ring. If it was urgent, people knew to contact Chelsea. If it was life or death, she had the only other key to the house. She'd never once used it.

There was a lot of wild speculation in the media about what he did in the house during this time. His favorite theory was the one that had him lighting candles and incense, attempting to commune with the spirits of the previous Chance Harkers. In one tabloid version, he supposedly watched the recordings naked and smeared himself with the blood of some sacrificial animal. The truth was far more mundane, more akin to an audit than a séance.

He always started at the end of the recordings and then jumped back to the beginning. As morbid as it was, seeing himself die was the final step in accepting that this was all real. He watched himself throw a parachute out of the plane and leap after it. The screen split into three panels, so he could watch footage from his helmet camera, the cameraman who'd jumped after him, and the view from the ground. He took a good line after the parachute, and even though he'd been told how it ended, he still held out hope that he would catch it. The strap of the runaway parachute danced wildly in the wind. He practically flew right into it. How could he possibly miss? But the parachute seemed to bounce away from him, and as he turned in midair to reach back desperately for the strap, it was already too late.

The rest was difficult to watch, but Chance didn't look away. Not until the cameras on the ground spotted his plummeting form and the abrupt, awful way it all ended. He began to cry; it always made him cry. Not in sadness, exactly, but out of relief that he had no more excuses to deny what had happened.

After he had accepted the reality of his death, Chance went back to the beginning. A voyeur to his own life. His one rule was that he would watch everything once through. However much there was, he then spent the next few days watching and rewatching the footage until it began to feel like actual memories. That was his reality. No candles, no blood sacrifices. He could skip past most of his sleep, so that cut out a third of the recordings right there. And if nothing interesting was happening, he would watch on double or even quadruple speed. The program scanned for keywords and automatically slowed the playback if anything important was said.

Going in, he'd been concerned about having seven days' worth of recordings to watch and sort through. Turned out he didn't need to be. There wasn't anywhere near that much footage. There were always gaps, of course. Not everyone appreciated being filmed, and some places, like Palingenesis, forbade recordings entirely. Chance did his best to respect their wishes and left himself notes with summaries of what was missing. In theory, the process left him with a fairly seamless document of his life.

This went way beyond that.

There were monumental gaps in the recordings. Actually, to call them gaps was a disservice. All of Thursday was missing. A compiling error? Had to be it. But when he checked the backups, they'd been wiped too, which made no sense. There only one person with access—him. And he'd never do such a thing. But when he checked the server log, he found a time stamp for a series of systematic deletions, all dated the night before the big airplane stunt.

Chance skipped forward through the recordings to the mass deletions. He expected the footage also to have been deleted, but it was there. And so was Chance, the previous one anyway, caught red-handed deleting days' worth of recordings. His predecessor had clearly wanted Chance to see him do it. To know it had been him.

On-screen, the former Chance finished his task and looked up at the camera. "I know you're probably upset, but this is for the best." And then, as an afterthought: "Good luck."

The recording went blank. Chance stared at the screen, willing it to restart and confused when it didn't. But that, as they said, was a wrap. He swore at the blank screen. Upset? Of course he was upset. What the hell was that? First he'd canceled his last refresh, saddling himself with a whole week of lag, and then he'd intentionally deleted all the footage from that week. He'd locked himself out of his own life. It was an incomprehensible betrayal. Of course, it was hard to know what to do with that when the person who'd betrayed you was you.

He swore at the screen again.

Then he did the only thing he could. He went back to the beginning and watched it all again.

CHAPTER SEVEN

Chance was sitting out by his empty pool nursing a half-empty beer when the house announced the front door had been opened. Since the alarm hadn't tripped, he knew it must be Chelsea. The arrangement was that she would wait to hear from him unless it was life or death. Her heels echoed on the stone floors, getting louder, and he heard her calling his name.

"Didn't you hear me calling you?" she said, stepping out onto the lanai. A magazine was rolled up in her hand.

"What are you doing here?" He'd been done since this morning but didn't see any reason to share that with her. He'd obsessively watched and rewatched the fragments of his missing week, trying to guess what had been purged from the recordings and why. It was a little embarrassing how long it took to recognize the major theme of the deletions—Imani Zari Highsmith. All traces of the reporter had been erased, like she'd never been there that week. It wasn't until this morning that he'd admitted that there was nothing more to see. Since then, he'd been sitting out here by the pool soaking up the peace and quiet. He still wasn't quite ready to rejoin the world, but the world was apparently determined to rejoin him.

"It's been a week, Chance."

That caught him off guard. He'd have sworn it had been only half that. His moral superiority wobbled beneath him. Looking to regain the high ground, he asked who'd died.

"No one yet, but we're on life support here." Chelsea dropped the magazine in his lap, where it unfurled like a battle streamer. Highsmith had said the odds were fifty-fifty whether he got the cover. Well, he had, and it was a doozy.

His father kept framed copies of all his own magazine covers in his office, but even though this was Chance's first, he wouldn't be hanging it on any wall. In the kindest possible terms, the photograph was unflattering. Taken from way, way too close up, it had a harsh, fluorescent quality that made him look like he had the plague. His pores were the size of canyons. It was the kind of cover reserved for divisive public figures. *Buy me,* the magazine promised, *and learn the unvarnished truth about this ugly man.*

In bold typeface, the issue's tagline read: "Meet the New Gods." It didn't sound like a compliment.

"What did you do?" Chelsea demanded, the anger and frustration in her voice red-hot.

"Is it really that bad?" he asked, although the feeling of uncertain excitement had returned. What *had* he done?

"Jesus, Chance. Yes, it's that bad. Highsmith basically painted you as the poster child of anti-democratic late-capitalist excess in America."

"Come on," he said, knowing Chelsea could be hyperbolic at times.

She pointed a manicured finger at the magazine. "Read it." And when he didn't immediately, she added: "Now."

They stared at each other for a long moment. Chance shrugged and thumbed through the magazine until he came to the article. He intended to skim it to get Chelsea off his back, but the first few sentences landed like haymakers:

To meet Chance Harker is to meet a god. You likely know his name, not because he's talented or gifted, but because he is the most privileged human being in history. He inhabits a world where death has lost its meaning. How do I know this? Because recently I watched him plummet to his death from an aircraft without a parachute. Shortly thereafter, he awoke in a glorified laboratory none the worse for wear. In an earlier age, it would be called a resurrection, a miracle, and Chance Harker worshiped as a god. Now the miraculous is known as revival, and Chance Harker is simply another obscenely wealthy client of Palingenesis. But I couldn't help but wonder, as he leapt willingly from that plane, if our ancestors were closer to the truth. Because what else but a god do you call a person who dies again and again without repercussion or responsibility? And what does that mean for the rest of us, for whom dying still means death?

Chance stopped and looked out over the city. This was the first time a magazine article had ever given him chills. It was more unsettling than reading his own autopsy.

"Keep going. It gets worse," Chelsea assured him.

He nodded and started over again, more slowly this time. Word by word, paragraph by paragraph, page after page, Highsmith tore him apart with her eloquence, rearranging his pieces to build her case. A beautiful, well-reasoned argument that made him out to be a narcissistic, spoiled clown. Charitably, he couldn't see anywhere to argue that she was wrong. And if the clown in question was convinced, how compelling would the rest of the world find her?

But it wasn't just that. She included details about the kidnapping that only a handful of people in the world knew. He'd discussed his secret fears and suspicions about the kidnapping that he'd never dared speak aloud. There would be hell to pay when his father saw it. But by far the biggest bombshell was Marley.

"My brother was out of bounds," he chided himself.

"Well, apparently *you* didn't leave him there," Chelsea said, the accusation hanging in the space between them like a fist. She'd warned him not to engage with Highsmith and, once he had, begged him not to talk to the experienced reporter alone, the implication being that Highsmith would easily manipulate him into saying more than he should.

"Where is she?" he demanded.

"I have no idea. Hell, if there's any justice."

"Then find out. I want to see her."

"Chance," Chelsea said, that mothering tone that he detested creeping into her voice. "I don't think that's such a good idea."

"I don't give a damn," he said, flinging the magazine into the empty pool like a bomb that might go off at any moment. He got up and stalked into the house.

Chelsea trailed him into the bedroom. "What we need to do is sit down and strategize," she said. "Get out ahead of this thing. Not make a public scene that will only make things worse."

"Worse than what?" he asked, pulling on the first clothes he found.

"We've been dropped by four of our sponsors."

That wasn't an insignificant number, given he had only six sponsors total. "Why? What for?"

"Why? Because you said, and I'm quoting you here, 'People say clones have no souls, but what about my audience? What kind of ghouls tune in to watch something like this? It says more about them than it does about me.'"

"You memorized it?"

"Your words are kind of hard to forget, Chance. It's not every day a client lights their career on fire."

"So who's left?"

"Just Durango and Lethal Injection energy drink. I think they can be convinced to stay on board, but only if we sit down with them and offer reassurances. And I'm getting swamped by the media with requests for comment, but I can't keep stonewalling. We need to issue a statement."

"I'm going out for a while," he said, with no clear idea of where he was going, only that he needed to drive and clear his head. He snatched up his LFD, wallet, and sunglasses. "Find Imani Highsmith."

"Chance, stop. Think," Chelsea said, blocking his path to the front door. "What is it going to get you?"

"Stop trying to handle me. You're starting to piss me off."

"Why'd you do it?" she asked, a whole new tone slipping into her voice, one of disappointment and betrayal.

"I have no idea. I wasn't there, remember?"

"Are you really going to hide behind that now? You're a clone, so you don't remember anything? How convenient." As soon as she said it, her face registered that she knew she'd gone too far.

"Get out of my way, Chelsea."

"Fine," she said, stepping aside. "Should I just wait here, Your Highness?"

"I honestly don't give a damn what you do," he said over his shoulder.

"Fantastic. I'll just start organizing your bail now."

———

The car asked for a destination, but he didn't have one. He told it to take him in the direction of Santa Monica because the drive was long, which would give him time to figure out what to do next. Talking to Imani Highsmith wasn't really on his list of things to do. Nervously, he powered on his LFD for the first time in seven days.

He had a metric ton of messages, way more than normal. Besides Chelsea, who'd called twenty-three times before resorting to breaking into his house, his father had also left six messages. Six more than

Chance had gotten in the last twelve months combined. He mass-deleted them without listening. No doubt his father was furious, and Chance was looking forward to having it out with him. The entire interview had been a thinly veiled "Fuck you" to him. Unsurprisingly, there were no calls from his mother, whom he actually would have enjoyed talking to. But he wasn't even sure what continent she was on this week. What were the chances she knew the article even existed?

He scrolled through the rest of his messages. Most were either journalists trying to sidestep Chelsea or people he would call his friends, if anyone asked him who his friends were. It was more honest, and accurate, to say they were his acquaintances. People he socialized with who barely knew him and, happily, vice versa.

Wait. What was that?

He stopped and scrolled back. There, mixed in with the dross, was a call from Maggie.

Her message was typically brief and to the point. "Call me," she said, her tone as light as a summer breeze, as if not a day had passed. No mention of the horrific argument that had ended things.

Not that Chance thought she'd forgiven him. She'd made her career playing the ingenue. One critic said she had the face of an angel, but you'd be a fool if you thought Maggie Soto was a pushover. She was as strong as they came. Despite all the terrible things he'd said to her, Maggie hadn't yelled, hadn't screamed, hadn't said a single word. She'd just stood there, making up her mind about them, while he'd actually been fool enough to think he was winning the argument. By the time he was done making an ass of himself, their relationship had been over.

If he'd learned anything since, it was to never underestimate the stupidity of a man who believes he's in the right.

He'd regretted their fight every day, of course, and just wanted things to go back to how they'd been. But that would have taken him stepping up and actually apologizing for the awful things he'd said. Thing was, apologizing wasn't a part of the bridge-burner's code. He'd done what he always did when someone crossed him—he'd dug in his heels and set to work cutting off his own nose. And for what? Because she loved him enough to ask him to stop . . . to stop taking such terrible risks, to stop traumatizing himself over and over, to get some real help. It had felt like a monumental betrayal at the time.

None of that mattered now, though. She had called, and all he felt was relief.

She picked up on the first ring. "Hi," she said delicately.

His heart fluttered. "Hi. I didn't think you were talking to me anymore."

"Is that what you thought?" she said, letting him know with her tone that the assumption had been mutual. "Are you okay?"

He realized why she was calling, and his heart fell silent. "You read the article."

"Everyone's read the article. It's all anyone is talking about. The talking heads are having a field day with it on the news."

"My dad is apoplectic."

"Well, you kind of emptied the teapot over his head. Anyway, isn't that what you wanted?"

That slowed him down. They hadn't spoken in almost seven months, but Maggie still knew exactly what he'd done and why.

She said, "I assume you're done watching your movies? Are you still lurking around your house?"

"I'm in the car."

"Making a run for it?" Maggie said, sounding amused at the idea.

"No. Maybe. I don't know. I miss you," he said, and then immediately regretted the words, feeling like he'd just given away a state secret.

"Well, if you don't know where you're going, you can come over here. We can figure it out together."

"Just like that? All is forgiven?"

"There was never anything to forgive," she said matter-of-factly. "I'll be here."

CHAPTER EIGHT

Chance woke with the rising sun, even though the curtains mostly shut out the light. They'd stayed up talking late into the night, and more sleep would have been welcome, but he'd always been an early riser even when he didn't want to be. Once he was up, he was up. Beside him, Maggie rolled onto her side but didn't wake. She'd kicked off the covers. She fell asleep cold but slept hot as a furnace. He watched her with a half smile on his face. Not everyone looked good in the morning, but she slept as if posed by an artist . . . peaceful and serenely beautiful.

He slipped out of bed and padded into the bathroom. He lifted the seat and stared sleepily down into the toilet. Dried pee was all around the lip of the bowl. There was a bathroom by the front door, so there was only one reason a man would use hers. Whoever it was had lousy aim. Chance stopped himself right there. What business was it of his? He hadn't seen Maggie since before his fifth stunt. And he had the audacity to feel jealous? What was she supposed to do, go into mourning and take a vow of celibacy?

In the kitchen, he poured himself a glass of water, drank it over the sink, and poured himself another. Her little bungalow hadn't changed. Maybe a few more photographs? She collected old picture frames, and the living room overflowed with them, so it was hard to be sure. How long had it taken him to notice that they were arranged chronologically? Too long. Working clockwise from the antique clock, they told the story of her life and the acting career that had begun so brightly but floundered over the last few years.

It began with a cast photo from *Our Crazy Family*, the show Maggie had starred in for four seasons as a little kid. She'd made him promise to never watch it. He had anyway. It wasn't good, but her talent was obvious, and by the last two seasons her character's storyline had dominated. The wall of red-carpet photographs of her alongside Hollywood royalty attested to that. Anton Brätt, the disgraced director, featured in many of them. Depending on who you asked, he was a genius or a monster, possibly both. Maggie had been in two of his films and starred in his fourth and final production, *The Redwood Code*, when she was fourteen. It had been nominated for eight Oscars and earned her a Best Supporting Actress nod. In Chance's opinion, she should have won, but Hollywood loved handing out makeup Oscars to seventy-nine-year-old legends who should have won in their prime.

Maggie had seemed poised for greatness, and everyone had assumed her time would come, but the nomination had marked the beginning of the end. She described her life after *The Redwood Code* as a bullet train with dirty windows. At sixteen she'd sued for emancipation from her parents, who'd been using her career earnings as their own personal piggy bank. Then there were the nasty rumors about the inappropriate nature of her relationship with Brätt. Her steadfast defense of him even after he was caught with another underage actress did little to help. She freely admitted that she'd become impossible to work with after that.

The arrest for shoplifting, being kicked off the sets of her next two movies—the parts quickly dried up. Swallowed whole by the LA party scene, she'd checked herself into rehab at eighteen, come out clean, and applied to USC the following year. She'd graduated high school thanks to an array of private on-set tutors but decided she wanted a real college experience. Despite her parents' mismanagement of her career, she'd owned this bungalow in Mid-Wilshire, with enough money put aside to live on. All she needed was an acceptance letter. That hadn't proved to be a problem. Turned out she was as smart as she was talented.

That's where she'd met Marley, who intended to major in economics with a cinematic arts minor. He wasn't especially creative himself and was self-aware enough to know it. What he had done was inherit his father's business savvy and effortless charisma. He loved being around creative people and had dreams of becoming a producer. That he'd immediately started dating a famous actress made for easy jokes at first. But anyone who saw them together knew it was the real thing. They'd met during freshman orientation and been inseparable from the start.

Maggie and Marley—you couldn't say one of their names without the other. He brought her home to meet the family, and the Harkers adopted her as one of their own. They became her family, and Chance her little brother. He picked up a photograph of them all together, the rolling hills of Napa in the background. His mother and father were smiling, arms around each other, still very much in love. Maggie and Marley radiated enough light and energy to form a new sun. And in the middle, awkward fourteen-year-old Chance Harker, happily oblivious to what the future held in store. They all were.

Those were golden memories for Chance, even now. After the kidnapping, when Marley had slipped away from all of them and his parents' marriage had disintegrated, Maggie and Chance had been all that had survived. Maggie had been heartbroken, but as great as her own grief had been, she saw it was nothing compared to that of her boyfriend's little brother. She'd taken care of Chance, and he'd clung to her like a life preserver in a typhoon. Maggie was the only person in the world who could maybe understand what he was going through.

Marley had been gone for four years before they became involved. Maybe it had been inevitable; Chance had been not-so-secretly in love with Maggie for years. That still didn't make the relationship healthy, and they both struggled with whether falling in love was a betrayal. The weight of their shared history was simply too great to overcome, even though that same history bound them together.

Maggie was awake when he came back to bed. "I thought maybe you'd left."

"Not without my jeans." He picked them up off the rug as evidence but didn't put them on.

She watched him from the bed. The euphoria of reunion energy had granted them one night, but their time-out hadn't survived the unflinching light of dawn. Tension was creeping back between them. What happened next, what they said next, would matter infinitely more than anything that had happened in the night. Chance was young and often stupid, but he knew that much.

"Who are the Black Microns?" he asked, the pressure of the moment getting to him. It was printed on the oversize T-shirt she'd put on while he was in the kitchen.

"A band."

He made a face, letting her know he'd guessed that much. Live music was Maggie's happy place, and she went to three shows a week minimum. Large crowds made him sweaty. What if someone recognized him? Someone who didn't like clones. What if the crowd happened to agree?

"I'm going to the Con D'Arcy concert tomorrow night," she said.

"The clone singer?" he asked, although he knew full well who and what Con D'Arcy was.

"She did three shows at the Forum this week. She's wrapping up her tour tonight at the Troubadour. Should be special."

"Shouldn't she be off somewhere waxing her halo?" When Con D'Arcy wasn't singing, she was advocating for clone rights and generally trying to make the world a better place. Call him a cynic, but he didn't buy it. Celebrities all had their pet causes. It didn't make her special.

Maggie raised an eyebrow. "Aren't you contractually required to be a fan?"

"She's just annoying. I haven't actually listened to her stuff."

"That's too bad. It's brilliant." That was high praise from Maggie Soto, who wasn't an easy convert.

"Can I come with?" he asked, much to his own surprise.

Maggie rolled on her back as if trying to decide if he looked any better upside down. "*You* want to go to a show? Of a singer you find annoying?"

"Yeah?" When she put it that way, it didn't sound like a very bright idea.

"That's sweet of you, but . . ."

"But we haven't really talked about the other thing," he said.

"No, we haven't."

The other thing was her ultimatum. The cause of their big blowout seven months ago. He'd been deep into prepping his fifth stunt. It had involved driving a car with bald tires, faulty brakes, and no seat belts or airbags down a stretch of California State Route 138, a notoriously dangerous highway in the foothills of the San Gabriel Mountains north of Los Angeles. Out of the blue, Maggie had begged him not to go through with it. Said she didn't think she could stand by while he risked his life again and that he had to choose—her, or his stunts.

He hadn't taken it well. Especially not from Maggie, whom he'd always trusted to have his back. A master of the preemptive strike, he'd said unforgivable things about her career and her life. The gift of being close to someone was knowing them intimately. The danger was that if you happened to be a thin-skinned, insecure child who thought the best defense was a cruel offense, you might use that intimacy against them. Chance had a gift for it. When you'd been abandoned by your own family, it was easy to become a knee-jerk bridge burner, sometimes while you were still standing on the bridge.

How naïve was he? So naïve that he'd walked away thinking he'd actually won because Maggie hadn't fought back: in his mind an iron-clad admission of guilt. He'd thought that after he finished his fifth stunt, everything would go back to the way it had been. What hadn't occurred to him until much too late was that Maggie might not fight his way. She didn't throw tantrums. She'd simply walked away and shut her door to him.

He'd gone through with number five, acquitting himself well—that's how one gearhead online had put it—before losing control of the car and skidding off the road. Miraculously, he'd survived, and the stunt earned huge numbers among his target demographics. He'd made a panicked face right before he'd lost control of the car, which had become a favorite meme online—shorthand for regretting a decision. Chelsea had loved that and immediately started talking about how to raise the stakes even higher for number six. When he'd called Maggie to tell her about it, she hadn't answered, not then, and not ever again. He hadn't heard a single word from her, until yesterday.

"Why did you leave?" he asked. "What changed?"

"You left," she reminded him and then sat up seriously. "And nothing changed. That was the problem. You were exactly where you were three years ago. In the past. That's where you live. But you don't live, not really. After three years of trying, why don't you see that?"

"That's not fair."

"How many times could you watch *me* die?"

A lump formed in his throat at the thought. "It's different, though. I don't really die."

"You do, though, Chance. We both know the toll it takes on you."

"So why'd you call me? What makes you think I could agree to stop any more than I could seven months ago?"

"This," she said, reaching under her nightstand to retrieve a copy of the magazine. She laid it on the bed between them and smoothed out the cover with her hand. "This was different. This was something new."

"Do you know how much trouble I'm in because of it? Most of my sponsors dumped me. Chelsea's furious."

"Yeah, that's too bad," Maggie said, sounding very much the opposite. "But the other stuff. Chance. You finally worked up the courage to ask the big questions. You did it."

"Dad's going to throttle me."

"Wasn't that the point?" She studied him. "This is a bomb, baby. The question you have to ask is, What are you going to do now that it's gone off?"

"I have to go," he said, casting around for his underwear, which he found still nested in his jeans. He tried putting both on together, got them tangled up in his feet, and had to steady himself against the wall before trying again.

"Let's go away," she said.

He paused with his jeans around his knees. "What?"

"You and me. Let's leave LA."

"And go where?"

"I don't care. You pick."

"And live like my mom?"

"No, she runs to run. She can't stop moving. I want to go somewhere and make a home."

"This is your home."

"This is where I live. It's not the same thing. I'd like to have a real one."

"With me?"

"I'd leave tomorrow."

Chance remembered his jeans and pulled them the rest of the way up. "I have to go."

"Yeah, I know. Will you think about it? Being here is half our problem."

"I will," he said, and then kissed her on the forehead to let her know he meant it.

"Chance," Maggie said as she sat cross-legged on the bed, studying him, "is Marley alive?"

"You have to let that go." He sighed. Of everyone who'd known and loved his brother—and there were many people on that list—Maggie had clung fiercest to the possibility that Marley might not have drowned in the ocean off El Matador.

"But in the article, when Highsmith asked about Marley, you talked about him in the present tense. *Is*, not *was*."

"Yeah, I probably did," he admitted. "I still think of him that way."

"So you haven't seen him?"

"Marley's dead. He killed himself." They were awful words to say.

"We don't know that. Not for sure," she said, but lay back on the bed, going slack like a sail that had lost the wind.

"The police seemed pretty sure."

"You'd tell me if you hear from him?"

"Why would I hear from him?"

"If he saw the magazine. Maybe he'd reach out. You'll tell me if he does?"

Chance sat down on the bed beside Maggie and ran his fingers through her hair. "Of course."

"Swear it," she said, searching his face.

"I swear."

That seemed to mollify her, and Maggie rolled onto her side, curling up into a ball, back to him. "I miss him. The way things used to be."

All the air seemed to leave the room. Chance stood up to go.

"Chance?"

"Yeah?" he said, pausing at the door without looking back.

"I shouldn't have said that."

CHAPTER NINE

Leaving Maggie's bungalow, Chance saw the Mercedes SUV parked behind his Aston Martin. He felt the flutter of nerves that usually accompanied the creak of floorboards in a supposedly empty house. Maggie had called the article a bomb. She was right as usual, and Chance had set it off like a terrorist with the aim of inflicting maximum pain and suffering. The Mercedes was proof it had hit its target, that he wasn't prepared to deal with the repercussions first thing in the morning. He'd wanted more time to prepare.

The second thing he noticed was the girl. She was standing—no, the only word for it was *lurking*—on the sidewalk by the manzanita tree that demarked the property line between Maggie's bungalow and her neighbor's place. The girl was maybe seventeen, plain, with pale, freckled skin and straight brown hair that fell evenly on both sides of her head like twin waterfalls. Only her eyes made an impression, dark, unblinking spikes set back in her face. It was obvious she'd been watching the house. He didn't like that at all. He was accustomed to the odd nutjob turning up at his place but never wanted that craziness to follow him to Maggie's doorstep.

The girl started toward him, on a course to intercept him at the end of the walk. That was fine. He had a few things to say to her too. He was in no mood today. But about halfway down the sidewalk, the girl hesitated and seemed to lose her nerve. She made an ungainly pirouette and scurried back the way she'd come like a roach caught out in the open. Chance made a halfhearted attempt to pursue her, but the girl darted around the corner. He stopped. It was too early in the morning to be chasing teenagers around.

Up the street, a man sat astride a scooter snapping pictures of him. Was that what had rattled the girl? Maybe stalkers didn't like paparazzi any more than celebrities did. Chance yelled at him to quit. The paparazzo didn't. Chance broke into a run, gesticulating wildly. A car was coming, but Chance kept running, forcing it to brake hard to avoid hitting him. The driver leaned on her horn.

"You looking to die?" she yelled out her window.

"Not today," Chance called back without breaking stride. He closed on the photographer, who was struggling not to laugh. At the last moment, Chance pulled up short.

"Dude," the paparazzo said in wonder.

"How'd that look?" Chance asked, trying to hide how winded that short sprint had made him. It took time to build up cardiovascular endurance after a revival.

"Like a wild man," the paparazzo said, and then offered Chance a fist bump.

"And they say I can't act."

"You looked mean enough. People will think you're a menace. Want me to erase them?"

"Darsh, would I do that to you?"

"You're the man, Chance. I need this."

"Do me a favor? Leave out any where the house is identifiable?"

"For sure," Darsh said, scrolling back through the pictures on the camera. He frowned.

"What?"

"Nothing. Some kind of glitch, I guess," Darsh said, showing Chance the viewfinder. The first good picture was of Chance charging across the street. Everything taken before then was blacked out as if

Darsh had forgotten to remove the lens cap. Darsh fussed with the camera for another minute. "Great. Maybe there's a firmware update."

Originally from Pushkar, Darsh Desai and his family had immigrated to America when he was two. He had no memories of his home country and had drunk deep from the SoCal vibes. He wasn't cool in any of the ways that conferred status in Los Angeles, but he knew exactly who he was and what he wanted from life. In Chance's book, that made him cooler than 99 percent of the people he encountered.

Darsh was in school at UCLA studying political science with an eye toward taking the foreign service exam one day. He'd grown up working in his family's jewelry store in San Diego. His parents had taken a dim view of Darsh pursuing his so-called passion and told him bluntly that he could waste all the money he wanted on such a frivolous degree, but it would be his own. To make ends meet, he had about a dozen side hustles, including moonlighting as a paparazzo. In the last few years, he'd become known as a Chance specialist: if you needed a good shot of Chance Harker, call Darsh Desai.

It had been Chelsea's idea to put Darsh on the payroll. He wasn't paid a ton of money, but just enough to encourage a congenial quid pro quo. Chance would tip Darsh off to photo ops, and in return, Darsh would respect Chance's privacy when asked. It was as honest a business relationship as there was in Los Angeles, and they'd even become friendly in a symbiotic sort of way. Chance even thought about inviting Darsh to hang out but wasn't sure that was allowed. Could you be friends with your paparazzo?

"Thought there'd be more of you vultures out this morning."

"Oh, they're out," Darsh said with a handsome grin. "But they're all staked out over at your joint. Suckers."

"How'd you know I was here?"

"My dude, you drive a bright-red Aston Martin with your name on the vanity plate. Doesn't take the NSA to track you down," Darsh said before turning serious. "Why'd you let them do you like that?"

"Like what?"

"That article. You need to fire your PR. Who green-lit that travesty?"

"I did."

Darsh took that in with a professional lack of surprise. "I know taking crazy risks is kind of your jam, but I didn't know you had a death wish."

"That's funny," Chance deadpanned.

"Just saying. You know how to stir a pot."

"I didn't know you cared. Isn't it good for business?"

"Yeah, you'll pay the bills this week, but I don't like seeing someone hit bottom."

"Oh, you think this is bottom?" Chance said it as a joke, but it landed with an uncomfortable ring of truth.

"Hey, you right, you right. What do I know? Who am I to say why you do what you do anyway? Just hope *you* know." Darsh started his scooter. "So where to now?"

"Shopping."

A pained look passed across Darsh's face. "Shopping?"

"Yeah, need some new clothes. You're welcome to tag along."

"I think I'll pass. Can you hook me up later?"

"How about I text you if anything interesting happens."

"That'd be cool. Anything with a brawl would be appreciated. Maybe throw a drink at a waiter? I need to bank some cash before next semester. Hey, speaking of, do you need any weed?"

"Credit for diversifying, but pot's *been* legal, Darsh."

"Yeah, but you'd be amazed how many celebs don't want their picture taken going into a dispensary."

Darsh had a point. "I'm not that kind of celebrity."

"True, true. Alright, see you when I . . ." Darsh revved the engine in lieu of finishing his thought and accelerated away down the street.

Chance waited until he was sure Darsh was gone before walking down the block to his Aston Martin and the black Mercedes SUV parked on its bumper like an unwelcome kiss. He was just glad Darsh hadn't recognized it. They might be symbiotic friends, but it wouldn't have counted for much if Darsh had known the vehicle belonged to his father. And that would *not* have ended well. In the years since the kidnapping, Brett Harker had become protective of his privacy to the point of paranoia. A paparazzo snapping his picture would have sent him straight over the edge. Chance had to laugh at his optimism; after the Highsmith article, his father wouldn't even be able to *see* the edge.

Maggie hadn't been wrong. Much of his motivation for granting the interview had been to provoke this confrontation. Three years of making an ass of himself in the public eye had lost its shock value with Brett Harker. The interview had all been a calculated move to pour fresh salt on their collective wounds. The family didn't have many secrets left, but his father guarded them like a junkyard dog. Chance had spilled every last one in the pages of the most respected publication in the country. His father's favorite, as it happened.

He was even looking forward to facing his father in the same perverse way a boxer needs to take that first punch. But he also hadn't thought the confrontation would happen this soon, and not outside Maggie's house. He didn't know his father knew he'd even been seeing her. Brett Harker, deliverer of life lessons, had always preached that half of any battle was dictating the where and the when. He wasn't wrong. Chance was embarrassed, rattled, and on the defensive. He considered getting in the Aston Martin and just fleeing the scene. A "tactical retreat," if anyone cared enough to put a positive spin on it. Running away would buy him time to regroup, but he also knew it would cost him the high ground, now and forever. Could he really afford that? After this, Chance would have nothing left to provoke his father with, to shake him out of his carefully cultivated poise. No, he decided, there'd be no more running away from this. It was now or never.

He tried the back door of the SUV. It didn't open. He rolled his eyes and rapped on the tinted windows with his knuckles. Still nothing.

"Really?" he said, trying for a bemused attitude but only succeeding in sounding nervous.

The window rolled down an inch.

"Turn off that ridiculous camera," his father said through the crack in a tone of weary disappointment that Chance believed had been rewriting his DNA ever since childhood. The camera wasn't even on. He'd forgotten to restart it when he'd left Maggie's, but his father didn't know that, so Chance did as he was told, slowly and dramatically, as if disarming himself for a trigger-happy cop.

"Everything's always a production with you," his father said, an audible thunk signaling that Chance had been granted admittance. He got in next to his father, who stared straight ahead as if searching for a familiar landmark.

"You look good," Chance said, and he immediately regretted being the first to break the silence, even if his statement was true. Brett Harker was sixty but was as well preserved as a mosquito in amber, a fact that irritated his ex-wife to no end. His father took his diet-and-exercise regime extremely seriously, in the same way that cult members took being cult members. He had one of those absurdly fit bodies that only actors training for a role in a superhero movie maintained. Even in youth-obsessed Southern California, Brett Harker was a living, breathing inspirational anecdote.

"Gentlemen, give us a minute, please," his father said to the driver and bodyguard sitting up front. Ever since the kidnapping, he never went anywhere—on the rare occasions he left his fortress of a home—without security.

"Yes, Mr. Harker," they said in unison before hopping out.

"How long has this been going on?" His father gestured toward Maggie's bungalow. Then, without waiting for an answer, he said, "You should be ashamed of yourself."

"Why, when I have you to be ashamed for me?"

His dad looked affronted but didn't dispute the point. "Who was that you were talking to?"

"Darsh."

"Darsh? You know paparazzi by name? Getting awfully chummy with the enemy."

"I'm a friendly guy, Dad."

"So it would seem," his father said, gesturing to a tattered copy of Imani Highsmith's magazine on the center armrest. It looked as if an angry dog had ripped it from the mail slot. His dad didn't own any pets. "Did you stop to think how your mother would feel reading this?"

"Oh, give me a break. Like you give a damn about Mom."

His father's voice became an anvil's crack. "You don't know the first thing about my feelings toward your mother. Do you have any idea what you're doing to her with this grotesque spectacle of yours, getting yourself killed over and over like some circus freak? What exactly are you trying to accomplish, except embarrassing yourself and your family?"

"What family?" Chance spat back, warming to the opening salvos of their long-standing war of words. "At least now I know what it takes to get you to descend from Valhalla."

Valhalla was Chance's nickname for his father's winery, Red Valley Vineyard; his mother wasn't the only one with literary pretensions. After the divorce, his father had pulled up stakes, stepping down from Palingenesis and divesting himself of his business holdings. He'd bought a vineyard two hours up the 101 from Los Angeles in the rolling foothills of Santa Ynez, near Solvang, a town that looked like it had been transplanted from a Danish postcard, windmills and all. His father didn't drink, but the lifestyle of gentleman farmer suited him and gave him a pretext to retreat from public life. And his son. Chance never missed an opportunity to remind his father of that.

"Don't be an infant. You know you're welcome anytime." His father pivoted in his seat to face Chance, tapping the magazine with a manicured index finger that had never once picked a grape. "This, however, is another matter. You've crossed the line."

"Your line," Chance shot back. They'd been sparring up until now, feeling the other out the way they always did, but now they were dropping their gloves.

"Our line, Chance. Maybe you've lost sight of that, carrying on the way you've been. Do you have any idea what you've done? I need you to issue a retraction."

"Sure, I'd be happy to."

"Really? Well, that's good to hear. I'll pay for any—"

"As soon as you tell me what really happened that night."

Brett Harker's face darkened. "We've been over and over this."

"No. *We* haven't. I've asked, and you've dodged the question. For five years, you've been dodging me. So just tell me the truth. Tell me the truth, and I'm done. I'll retract every word and issue a statement that I was on drugs. I'll even quit jumping out of airplanes."

"Chance. There is nothing to tell."

"Come on, Dad. Here, let me make it easier for you. Why'd it take you so long to pay the ransom? Why'd you stonewall the police? Why were you the only one to communicate directly with the kidnappers? Take your pick."

His father fell silent.

"What happened that night?" Chance demanded, hammering away. "What happened with the ransom?"

"You need to let this go," his father said, an unfamiliar note in his voice. In anyone else, Chance would have called it fear.

"Was there even one?" Chance plowed ahead. "The kidnappers asked for fifty million. You claim you paid it."

"Chance," his father said in a cautioning tone.

"But in the divorce, Mom's forensic accountant found no trace of a missing fifty million." When Maggie called the article a bomb, she'd meant this specifically. It had never been disclosed publicly before. His mother had used it as leverage in the divorce to force his father to accept her extortionary terms. Nondisclosure agreements had followed.

Chance had never signed one.

"Did you even pay?" Chance demanded.

"I gave them what they wanted," his father said stubbornly.

"So you hand them fifty million and they shoot Marley for shits and giggles; is that how it went down? Not because you were too cheap to part with the money."

"I am your father!" he snapped as if his parentage were what Chance had questioned.

"Were you involved?" The question of Brett Harker's involvement in the kidnapping of his sons had been asked many times, both in the media and by the LAPD, who still considered him a person of interest, even if they'd never made any progress in connecting him to the kidnapping. This was the first time Chance had dared to say it out loud.

His father slapped him so hard he saw stars that Van Gogh would have admired. It hurt like hell, but Chance didn't raise a hand to his face.

"How dare you?" his father said, voice cold and indignant. "Listen to me, you little shit, I had nothing to do with the kidnapping. Why would I kidnap my own sons?"

"I don't know!" Chance yelled, although it sounded more like a roar in the closed confines of the SUV. Chance let the SUV fall silent, then spoke quietly. "Why didn't you pay them right away? Why did you spend days haggling with them? Why didn't we matter to you?"

"I got you both back, didn't I?"

"You call this being back?" Chance pounded all five fingers against his chest, his eyes hot with tears. "Marley is gone. I'm . . . I'm like this. We never came back. They killed us."

"They were always going to kill your originals," his father said in a hushed, cathedral tone.

"Bullshit."

"Think about it. Why do you think they cut the biometric Palingenesis chips out?"

"So you couldn't track us."

"Well, yes, but only in part. The kidnappers knew that Palingenesis won't revive a clone without a verified death event. You know their protocols. There can't ever be two of someone, ever. Without the monitoring chips, the only way Palingenesis would approve a revival . . ."

"Would be with a body," Chance said, finishing his father's sentence.

"The ransom was never to get you boys back alive. It was to get your bodies back."

Chance slumped back in his seat. The possibility hit him hard. He'd always believed the kidnappers had executed him and Marley because his father had dragged his feet. But this alternative was ingenious. Chance's last upload had occurred a week before the kidnapping; Marley's was nearly three months old. Killing them eliminated any possibility that they could identify their captors. It was diabolical. If true. He had no good reason to accept his father's story as anything but self-serving.

"But there was no ransom. You're still lying."

"I gave them what they wanted," his father repeated.

"I don't believe you," Chance said, opening the car door.

"Chance," his father said, taking hold of his arm, "you need to let this go."

"Tell me the truth, or get your hands off me."

His father's grip tightened. He was shaking his head as if locked in a silent argument with his ghosts, and for a moment, it looked like he might finally say something that was true. But then the other side of the argument seemed to win out. Chance felt his father let him go.

Even after five years, he couldn't believe it. He'd set off the bomb for nothing.

CHAPTER TEN

Twenty years ago, the trendy shopping co-op would have been called what it was—a mall—but that word had long since fallen out of fashion. It had the kinds of stores people assumed Chance liked and could afford. It made "going shopping" a good cover story, but the real reason he "shopped" there was that its garage offered long-term parking, another relic that had never been discontinued.

The Aston Martin parked itself on the top level in a spot shielded from easy view behind a concrete pillar. Someone would need to be highly motivated to come poking around up here. He twisted Marley's ring off his finger and rubbed it for luck. There were only two times it ever came off—this was the other. He put it safely in the glove box, along with his LFD, which he powered off. He didn't want a GPS trail of where he was headed, not that the LFD would get any service out there anyway. He took the portable jump-starter from the trunk and left his body camera in its place. He'd never turned it back on after meeting his dad and had also disabled the recorders in the Aston Martin before driving here. No cameras, no recordings, a hard-and-fast rule.

Patting himself down until satisfied that he wasn't carrying anything that could be tracked, Chance went down two levels to the parking spot he rented by the month. He peeled off the car cover, the kind people used to protect vehicles from the elements. In this case, the cover was protection against prying eyes. For anything cosmetic, it was far too late for the

Chance

2017 Toyota RAV4. Twenty-five years in the California sun had long ago bleached out all the plastic. The paint job had faded to memory, the hood a mottled archipelago of UV damage. When Chance bought it at the junkyard, it had been missing three doors and a back seat. He'd replaced them with whatever mismatched spares he could salvage, giving the car a patchwork-quilt look that Chance empathized with. One of the back doors had been welded in place and didn't open at all. But pop the hood and the engine was shiny and well maintained. The only thing he'd put any money into. The last thing he wanted was to get stranded out in the desert.

The RAV hadn't been driven in six months, so the battery was dead. He connected the jumper cables and started the engine. While the engine warmed up, he checked the tires and stowed the jump-starter in the back seat. He was eager to get on the road. It was at least a six-hour drive, and he wanted to get there before sundown. In the Aston Martin, it would have taken a little over three, but the 10 was auto-drive only until the other side of San Bernardino, so he would have to stick to secondary roads until then.

Once at Redlands, his obsolete, gas-powered beater was finally permitted to join highway traffic heading east. Windows down and music up, he pushed the RAV up to ninety to make up for lost time. The little car vibrated like it was attempting to reenter earth's orbit.

The drive gave him time to think about his father. The so-called bomb hadn't made a dent in the old man's armor. He'd just stonewalled his son as he always did, claiming there wasn't anything to tell while simultaneously insisting that Chance needed to let it go. The certainty that his father was lying had been the unbearable rock in Chance's shoe for five years now. The interview had been his last-ditch effort to shake it out. Might be time to admit that the truth, whatever the truth might be, was beyond his reach. But what came next? Pick up where he'd left off? Start planning his next stunt? The thought sickened him. What else did he have?

There was Maggie's offer, if it still stood. Was it in him? Could he run away with her, leave LA behind, and just let go of the past? And if he did, would the past let go of him?

Chance drove on, trying to picture his life with Maggie. Could he make her happy? Maybe they would settle in Montana. Maggie had filmed a movie in Bozeman once and still talked about how much she loved it there. They could find a peaceful spot on the bend of a river somewhere and build a life together. He could go to college. Maybe she would act again. There would definitely be dogs; he'd always wanted a pet.

What about kids?

Okay, settle down, he cautioned himself with a foolish grin, but the daydreaming kept up until he saw the signs for Palm Springs.

At Indio, he stopped at a generic big-box hypermarket. He filled two grocery carts to overflowing with canned goods, bottled water, batteries, clothes, propane tanks, and other nonperishables. Fresh produce only went to waste. At the checkout, he paid cash. In Los Angeles it would have raised eyebrows, but out here, at the edge of the Sonoran Desert, cash was still a way of life.

He continued, south and east, deeper into the desert. Civilization thinned and fell away behind him. There were fewer and fewer cars on the road, and those he saw were old. Not vintage, old. Junkers. Cars that predated the switch to electric auto-drive vehicles. In LA, there were collectors who prized them for the independence they represented. Out here it was a necessity. His RAV went from being an eyesore to fitting right in, the idea all along.

The smell of rotten eggs filled the RAV well before the Salton Sea appeared off to his right, broad and still. Almost everyone who lived out here had respiratory problems, a legacy of decades of suffocating pesticide use in the Imperial Valley. It was on these shores where Marley had died. Chance knew exactly where but had never visited.

Walking alongside the road, a man dressed in black turned at the sound of the car engine. He wore an enormous papier-mâché crow headpiece and began to flap his arms wildly as Chance passed, dancing out into the road, cawing wildly. Chance watched him warily in the rearview until the crow-man passed out of sight. He was getting close.

The road delivered him to Niland, an unincorporated four-block grid of scrub brush, defiant salt cedar trees, rusted chain-link fences, and a scattering of ranch-style houses. A woman of at least sixty rode by on a beleaguered horse fit for Don Quixote. She was topless from the waist up. A small dog sat proudly in her lap. She nodded a neutral greeting to him. He nodded back. Niland drew people not for what the town offered but for what it didn't. There was no law, no order. No school, no post office. Half the town had burned to the ground twenty years earlier, but it still had no fire department. It was a dusty plot of land that no one in their right mind could want, and that suited the people here fine. Unfiltered freedom far from the constraints of civilization.

Salvation Mountain, with its interlocking murals painted on adobe brick, rose up to announce he had arrived at Slab City. It was only a few minutes north from Niland, but it might have been another world entirely. Named for the concrete foundations left behind when the marines abandoned Camp Dunlap in 1946, Slab City was home to people who found Niland too uptight. No one knew exactly how many souls called it home because there was no one foolish enough to attempt a census. Some called Slab City an artists' colony, but to Chance it felt more like the arts-and-crafts room in an asylum. Art therapy for trauma that would never be resolved. Fair to say, he hated this place, maybe because part of him feared he belonged here.

Slab City had no electricity except what the locals drew from the sun. No running water. People lived in broken-down campers or corrugated lean-tos built from refuse scavenged from someone else's abandoned campsite. People came, people went. From where? To where? No one asked and no one told. It was a transient place. A way station between worlds, and the right to disappear was revered above all others.

At the far side of the settlement, Chance turned off onto a hard-packed dirt road that twisted up toward a low mesa. Twenty minutes later, the faded yellow of an ancient school bus caught the afternoon sun. He made for it, leaving the road behind and kicking up a plume of dust behind him. Off to the right, a small army of metal figures stood in precise rows. The figures were paired together, one slightly taller than its companion. From a distance, the statues looked surprisingly lifelike. It was only when you got up close that you saw they were welded together from scrap.

As he pulled to a stop near the bus, a man stepped out from beneath an awning fashioned from a tattered brown tarp. He cradled an old rifle in one arm like a baby. The man raised a hand in a kind of greeting and approached the car. Propping the rifle against the side of the RAV, he rested his forearms on the door's frame and leaned in to peer inside. His heavy beard couldn't hide the damage that years in the desert sun had done to his leathery, cracked skin. It made it all but impossible to judge his age, but Chance knew the man was only twenty-five. He would have forgiven someone guessing forty.

Satisfied, the man looked at Chance for the first time. "Hello, little brother," he said as if they'd seen each other only the day before yesterday instead of six months earlier.

"Marley."

"What are you doing here?"

"Brought supplies."

Marley gazed toward the trunk. "Remember the propane this time?"

"I told you they were out."

"Were they out again?"

"No, it's in the trunk."

"And the bourbon?"

That Chance *had* forgotten. "Store was closed. Next time."

"Dammit, Chance. The one thing I asked for." Marley sniffed the air in disappointment. "Alright then, let's get it unloaded."

CHAPTER ELEVEN

Unloading consisted of Chance sitting on a moldy couch in the shade of the awning while Marley made umpteen trips from the RAV to the bus. Things would have gone faster with Chance helping, but doing it himself gave Marley time to acclimate. Marley didn't spend a lot of time around people anymore, and having his brother show up unannounced was always a shock to his system. Chance could hear him fussing around inside the bus, arguing with himself about where to store it all. He sounded irritated, as if this was all a massive pain in the ass and he was doing Chance a favor by taking it off his hands. His arrival went this way every time, and he had learned not to take his quarantine personally. Honestly, he needed the time too. It wasn't easy to accept that this was who his brother was now.

Marley stuck his head out of the bus, holding a pack of boxer briefs. "You think I need underwear?"

"Clean ones."

"Fuck you," Marley said, and then disappeared inside again.

It was hard to see now, but growing up, Marley Harker had always been the golden boy. Smart, handsome, effortlessly charming, he made friends wherever he went, every single one of whom would have sworn that they were his best friend in the world. When Marley's attention was on you, he made you feel as if you'd known him all your life. That you were the only person in the world who mattered. And it wasn't an act; Marley genuinely loved being around people and found them fascinating. To Chance, the bookish introvert, such behavior had been witchcraft. He'd grown up idolizing his big brother and wishing he were more like him.

The moment Marley left for college, he'd stopped keeping his appointments at Palingenesis. Without his parents to remind him, that all fell by the wayside. He was a busy freshman at USC and madly in love with Maggie Soto. It was unreasonable to expect him to give up a whole day to do regular refreshes. Anyway, he was eighteen and in perfect health. What was the worst that could happen? It was only when he came home on breaks that his parents could strong-arm him into keeping the appointments they'd made for him.

Everything changed the Thanksgiving of Marley's sophomore year. Maggie, by now a mainstay at the Harker household, had come home with him for the holiday. His mother adored her, treating her like the daughter she'd never had. On Wednesday, she'd declared it a girls' day and taken Maggie shopping and then to lunch. The brothers had taken the opportunity to drive up PCH to El Matador Beach. It didn't have the biggest waves in California, but it had good breaks in late November, and unlike his brother, Chance wasn't a natural surfer. According to witnesses who came forward, the brothers had surfed all afternoon, but no one remembered seeing anything out of the ordinary. The kidnappers had taken them at the car when they'd come up from the beach after sunset. The biometric Palingenesis chips that had been cut out of their necks were found in a puddle of blood on the hood of their car. The irony was that his parents had scheduled Marley for a refresh at Palingenesis for the Friday after Thanksgiving. Two days late and a lifetime short.

"You need anything?" Marley said, striding back to the RAV for another load.

"Do you have anything cold?" Chance asked. Even in the shade of the awning, the late-afternoon heat was intense.

"My solar crapped out."

"When? I wish I'd known. I could've brought a new unit."

"The store probably would've been closed," Marley said before disappearing back inside the school bus with a case of canned beans. Chance picked up a rock near his feet and threw it as far as he could.

Knowing the answer, he asked anyway: "You sure you don't need any help?"

"I'm sure," Marley said. "How's Mom?" Marley always asked about her, but never Maggie or their father.

"The same. I think she's in Europe. It sure would be good to tell her you're alive and okay."

"Only if you want me to move," Marley warned.

Marley had been "dead" for two and a half years when the postcard arrived addressed to Chance. It had come a few months after Chance had fallen off the Ritz-Carlton. Chance didn't get much mail, so the postcard caught his eye. On one side was a picture of Death Valley. The family had taken a trip there when Chance had been seven and Marley eleven. It had been a disaster from the start, involving a broken-down car, awful cell reception, and Chance getting apocalyptically sick from a roadside burrito. In the years since, the vacation had become a foundational piece of Harker lore, transformed from traumatizing horror story to beloved family comedy through constant retelling and embellishment. Suffice it to say, Death Valley was the first and last family trip to a national park. *Death Valley* also became family slang for anything that went wrong.

"How'd the exam go?"

"I Death Valleyed it."

"Sorry."

The flip side of the postcard had been blank, apart from a date and a time. His parents, locked in their marriage's death roll, hadn't even noticed when he'd borrowed a car. Chance had waited for two hours at the park entrance without realizing the filthy vagrant huddled beneath the welcome sign was Marley. His brother had made him swear not to tell anyone he was alive. If he did, Marley said he would disappear again, for good this time. It hadn't been easy not telling his parents or Maggie, but he'd believed his brother and kept his secret.

Every six months or so, after each of his stunts, he would load up the RAV and bring his brother supplies. Sometimes he spent the night; sometimes he turned right around. Marley wasn't exactly the host with the most. He became more and more antisocial and withdrawn with each passing year. But Chance understood what he was going through in a way that no one else could, and that kept him coming back.

Marley disappeared into the bus and emerged with two unlabeled beer bottles. He pressed one into Chance's chest.

"What's this?" Chance asked.

"Old Sheila started brewing beer."

Chance had no idea who that was. "Yeah, but it's hot."

"They had beer before refrigeration, you know. Room temperature is historically normative."

"This," Chance said, waving a hand at the desert, "isn't room temperature!"

"I'd offer you bourbon," Marley replied, pulling up an aluminum beach chair, "but I'm fresh out."

"They were closed," Chance said, sticking stubbornly to his story. "I brought propane."

"Can't drink propane," Marley said while twisting open his beer. He held it out to Chance, who stared moodily before grudgingly extending his own. The two brothers touched bottlenecks and drank. It was awful, even worse than Chance expected, but he held the bottle and took the occasional sip to keep Marley at bay.

"Saw the sculpture on the way in," he said. "You've done a lot of work on it since last time." Marley had been toiling away on the same piece for two and a half years now. Whenever Chance asked how much he had left to go, Marley always answered the same: "It'll be done when it's done." But it would never be done. That was the truth of it. Marley would keep on adding new figures to his army until he dropped or the world ran out of scrap metal.

"It's not done."

"Looks done."

"It's not," Marley repeated.

They sat a piece in silence, staring out at the desert as the sun lost its grip on the horizon. The sculpture cast spectral shadows across the desert floor. If he hadn't been the inspiration, Chance would have found it beautiful.

"What if it was?" Chance asked.

"If what was what?"

"The sculpture. Done."

"It'll be done when it's done," Marley said with the weariness of a father grown tired of a child's endless questions.

"You could maybe start something new. Ever think about that? Starting something new?"

"What are you really doing here?" Marley asked.

"I haven't seen you in six months. We were due."

Marley just stared back levelly, waiting him out. Chance took a sip of his skunk beer and regretted it immediately.

"I'm thinking about leaving LA," he said, leaving out the part about going with Maggie.

"And go where?"

"Anywhere."

Marley drained his beer and went back into the bus for two more beers. He didn't offer either to Chance.

"Are you the same one I saw last time?" Marley asked.

"I'm always the same one."

"I admire how you're sure," Marley said. "How many of you has that been now?"

"Five. Jumped out of a plane last week. Didn't work out."

"Five is a lot."

"Yeah, I'm getting sick of it."

Marley nodded thoughtfully. "So stop."

"Stop making sculptures of us in the desert."

Marley finished his beers and went into the bus and returned with a small portable cookstove. He heated up two cans of SpaghettiOs (with meatballs, so Chance knew it was a special occasion) in a crusty pot. He ladled it into metal mugs and passed one to Chance. It was surprisingly good, and they ate in silence. Afterward, Chance smoked half a cigarette while Marley built a fire, the desert air chilly now that the sun had gone down. A small army of empty beer bottles were assembling at Marley's feet.

"You think you could quit jumping out of planes if you were somewhere else?" Marley asked, breaking the silence that had built between them.

"Honestly, I can't remember why I was doing it in the first place."

"Yeah, you do."

"Well, it's not working anymore."

"Yeah," Marley agreed, then stood on unsteady legs, knocking over a good part of his army. "Alright, I'm racking it. You staying the night?" As if Chance might seriously be about to drive back to LA now.

"If that's okay."

"I guess. There's a spare sleeping bag. I'll get it." Marley disappeared inside the school bus of infinite storage and returned with a ratty sleeping bag and bedroll.

"Thanks."

"Go," Marley said. "If you got to go, go. Get the hell out of LA. See if you can live."

"What about you?" Chance looked up questioningly at his brother.

"I'll be fine. Got my statues, don't I?"

Marley patted Chance on the shoulder and stumbled into the bus. At the door, he paused to piss into the wheel well. Chance marveled at how unrecognizable Marley had become. He loved his brother, going to enormous lengths to protect his privacy and keep him safe, but he didn't know him. In the five years since the kidnapping, they'd spent no more than a few days together. Still, coming out here always made him feel a little better about life. Maybe they didn't know each other any longer, but Marley understood what he'd been through better than anyone, and that counted for something.

Chance slept out by the fire, under the stars. In the morning, Marley was gone. Chance climbed up on the roof of the bus and shouted his brother's name, but either he was out of earshot or wasn't answering. It was like that sometimes when Chance visited. Marley was no good at goodbyes or people and would disappear rather than say one word more. Chance couldn't blame him but wished he'd been able to say goodbye. He didn't know if he'd be back.

———

The drive back to Los Angeles took twice as long as the trip out to Marley's camp. That was probably because he drove five miles an hour below the speed limit the whole way. He'd reached a monumental decision about his future out in the desert, the culmination of conversations with Maggie, his father, and finally Marley. What happened if he was killed in an accident? He would lose all those memories, and there was no guarantee his clone would reach the same conclusion again. That was why the first thing he did when he got back to the Aston Martin was call Palingenesis for an appointment to refresh his upload. He needed his decision locked into his upload, part of the permanent Chance Harker. As luck would have it, Holifield said there'd been a cancellation and they could fit him in immediately. Could Chance be there in thirty minutes? Overjoyed, he assured Holifield that wouldn't be a problem as he started the Aston Martin's engine.

Palingenesis recommended clients refresh uploads at least once a month. It was a whole production and took at least six hours, which was a meaty chunk out of a workday for their highfalutin clientele to sacrifice. To compensate for the inconvenience, Palingenesis had designed the experience to be as luxurious as possible. It was all the brainchild of his dad. The two founders of Palingenesis, Vernon Gaddis and Abigail Stickling, had brought him aboard as the chief marketing officer, and his first job had been to design the client-facing experience.

Chance had met them once. Palingenesis was headquartered in Washington, DC, but his dad had hosted a party at the house to celebrate the grand opening of the Los Angeles branch. Chance remembered Vernon Gaddis, the business acumen behind Palingenesis's remarkable ascent, being remarkably charming and debonair, even by LA standards. Drifting among the guests, working the room in his three-piece suit, he seemed to Chance like something out of the old black-and-white movies his brother made him watch sometimes. Brett Harker was typically the center of any room he was in, but Vernon Gaddis had a presence and star power that belonged in Hollywood.

Abigail Stickling, on the other hand, had been a strange, intense woman who stood stiffly in one corner nursing a drink. Even a twelve-year-old could see that human interaction wasn't her forte. The scientific genius behind human cloning, Stickling seemed irritated about wasting an evening on anything so prosaic as socializing with other humans. The story went that she'd been turned down by dozens of venture capital firms before Vernon Gaddis recognized her potential. Together, she and Gaddis had built the company into a phenomenon before a dramatic Christmas Day suicide at the age of fifty-four ended her life. The cruel irony was that the inventor of human cloning had never been able to have a clone herself. A rare condition called Wilson's disease, which causes a buildup of copper in the brain, interfered with Palingenesis's upload technology.

His father had built his reputation as a customer service genius. His guiding principle had been simple: no one liked going to a doctor's office. That was why the nurses were called *stewards* and the receiving area looked like the lobby of a swank five-star hotel.

When Holifield appeared, he was wearing a handsomely tailored suit, not scrubs, which would've clashed with the whole day-spa vibe.

First stop was the changing room, where Chance traded his street clothes for a plush bathrobe over a designer medical gown. They returned to the receiving area, where Holifield reviewed the menu options for him. In addition to the Michelin-starred chef, Palingenesis also offered a dry cleaner, a hairdresser, a massage therapist, a nail salon. Every conceivable amenity. Right now, his Aston Martin was being detailed in the garage. Normally, Chance skipped all the pampering, but he hadn't eaten yet this morning and would be ravenous after the refresh if he didn't eat something now.

A handful of other clients also waited in the receiving area. Some ate, while others took care of last-minute business before their refreshes began. LFDs were forbidden in the refresh suites, and anyway it was hard to take work calls while having one's consciousness copied to a quantum hard drive. It was both funny weird *and* funny ha-ha when put like that. Chance figured that was why Palingenesis also kept the massage therapist on staff. Thinking too hard about the existential nightmare of what went on here could put one hell of a crick in your neck.

Chance had spent a lot of time in this room. The one constant was that clients never acknowledged each other. In a town built on relationships, there were still a couple of places you didn't pause to hobnob . . . on your way out of your plastic surgeon's office, on your way into a brothel, and in the lobby of Palingenesis. Who did or didn't have a clone stored at Palingenesis was a closely guarded secret. The media loved to speculate, and there could be unforeseen consequences—public, professional, private—for anyone who was outed.

More than one career had been ended that way. Maybe that was why Chance liked to catch other clients' eyes and give them a wave or a wink. It was childish, but sometimes, if they were especially famous, he'd give them the finger guns. The gesture never failed to freak them out, and he'd received letters from expensive law firms threatening legal action if he was anything but discreet.

Rare were the cases of someone broadcasting their status, and no one was as in your face about the fact they were a clone as Chance Harker. Well, except perhaps Con D'Arcy, the musician Maggie had tickets to see tonight. Except that D'Arcy wasn't doing it to draw attention to herself, but to raise awareness about the discrimination that the first generation of clones had faced. The so-called first generation had been soldiers, predominantly special forces, who'd been enrolled in Palingenesis's top-secret military program back in the twenties. After the *Washington Post* and the *New York Times* had broken the story, those soldiers had been disowned and forgotten by everyone: family, friends, and country. An uneasy footnote that America had been keen to leave out of its history.

Con D'Arcy had made it her mission to make sure that didn't happen. She was the niece of Abigail Stickling and had inherited her aunt's fortune after the suicide. D'Arcy had used that money to provide outreach and support for the first generation, many of whom had drifted into drug addiction and homelessness when their families had turned their backs on them. Maybe that was why Chance found her so irritating. He didn't trust anyone who appeared to be that noble, which probably told him more about himself than he cared to know.

Holifield returned with a tray. On a cloth napkin beside his food were several pills. The patented Palingenesis chill-out cocktail of pharmaceuticals that made clients' brains more amenable to having their consciousness vacuumed up. Chance swallowed the pills under Holifield's watchful gaze. Clearly satisfied, he left Chance to his food. While he ate, Chance filled out the paperwork that Holifield threw to his LFD. Holifield insisted on going through the charade every damn time, even though Chance had had hundreds of refreshes at this point. Chance checked off the boxes automatically without reading the boilerplate language that warned of potential side effects.

Appropriately fed and chastised, Chance got into the wheelchair and let Holifield roll him back to the refresh suites. His steward helped him into the chair—the drugs made balance and depth perception a challenge. While Holifield fine-tuned the refresh, music filled the room. Palingenesis encouraged clients to make individualized playlists because music had been found to facilitate the upload process. Chance regularly updated his, but the first track was always the same: "Smiling Faces Sometimes," by the Undisputed Truth.

Above him, a white cylinder descended silently from the ceiling. He felt a familiar hum in the back of his head as the refresh began. His fingers tingled pleasantly. He yawned, although he wasn't a bit sleepy. A sign he'd be unconscious soon. His thoughts drifted back to Maggie. He couldn't believe they were actually going to do it—leave Los Angeles and the past behind. No more stunts. Start over fresh. Take a stab at asking questions about life that might actually have answers. And with a woman who loved him. Despite everything.

He grinned to himself and probably looked pretty damn foolish doing it. He really didn't care. Maybe it was the drugs talking, but he felt so unbelievably light, like he could float away into the sky and get carried away on the Santa Ana winds. What surprised him most, though, was how sure he felt about his decision, now that it was made. How calm. He couldn't wait to see Maggie. Maybe they would go out and celebrate, see Con D'Arcy and then hit the town. He didn't usually like concerts, but he didn't mind that idea one bit. Not one bit.

CHAPTER TWELVE

Chance woke to thoughts of Maggie. Missing her desperately and feeling like he hadn't seen her in a thousand years. It happened sometimes after a refresh; his last thoughts before the procedure began would be waiting for him on the other side, amplified a hundredfold. Sometimes it left an emotional hangover, but Chance didn't mind having Maggie stuck in his head. Not at all. There was nothing else he wanted there. He would call her the second Holifield gave him back his LFD.

He went to sit up and couldn't. That's when he knew something was very wrong.

Although his vision was still blurry, he could see one thing clearly: This wasn't a recovery suite. It was almost certainly a Palingenesis hospital bed in a Palingenesis hospital room. The ones used for revivals, not refreshes. He should know; he'd been in enough of them. Except it couldn't be. The last thing he remembered was visiting Marley in the desert. He'd decided to quit doing stunts and to leave Los Angeles with Maggie. He'd been anxious to break the news to her. So how could this be a revival? It just didn't make any sense. At least none that he wanted it to make.

Desperate to anchor himself to reality, he felt for his ring. It wasn't there. A wounded moan escaped him. The awful feeling of being a trespasser in his own body swept through him. Even his skin hated him and wanted to peel itself off. There were only two times he ever took the ring off, and a refresh wasn't one of them. So now he just had to work up the courage to admit the truth to himself. Admit that he'd died. Admit that this was his revival and that it had arrived far too soon.

Easier said than done: he was generating far-fetched alternatives faster than he could rule them out. Auditioning for the role of the other shoe, Holifield sat nearby, fingers tented as though a team of fussy mountain climbers had established base camp on his chest. When Chance stirred, his steward stood and approached the bed with all the enthusiasm of a terminal patient submitting to a painful treatment he knew would do no good. An unconvincing smile appeared on Holifield's face. The man wasn't Chance's biggest fan, but he usually did a better job of hiding it.

"Welcome back, Chance. This is your download, not your upload." His steward had a deep, soothing baritone that belonged in commercials for hearty, homestyle soups.

"What's going on? Why am . . . here?" Chance asked, stuttering over the possessive pronoun, his panic too great to be more careful in choosing his words.

"This is your revival," Holifield said, although Chance had stopped listening. Javier Paloma, in his off-the-rack suit and cheap shoes, was standing by the door. Why was someone from legal here? Normally Palingenesis didn't sic its lawyers on him until he'd had time to acclimate. For now it was supposed to be just Holifield. This was a well-rehearsed scene for two actors, not three.

"That's Javier Paloma, our legal counsel," Holifield explained when he saw Chance's panic.

"Good for him. What's he doing in . . . room?"

Holifield looked at the lawyer as if seeing him for the first time. "He's here as a witness."

"Witness to what? Where's Chelsea?" She would sort everything out. Chelsea lived for exactly this sort of confrontation, so she could remind Chance how essential she was to his well-being.

"She's in the waiting room," Holifield answered.

"Well, send her in," Chance said, happy to be back on script, even if the lawyer was stressing him out.

"Presently," the lawyer said.

"What the hell does that mean? Send her in," Chance said, struggling again to sit up in the bed. It was hard to sound authoritative while flat on his back like Fredo Corleone demanding respect, but Chance couldn't get his arms to do what they were told. He badly needed his ring.

"There's been an incident," Holifield said.

"Incident?" Chance was on high alert now. He didn't like that word at all, pregnant with vague menace. "What's going on, Holifield? Why can't . . . remember the last five months?"

"Because there aren't five months to remember," Holifield said. "It's been twenty-four hours. You came in yesterday."

Chance didn't take the news well, and his body tried to retch. Nothing came up, probably because this body had never eaten anything. From across the room, Paloma watched intently.

"Yesterday . . . ," Chance echoed. "What happened?"

"That's what we're trying to understand," Paloma said. "But unfortunately, Ms. Klos is being uncooperative, so I'll be sitting in until I have a clearer picture of Palingenesis's exposure."

Exposure to what? Chance wondered, but he was done asking questions they wouldn't answer. "Fine, fine, whatever. Just get her."

Holifield left and returned with Chelsea, who looked exhausted and disheveled. If you knew Chelsea Klos the way Chance did, then you knew it would take a drone strike for her to have so much as a hair out of place. She came straight to his bedside and pressed the ring into his hand. He slipped the ring onto his finger, immediately feeling steadier.

"We need to talk," she said. "Alone."

"As we explained to Mr. Harker, that's not going to happen," the lawyer said.

Chelsea not getting her way usually released her inner Kraken. Instead, she wilted and pleaded mutedly for five minutes.

"Not possible. We need to assess if Palingenesis has legal liability here or if we're only facing a public relations nightmare."

"For what?" Chance said. "Chelsea, just tell . . . what happened."

"I don't know exactly," she said, making eye contact with the lawyer before continuing. "You called me. Late last night? It was four, maybe five in the morning. You told me to meet you at the house with a cameraperson."

"What did . . . need with a cameraperson? The house is wired with cameras."

"I asked the same question. You just yelled at me to do it, so I called Trang, who never sleeps anyway. When we got to the house, you seemed way off. Angry. There was a gun."

"A gun?"

"I know," Chelsea answered, well versed in his gun phobia. His body, his original body, had been found in a culvert north of Frogtown. Cause of death had been a single bullet to the back of the head at a downward angle, suggesting Chance had been on his knees. *Execution-style*, in the parlance of police reports. A year after the kidnapping, just when public interest had begun to wane, the crime-scene photographs leaked. Everyone warned him not to look, but there'd been no chance of that. He'd needed to see. It had been a compulsion: a preview of the stranglehold that the lag surrounding the kidnapping would hold on his life for the next five years.

The pictures had made him sick. Then he'd gone back to look at them some more. The sight of his own lifeless face in the dirt burning a hole in his still-fragile sense of self. Six months later, he'd run laps around the roof of the hotel. Was one connected to the other, or had he already been on that track? He didn't know that either, but does a chicken sitting on a cracked egg really give a damn which came first?

". . . don't own a gun," he said.

"Well, you had one. An old-fashioned revolver. You were sitting at the dining room table." She took a deep breath before continuing. "Trang started filming. You made a big show of dumping out all the bullets, rambling about how you wanted to give people something different. You chose one bullet, kissed it, and put it back in the gun. Then you spun the cylinder, put it to your head, and pulled the trigger. No hesitation."

It was absolutely silent in the hospital room. Holifield and the lawyer exchanged a look.

"Did the gun go off?" Chance asked, although the answer should have been obvious to him, under the circumstances.

Chelsea flinched at the memory as if seeing it replay before her eyes. "Not that time. What can I say? You're a very lucky guy." She laughed but it was tense and humorless. She'd seen him die four times without batting an eyelash, but now her voice choked. "You just kept spinning and firing, spinning and firing, until it went off."

"And you didn't ask why?"

"You weren't exactly taking questions."

"Did he say anything else?" Paloma asked.

"No, but . . . ," Chelsea said, and then looked to Chance. "There was blood on your T-shirt. It wasn't yours."

"How do you know it wasn't his?" the lawyer demanded, giving Chance a glimpse into what he would look and sound like in a courtroom.

"Because he wasn't bleeding."

"That doesn't prove anything. He could have had a nosebleed earlier, for all you know," Paloma said, clearly determined to contest the point.

A commotion in the hallway brought his cross-examination to a premature halt. The door burst open, and two Palingenesis security guards backed into the room. Neither looked to be having their best day.

"LAPD is here," the less flustered of the two announced as a plain-clothes detective flanked by two uniforms pushed them aside with strong first-person-through-the-door energy. The detective was a solidly built Black woman, perhaps fifty, with a face that had seen things, and those things had left their mark. The downward curl of her lips suggested she made it her mission in life to return the favor.

"Appreciate the formal introduction, gentlemen," she said as Paloma positioned himself between the detective and Chance. It was a brave thing to do, because judging by the way her eyes narrowed, she classified ingrown hairs and young know-it-all lawyers in the same category of irritant.

"Can I help you?" the lawyer asked.

"Who are you, besides in my way?" she said, eyes never leaving Chance.

"Javier Paloma, legal counsel for Palingenesis. And you are?"

"Here for him," she said, holding up her badge so close to Paloma's face that the man had to step back to see it clearly. "Chance Harker, you're under arrest for the murder of Lee Conway."

"Who?" Chance asked. The name meant nothing to him.

The detective seemed disinclined to elaborate, instead directing the two uniformed officers to get Chance out of bed and ready to move. Raised voices swirled around him, but they sounded far away and indistinct, as if someone had a grip on his neck and had forced his head into a bucket of water. The first few hours after a revival were supposed to be as calm as possible, and this was a lot of stimulation. The two uniforms circled in slow motion on either side of the bed as the detective read him his rights. The machines that monitored Chance's vitals began to squawk like carrion birds.

"Shut those off," the detective ordered.

Holifield, who had already navigated around the officers and was checking the machines, insisted that wasn't possible and that Chance couldn't be moved.

"And why's that?" she asked.

"He's not medically cleared."

"So clear him. I'm not here over a parking ticket," the detective said.

"I don't doubt that, but it's not possible."

"He looks fine. Is he sick?" the detective asked suspiciously.

"No, but a clone needs a period of adjustment to stabilize after a revival. Body and consciousness require time to sync."

"If you take him now, there's a risk of neurological complications that the LAPD simply isn't equipped to handle," Paloma chimed in. "You want to be responsible if he dies in your custody?"

"Don't play me, Counselor. How long until he's ready to move?" the detective said.

"A little less than a week," the lawyer said, but quickly followed that up with "one hundred and twenty hours" when he saw that wouldn't be good enough for her.

"Why don't you just say five days like a normal goddamn person?"

"Five days," the lawyer amended. "Typically."

The detective laid a look on the lawyer that would have parted the Red Sea before setting out her terms in a solemn, low tone. "Two of my people are posted at the door at all times."

"This is private property."

It was at this point that the room degenerated into an ugly shouting match. One that Chance was happy not to be a part of. Even Chelsea, usually no stranger to a good throw-down, stepped back out of harm's way as the detective and the lawyer dug in their heels. From the cheap seats, it didn't seem as if either had ever met anyone who could out-argue them, but, having finally met their match, it didn't appear that this was going to be a case of game respecting game.

"Do you realize what'll happen when word of this gets out?" the detective demanded. "A clone being arrested for murder? You think you people have protesters now?" For a moment, the only sound was the rhythmic beeping from the machines monitoring Chance. Confident now that she had the floor, the detective continued. "The LAPD talks to the press later this afternoon. The only question is, Will we be saying that Palingenesis is cooperating, or will we be informing the public that you're allowing a clone wanted for murder to go unguarded?"

The lawyer transitioned from confrontational to congenial with whiplash speed. "Detective, Palingenesis intends to cooperate fully. Your people are, of course, welcome here until Chance Harker is discharged, and we will extend you every possible courtesy."

"The city of Los Angeles appreciates your assistance," the detective said, hand extended for Paloma to shake.

Under the detective's watchful eye, the two officers handcuffed Chance to the bed rails. It seemed a little excessive since he couldn't sit up on his own, much less mount a daring escape. Still, he kept his mouth shut in an uncharacteristic show of self-restraint. Cuffs weren't comfortable, but they beat jail all to hell. Chance had spent a night in juvie lockup when he was seventeen for vandalizing his high school, an experience he was not anxious to repeat. And the speed at which Javier Paloma had rolled over for a belly rub from the detective didn't fill him with confidence. Best to remember that Paloma was Palingenesis's lawyer, not his.

Satisfied that Chance wasn't going to pull a Shawshank, the detective left with Holifield and Paloma in tow. Chelsea looked shaken. She backed up against a chair and sat down hard.

"What do you need me to do?" she asked.

". . . need a lawyer. Someone good."

"Someone very good," Chelsea agreed. "I'm on it."

"And will you reach out to Maggie? Tell her where . . . am and what the situation is . . . really need to talk to her as soon as possible."

"Will do. Anything else?"

"Yeah. Find out who the hell Lee Conway is."

CHAPTER THIRTEEN

The next few days were *weird*. Not a word that would impress his mother, whose vocabulary erred toward the flamboyant, but Chance didn't know what else to call it. Recovering from a revival was always hard. Doing it in handcuffs while chaperoned by the police, with a trip to jail awaiting him upon his release, was torture. Holifield had never been his biggest fan, but things had turned arctic between them. As they moved through the daily schedule of physical and talk therapies, the two men barely spoke. Palingenesis was quiet and austere by design, but a hush still managed to fall wherever Chance went.

He was the center of the hurricane, and the entire staff was holding its breath for what waited on the other side of the eye wall. To be safe, all nonessential personnel had been placed on leave, and only a skeleton crew remained. All refreshes were suspended until Palingenesis could ensure client safety. Any scandal involving a clone invariably cranked up anti-clone sentiment, and now one had been accused of murder. Still, Chance thought it was overkill.

Then, on the second day, he heard it for himself—the low, steady rumble of protest. Even deep inside the building, he still felt the vibrations through his feet, as if Palingenesis had been surrounded by a hostile army, a hostile army that was here for one reason: him. All the hairs on his arms and neck stood up, and he caught himself looking around for somewhere to hide.

So, yeah, things were weird. And tense. And more than a little unnerving. The days passed in a strange limbo between fear and anger. Chance moved through his therapies on autopilot, counting the minutes until Holifield took him back to his room. The estuary of drugs that helped his new body to not reject the implanted consciousness also knocked him out. It was a restless, frustrated sleep, but it took him far away from Palingenesis. He always went somewhere different in his dreams, and Maggie was always there waiting for him. She'd take him by the hand, and they would walk toward the sun. He would ask if it was rising or setting, but she would only smile and squeeze his hand. In the morning, he woke exhausted, hoping to find his situation was all a bad dream.

No luck there.

Most of all, what he felt was lonely. That, despite the company of two of LA's finest twenty-four hours a day. He peppered them with questions about Lee Conway, but they were under orders not to talk to him and wouldn't even acknowledge him. Desperate to learn anything about this man he was accused of killing, he also tried to bring up his arrest with Dr. Hughes during therapy, but the good doctor sidestepped any attempt to deviate from the business at hand—getting Chance out of Palingenesis with all due haste. Suddenly, there were two physical therapists at every session instead of one.

Without access to his LFD, contact with the outside world was severely limited. His carefully staged, made-for-social-media life had its drawbacks. No friends visited him because he had no real friends. Notable no-shows included his mother, and his father, which, despite their last meeting, still managed to hurt. He wondered if Marley, out there beyond the edge of the world, would ever know his brother had been arrested for murder. He'd probably assume Chance had moved away like they'd discussed, if his brother even gave him that much thought.

And then there was Maggie. Apparently his arrest was all over the news, so there was no way she hadn't heard. Where was she? His plan had been to go see her after his last refresh and ask her to go away with him. Had he screwed it up somehow? He just needed to hear her voice, and for her to tell him what had happened. Under the circumstances, this was probably the wrong thing to be worrying about, but she was infinitely more important to him than Lee Conway. Chance didn't know the man. The idea that he'd killed anyone, much less a stranger, seemed surreal.

It took three days before Chelsea was allowed to visit. The silver lining to all this was that for the first time in a long time, Chance was happy to see her.

Ironic, considering he'd been close to firing her only last week. All it had taken was a little homicide. Not that she was all puppies and sunshine, far from it. She dutifully delivered the news, and the news was grim. The demonstrations outside Palingenesis were growing in size every day. Violence was in the air, and the police were braced for things to turn ugly. Chelsea described running a gantlet of protesters to get into the parking garage. She used phrases like *powder keg* and *tipping point*. Now, embellishment and Chelsea Klos were old and loyal friends. Chance wanted badly to discount her as an alarmist, but, judging by the mood around Palingenesis, he suspected that for once she might even be underselling the situation.

She explained that due to mounting civil unrest, the LAPD hadn't waited for Palingenesis to release Chance and had charged him in absentia. That in turn had started the clock ticking over at the DA's office, which had only forty-eight hours to make a charging decision. A decision had been made to hold the arraignment at Palingenesis, with the judge conferencing in remotely. In the meantime, LAPD had obtained a search warrant for his house and seized the hard drives that stored all his recordings.

"What do we know about Lee Conway?" he asked.

"Not a lot," she replied. "He was twenty-nine. The media keep talking about how he was an aspiring DP, but he has no credits as a director of photography that I could find. Mostly he was unemployed. He was sleeping on someone's couch. Sounds like a bum to me."

That was all vague and unhelpful. "What's his connection to me? How do I know this guy?"

"I don't know. The cops are still investigating," she said.

"What exactly do they have on me, then?" His frustration at being in the dark about his own case was finally boiling over.

"They haven't deigned to share that with me," she said, clearing her throat like a sapper who'd just stumbled over a land mine. "Good news on the lawyer front, though."

"Oh?" As far as Chance was concerned, the money it took to hire a good criminal lawyer should have been a crime in itself. Best-case scenario, they would keep Chance out of jail but would put him out on the streets doing it.

"Your father hired you a lawyer," Chelsea said. "He also agreed to cover bail, if there is any."

"What? Did you call him?" Chance was immediately suspicious that she'd gone to him behind his back.

"No," she answered emphatically.

"He just offered out of the goodness of his heart?"

"He offered. I don't know anything about his heart."

Chance knew how that was. "Did he get someone decent?"

"Sy Berger."

Now he really was speechless. Sy Berger was probably the most famous criminal defense lawyer in California. He'd been dubbed the "Champion of Lost Causes" by his admirers, the "Antichrist of the Legal System" by his detractors. He was a showman and a shameless provocateur; the oversize portraits of Melvin Belli and Johnnie Cochran that hung side by side in his office spoke to his influences and role models. Most famous for convincing a jury to acquit former congresswoman Marjorie Hackman in the murder of her husband and three children—a case most of America had viewed as open and shut—Sy Berger had been the scourge and boogeyman of the LAPD for the better part of three decades. He did take pro bono cases, but his legion of critics insisted that was determined by potential media attention. For everyone else, the price tag was staggering. For his dad to foot the bill after what Chance had said to him felt like some sort of message.

"Did he say anything else?" Chance asked.

"I didn't speak to him directly. Everything was communicated to me through an assistant."

And there was the message, loud and clear. Always media savvy, his father knew how it would play if he didn't help his youngest son. This was damage control, nothing more. He'd probably figured out a way to write off the legal fees as a business expense.

"Any word from my mom?"

"Haven't heard from her. Could she be traveling?"

More than likely. Emelia Harker had spent the better part of her postdivorce life in a first-class airplane seat. There was a real possibility the news of Chance's arrest hadn't reached her. Would she come home if it had?

The arraignment was set for the evening of the fourth day. Chance was up and moving more easily, although it still felt like there was a delay between thought and action, like an old computer trying to run new software. Palingenesis had negotiated to have Holifield and Paloma present but merely in an observational capacity. They clearly wanted nothing to do with Chance. Holifield hovered by the window almost apologetically, while Paloma sat in a corner typing furiously against his thighs, immersed in his LFD.

A large monitor had been set up at the foot of the bed for the judge to conference in. The detective was first to arrive. Although she hadn't given her name during his arrest, Chance overheard the officers guarding his room call her either Val Wolinski or "Butcher," which seemed unnecessarily intimidating. True to form, she offered no greeting and stood by the door glowering at Chance as though she'd found him tunneling to freedom.

The team from the district attorney's office arrived next in a fast-moving, agile peloton of dark suits and power ties. They were all roughly the same age, midthirties to early forties, two men and two women, but it was easy to pick out the assistant district attorney, who directed his people to arrange chairs to the right of the bed, in view of the monitor. His name was David Li, and he had a hard-nosed reputation as a courtroom killer. Chance didn't like how competent and focused they seemed. And even though he was the reason they were here, none of them acknowledged his presence.

Where was his lawyer?

Chance had yet to have any contact with the man, the myth, the legend that was Sy Berger, which seemed bizarre. His own lawyer hadn't talked to him before the hearing. Chance was the client, wasn't he? Or was that his father? Chelsea had assured him that Berger was hard at work and would arrive early to prep him. Well, early had come and gone; Chance would settle for on time.

"I'm here, I'm here," Sy Berger announced, sweeping into the room as if taking the stage for the opening number of a popular Las Vegas revue. The shock of silver hair on his head swirled like a blizzard. In contrast to the opposition, he wore a sky-blue three-piece suit over a peach dress shirt and a blue-and-silver pastel necktie. His cuff links were golden coins from the Roman Empire. He paused in front of the detective. "Val Wolinski? Detective Wolinski?"

"Yeah," she replied warily.

"Sy Berger," he said. "I must ask: Why do they call you the 'Butcher'?"

"My parents own a butchers' in Torrance. I worked there as a kid."

Sy nodded as if this explained the mysteries of the universe. "Anticlimactic but fabulous," he said, and then turned his attention, at last, to Chance. "How are you, my boy?"

"I thought you'd be here earlier. Aren't we going to go over my case?"

"Not to worry, this won't take but a minute. Are they treating you well?"

Chance held up his handcuffed wrist.

"David?" Sy said with the grave solemnity of a deeply disappointed spouse.

"Detective Wolinski will remove them before the judge logs on," David Li said as he shook Sy's hand across the bed, only reinforcing Chance's feeling of being the main course.

"So you're really going through with this?" Sy asked rhetorically.

"Don't start with me, Sy."

"It is, as they say, your funeral."

"I'm not granting him bail."

"I'm not going to need bail."

David Li regarded Sy suspiciously. "We've got your client cold."

"Do you?" Sy said in feigned wonderment.

"We have photos of Chance Harker leaving the scene."

That was alarming news to Chance, who looked at his lawyer for any indication that this was true.

"There's no law against leaving a place," Sy replied in his soothing baritone.

"He had the victim's blood on his clothes."

"And please keep them, with our compliments. You know how hard it is to get bloodstains out."

Li snapped his fingers at one of his associates, who then put a folder in his hand. "We are still waiting for ballistics to come back."

"I can hardly wait."

"But we have video of Chance Harker playing Russian roulette with a Ruger GP100. The same weapon he was photographed leaving the scene carrying."

"Yes, but whose prints are on it?"

Li paused. "What?"

"It's a simple question, David. Whose fingerprints are on the Ruger? And have you matched those fingerprints to my client?"

"You know damn well the police won't be able to process him until he's medically cleared to leave here. We'll take fingerprints then. But they'll match."

"Didn't one of your eager posse here do their homework?" Sy said, and then snapped his fingers at Chance's steward. "You're Holifield, yes?"

"Yes?" Holifield said with all the enthusiasm of a kid who hoped the teacher wouldn't notice him at the back of the classroom.

"Would you be so kind as to enlighten Mr. Li on the peculiarities of clones and fingerprints?"

"Clones do not share fingerprints with their originals."

"What are you talking about?" Li said.

Holifield sighed, clearly wishing to be left out of this. "Fingerprints are created by pressure in the womb. It's the same reason why identical twins don't have identical fingerprints."

Li fixed a withering look at his underlings. "How the hell did you miss this?"

"Oh, it's not their fault," Sy said, enjoying the moment. "How often do the wealthy submit themselves to fingerprinting? There's simply not much case law on the subject. As yet."

"This is bullshit, Sy."

"I assure you it is not. And if you hurry, you should be able to catch your perp in the morgue, where you'll find that justice has already been self-inflicted."

Detective Wolinski had reached her limit on fancy lawyer talk. "Fuck you, he did it."

"My client did no such thing," Sy replied, apparently no stranger to hostile law enforcement. "He doesn't know Lee Conway, has no knowledge of the crime, and will happily sit for a polygraph to prove it."

Li turned the angry color of an overripe eggplant. "The Supreme Court ruled in *Gaddis v. Virginia* that clones are legally recognized as their originals, which means this Chance Harker is that Chance Harker. There's no difference between the two. That means your client is legally responsible for the actions of the previous Chance Harker. So stop with your horseshit."

"Let me see if I have this straight. You can't physically place my client at the scene of the crime. You can't connect him to the murder weapon. And you have no motive. All you have is his downloaded consciousness, which has no memory of the incident in question," Sy said with a melodramatic and confounded sigh. "Seems mighty thin, but alright, have it your way. Let's take it to the judge. He didn't seem overly impressed with your case when I saw him at the club yesterday, but today, as they say, is a new day."

There was a profound and interminable silence. All eyes were on Li, who didn't appear to be relishing his moment in the spotlight. The monitor chose that moment to announce that the judge was joining the hearing.

"Good afternoon, counselors. Are we about ready to begin?" the judge asked.

What had been shaping up as a very bad day for Chance turned into an absolute rout for the district attorney's office. Once Li stammered out that his office was declining to press charges at this time, the judge let him know exactly how little he appreciated having his time wasted. The beleaguered assistant district attorney pleaded for more time to prepare, but the judge was having precisely none of it.

Paloma was the first out of the room, already on a call to his superior. The ADA and his crew weren't far behind, packing up and beating a hasty retreat. Detective Wolinski uncuffed Chance and offered a simple warning: "There's an old Polish saying: 'Don't praise the day before sunset.'"

"What's that supposed to mean?" Chance asked, rubbing his wrist.

"I wouldn't leave the state."

"He's free to travel as he likes, Detective," Sy reminded her, but she was already out the door, slamming it behind her.

"Well, that was unusually satisfying, don't you think?" Sy said. "Apologies for my dramatic entrance, my boy. I wanted to be certain our ducks were lined up in precise military fashion."

"That . . . that was incredible. You saved my ass."

"Well, I wouldn't bet on this being over. The DA will regroup. My guess is he'll be under enormous political pressure to bring new charges."

"How soon?"

"Time will tell, but we have a reprieve for now."

"Thank you again," Chance said, putting out a hand. They shook. Sy had the softest hands Chance had ever felt, like a friendly veal cutlet.

"My office will be in touch so we can review our strategy. Must fly for now."

On that note, Sy Berger left the same way he'd arrived, loudly and in a cloud of expensive cologne. His wake left behind a vacuum into which poured an anticlimactic silence. Chance wanted to celebrate not going to jail, but only Holifield was left. His steward wouldn't make eye contact and fussed with the machines arrayed around Chance as he got him settled for the night. The steward's attitude was a little unfair, since he was no longer under arrest. Couldn't they go back to not liking each other and giving each other crap instead of this nasty silent treatment?

Maybe one of them just needed to break the ice. Fine. Chance could be the bigger man for once.

"Bet you didn't see that coming."

Holifield finally looked at him. "I'm going home. Been a long day. The overnight staff will be along shortly. I'll see you in the morning."

"Come on, man," Chance said. "Enough already."

Holifield paused by the door. "You really don't get it, do you? What you and your lawyer just did here."

Chance asked him what he meant, but Holifield wasn't in any mood to elaborate. It wouldn't be until he left Palingenesis that Chance began to understand.

CHAPTER FOURTEEN

On Chance's last morning, after Holifield had finally cleared him to leave, the entire staff seemed to breathe a collective sigh of relief. Chance was right there with them. Being silently despised and judged had worn him down. He needed to breathe fresh air, literally and figuratively.

So much had changed since his revival. His first and only thoughts had been of Maggie: finding his way back to her, leaving Los Angeles together. But that was before he'd been accused of murdering Lee Conway. Maybe he hadn't taken the allegations as seriously as he should have at first, but that was only because the whole thing sounded absurd. He'd done a lot of questionable things in his life, things he didn't look back on with any pride, but they'd all been self-inflicted mistakes. Murder was a whole other thing. He'd never been a violent person, never even been in a fight, at least not one he'd started.

At the hearing, Chance had been grateful when Sy Berger had the charges dropped. But he'd had time to think things through in the days since. There'd been no real debate at the hearing that his predecessor had killed Lee Conway. The assistant district attorney had talked about bloody clothes and photographs of Chance leaving the crime scene carrying a gun. Sy Berger hadn't argued with any of it, instead relying on a technicality over fingerprints and memories. But they all still believed he'd done it, especially Holifield, who continued to perfect his impersonation of a sentient glacier.

So what if Chance had killed Lee Conway? It still didn't seem possible to him, but hypothetically speaking, what if? That's why he needed to get out of here now. Not to see Maggie, not to make plans for their future, but to find out what had really happened in the eighteen hours between the time he'd left Palingenesis after his last refresh and when he sat down at his dining room table and shot himself with a gun he didn't own.

———

Chance was sitting on the edge of his bed waiting when Holifield arrived accompanied by two security guards. That was a first, but Chance didn't mention it. He followed Holifield down to be discharged. Neither man spoke, but Holifield lingered while Chance filled out his exit forms. That was another first. Chance wrote it off as nerves. Then Javier Paloma arrived just as Chance was finishing up. It surprised him a little. He would've expected Palingenesis to forgo the usual admonishments to speed his departure, but if nodding agreeably got him out the door more quickly, then Chance would be an obedient bobblehead.

"Mr. Harker. All set?" Paloma asked.

"Javier, aren't we on a first-name basis by now?"

"You remember my name. I'm touched."

"Are we really doing this again so soon? We just had this conversation."

"I imagine it feels that way to you. This will be slightly different, though."

"Oh?" Chance didn't like the sound of that one bit.

"I've been asked to inform you that as of now, you have no clones left at Palingenesis."

Chance hadn't thought of that. Most clients kept only one backup at a time. His father's policy allowed for two, a perk of the Palingenesis Platinum Protection package. The fabled Triple-P. Clones took time to grow, roughly six months. Having a second clone in storage insured top-tier clients against the risk of a second, permanent death after a first revival. Only the absurdly wealthy (and Palingenesis executives and their families) were enrolled in the program. Chance had now burned through both his clones in a matter of weeks.

"How long will it take to grow a new one?" Chance asked.

Paloma shook his head. "No, I apologize for the misunderstanding. What I should have said was there won't be another clone."

It took Chance longer than it should have to comprehend what the lawyer was saying. Having a clone in waiting had been a fact of his life since before puberty. He wasn't ready to hear that that privilege might be taken away.

"Why not?" Chance finally asked.

"In light of recent events, the decision has been made to terminate your policy."

Chance felt light-headed, as if he'd stood up too quickly. "Because of the Lee Conway thing? The police dropped the charges."

"That did not exactly win you any points with us," Paloma said.

"I want to talk to your boss."

"This comes directly from Mr. Gaddis himself. He told me personally not fifteen minutes ago."

That caught Chance by surprise. "Gaddis is here?"

"He flew in last night."

For the man to get on a plane told Chance how serious Palingenesis was taking this. Vernon Gaddis, the reclusive CEO, was famous for never venturing far from his Maryland compound and for never, ever flying. Seven years ago, he and his wife, Cynthia, had died when their private jet had crashed in the Atlantic while returning from Europe. Vernon had a clone; Cynthia did not. Her death had triggered an ugly custody battle between Gaddis and his wife's family over guardianship of his three children. The family contested that the clone of Vernon Gaddis wasn't legally a person, much less a father. Under Virginia law,

Vernon Gaddis had died in the plane crash along with his wife, and therefore their children belonged with the next of kin, as stipulated in the will.

The legal battle had raged for years, culminating just last summer in the landmark five-to-four Supreme Court decision *Gaddis v. Virginia*. It recognized the civil rights of clones at the federal level, wiping away anti-clone laws in dozens of states. Vernon Gaddis was declared sole guardian of his three children.

"I want to talk to him."

"That's not possible," Javier said, choosing his words carefully, although his tone was far less politic. It dawned on Chance this was why Holifield had hung around. His steward must have been turning cartwheels at the prospect of finally being rid of him. It also explained the two security guards lurking nearby like Chekhov's bouncers and just waiting for an excuse to go off.

"I didn't kill Lee Conway."

"No, you just have no memory of killing him. Which is convenient, isn't it?" Paloma said.

"Doesn't feel convenient. What am I supposed to do now?"

"Try not dying," Paloma suggested. "Like the rest of us."

Chance didn't know why he needed someone to point out the obvious, but he seemed determined *not* to put two and two together. But anything that happened now was permanent. He looked at the counter and put a hand out to steady himself. If he slipped and fell and hit his head, he could die. Freak accidents like that happened all the time. And now it could happen to him too. For the first time since he was a kid, if he died, he was dead. There would be no coming back.

———

Chelsea was waiting for him, per usual, although it had taken some aggressive arm-twisting to persuade her to return to Palingenesis.

Not until he got to the garage did he fully appreciate her reluctance. What had been a faint rumble of distant thunder from the safety of the Palingenesis offices became a lightning storm when he got to the deserted parking garage. The sound was unbelievable. He had to force himself to get off the elevator before the doors closed again. Chelsea's Tesla was idling nearby. Why had she brought her car and not his? When he got in, she anticipated his question, saying his car was too recognizable and would draw unwanted attention.

"What the hell's going on out there?" he asked.

Chelsea only shook her head, as if there weren't words to describe it. They circled the garage and stopped at the entrance. The reinforced roll-up gate was down, which was a first. A Black man in a sports coat stepped out of the booth. Slung casually across his chest was a wicked-looking tear-gas launcher. He knocked on the glass. When Chelsea rolled down the window, he introduced himself as Bill Roberts, head of security for Palingenesis.

"How dark can you make these windows?" he asked Chelsea, who adjusted the tint to maximum. Roberts nodded approvingly. "That ought to buy you some time. We've got barricades set up in the street, for all the good they're doing, but there's a clear lane out of the garage. Make a hard left and floor it. Do not stop for anyone. If the first light is red, run it. You got me?"

"Got it," Chelsea said through clenched teeth.

Roberts reached through the window and squeezed her shoulder. "It's going to be alright, long as you don't dillydally. And no sightseeing."

"No dillydallying," Chelsea repeated.

"No dillydallying, that's right. And we'll be watching. I'll be watching." He patted his weapon reassuringly.

"How many are out there?" Chance asked.

Roberts shrugged as if Chance had asked him to count the sand on a beach. "Fifteen hundred? Two thousand? Give or take. I mean, they just keep coming."

"There are that many Children of Adam?" CoA was mainly an East Coast organization. Chance had no idea it had that many members in California.

"No, this is way past Children of Adam. Not sure this is even about cloning anymore. You sure stirred up the hornet's nest, boy."

"What about the police?" Chance asked. "Why aren't they here?"

"Oh, you know the police. They're here. They just won't get involved 'less things take a turn. And you don't want to be that turn, believe that," Roberts said ominously. He clapped his hands together. "Now let's do this!"

Roberts walked alongside the car up to the foot of the gate, which retracted slowly into the ceiling. Each foot it rose, the noise from outside seemed to double and then double again. When the gate was high enough to drive under, Roberts tapped the roof and gave them a reassuring thumbs-up. It didn't reassure. Chelsea had the steering wheel in a white-knuckle death grip. Chance reached for his seat belt, a numbing realization settling into his frame: there were fifteen hundred people out here who wanted his head, and he didn't have a backup clone. He wanted to go back inside, where it was safe.

The car nosed out of the garage, like a rabbit timidly coming out of its burrow, sniffing the air for trouble. Trouble didn't look to be in short supply. The street was a war zone. A furnace of anger and frustration. The air sizzled with chants and desperate cries. To the right, the front entrance of Palingenesis was a wall of humanity that clogged the sidewalks and streets. Crude bonfires lit up the protesters like a medieval army laying siege to an enemy castle. At the end of the block, riot police stood in formation but made no move to disperse the crowd. Probably wise. The police were badly outnumbered, and Chance didn't see things going well for them if they attempted to clear the street.

Heads turned as the Tesla pulled out of the garage. Roberts was right: the barricades weren't good for much. People were everywhere.

A bottle hit the side of the car and shattered. Chance found himself wishing that Chelsea drove something a little sturdier . . . like a tank.

"I thought they didn't know your car," Chance said.

"They don't care whose car it is," Chelsea said, making a slow left onto the street. A young woman darted out and slapped her palms on the hood, digging in her heels as if she were singlehandedly going to push the vehicle back into the garage. She grinned wildly at them through the windshield, and Chance reminded himself that she couldn't actually see them through the tinted glass.

Chelsea tapped the brakes. They came to a precarious stop.

"You have to keep going," Chance said.

"I'll hit her."

"She'll move."

"If I hurt someone, they'll tear the car apart."

The protesters looked of that mind already. Emboldened, they began to swarm around the car, pounding on the roof and yelling indecipherable threats at whoever was inside. The Tesla began to rock back and forth like a dinghy caught in a gale.

"We're going to die," Chelsea whispered, tears welling in her eyes.

"No, we're not," Chance said, hoping to sound inspiring.

"Well *you're* not, so easy for you to say." She didn't know that Palingenesis had canceled his policy and thought he was being characteristically glib about death. He'd almost told her when he got into the car, but then kept it to himself.

Another bottle shattered on the side of the car. Chelsea screamed. Chance was about to lose it as well. *The police will stop this,* he told himself. *They have to step in.*

There was a hollow popping sound. Something arced overhead and landed in the crowd. Gas billowed up, scattering coughing, spluttering protesters in all directions. Chance said a silent prayer to Bill Roberts. Another tear-gas canister landed and skittered in circles, sending out plumes of gray smoke. A path opened in the thinning crowd. Chance pointed excitedly, but it wasn't wide enough for a car. Chelsea leaned on the horn. Call it a miracle or simple muscle memory, but people jumped out of the way. The car rolled forward, forward, slowly forward, and then they were through and in the clear. Chelsea accelerated. Neither of them saw or cared whether the first or second light was red.

The riot police never moved.

Once they were safely away, Chelsea switched the car to auto and sat back in her seat. She was breathing hard, as if she'd just finished running a race.

"What was all that?" Chance asked, mostly to himself, a way to express and give voice to his disbelief, but Chelsea heard him and had an answer.

"What do you think? Your lawyer created a loophole where a clone can get away with murder. People are sick of it."

"Wait, sick of what? Of murder?"

"Of rich people," she answered. "Fucking rich people."

Chance had never thought about it that way. The tension and controversy surrounding human cloning had always been about clones' humanity, or lack thereof. Did they have souls? Were they really just "pretentious meat," as Franklin Butler, the founder of Children of Adam, had labeled them? The class warfare themes in Imani Highsmith's piece were suddenly prescient.

"I'm not rich," he said sulkily.

"Oh, Chance, please! You come from money. Do you think Sy Berger is representing you out of the goodness of his heart?"

Chance frowned, her words sharp, piercing. Accusatory. "Just take me home," he said. All he wanted was to lock his front door and never open it again.

"You can't *go* home."

"Try and stop me."

"It's not me you have to worry about." Chelsea described the scene outside his house. The protesters. The media. The mess the police had made during their search. "I don't think it's safe for you to be there right now."

He hated to admit it, but she was right. He'd be a sitting target. "So what do you suggest?"

"I rented you an apartment for a week through your holding company, so it's not in your name. Furnished. Low-profile neighborhood. Maybe things will blow over in a couple of days."

"How low profile?"

"West Adams."

"What the hell is West Adams?" he asked.

Chelsea gave him a second look to see if he was kidding. "West Adams. It's a neighborhood. South of the Ten?"

"Are you kidding me?" Chance knew where she meant but had no idea it was called West Adams. *Low profile* was an extremely generous way of describing the area. It had never been trendy and had become severely depopulated in the last ten years as families migrated east searching for affordable water.

"Hey, I'll drop you anyplace you want to go. Just say where," she said, sounding like a person who'd picked up a hitchhiker but now regretted the decision.

"What about my stuff?" he asked.

"I packed you a bag. Toiletries. Change of clothes. It's in the trunk."

"I mean the recordings." The police might have taken the hard drives, but they wouldn't have found the backup. Chelsea had described what had happened the night he shot himself, but he needed to see for himself.

"It's at the apartment."

"Alright," he said as though he had a choice. "Let's go."

They drove the rest of the way in silence. Chelsea kept shaking out her hands as if all her stress had settled in her fingers. Chance powered on his LFD and checked a week's worth of missed messages. Most were from media vultures hoping for an exclusive. He skimmed through them, looking for any of the names he cared about. He didn't expect to hear from his mother or father, and he hadn't. Harder to take was that Maggie hadn't called. He'd invented a plausible explanation for why she might avoid Chelsea, but he couldn't come up with a comforting story for her ghosting him entirely. He wanted to call her but was afraid of how it would go. What had happened in those eighteen hours?

He was still mulling that over when the car pulled up outside the apartment building. Chelsea left the engine running when they got out.

"Aren't you coming up?" he asked.

She didn't answer. She popped the trunk and put Chance's bags on the sidewalk. It took only a moment to transfer the apartment's door codes from her LFD to his, but then she lingered at the curb. He realized she hadn't asked him one question, or brainstormed how best to handle this situation. She hadn't said a word.

"Chance," she said, his name a mere preamble to a speech he could tell she'd been rehearsing. But at the last moment, she paused as if throwing out her prepared remarks to speak from the heart. "I quit."

"You what?" He'd heard her fine, but sometimes saying something stupid was preferable to standing there with your mouth hanging open.

She was already walking back to her car. "If you have any questions or need help with the transition, you can contact my office. Cais will be able to—"

"We're in kind of a crisis here," Chance said.

"No, *you* are. I'm done."

"You said you had my back," he said, unable to keep the hurt from his voice, which only angered him further.

"That's a figure of speech, and it only extended to our business. You killing someone is not in my job description."

"I didn't kill anybody."

"Sy Berger is a hell of a lawyer. You're lucky to have him."

"I did not kill anyone," he repeated, slowly this time, in case she'd missed the gist of what he was saying.

She gave him a pitying look. "Watch the recordings."

"Chelsea," he said as she got back into her car. He rapped a knuckle on the passenger window until she rolled it down exactly one inch. "You can't do this to me." He hated himself for sounding like such a cliché.

"Know what the funny part is?" she asked.

"What?"

"After I'm gone, you'll turn this around so that I'm the one who let you down."

"Aren't you the one that's quitting?"

"See?" Chelsea said with a weary laugh. "It's started already."

CHAPTER FIFTEEN

The Tesla pulled away, marooning Chance on the curb with nothing but two suitcases and a long list of unanswered questions. Life without Chelsea Klos had been on his mind for some time, but he always assumed he'd be the one to do the firing. He'd never gotten around to it because, well, she was the devil he knew. She kept the trains running on time, which left him ample time to do whatever it was he'd been doing with his life. A nasty little codependent arrangement, which he saw now had been one-way traffic all along. She'd picked a rough day to teach him that lesson. Chance wondered if he'd accumulated enough credits now to graduate with that degree in irony he'd been working toward all his life.

A couple walking their dog passed him, or at least tried to. Their hyperactive terrier had other ideas, and in its enthusiasm over meeting a new person, the dog wrapped its leash around Chance's ankles. "Sprinkles!" the man scolded as the three of them did an awkward dance of apologies while trying to untangle his legs. As the couple walked away, the woman glanced back as if trying to place him. Had she, or was he just being paranoid? If he was just going to stand on the sidewalk all day, he might as well post a START RIOT HERE sign and be done with it.

Gathering up his suitcases, he looked up and down the street to get his bearings. Most of the businesses were boarded up, but there was a takeout chicken joint across the street if he got hungry later.

Outside the restaurant, a teenage girl with the kind of pale-white skin that didn't age well in Southern California loitered under the faded awning. An Angels baseball cap was pulled down low over her eyes, but it got in Chance's head that she was watching him. She lifted her head and stared right at him. It was the girl from the other morning. The weird one who'd almost but not quite confronted him outside Maggie's bungalow. He'd had his share of obsessive fans, and all but two had been harmless. It was one thing for her to track him to Maggie's. Like Darsh had said, his car wasn't exactly subtle. But her being here? That was something else. He had no connection to West Adams. Chelsea had just rented the apartment. So how had she gotten here first?

Uneasy at the question, he snapped several photos of the girl on his LFD. He knew from experience that if she turned out to be a headache later, it would be better to have a record of his interactions with her. But the pictures were all black rectangles, as if he'd left the lens cap on. (LFDs didn't have lens caps.) He tried again, same result. Frowning, he checked the settings. This was a great time for his LFD to shit the bed. He took a picture of his feet. It came out a picture of his feet.

Okay, now that was weird.

Across the street, the girl was shaking her head as if chastening a disappointing child. He took one more picture of her, but it was tar black, like the first batch.

He gave the girl a longer look. Celebrities often carried surveillance-suppression equipment when they wanted privacy. Paparazzi (like Darsh) countered by sometimes shooting with old-fashioned film cameras in what had become an escalating arms race between celebrities and the media. But surveillance suppression was expensive, and the girl's gear had to be high end to defeat his LFD at this distance. She jaywalked across the street toward him. Up close he saw that her plain, mousy face had a faint dusting of freckles. The only thing at all remarkable about the girl were her eyes, which were fiercely intelligent.

"I've seen you before," he said. "How'd you find me again?"

"Followed you. Wasn't that hard."

He didn't believe her. There was something in the way she'd been leaning against the wall that made him think she'd been waiting on him to arrive.

"Who are you?" he asked.

"I'm just a big fan. The fabled Chance Harker."

He glanced up and down the street again, checking for anything or anyone out of place. It didn't feel safe out here. "What do you want?"

"How about a picture?" she teased.

"Yeah, sure," he said, hoping to placate the girl and send her on her way quickly.

She struck a pose beside him and told him to smile, although she herself wasn't. She took his hand and gave it a familiar squeeze, rubbing the back with her thumb.

"Okay, that's enough," he said, stepping away from the girl. What was he doing taking pictures with obsessive fans? If she posted it somewhere, the place would be swarming with Children of Adam fanatics. Hell, maybe he'd been too quick to write her off as a fan; she could be Children of Adam. Did they have their own little brownshirt brigade now?

"That was perfect," she said.

"Are you going to tell anyone I'm here?"

"Why would I ever do a thing like that?" she asked mischievously.

After collecting his things, he retreated into the small, dank lobby of the apartment building. Through the leaves of a potted palm tree, he looked back at the street. The girl was nowhere in sight, although that didn't mean she was gone. He'd been here all of five minutes, and already he didn't feel safe. He needed somewhere else to hole up and think.

The safe and sensible answer was Valhalla. It was a couple of hours outside Los Angeles, and his father had turned the vineyard into a fortress since moving up there. Chance knew that wasn't happening, though. Call it foolish pride, but after their last conversation and the anonymous dispatching of Sy Berger to tidy up, Chance would rather roll the dice in West Adams than go begging for his father's protection.

His heart was lobbying for him to go to Maggie. He might have been sidetracked by Lee Conway, but he still held out hope that after he'd figured this thing out, they might still get out of this town. If her offer was still on the table. Her silence suggested maybe she'd had a change of heart. He got as far as dialing her number but hung up before it could ring.

So who did that leave that he could count on, now that Chelsea had set sail? It wasn't a long list on the best of days. He scrolled through his contacts, rarely slowing down. As a last resort, he decided to call his mother. Her house would be a perfect place to lie low, and she almost certainly wasn't home.

She always answered the phone managing to sound like she'd just been dialing his number. "Chance. What a nice surprise. Happy birthday, baby boy."

His birthday had been weeks ago, but Chance didn't want to spoil the moment by being a stickler for details. It was a surprise she'd remembered at all. Emelia Harker and calendars had never been on the best of terms, but ever since the kidnapping, she'd become unmoored from the calendar. If she knew the month she was in, it was a minor miracle.

"Thanks, Mom." He could tell from her tone that she didn't know anything about what was happening in Los Angeles. Postkidnapping, his mother had also become news agnostic: it might exist, but Emelia Harker didn't believe anything good came from following it.

"Did you get my transfer?" she asked, eager to keep up the momentum of their small talk lest anything real slip in during the pauses.

"I did. Thank you."

"You only turn twenty-one once. Buy yourself something special."

"I will. Where are you?"

"Split," she said. "Didn't I tell you?"

"No. Where's that?"

"Croatia. On the Adriatic. It's gorgeous. There's a whole Roman palace. You've got to visit one day."

"You know I can't go to Europe, Mom." The European Union had an outright ban on human cloning, which made travel there extremely complicated.

"Well, yes," his mother said, flustered to have reality intrude upon her lighthearted catch-up with her son. "But someday."

"When will you be home?"

"I'm not really sure. Perhaps next week, although Richard is trying to talk me into flying on to Istanbul. A friend of his is opening a new restaurant there that's getting lots of buzz."

Chance wasn't sure who Richard was, only that they'd never met. His mother didn't date so much as keep company with various men. "That sounds nice."

"How is everything there?"

Mom, I've really screwed up. Can I stay at your place? Please help me.

Instead he said, "Same old, same old."

"Well, try and get some rest, you sound tired." That was her advice for everything.

He wiped his eyes. "I will."

"Alright, well, must run. Love and kisses. I'll let you know when I'm back. We should have dinner and celebrate properly."

"I'd like that," he said, but the line was already dead.

Why hadn't he asked her if he could stay at her place? It was complicated. The hardest thing for him to reconcile was the difference between the warm, loving memory of his mother and who she became in the wreckage of the kidnapping. Rising from the ashes like an alcoholic phoenix . . . he remembered how much she drank in those days. A ghost wandering the halls of the family home. She'd had to endure watching Marley fall apart, unable to reach or help her eldest son. His apparent suicide at El Matador had been the end for her. The divorce, already vicious, turned toxic. Her way of punishing her husband for failing them all.

Chance had simply gotten lost in the shuffle. The forgotten child. He would've liked to say that he'd handled it gracefully. That he'd understood that they were all devastated by what had happened. But he was only sixteen, and wasn't, in that moment, capable of that depth of insight. They were his parents. He was their son. It wasn't that complicated. He'd become sullen and withdrawn. A raw nerve of a boy who'd desperately needed his parents, who were too lost in their own grief to notice.

He remembered how exhausting it had been being that angry all the time. Torturing himself with questions like, Did his parents not love him anymore because of what they'd all been through or because they didn't think he was really their son anymore? He'd read the stories in the media; it wouldn't be the first time a clone was rejected by their own family. To this day he still wondered, but he'd never dared ask the question. Sometimes it was better just to be heartbroken than to know the truth and have your heart die altogether.

His court-mandated therapist had said that was why he kept everyone at arm's length. Classic abandonment issues. Whatever. He'd needed her then, and she hadn't been there. Maybe it *had* made him wary of asking anything of her again, but that was just common sense. She hadn't helped him then; he wouldn't make the mistake of asking now.

Without a better option, Chance took his bags up to the apartment, which at least offered privacy. Otherwise it wasn't much of an improvement on the lobby, little more than four cinder block walls, two wooden chairs at a bowlegged particleboard table, and a twin bed that sagged in the middle like a tired, worn-out pony. In the alcove that passed for a kitchen, an old food printer sat next to a microwave and a hot plate, three generations of food preparation side by side by side. It was like the saddest museum in the world. The sole attempt at decoration was one of those generic office paintings that took the worst bits of mid-twentieth-century art and mashed them up on one canvas. On the bright side, the lock on the front door worked just fine, which felt priceless right about now.

He dropped his suitcases in the cramped bedroom and circled the apartment, closing all the blinds. Down in the alley below, a man rested his head against a dumpster to keep from tipping over while he urinated. It certainly wasn't the view from the Bird Streets, but he wasn't here to take in the sights. Ever since being accused of killing Lee Conway—a man he still knew next to nothing about—he'd been hearing secondhand about the recording he'd made at the house. The police considered it as good as a confession, and it had been enough to make Chelsea quit. The need to see the footage for himself had steadily built up in his blood like a junkie's habit. If he was lucky, there might be some indication of how Lee Conway had come into his life.

There were eighteen hours between the time he'd left Palingenesis and the moment he played Russian roulette with a loaded gun. But when he loaded the footage to his LFD, the total run time was less than an hour: fifty-six minutes, to be exact. He hoped maybe there'd been a transfer error, but after hitting "Play," he realized he'd done it to himself again.

The fifty-six minutes were his last. The recording began with his predecessor arriving home. He looked like hell. The gun was in his hand, and the front of his T-shirt was a livid smear of dried blood. Chance watched himself go into his private room and methodically delete everything before opening his front door, never once putting down the gun, as though it were an extension of his hand now. Once that was done, his predecessor looked directly at the camera mounted in the ceiling. Chance thought he knew all his own expressions, but this was a new one. He couldn't put his finger on just one emotion behind those eyes. Regret? Resignation? Rage?

The doorbell rang. It was Chelsea and Trang, who looked decidedly unthrilled by life. Chelsea looked startled at Chance's appearance and had a thousand questions, none of which received answers. His predecessor led them into the dining room and took a seat at the head of the table. He told them to set up at the far end. It was exactly the way Chelsea had described. His predecessor shook the revolver empty. Bullets and empty shell casings danced across the table like the first heavy drops of a hard rain. He gathered them up and made two neat rows: three empty shell casings, three unfired bullets. He assessed each one thoughtfully as if tasting wines, looking for the perfect pairing. All this time, Chelsea was asking him what he was doing. She begged him to stop and talk to her, but he paid her no mind. The second bullet in line caught his eye, and he held it up to the light. Satisfied by what he saw, he touched it to his lips and slipped it into one of the six empty chambers. With a flick of his wrist, he snapped the cylinder shut and gave it a healthy spin.

"So, who's ready to see me do something reckless?" his predecessor began, momentarily flashing his trademark showman energy, but it vanished before the words had faded to silence. "You know what? Forget all that." He looked directly into the camera. "People are going to be asking a lot of questions about Lee Conway." The disdain in his voice was like curdled milk. "I know it'll make you curious. You're going to want to go sticking your nose in. All I'm going to say is he had it coming. Beyond that, trust me, you don't want to know."

Preamble complete, his predecessor pressed the gun to his temple and pulled the trigger. No hesitation, no fear.

Click.

In the here and now, Chance flinched. Back then, his predecessor barely reacted and only gave the gun a disappointed look.

"What are the chances?" he asked rhetorically before trying a second time.

Click.

Even though he knew how it ended, Chance sat on the edge of the bed, holding his breath. After the third attempt, his predecessor paused to compose himself.

"Stay out of it," the Chance on-screen warned, then pulled the trigger a fourth and final time. In the recording, Chance lurched to his left and collapsed forward onto the table like a marionette whose strings had all been cut at once. There was a moment of silence, then Trang put the camera down on the dining room table, announced that he was quitting, and stalked out. In the background, Chelsea could be heard calling the police. Then she fumbled with the camera. The recording ended.

Chance ripped his LFD from behind his ear and threw it on the bed. Then he was up, pacing around the small apartment, trying to walk off the queasy feeling in his gut. He went to the bathroom and splashed water on his face as if trying to sober himself up. It didn't work. Back at Palingenesis, he'd held out hope that the police had jumped to the wrong conclusion about him. The idea that he'd killed someone had just been too much to wrap his mind around, especially some guy he'd never heard of before a few days ago. Now he saw why the detective had been so certain she had her man. He'd all but confessed to his murder in the recordings.

Like hell he was staying out of it. Who was Lee Conway?

He went back and fished his LFD out from behind the bed where it had fallen. He searched Lee Conway's name. It would have been just as fast if he'd typed his own. In the endless scroll of news stories, one name didn't appear without the other. From the internet's point of view, it wasn't entirely apparent that Lee Conway had even existed before last week.

From Sacramento originally, twenty-nine-year-old Lee Conway had no living parents and an older brother whom no one knew where to find. He'd been kicking around Los Angeles for over a decade trying to catch on in the film business. He'd started at USC but hadn't finished. Six addresses in the last eight years, he'd recently been crashing on a friend's couch in Panorama City. The friend spoke highly of Conway, whom he called an aspiring director and an extraordinary talent. Now if any of that was true or simply polishing the memory of a recently deceased friend, the media offered no opinion, although Chance picked up a hint of relief from the friend at having his couch back.

To Chance, Lee Conway sounded like every other hustler in Los Angeles—lots of talk, very little to show for it. Conway's only professional credit on a feature was working as a grip. The high point of his career had been as cinematographer on a pair of low-budget shorts seven years ago. There was nothing to suggest a connection between them, much less a motive for murder. It wasn't until he pulled up the picture that every story was using of Lee Conway that Chance felt a prickle of recognition. That humorless smile was familiar, as were the sun-damaged skin and the shaggy head of blond hair looking like an overgrown lawn. But from where and from when? The problem with his memory was that their encounter might've been ten years ago or last week. But whenever it was, he knew that face.

So, it appeared, did a lot of people now. Lee Conway was the newly anointed poster child for any number of societal sins. Sy Berger had warned Chance that this wasn't over. That looked to be an understatement. At the local level, protests had expanded far beyond Palingenesis. Los Angeles had always been an angry city, and as the environmental crisis tightened its grip, protests had become an annual ritual. Ever since the charges against Chance had been dropped, riots had engulfed downtown Los Angeles, escalating each night. The mayor, the chief of police, and the district attorney's office were all vying to lay the failure to prosecute Chance Harker at the others' doorsteps. Meanwhile, the governor seemed on the verge of returning Los Angeles County to Mexico. The story had even made its way to a White House press briefing, and the president was said to be monitoring the situation.

But the good news was that Chance had succeeded in uniting the punditry industry on all sides of the political spectrum. What was the media term for torches and pitchforks? They were calling it the "crime of the century": legalized murder, a Get Out of Jail Free card, a stain on the American judicial system. Opinions on human cloning were still incredibly divisive, but everyone agreed that Chance Harker was scum who thought he was better than everyone. Now, whether he was human scum or some other kind remained very much up for debate.

Even for someone who was a professional pot stirrer, it was too much for Chance to take. Sy was right. The city wasn't about to take the fall for him. They would build a fresh case, and then they would come for him again. It wasn't a question of if, only of when. That meant he was on borrowed time. His predecessor had warned him to leave it alone, but he wasn't about to do that. So assuming he had killed Lee Conway, the question now was why. And how. How had he crossed paths with Lee Conway that night? Unfortunately, his predecessor's deletion of all the recordings made that a very hard question to answer.

At a dead end, he went back and read the news reports of Lee Conway's murder that he'd only skimmed before. LAPD said it had pictures of him leaving the murder scene. Turned out those pictures had first appeared on a tabloid site that Chance had appeared in many times before. He had a pretty good idea who'd taken them.

Darsh answered on the first ring.

"Can we meet?" Chance said in lieu of a greeting.

"That depends. You still have the gun?"

"The police took it."

There was a pause as Darsh did some sort of calculation. "Okay then. Where'd you have in mind?"

"Wherever it was you took those pictures."

"Oh, there," Darsh said, but he gave him a location not far from Dodgers Stadium in Elysian Park.

Chance cursed quietly. He knew exactly where Darsh meant and had sworn never to go there again.

CHAPTER SIXTEEN

The old drainage ditch was a steep, treacherous climb, but it beat bushwhacking up the hillside through the thick, withered chaparral. Thankfully the moon was out, or it would have been impossible. Halfway up, Chance slipped and nearly tumbled back down. With an undignified cry, he squatted down and put both hands in the dirt, searching for his balance. He felt paralyzed, afraid to move forward, afraid to go back.

Ever since the drive through the protest outside Palingenesis, the facts of his own mortality had continued to intrude. He could barely remember his life before clones. He'd been so young when he'd gone in for his first refresh that death had still been largely theoretical: a thing that happened to other people but not to kids his age. Now death was frighteningly real, and the reality was that all it would take was one careless step, one stumble, and he could die. Once-easy decisions had become difficult—everything was a gamble. How did people live like this? Was he just supposed to accept the fragility of his existence and hope for the best? What an insane way to live.

Up above, Darsh had stopped and was looking back at him. "You alright?"

"I slipped."

"Yeah, I definitely wore the wrong shoes for this," Darsh said, and he stood on one leg and then the other to knock dirt out of the soles. It made Chance very nervous, but he resisted the urge to ask Darsh to be careful. He didn't think *protective parent* would be a good look on him. Darsh tried to take pity on him. "You know, we really don't have to do this. There's plenty of dirt and dead sticks at the bottom of the hill."

"You took those pictures of me coming down this hill?"

"Yeah."

"Then let's go," Chance said, standing up to signal he was good to carry on. It was tempting to take Darsh's out, but he'd come this far. There was no turning back now. Darsh shrugged and led the way.

They made it to the top without any more near-death experiences. Chance scrambled over the lip of the culvert and tried to catch his breath. Darsh was already rummaging through his camera bag.

"You didn't have to lug all that up here," Chance said. He would have preferred some privacy, but pictures had been the deal for Darsh to meet him here. Killer returns to the scene of the crime, that kind of thing. Darsh probably already had a buyer lined up.

"What kind of paparazzi would that make me?"

"The kind that doesn't need a shower now."

Darsh adjusted his camera's settings and snapped a few test shots. The flash lit up the ancient culvert and the surrounding trees. Chance shivered, emotions getting the better of him. Everything was dead or dying, like something out of a Beckett play. It looked like it'd been a thousand years since water had last flowed through the cracked and broken concrete. Living in a neighborhood like the Bird Streets, where residents could afford to flaunt water restrictions, it was easy to forget how barren Southern California had become. Los Angeles had been carved out of the desert, but the epidemic of wildfires and droughts over the past decades had seen the desert begin to reclaim it. The eastward migration of the middle classes in the thirties had thinned the populace, creating an even starker divide between rich and poor and giving Los Angeles the feeling of a city in decline. Some smartass in the media had called it the "Detroit of California." Civic pride hadn't taken that well at all.

The pictures continued as Chance looked around. It was smaller than he'd expected. Whatever signs Lee Conway's death might have left behind had already been scrubbed clean by nature and the LAPD.

"For real, why are we up here?" Darsh asked.

"This is where they found the body."

"Yeah, I know. But the police have been all over this place. You've seen too many movies if you think you're going to find something they missed."

"No," Chance said. "No, not that body. *My* body."

"Your body? No, man, you went home before you pulled the trigger on yourself."

"Different body."

"I'm so lost," Darsh said.

That was alright. Chance knew exactly where they were and felt lost too. In the five years since the kidnapping, he'd never worked up the courage to come up here. He'd thought about it a million times, but when he got right down to it, he'd always chickened out. Too many ghosts. A man shouldn't visit the scene of his own murder. Yet here he was, five years and six bodies later, still with more questions than answers. But now he had a new and interesting question to add to his list: Why had he killed Lee Conway in the same place that Chance Harker's kidnappers had killed *him*?

"Did you follow me or see me go up the hill?" Chance asked.

"No, I got here after."

That was disappointing. He'd hoped Darsh would know where he'd been before coming out here. Had he met Lee Conway here, or brought him at gunpoint? "Was I alone? Did anyone come down after me?"

"Not that I saw, but I didn't exactly hang around," Darsh admitted.

"Did I see you? Say anything?"

Darsh shook his head. "If you saw me, you didn't say. You just got back in that weird-ass car and drove away."

"Weird car?"

"Not weird, well, yeah, weird. For you anyway. Thing was old as dirt. Looked like about three different cars stitched together, Mad Max–style."

That had to be the RAV, but Chance drove that only if he was going to visit his brother. But he'd just been out there, so why drive the RAV instead of the Aston Martin? The answer was obvious—it didn't have GPS and couldn't be tracked. For someone who'd never killed anyone before, his predecessor had sure put a lot of thought into it.

One thing was still bothering him. "Hey, Darsh, weird question."

"Sure."

"If you didn't follow me, how'd you know I'd be here?"

"Got a tip."

"From who?"

Darsh seemed embarrassed to say. "From you, man."

"I told you I'd be here?"

"You told me you *were* here."

That put a pin in anything else Chance might have had to ask. What kind of cold-blooded killer called the paparazzi to photograph himself leaving the scene of a crime? The same kind who recorded a semiconfession in a T-shirt stained with the victim's blood. But if he wanted to get caught so badly, why hadn't he just called the police? Why call Darsh and Chelsea and stage an elaborate pageant? He could feel a piece of the puzzle was missing but had no idea what it was.

He kept turning it over in his head on the way back down the hill with Darsh. Detective Wolinski was waiting for them at the bottom.

She was leaning against her car, coffee in one hand, the other resting lightly on the butt of her service weapon. The strap that held it in the holster had been unsnapped. Darsh put up his hands, but she shook her head wearily.

"Richie Rich. Nice night for a walk," she said to Chance.

"Good to see you again, Detective."

"Good to see you coming down this hill with as many men as went up it. Personal growth is important."

"Are you following me?" Chance asked.

"You triggered the motion detectors," she said, nodding up the hill. "We set up cameras to see if anyone comes back to the scene. You'd be surprised how often it works."

"Cool," Darsh said.

"Beat it, pap," Wolinski said without taking her eyes off Chance. "Don't think I've forgotten you sold evidence to a tabloid instead of bringing it directly to the police. When I get a minute, I'm going to see if I can pin an obstruction charge on your narrow ass."

For a moment, Darsh looked like he was going to argue his case but then thought better of it. With a wary nod to Chance, he took off on his scooter.

"So what are you doing out here?" Wolinski asked when they were alone.

"Just trying to understand what happened, if that's alright with you."

Wolinski frowned. "How long exactly are you going to keep playing the I-didn't-plan-the-whole-thing card?"

"Whatever my predecessor did—"

"Your predecessor?" Wolinski said. "Fucking rich people. Your predecessor? Are you serious right now?"

"That's how it works, Detective. I don't have any memory of what happened to Lee Conway. And whatever happened, I didn't plan any of it. I'll take a polygraph on that anytime you want. Shouldn't that count for something?"

"It can't."

"Why not?" he asked.

"Because the alternative is unacceptable. Chance Harker killed Lee Conway. I don't care what body you were in at the time. The consciousness, the soul—whatever you want to call it—that pulled the trigger is in your head right now," she said, jabbing a finger in his direction. "You might not remember doing it, but you're responsible, Richie."

"You know I'm not actually rich." He thought he had thick skin, but her calling him that was getting to him.

"Uh-huh. That your Aston Martin parked in the driveway of your house in the Bird Streets?"

"The car's for show. And the house belongs to my mother."

"You know my least favorite kind of obscene wealth? The kind that wants to believe it has it tough," Wolinski said. "But, hey, if you want to complain about how hard it is being a struggling white boy with rich parents, head down to the city jail and tell any of the inmates how your pops bankrolled Sy Berger."

Chance tried not to say something that would land him back in handcuffs. He'd been in them enough lately to know he didn't enjoy the experience, and Wolinski didn't seem like she'd need much of an excuse.

"So what now? You arresting me again?" he asked.

"Not until the DA relocates his balls."

"Will he?"

"Has no choice in the matter. The city is on fire over this. Somebody has to be responsible."

"And until it's me, it's them."

"That's how politics works—your neck or theirs."

"You don't know for a fact it was me."

"Don't need to, just beyond a reasonable doubt. And I don't have any of those. The pictures of you coming down the hill covered in Lee Conway's blood, holding the murder weapon, are pretty compelling."

"The paparazzi who took those pictures, guess who called him?"

"You did," she replied.

"You already know?"

"I do my job."

"And that doesn't sound weird to you?"

She blew on her coffee. "I don't deal in weird, just facts. But you know what *is* weird? Jumping out of a plane without a parachute for a live audience. Who knows why you do what you do."

Chance couldn't argue with her there. He hadn't exactly cultivated a reputation as a rational actor. How hard would it be to convince a jury that he'd been so sure he'd get away with murder that he'd called Darsh for the publicity? Didn't that sound just like him, or at least the person he'd been playing for the last few years?

"So you don't care about my motive? You know what this place is?"

"Yeah, I know what happened here," she said. "Like I said, I do my job."

"Doesn't that make you at all curious about Lee Conway?"

"Go on home. Let the professionals handle it."

"I can't."

"Why's that?"

"Because you don't care what happened."

"Oh, I don't?" Wolinski said, pushing off from the car, as if the affront to her honor had given her wings.

"No, and no offense either. It's just not your job."

"And what is my job, Mr. Harker?"

"To build a case," Chance said. "You've already taken it as far as you're going to take it. You deal in reasonable doubt, not weird. Isn't that what you said? The things I need to know aren't about building a case. For you they'd fall under *weird*."

Wolinski blew a second time on her coffee, which was probably plenty cool by now. "You think he was involved in your kidnapping?"

"If my predecessor . . ." He paused at the face she made. "If I killed Lee Conway, there was a reason. I need to know what it is."

"Alright, I can respect that. So long as you know it makes no difference to me."

"Why not?" He was genuinely curious.

"Because you killed a man, and that's a crime, no matter what happened five years ago. The state of California doesn't currently have a revenge exception when it comes to murder. But if it helps you sleep at night, go ahead."

At least she was honest; he had to give her that. "Anything you can tell me about him?"

"Not a lot to tell that's not already in the press. Bit of a drifter. Odd jobs. No regular address. Didn't leave much of a footprint in the world."

"Any idea where I crossed paths with him?"

"Not yet. We're having a hell of a time tracking your movements that night. Reminds me, though, did you have tickets for the Con D'Arcy show?"

"No, why?" he answered cagily.

"The T-shirt you were wearing—"

"The one covered in blood?"

"Yeah, the one covered in Lee Conway's blood. It was a limited-edition print commemorating her final show at the Troubadour."

"I was at the show?"

"We're working on establishing that. Problem is, we can't find you on surveillance footage from the venue. Place was mobbed. It was the last night of the tour, so Children of Adam put on their own show outside."

"I don't even listen to her music." He didn't, but he knew who did—Maggie. If he'd been wearing a Con D'Arcy T-shirt, that meant he'd seen her that night. There was no other explanation. He'd been too nervous to call her before, but they needed to talk now, no matter what she had to say.

Wolinski was squinting at him as if she could tell he wasn't being entirely forthcoming. She held out her card to him.

"What's that for?"

"In case," she said.

He considered the card, then took it and tapped it against his LFD, downloading her contact information.

"Am I free to go?" he asked, hooking a thumb toward the main road.

"For the time being. Now get on home. Mayor ordered a curfew starting at midnight. Tonight's going to be bad."

"Alright," he said, starting away toward the main road. "I'll be seeing you."

"Count on it," Wolinski said, and then: "Hey, Richie."

"Yeah?"

"Be careful, hear? There's a reason I don't concern myself with weird. Shit ain't safe."

He said he would and walked away. When he glanced back at her as he turned the corner, she was still standing there staring after him, her expression unreadable.

CHAPTER SEVENTEEN

Judging by the packages stacked by the front door, Maggie hadn't been home in days. The house was silent but, more than that, felt abandoned. There was no answer when he rang the bell, and after his third try, the house asked if he'd like to leave a message. Chance declined. He'd tried Maggie's LFD on his way over and left a message when she didn't answer the third time. That didn't mean she wasn't home. It wasn't unlike her to draw the curtains and unplug from the world if she needed time to herself. They had that in common.

The side gate was never locked. He went around back in case she was in the garden. All he found was an antique glass ashtray and an empty bottle of wine. She'd quit smoking years ago but would sneak a cigarette when she was stressed out. Judging by the pack's worth of butts in the ashtray, she'd been in a very bad way. He cupped his hands to the sliding glass door and peered inside. The house was dark and still. As an afterthought, he tried the door, but it was locked. Fussing with it would only set off the alarm.

"What are you doing back here?" a voice from behind him asked.

In the reflection of the glass, he saw a white woman had followed him into the backyard. She was older, perhaps fifty. It looked like a crow had done an angry dance at the corners of her eyes, or maybe she was only squinting to better aim the gun she was pointing at him. It wasn't big and looked small even in her small hands, but the way she held it told him she'd been to a shooting range more than once. He also got the impression that she'd never pointed a gun at a person before and was more than a little excited that the opportunity had finally presented itself.

"I said, what are you doing?" The woman shook the gun to remind him of the pecking order.

He wanted to answer, but he'd also never had a gun pointed at him before, at least not that he remembered. It wasn't like in the movies, where people coolly carried on entire conversations like it was nothing. He was one false move away from dying. Really dying. His legs went rubbery with fear.

"I'm not going to tell you again. Turn around."

He turned slowly and showed her both his palms. In the gloom, he couldn't tell if her finger was on the trigger or the trigger guard. "I'm a friend of Maggie Soto. She lives here."

The woman made a face as if he'd told her he'd been a passenger on the *Titanic*. "She's not home. So what are you doing in the backyard, Maggie Soto's friend?"

She stepped forward into enough light for him to place her: the next-door neighbor. He'd seen her in passing lots of times, though they'd never spoken. Her husband was the social half of the couple.

"Haven't been able to reach her," Chance said. "With everything going on this week, I was worried something might've happened. You or Frank haven't seen her?"

"You know Frank?" she said cautiously.

"Maggie introduced me one time when he was working in the yard. He's always gardening."

His familiarity with her husband's name and hobbies seemed to placate the woman, who lowered the gun, pointing it at his legs instead of his chest. Not ideal, but progress.

"Sorry about that," she said. "Ever since that damned clone killed that man, things have been going to hell. What if those animals get tired of looting and rioting downtown? Whole neighborhood's on edge."

Since she still had the gun, Chance nodded as if her thinking were the most sensible thing in the world. "I know Maggie would appreciate you watching out for her place this way."

"Who else is going to do it? The police? They're too busy protecting their rich overlords. I saw this strange car parked on the street last night, called 911. They left me on hold for a half an hour. Said they'd send a patrol car. Did they? No. You believe that? Probably too busy with some billionaire who had a splinter needed tweezing."

"Have you seen Maggie?"

"Not for about a week. She came home real late one night and then left with a suitcase about an hour later. Girl was in a terrible rush, Frank said." The woman looked around to make sure they were alone, then added confidentially, "Frank has insomnia something awful. Sometimes he jogs when he can't sleep."

Chance commiserated that insomnia was indeed a curse, then asked, "Did she say where she was going?"

"Visit her parents, Frank said."

Maggie's parents lived in Roseville, outside Sacramento, but she hadn't spoken to either of them in years. There was a better chance of her being on the International Space Station than enjoying the hospitality of Oscar and Siobhan Soto. So why had she bothered lying to a neighbor, and where had she really gone? The bungalow was more than a home to her; it was a sanctuary. She wouldn't abandon it for no reason.

He'd come here to find out what she knew about the bloody Con D'Arcy T-shirt, but now he wondered how involved she'd been that night. The omnipotent Frank said she'd pulled up stakes a week ago. Could she have been packing a suitcase at the same time he'd been playing Russian roulette? What were the odds the two things were unrelated? He checked his missed calls during the eighteen hours before he'd shot himself in front of Chelsea. Nothing to or from Maggie. That made him more than a little suspicious. Calling Maggie had been his only priority before his last refresh. Was he supposed to believe he'd had a complete change of heart? His predecessor had gone to extremes to prevent him from retracing his steps. Had that included erasing his phone history?

He really needed to find Maggie.

The neighbor escorted him out to the front of the house while carrying on about the riots and the sorry state of the world. It seemed like she needed someone to vent to, and Chance figured he owed it to her to listen for not shooting him. She asked him if everything was going to be okay. He thought for a moment she meant Maggie, but then realized she meant the world at large. Sometime between pointing a gun at him and now, he'd become a person whose opinion she valued.

"Things just seem to be getting worse and worse, you know?" she said, reaching the conclusion of an argument she'd been formulating her entire life.

"It always feels like that," he answered.

"No, this is the worst things have ever been."

"If you had to choose between living now and in Nazi-occupied France in 1942, which would you pick?" he asked.

"France," she answered without hesitation, and then looked confused at how she'd reached that conclusion.

"You know why?"

She shook her head.

"Because you know how that turned out. But I guarantee people back then were wringing their hands saying the same exact things you are. Only in French."

That got a courtesy chuckle out of her. He couldn't tell if he'd made her feel better or worse, but she didn't argue with him. With a wave, he left her standing on the curb and started walking without any clear destination in mind. His body hurt and was only grudgingly doing what he told it. A new clone was encouraged to take things easy at first, and he'd pushed himself too hard. He needed his pills and about three days of sleep.

His LFD flashed up an alert from his home-security system. The front-door alarm had been triggered. Moments later, sensors tripped on the front windows, and the sliding doors that led out to the patio. Chance pulled up the camera feed from inside the house. Dozens of people had broken in, with more flooding in every moment. All wore masks to hide their faces. They fanned out through the house, hunting, the motion-activated cameras jumping from one end of the house to the other and back. A disorienting perspective. Maybe that was why it took him so long to see that what they were looking for was him.

Soon realizing their quarry wasn't home, the pack met in the living room. They faced each other, frustrated and angry, but for a moment it looked as if they might have exhausted themselves. Then someone picked up one of his plants and flung it against a wall. The pot shattered, and with it the momentary calm.

All hell broke loose.

Chance stood in a daze watching them rampage through the house, destroying everything in their path. Someone spray-painted ABORT ALL CLONES on the living room wall in jagged red letters. Two men wrenched the kitchen cabinets from their moorings and dashed them on the ground. The mob screamed in delirious jubilation. Down the hall, a frustrated trio took turns ramming the one locked door in the house. Chance prayed for it to hold; he didn't want them in there. They had no right. The door trembled but held until the frame ripped loose from the wall. With one last heave, the door buckled and collapsed. The trio almost fell into the room and looked around in disappointment. They'd expected treasure, not a roomful of old junk. They set to destroying it anyway.

He didn't see how the fire started, but suddenly it was everywhere, licking up the walls. The sprinkler system kicked on, but the water pressure was too low to slow the growing inferno. Suddenly, the mob went from exultant to panicked. There was a stampede to get out. The outdoor cameras picked up the action as flames blew out the windows of the house on Blue Jay Way. The roof went up like dried tinder, a beautiful bonfire framed against the Los Angeles skyline. It was a sharp contrast to the ugly laughter and celebration of the protesters dancing around the house like pagans at the birth of a new year. Had any of them thought to bring marshmallows?

A cinder block entered the frame like a lonely asteroid and exploded into the windshield of the Aston Martin. The crowd went wild.

Off to the side, at the edge of the frame, two squad cars blocked the street. Four cops were leaning against the hoods watching the destruction, not doing a thing to stop it. One of them said something, and the other three laughed. Chance couldn't help wondering about the cinder block. For once there wasn't any construction on his block, so where had it come from? Had someone lugged it up the hill to his house? That was dedication to the bit; he'd give them that.

He couldn't say how long he sat on the curb watching the fire burn. The power must have died because all the camera feeds dropped at once. His mom was going to be so happy; she hated that house. As for Chance, his feelings were mixed. Watching the house burn and his things with it was like attending the funeral of a family member he loved but knew wasn't good for him anymore. It felt cathartic, a necessary severing of his connection to that time in his life. On the other hand, even though he was coming to accept that living in the past wasn't healthy, the past was all he'd had for so long that he wasn't entirely sure what to do without it.

A car pulled up beside him, silent apart from the soft crunch of gravel beneath its tires. Detective Wolinski looked over at him from behind the wheel.

"It's after curfew," she said.

"How do you keep finding me?" he asked, both frustrated and a little awed.

"You need to stop being surprised the LAPD is better at this than you."

"My house burned down."

Wolinski nodded. "Yeah, it did."

"The cops just stood by and watched," Chance said, remembering trying to drive through the protest and the riot police who didn't lift a finger to help. "You guys just tourists now? Do a little sightseeing, punch the clock?"

"Yeah, well, it's not the only house on fire tonight," Wolinski snapped back. "An entire block is on fire in Century City. We're stretched a little goddamned thin. There were over two hundred protesters at your place and only a couple uniforms. What do you think happens if they'd intervened? You know how many officers are already riding hospital beds over your mess?"

Chance stood up and started walking. He was in no kind of mood to have the societal ills of Southern California laid at his size nines. The car rolled along next to him. They went on like this for fifty feet before Wolinski broke the silence.

"Let me drive you back to West Adams. It's not safe out here tonight."

"You know about West Adams?" he asked without breaking stride.

"Again, good at my job."

"What are you really doing here?" Chance asked. "I mean, you're stretched pretty thin, right? Shouldn't you have better things to do than chauffeur my ass around the city?"

"Well, we need to talk, and I have the time because I was placed on leave an hour ago," she said with such practiced neutrality that Chance couldn't tell if she'd been rewarded or punished.

"So you're violating curfew too."

She laughed. "Guess that's right. So c'mon, get in."

He shrugged and did as she asked.

As a rule, cops hated auto-drive with a passion, arguing that real policework required the experience of human hands. Their union had fought for an exemption everywhere except on federal highways. Wolinski drove them toward West Adams the old-fashioned way. After a couple of blocks, the car chimed to remind him to put on his seat belt. It used to be the kind of thing he'd roll his eyes at, but now he buckled up guiltily.

The streets were apocalyptically deserted, with only the odd car and virtually no people. The city felt like it was holding its breath for whatever came next. Away to the west, the sky was a hellish red, lit by the Century City fire. The only sound was the distant, plaintive wail of sirens, a coarse mixture of police, ambulance, and fire. And maybe his ears were playing tricks on him, but it didn't sound as if anything was headed in the same direction.

"Is *placed on leave* cop code for *suspended*?" he asked.

Instead of answering, she said, "Got the report back from ballistics."

Chance didn't respond. She was working up to telling him something and was clearly conflicted. Interrupting would only reset her oven timer.

"You know I was detailed to your kidnapping back in the day?" she said.

"Really?"

"Yeah, I'd just taken the detectives' exam and was waiting on the results. It was grunt work, but I took it as a good sign they'd asked for me by name. About a week after your father went cowboy at the ransom drop, I found out I'd made detective one. I've seen a lot of crime scenes since then, so it took me a minute to put it together. How I knew that place earlier."

"You were actually there?" he said, feeling suddenly shy and embarrassed, as if she'd seen him in a compromising position. Maybe she had. What was more compromised than your dead body?

"Wasn't first on scene, but yeah, I was there. It was a tough night," she said, reaching a decision about the other thing. "Alright, here's the thing. That revolver has itself quite some history."

"It's been used before?"

"At least twice that we know of."

"Well, I didn't do that either."

Wolinski let out a tired, judgmental laugh. "Yeah, I know. The firearm recovered at your house . . ." She paused, steadying herself at the edge of the cliff for the final step. "It's a match for the weapon used in your kidnapping five years ago."

"What?" he said, the world falling silent around him.

She dumbed it down for him. "That gun's killed you twice now. Your brother once."

"Stop the car," he said, opening his door and trying to get out. Only the seat belt kept him from hitting the asphalt at forty miles an hour.

Wolinski cursed and slammed on the brakes. Fortunately, the streets were all but deserted. Chance fumbled with the buckle and stumbled away from the car. He heard himself screaming. Then someone had him by the arm and was guiding him gently down to the ground. A familiar voice told him to put his back against a trash can and his head between his knees. Gradually his vision cleared. He looked up at Wolinski, who was squatting down by his side. For the first time, she didn't look like she wanted to throttle him.

"You're alright," she said, before putting a bottle of water in his hand. "Don't talk a minute. Just breathe."

Chance nodded and sipped the water. Wolinski waited patiently, letting him work it out.

"Lee Conway was one of the kidnappers." He'd been thinking it, but having proof was a whole other thing.

"A fair assumption at this point."

"I had him," he said. "I fucking had him."

"Yeah, you did. Look me in the eye and tell me you wouldn't have killed him if given the chance."

Chance met her eyes but couldn't deny it. She patted his knee as if thanking him for his confirmation and looked back up the street.

"So you're going to find out who this guy was? Who the others are?" he asked.

"I'm on leave," Wolinski said as she stood up.

"But someone is, right? Someone's on it."

"At this time the department feels it has sufficient evidence to move forward with a case against Chance Harker," she said as though reciting someone else's words. "My request to continue the investigation was denied. When I persisted—"

"They put you on leave," he finished for her. "Why?"

On cue, three police cruisers blew past in tight formation doing at least seventy, no sirens, no flashing lights. Wolinski gestured after them. "Because the city can't afford a war, and that's what we're headed for. Saw one estimate, put damage north of two billion already. Sorry to say, but you're a small price to pay for peace."

"How long do I have?"

"Not my circus, not my monkey. Not anymore. But I'd guess a day or two. Three, tops. Wouldn't waste any time, I was you."

"Why are you telling me all this? This whole time you've been on me like the Inquisition. Why are you helping me now?"

"Because it's my job. Should be anyway. I didn't sign up to railroad you or anybody else."

CHAPTER EIGHTEEN

Chance fell into bed fully clothed, expecting to fall asleep in seconds. An hour later, he was still studying the topography of the cracked ceiling. His mind was restless and kept arranging and rearranging what he'd learned, hoping to find a recognizable shape. What he badly needed was rest. He'd pushed himself too hard since leaving Palingenesis, and his body was in open rebellion. But how was he expected to sleep?

After five long years, he'd finally tracked down one of his kidnappers. But instead of answers, his predecessor had methodically covered his tracks, making it nearly impossible for Chance to follow. Lee Conway was dead. His predecessor had called Darsh to take pictures that would hang the murder around his own neck. Then he'd gone home and put a bullet in his own head, a blunt, grisly surgery to excise everything he knew.

Ironically, if it wasn't for the bullet, the plan would've worked. Without the ballistics, he still wouldn't know his connection to Lee Conway. He remembered the haunted look in his predecessor's eyes when he'd begged Chance to leave it alone. Well, he couldn't do that. Perhaps the fact that he'd known—and, knowing, had gone to such extremes to unknow it—should have given Chance pause, but that wasn't how things worked. That wasn't how things worked at all.

A faint rapping at the front interrupted his thoughts. He lifted his head from the pillow and listened to the silence. There it was again.

The unmistakable sound of the latch against the strike plate as someone gently eased his front door closed. He sat up. Someone was inside the apartment. They had knocked and then broken in. That wasn't how these things usually went. He knew for certain it wasn't the police. They didn't come for you quietly.

There were only two ways out: a three-story jump from the window or out through the bedroom door, where an unknown intruder or intruders waited. Not so long ago, he might have opted cavalierly for a dramatic fall, but times and his circumstances had changed. He cast about for a weapon. The best he could come up with was the bedside lamp. He tested the weight in his hand and put it back. If he was going to die, it wouldn't be brandishing a turquoise lamp.

He cracked the bedroom door an inch to peek out, felt foolish doing it, and opened the door the rest of the way. It had been too strange a day to end it sneaking around in his own rented flophouse. The living room was dark, but light from the street drew the unmistakable outline of someone standing at the kitchenette. He flipped on the lights. The strange girl from the street was fussing with the food printer.

"Is this thing kaput?" she asked as if frustrated he'd lent her something broken.

He'd meant to take her by the arm and throw her out into the hall, but the banality of her question threw him off. Instead he asked, "What are you doing in my apartment?"

"A bit of a comedown, isn't it?" she said, gesturing at the drab living room. "A long way from the Bird Streets."

"What are you doing in my apartment?" he asked a second time. It felt important that they establish a ground rule that she should answer his questions.

"We need to talk."

"That's usually when I break in somewhere too."

"If I'm not welcome, I can always go back outside and pass out fliers with your address," she said with the self-assurance of someone older. The way child actors, forced to grow up too fast, sometimes did, becoming miniature, robotic adults.

"Who the hell are you?" He didn't know who this girl was, but she wasn't some obsessive fan. Nor did he get a rabid anti-clone vibe off her. He didn't know what options that left, but he was curious to find out.

She considered the question while making herself at home on one of the stools at the little kitchen table. "You can call me Mary."

"Alright, 'Mary.' And you're what? Sixteen, seventeen?"

"I'm older than I look," she allowed with a faint smile.

"Great, you can buy the beer." He was curious about her but was wearying quickly of getting evasive, secondhand replies that almost but not quite addressed his questions. He sat down across from her and folded his arms across his chest. Chance was done chasing answers and was willing to wait her out.

The girl took a small device out of her pocket, powered it on, and placed it on the coffee table between them. He'd guessed right about why his LFD wouldn't photograph her; it was a portable surveillance jammer designed to block audio and video recordings. Not a cheap model either. She waited until its lights flickered from red to green before speaking.

"I've watched your channel. You come off like an imbecile," she said without a trace of cruelty, simply stating a well-established fact that she'd picked up somewhere. It wasn't the first time Chance had been called stupid, but it landed a little harder coming from a kid. "But you're smarter than you let on."

"Thanks?"

"I mean no offense. I only point it out because it means that perhaps we can help each other."

"How are we going to help each other?" Chance had taken enough meetings in LA to know when he was being pitched. The air became oily, and everyone had a buzzy, hypnotic look in their eyes. The girl had that look now, and he was convinced she was about to offer him a partnership in the ground floor of her revolutionary Ponzi scheme.

"What do you want most in the world?" she asked.

Definitely a Ponzi scheme.

"To be left alone."

She nodded seriously at his answer but disagreed. "At best that's second or third on your list. What's really first?"

"Apparently you're the expert on what I want. Enlighten me."

"Well, it's not that difficult to guess, Chance. I read Imani Highsmith's piece on you. The answer is there in every heartbreaking word. You want a way to rein in your lag. You want to know the truth about your kidnapping and what role your father played. You want that missing time back so you can feel whole. Tell me, all your stunts—are they just a way of getting back at your parents? Any attention is good attention, that sort of thing? Or is it just a defiant roar into the void?"

"You can go to hell."

"More than likely," the girl said with a jaded laugh. "But I'm planning on forestalling that visit for a while yet."

He didn't know what to make of that, so instead he asked, "So how can you help me?"

"Tracking down your kidnappers. But I get to talk to them before you send them to meet Lee Conway."

That was definitely a zig where he'd expected a zag. "That was five years ago."

"But they're back now, aren't they?"

"What makes you say that?" he said, trying and failing to keep a poker face.

"For one thing, the ballistics report connecting Lee Conway to your kidnapping. Something in that Imani Highsmith article must have gotten their attention."

"Who are you?" he asked with the kind of superstitious awe that a medieval man might have had for an airplane landing outside his hut. How did a teenager have access to police files?

"Not a book to be judged by its cover. I may look like a young-adult novel, but you'd be wise to keep in mind that I should be shelved in horror if you take me lightly," she said with the finality of a vault closing. "But I'm also big on DIY. I know things that would be useful to you."

"What do you think you know?"

"What do I know? I know the powers that be aren't planning to follow up on Lee Conway. I know they're going to parade you through the proverbial town square like a trophy to satiate the mob. What we both know is that you're running out of time, Chance, so the real question is, What else do I know?"

They sat studying each other across the particleboard table. What did he have to lose? Either she was bluffing or really could help him.

"I need to find the other kidnappers," he said. "There are at least three more. Can you help me do that?"

"No, but I can tell you where Maggie Soto is. How would that be?"

That caught Chance off guard, but not as much as it would have a few hours ago. "What does she have to do with it?"

"Honestly, I have no earthly idea, but she pulled her disappearing act the same night Lee Conway died and you played Russian roulette. I don't know about you, but I'm not a great believer in coincidence."

He'd had the exact same thought outside Maggie's bungalow. "Where is she now?"

"Do we have an understanding?" the strange girl countered. "If she leads you to your kidnappers, nothing adverse happens to them until I speak to them alone. Think you can restrain yourself that long?"

"What are they to you?" He couldn't make sense of it. At the time of the kidnappings, she would have been eleven or twelve years old. What could she possibly have to ask them?

"Do we have an understanding?"

In the end, he realized he didn't care what she wanted or why. Time didn't give him the luxury of being picky about his allies. If this girl could point him in the right direction, then that would have to be good enough for him. "Yeah, we do. Where is she?"

"Your Maggie went from her home to the Decameron. To my knowledge, she hasn't left since."

The Decameron. That made so much sense he kicked himself for not thinking of it himself. One of Nan Darrow's clubs. She and Maggie were friends from way back. If Maggie needed somewhere to lie low, Nan wouldn't hesitate to offer her sanctuary. The question remained, though: Sanctuary from what? Or whom? An ugly thought intruded, and he tried to hold it at bay like an uninvited party crasher. Was Maggie trying to stay safe from him?

He glanced over at the time on the food printer. So much for that good night's sleep. He wouldn't be able to close his eyes until he had an answer.

CHAPTER NINETEEN

The Decameron was tucked away on a discreet side street west of Sunset Plaza. By design, the club wasn't much to look at from the outside: a gray door set back in a gray brick wall. The name, spelled out in dull brass letters, was small enough to miss even if you were looking for it. Famously, a drunken Billy Chin had stolen the *c* after getting in a screaming fight with the owner, Nan Darrow, over his unpaid tab. The "De ameron" had never bothered to replace it. Chin kept the brass letter on a shelf alongside his Grammys like a trophy from a safari.

On a normal night, the velvet rope to the left of the door marked the starting line for the display case of beautiful nobodies. But looks alone weren't enough to be granted entrance to the Decameron. Every city had its currency, and Los Angeles traded primarily in fame; everyone felt better about themselves in its proximity. Usually the line snaked all the way down the block. Tonight, however, deep into curfew, the line was nonexistent, and only a solitary bouncer kept vigil from the shadowy alcove of the doorway.

Chance hadn't even bothered to check if the club was open tonight. He knew Nan well enough to be certain that she wouldn't close for anything as prosaic as a riot. Curfew was for little people.

"Name?" the doorman asked, clearly irked to have his sitting-around-doing-nothing time interrupted.

Chance

"I'm not on the list."

"We're closed."

"Tell Nan that Chance is here to see Maggie Soto."

For a second, Chance thought the doorman was going to keep on playing dumb and claim he'd never heard of any Nan Darrow. But then the big man sighed heavily and radioed inside. While Chance waited for the verdict, he bounced on his toes, trying to coax the last joule of energy from his tired body, psyching himself up in case Nan didn't let him in. He was talking to Maggie, one way or another. Looking at the size of the bouncer, he really hoped it wouldn't come to that, but he'd rather go to the hospital than leave without answers. Off in the distance, sirens howled like coyotes searching for their lost pack.

Maggie and Nan Darrow went way back. Nan had been an ethereally beautiful child actor in the early 2000s. Once the cruel alchemy of puberty made it clear that her looks wouldn't translate to adulthood, the parts dried up and her career foundered. It was an old, old story in Hollywood, but Nan hadn't been interested in being another cautionary tale. She'd seen the writing on the casting-room wall, quit the business, and opened her first club at twenty-three. From her apartment above the Decameron, Nan Darrow now oversaw an empire of ten bars and restaurants scattered across LA. Two of them were colossal megaclubs, but the smaller, more intimate Decameron was home. Everyone knew her, and no one crossed her twice. Just ask the permanently eighty-sixed Billy Chin.

Nan had taken Maggie under her wing one night when a producer with a sordid reputation showed up to an opening with a wobbly-legged Maggie clinging to his arm. Maggie was just sixteen at the time, the producer in the sunset of his forties. Nan had pried Maggie away and put the fear of the media gods into the producer. It had taken time, but Nan had shepherded Maggie through rehab, eventually teaching her how to manage her finances and run her own life. Nan had been the one who'd encouraged Maggie to apply to college. She'd always been kind to Chance—he wasn't a child actor, but she recognized a kindred pain—but he knew he came a distant second to Maggie in her affections. If Maggie didn't want to see him, then he wouldn't be getting through that door with all his teeth.

"Well?" Chance asked, bracing himself for the beating that would come when he tried to force his way inside.

The doorman eased off his stool and held the door open for him. Chance nodded thanks to him, as if it had never been in doubt. Inside, a host who would have been one of the ten most beautiful people in any other city greeted him like they were old friends and led him back into the club, a warren of plush couches and oak-finished alcoves that allowed its guests to be glimpsed without being disturbed. Despite the summer heat, twin fireplaces crackled at either end of the main room. It wasn't a busy night, but most of the tables were still occupied. Chance wasn't trying to make eye contact with anyone, but he recognized faces that were famous around the world. A violinist played a haunting cover of a Radiohead song that Chance recognized but couldn't name. On the small dance floor, a lone couple swayed their way through a box step. In this sacellum to cool, it was tempting to order a drink and forget the chaos raging outside.

At a red damask curtain, the host held it aside and ushered Chance inside one of the private VIP rooms with a nightly minimum more than most Americans made in a year. The funny thing was it didn't look any different from the rest of the club, didn't offer anything more than the rest of the club—it simply cost more as the result of being behind a curtain. Exclusivity was a hell of a drug. Maggie and Nan were alone on one of the couches, locked in an intense conversation. They looked up at Chance as if seeing a ghost.

"Thank you," he said to Nan. She'd dyed her hair purple since the last time Chance had seen her, and somehow she'd lost even more weight, although Chance didn't know how that was possible. Her eyes were several times too large for her face, and although it was impossible, he wasn't sure that he'd ever seen her blink.

"Thank her," Nan said, standing to leave. "I told her she should send you packing." Then to Maggie: "I'll be around if you need anything."

Nan paused on her way out and put a hand on Chance's arm. "Please be careful."

He didn't know what that meant but said he would. Nan nodded and went out, drawing the curtain behind her. Once they were alone, Maggie reached for a glass of red wine on the coffee table, then gulped it down like it was water at the end of a long race. She looked as tired as he felt.

"How'd you find me?"

"Everyone comes to Rick's," he offered lamely, not knowing exactly why he didn't tell Maggie about the strange girl who'd told him how to find her. It felt like too much to explain, and they had more pressing things to talk about. "I'm sorry. I had to see you."

"I know," she said sadly. "We should have left town while we could."

"I was going to ask you to."

"You did," she said, the memory of a smile on her lips.

"I really did?" he asked, voice full of wonder as if she were telling him a bedtime story full of fantastical mythological beasts that had never and could never exist.

Maggie nodded and crossed the room before throwing her arms around him. After a moment, he collapsed into her embrace. It was a miracle that he didn't cry.

"And you said yes?" he whispered into her neck.

"A day late, turns out."

"Where were we going to go?"

"Alaska to start. We didn't get any further than that."

It made him hopeful and sad knowing that he'd at least asked her . . . the melancholy of almost. "Always wanted to see it. Then maybe Montana? I know you love it there."

"We still could," she said, and stepped back so she could look him in the eyes. "I'll only suggest it once. Let's just go. Forget all this. Forget LA. You and me. Let's get the hell away from here."

"I wish I could."

"Why can't you?" She was almost pleading.

"Lee Conway."

"Fuck Lee Conway. He doesn't matter."

"Maggie, they're going to arrest me for his murder."

The news visibly rocked her, and she took another step back from him, studying his face. "What are you talking about? The police dropped the charges."

"Only temporarily," he answered, and then laid out everything that Wolinski had told him.

"I need to sit down," Maggie said when he was finished, leading him to one of the couches. He was grateful for any excuse. It was taking more and more concentration just to keep his balance. He'd been running on fumes to find Maggie, with nothing left in reserve.

"You don't look so good," she said.

"I haven't slept since Palingenesis."

"Chance," she admonished with a frown that would have made the mother of any five-year-old proud. "Have you eaten anything?"

"Not really," he admitted, and then tried to get back on topic. "Where have you been? I've been calling."

"I'm going to order you something."

She stood to go find a server, but he took her hand and held on with what strength he had left. "Why'd you stay away, Maggie?"

"Because you asked me to." Her answer surprised him enough that her hand slipped out of his. "I'll be right back."

"Swear?"

"I swear."

After she left, Chance made the tactical mistake of leaning back against the couch. His body saw its chance and started flipping the circuit breakers until his eyes closed and didn't reopen.

When he woke, it took a moment to reorient himself. Someone had covered him with a blanket and dimmed the lights. He'd even slept through someone taking off his shoes. He yawned and raised his head. The likely culprit was curled up asleep in an armchair across from him. Maggie must have sensed she was being watched because she stirred, opening her eyes and smiling at him.

"How long have I been sleeping?" he asked.

"Probably not long enough. Eat." She gestured at the half dozen dishes covered with metal cloches.

He didn't need to be told twice. The food was cold, but that didn't slow him down any. He ate all but one slice of a pizza, half a cheeseburger, and even some green beans like a good boy. He washed it all down with a pitcher of water.

"Better?" she asked when he was done.

"Why would I tell you to stay away from me?" he asked, anxious to hear the end of the story now that his head was clearing.

"I can't tell you."

"Why not?"

"I promised not to."

"Did that include me going to prison?"

"Even that." She nodded, tight lipped. "No matter what."

"Then I release you from your promise," he said as if he'd found a clever loophole in an ironclad contract. Then he saw her expression. "I said I'd say that, didn't I?"

"You know yourself. I'm sorry."

"Maggie, Lee Conway is one of the kidnappers."

Better than anyone, he knew she would understand the significance, how important it was, but she didn't seem surprised. More than anything, she looked disappointed.

"How did you find out?"

"The gun. The police matched it to the one that killed me and Marley five years ago."

"Damn," she said. "You really hoped you wouldn't put it together."

That was one of those ontologically eye-crossing sentences that being a clone sometimes produced. "So you knew already?"

"Not about the gun, but about Lee Conway? Yeah."

"Why would I try to keep all of this from myself? I've been looking for these people for five years. I don't understand."

Nan chose that moment to return.

"You. Up," she told Chance. "You've got to go."

"What's going on?" Maggie asked, standing with him.

"Someone recognized him last night. There's a video online of Chance Harker in my club. Protesters started gathering out front an hour ago. Plus I got a tip from a friend in the department. Cops are on their way to join the party."

"Are they coming for me?" he asked.

"Couldn't say. Maybe? Then again, they might just feel the need to bust me now that it's public that I stayed open after curfew. An example may need to be set. Either way, you can't be here when they arrive. Maggie, you're welcome to stay."

"I'm with Chance," she said.

There was no hesitation.

CHAPTER TWENTY

Nan led them through the now-deserted club to the kitchen and finally the back offices. A private staircase took them up to her apartment, which was uncomfortably bright and sunny after the perpetual twilight of the club. The apartment was smaller than Chance would have guessed, cozier. He would have pegged Nan as a Scandinavian minimalist, but there was an orderly clutter that belied her no-nonsense personality. If Nan kept mementos from her time as an actor, she hadn't hung any of them on her walls. On a couch stacked high with pillows and blankets, a woman about Chance's age lay sprawled out reading a book and balancing a mug on her chest. She sat up guiltily as they entered.

"Babe, I told you to stay in the bedroom," Nan said.

"I wanted to sit in the sun," the woman pouted.

"In five minutes, okay? I just need five minutes."

"Is that him?" the woman asked. "Hi."

"Hi," Chance said with an awkward half wave.

"Babe. Seriously. The police are on the way," Nan said.

"Fine," the woman said with a dramatic flourish, gathering up her things before not quite slamming the door on her way into the bedroom.

"Sorry," Maggie said.

Chance nodded but kept his mouth shut.

Matthew FitzSimmons

"That . . . ," Nan said with a sigh. "That is a whole other situation. Now let's get you moving."

In the kitchen, she pressed a key fob into Maggie's hand and gave them directions to her car.

Maggie hugged her, but Nan didn't appear to be in a hugging mood, keeping her arms at her side. "Just return it in one piece."

"Thank you," Chance said.

"Here," Nan said, handing him a Dodgers cap from a hook by the door. "Try not to get spotted leaving, huh?"

They went out and down a fire escape to the street around the block from the Decameron's main entrance. The low chorus of rhythmic chants echoed over the rooftop, while up on Sunset a steady stream of people marched east toward the club's entrance, all descending on the place because Chance had been seen inside. A daunting thought. He didn't like to think what would happen if someone saw him out here. Would they do to him what they'd done to his house?

No one was looking for Maggie, so she stepped out into the open to see if the coast was clear while Chance crouched behind a dumpster.

"I'm sorry I got you and Nan involved in all this," he said, since they had this moment alone.

Maggie shrugged without taking her eyes off the crowd passing by. "I was always involved. Nan'll get over it."

He asked her how it looked. She shook her head.

"That bad?" he asked, pulling the cap lower over his eyes.

"It's a lot of fired-up, angry people. Just be ready when I say go."

"Don't worry. I'm Usain Bolt down here."

"You really think the police are going to arrest you again?" she asked, returning to their interrupted conversation.

"Do they have a choice? Look what's happening out here," he said, gesturing toward Sunset.

"Even though they know now Lee Conway was one of your kidnappers?"

"That just gives them motive. It's just a matter of time before they arrest me again. That's why I'm in such a hurry. I'm this close to finally finding out what happened five years ago. Lee Conway is the key. So whatever you—"

"Now," she interrupted. "Let's go."

Exasperated by the eternal interruptions, Chance followed her across the street, angling away from the protesters and toward the garage.

"You have to tell me," he said. "I can't go to prison without knowing the truth."

"Can we talk about this later?"

"No. Now," he said, grabbing her arm and stopping her in the middle of the street. He'd had it with these constant interruptions and apparently also rational thinking as well. She was going to answer him, even if it meant bringing the mob down on his head.

"Are you out of your mind?" she demanded, glancing nervously up toward Sunset.

"Tell me what happened. What'd I find out?"

"You don't want to know what I know. Trust me. Why do you think you went to these lengths to keep it from yourself? Maybe you did all that for a reason."

Old maps had *Hic sunt dracones* written along the edges to warn travelers of dangerous, unexplored places. He knew on some level that was what Maggie was telling him. *Here be dragons! Stay away.* But this had been his sole preoccupation for years. With answers within his reach, he couldn't hear a word she said. "Well, it didn't work, and now I need to know the rest."

"I made you a promise," she answered with her familiar stubbornness.

"I'm going to find out. With or without you."

"Maybe you will," she said. "But I'm not helping you do it. I made a promise."

"Maggie."

"We need to get off the street," she reminded him, pulling her arm free. He followed her through the side door of the garage where Nan kept her car.

"Maggie," he called after her, the frustration in his voice echoing through the stairwell. This felt like a betrayal, but who exactly had betrayed him, Maggie Soto or Chance Harker? She was only doing what he'd asked her to do. So couldn't it be argued that she was being loyal by not telling him? See, it was exactly this kind of paradox that made being a clone such a mindfuck.

He tried a different tactic. "Will you at least tell me what happened that night?"

"Yeah, that I guess I can do," she said, stopping on the landing halfway up and hunting for where to begin. "You called me that afternoon, right after your refresh. Asked if we could talk. We talked. It was wonderful. We went to bed. Then we ate and started making plans to go away. You remembered I had tickets to the Con D'Arcy show and said we should go. I know you didn't really want to, but you insisted we have a night out. It was very sweet. The show was amazing, for what it's worth. D'Arcy sounded great. At some point, one of her people invited us backstage. I thought you'd say no, but again you surprised me."

"What was she like?"

"Exhausted but really gracious. Funny. Intense. Honestly, I didn't talk to her for long. She kicked everyone out of her dressing room so you guys could talk in private. She was very polite about it."

"Talk about what?"

"You never said. But when you came out, there was a message on your LFD from a blocked number."

"Lee Conway?"

"Turned out, yeah. Said he'd read your interview and had information about the kidnapping. He wanted to meet."

"Let me guess, at the culvert?"

"Yeah, I don't know why. Some kind of psych-out, I think. It all sounded like a terrible idea, but there was no talking you out of it."

"So I met him there?"

"Yeah, we did," she said reluctantly.

"You came with me?"

She made an offended face. "I wasn't letting you go up there alone."

Her fierceness made him smile, and he went up the stairs to join her on the landing. He took her hand gently. "I really love you, you know?"

"I know. I do too. Why do you think I'm trying not to tell you all of this?" Maggie said, leading him up the stairs and out to the garage. It was all but deserted, but Nan's black 2039 Mustang GT was there, parked beside a weathered, street-scarred panel van.

"So what did Conway want?" Chance prompted.

"In the message, he wanted money, but right away we knew that wasn't it. All he talked about was your brother. Where was Marley? Where was Marley? Where was Marley?"

"Marley's dead," Chance said reflexively.

"Not according to Lee Conway."

"And he thought I knew?"

"Remember how I asked why you'd talked about Marley in the present tense in the article? Well, Conway wasn't buying that it was just a slip of the tongue. He was sure you knew Marley was alive and where he was. When you wouldn't tell him, that's when the gun came out."

She stopped as if that were the end of the story and tried the door of the Mustang. The car recognized the fob but, since Nan wasn't with them, refused to unlock the doors or start the engine until she'd given it her permission. Maggie kissed him and held it for a moment.

"What was that for?" he asked.

The Mustang rumbled to life with a predatory roar. The engine on the GT was a whisper-quiet electric, so Nan must have sprung for the acoustics package that simulated an old-school combustion engine.

"Don't know when I'll get another chance," she said, immediately realizing the double and triple meaning of her words and mimicking a rim shot to cover the awkwardness.

"I see what you did there."

"Shut up. Come on, get in." She opened the door and eased behind the wheel.

He went around to the passenger side. The panel van was parked over the white line, crowding their spot, so Chance had to shimmy his way between the vehicles to get to the door. That was why, when the van's side door rolled open, he all but fell backward into it. Strong hands reached out from the dark and dragged him inside onto his back. A broad white face hewn from granite and framed by an untamed beard glared down at him like a Civil War general who'd chosen this place to rally his men for one last, hopeless charge. Chance fought to sit up, but the man, twice his size, pinned him effortlessly.

"Hello, dupe," the Civil War general said, spitting the slur for clones, the stink of whiskey unmistakable on his breath. He yanked Chance's LFD out from behind his ear and gave his captive a quick jab to the temple that made him see fireworks.

The back doors of the van were thrown open, and Maggie was dumped unceremoniously inside. Her hands were bound behind her back with disposable plastic handcuffs. With a groan, she rolled onto her side. The doors slammed shut while the general relieved Maggie of her LFD. A moment later the van started and lurched out of the parking spot.

"Be cool, man. Be cool. Ain't nobody chasing us," the general warned.

The van slowed.

The general manhandled Chance onto his stomach. A stout knee in the small of his back held him down as his wrists were also cuffed. The general tossed him into the back of the van like a half-full laundry bag. Chance tried wrestling himself into a sitting position, but the van turned sharply as it left the garage and toppled him into Maggie. He started again. He didn't know how Children of Adam had found them, but he had heard the horror stories of clones who'd been captured. Until *Gaddis v. Virginia*, some states had classified the killing of a clone as destruction of property, not murder. CoA had reveled in pushing that boundary, and Chance wasn't at all sure the group gave the new law of the land its due.

He asked Maggie if she was alright, but she was looking at the general, who was watching them from a backward-facing jump seat. Chance didn't know anything about guns, but the one resting on his knee looked lethal enough.

"Been a long time," Maggie said to the general.

"Hey, little sister," the general answered without a trace of affection.

Chance's head popped up like a coyote that had heard an unfamiliar sound. *Little sister?* Maggie knew this guy.

"Don't call me that," she said. "It wasn't true even when it was true."

"You're as lost as ever, aren't you?" the general said with a sneer. "Hiding away in that crappy bungalow of yours. Little young to go full Garbo."

"She had the right idea. At least I didn't run away to Mexico."

The general frowned. "That's enough talk."

"¿Cómo es tu español?" she taunted.

"In any language," the general said, leaning forward and smacking the side of his gun down on Maggie's hip. The breath hissed out of her, but otherwise she didn't make a sound.

"Leave her alone," Chance said, aware that as deterrents went, it didn't carry a threat behind it. But it seemed to be enough to divert the general's attention. The man looked down at him contemptuously. What Chance saw in his eyes scared him, and he was already plenty scared.

"Oh, don't worry, dupe, we're not here for her."

CHAPTER
TWENTY-ONE

Little sister.

The Civil War general had called Maggie *little sister*. Chance still didn't know what to make of that. The way the two had talked sounded as if they'd been close once upon a time. But why would Maggie know anyone from Children of Adam? She hadn't even sounded surprised: more resigned, as if she'd been expecting him. None of it made any kind of sense that he could see. He nudged Maggie, trying to get her attention, but she wouldn't make eye contact. The general caught him doing it and gave him a swift kick in the back. After that, Chance quit trying to get answers out of Maggie and focused on not getting his brains scrambled by the general's steel-toed boots.

Time was hard to track from the floor of a van, but they drove long enough to get on and off the freeway twice. Then came a long stretch of slower, winding road, although they rarely stopped at traffic lights. The van turned and then turned again and again until Chance lost track. He didn't hear many other vehicles and guessed they were well outside the city now. Eventually, the van left the paved road and bumped its way along a rutted incline that made his teeth rattle. The van skidded to a halt, then did a rough three-point pirouette that sent Chance and Maggie sliding around like butter in a hot skillet.

Chance

Footsteps crunched in gravel. The back doors opened.

"End of the line. Everybody out," the general said amiably and shoved Maggie out with his boot. She grunted as she hit the ground but otherwise didn't make a sound. Chance tried to fight back, but the general clamped a hand around his throat and dragged him out of the van. Chance landed hard in the dirt next to Maggie, knocking the wind out of him.

Wheezing, he looked around. The van was parked beside an old pickup truck the color of rust. Both vehicles were backed up to a derelict stable. The unmistakable smell of tired animals and ancient hay filled his nose. Off to their left stood a clapboard ranch house straight out of *The Grapes of Wrath*. It didn't look as if anyone had called the place home in years. The abandoned ranch was surrounded by barren fields of dead, brown grasses. A lot of the farms around Los Angeles had gone bankrupt as the water supply tightened. The properties had become virtually worthless, and many of the families had simply pulled up stakes and headed east.

"I'll make the call," the driver said.

"You do that," the general agreed. "I'll take care of our guests."

"Paul, can we talk?" Maggie asked the driver, who was already walking toward the ranch house. Apparently, she knew everyone here. "Paul Lin, I'm talking to you!"

"Talk to Bear, I'm busy," he called back over his shoulder.

The Civil War general's name was Bear? Perfect.

Maggie took Paul up on his suggestion and rolled over to confront Bear. "Does he know what you're doing?"

From the way she'd emphasized *he*, Chance could tell she meant someone further up the food chain. Beyond that, he still had no idea what was going on.

"He knows enough," Bear said, lifting them both to their feet with discouraging ease.

"I want to talk to him," she said.

173

"Nothing to talk about. You broke the truce," Bear said.

"Lee broke the truce."

Chance's head snapped up, alert and wary now. Lee? As in Lee Conway? It couldn't be anyone else, but also couldn't be him.

The big man shook his head in grave disappointment. "I didn't have nothing to do with that. You know how Lee was. All balls, no brains."

"He's still *your* brother, Bear."

"That he was," Bear replied with more than a hint of foreboding before shoving them into the gloom of the stable.

Chance stared at Maggie as if seeing her for the first time. In theory, he knew the words she spoke, but he struggled to make sense of what she was saying. It sounded like Bear was Lee Conway's missing brother. That meant that he hadn't been snatched by Children of Adam. His first thought was that Bear Conway had come looking to avenge his brother. Maybe, but the situation wasn't that simple. Bear and Maggie had been arguing about a truce, and who'd broken it. Bear said Maggie; Maggie said Lee. And Lee was one of his kidnappers.

Everything clicked into place. These were his kidnappers. Two of them anyway. There was one more, probably the call that Paul Lin had gone to make. And Maggie knew them. Maggie knew his kidnappers.

Chance spun around and lunged at Bear, which wouldn't have been a good idea even if his hands weren't tied behind his back. The man was twice his size, and with one huge hand, he palmed Chance's face and pushed him onto his back.

"I think pretty boy here is finally catching on," Bear said. "You're gonna have some 'splaining to do, little sister."

"Leave him alone," Maggie said, stepping between them.

Bear towered over her. "Lee's dead. No one's getting left alone today." He brushed Maggie aside and kicked Chance in the ribs. "Get up, or I show you what full strength feels like."

Chance didn't want to know. He could barely breathe as it was but rolled onto his knees and forehead before climbing unsteadily to his feet.

"Let's go," Bear said, then gave them a helpful shove in the right direction.

Chance stumbled forward, fortunate to keep his balance. Along the wall opposite the stalls, cabinets hung open and tools were scattered on the ground, mixed with a hail of nails and screws, as if the owners had left in a hurry. A haze of bugs hummed impatiently in the rafters, as if they'd been waiting for the show to start. The air was stagnant and sweltering. A blue plastic tarp had been spread out on the floor, and it was here that they were herded.

A boot in the back of his leg forced him to his knees. Maggie followed him down. She looked at him mournfully and mouthed, *I'm sorry*.

He could barely stand to look at her and started to tell her so. A cruel, metallic clack cut him short. Somehow he knew without knowing that it was the sound of a slide being racked on a pistol. It was the second time in twenty-four hours he'd had a gun pointed at him. The experience wasn't growing on him. He felt the barrel press into the back of his head, forcing him even lower.

"Welcome home, dupe," Bear growled in his ear. "Place hasn't changed much since last time you was here."

Warily, Chance looked around the stable, afraid that meant what he thought it did.

Bear snorted. "Oh, that's right. You don't remember any of this, do you? Well, let me give you the tour. See over there? Stall three? That was yours. Where we kept you. Lord, you were such a whiny little bitch. Crying for your mommy. Honestly, it was a relief to put a bullet in you."

"Fuck you," Chance whispered. His parents had taught him to keep his voice down in museums, and wasn't that where he was? A museum to the end of his life.

"What?" Bear said in mock concern. "I thought you were dying to know. Where's the gratitude, huh? Or maybe I should just put another bullet in you now and send you back to knowing nothing. Then I could walk right up to you on the street, and you wouldn't have the first clue. That would be fun. What do you think?"

Bear's taunts reminded Chance that no one outside Palingenesis knew his policy had been canceled. It wasn't something they would make public, so as far as Bear was concerned, Chance had another clone on standby. He couldn't decide if that was an advantage or a really serious problem.

"That'd drive you nuts, wouldn't it?" Bear continued warming up to his mind games. "I've read how well dupes handle not knowing a thing. You'd just be left to wonder why. At least until I get around to killing you again. Plus, it'll give you time to mourn little sister here. Because she ain't coming back from shit."

The gun swung away from him and toward Maggie. She turned her face away, as if not seeing might make the threat not real. If Bear expected her to beg for her life, he was in for a disappointment.

"Leave her out of this. I'm the one who killed your brother," Chance said, although he had no idea why he still cared. Maybe he hadn't had time yet to absorb the magnitude of Maggie's betrayal or to reconcile it with what he thought he knew about her. He wanted to believe there could be an innocent explanation for all this. In a few hours he might well feel differently, but for now he was still very much in love with her, and the idea that she might have been involved in his kidnapping was too much to take.

"Oh, I'm aware, dupe," Bear said. "That's why I'll be taking my time with you."

The gun came back toward Chance. He was going to die again—but for the last time. All he felt was disappointment. How was that for irony?

"Stop it!" a man's voice called from the entrance. Paul had made a timely return from his call.

Bear didn't take his eyes off Chance. "Go back to the house, Paul. I'll be up in a minute."

"Can't do it, man. Can't do it. We need them alive."

"Why? We know where Marley is. That's all that matters."

That got Chance's undivided attention. How had they found his brother? That was impossible. Wasn't it? Maybe he'd screwed up somehow. Could they have followed him the last time he'd driven out there? He would have noticed, though, wouldn't he? Then he thought about how easily the strange girl had followed him around the city. He wasn't exactly world class at spotting a tail.

Paul said, "We won't know what matters until we have them all together. I'm leaving now. Just wait till I get back with him. We'll sort it out then. We all know what needs to happen. I'm just asking you to wait. Can you do that?"

Bear cocked the hammer of the gun by way of answer. Chance felt his stomach fall away, like he was back up in that aircraft watching his parachute disappear from view.

"Or," Paul suggested, "you can deal with Anton when he gets here."

Whoever Anton was, his name was enough to rattle the only person with a gun in his hand. Bear cursed to himself and let the hammer down.

"Give me the gun," Paul said as gently as a kiss.

"Fine, but I'm staying here with them," Bear said, slapping the gun into Paul's outstretched hand.

"That's fine. I'll be back soon. Then we'll get to the bottom of everything. Just sit tight and be cool," Paul said.

"Take your time."

"Be cool. Just be cool. I'll be back with the cavalry in no time."

"And Marley," Bear said as if he'd ordered a steak, extra rare.

"And Marley," Paul agreed, and patted the big man on the arm.

The two men went out of the stable together, talking quietly. Maggie tried to get Chance's attention, but he shook his head and looked away. He wasn't ready to hear whatever she had to say.

Outside, the van started up. Bear stood in the open doorway of the stable, silhouetted by the sun. He didn't move until the sound of the van's engine had faded to silence. Then he turned to gaze upon his prisoners still kneeling on the blue tarp. Paul might've taken the gun, but Chance wouldn't put it past Bear to improvise if he got it in his head to finish the job.

Their jailer disappeared, and Chance heard the door of the pickup truck open and then slam shut. Bear returned with a bottle of whiskey and a baseball bat. Cracking the seal, he gulped down a quarter of the bottle without taking a breath. Chance had only seen people drink like that in movies. Whiskey dripping from his beard, Bear wiped his mouth with the back of his sleeve. He set the bottle down and took batting practice over their heads. The bat whistled through the air so close they flinched and ducked. Bear found that funny and imitated the crack of hard contact and a rapturous crowd cheering him around the bases. In between home-run swings, he paused for unhealthy pulls from the bottle. He was a big man, but no one was built to guzzle down hard liquor so quickly. The bottle was three-quarters empty in a matter of minutes.

When he wearied of tormenting them, Bear pushed them over on their sides. He found an old, overturned rocking chair in a corner and set it at the mouth of the stable. Chance and Maggie lay very still, like children of an abusive, drunken father, hoping not to draw his attention. After a time, Bear's chin settled on his chest. His breathing slowed, and a steady, rumbling snore filled the stable.

Chance lay there, listening for any sign Bear might wake up, but the big man appeared down for the count. He turned to Maggie to say it was time to go, but she was already sitting up and shimmying her wrists out from under her legs like an escape artist. She scavenged a pair of rusted pliers from the ground, cut off her plastic cuffs, and then did the same for Chance.

Single file, Chance followed Maggie cautiously past their captor. The stench of whiskey was eye watering, even from six feet away. Doing his best to watch her feet, Chance tried to step only where she did.

Keys, she mouthed, pointing at Bear's belt, where a key ring hung like forbidden fruit.

That was an awful idea for one massive, homicidal reason. But then the devil's advocate in him pointed out that they had no idea where *here* was or how long a walk it was to anything resembling help. And more than anything, he needed to warn Marley that he was in danger. Was he really going to walk all the way to the Slabs?

Chance took a tentative step toward Bear and the keys. Then another and another like a bomb-disposal technician approaching live ordnance, braced for it to go off in his face. He closed a fist around the keys and unhooked them from the belt loop with his other hand. The sleeping man's breath hitched, just in case Chance needed any more dramatic tension. But he had the keys now and backed away slowly, watching the sleeping man's eyes. If they opened, even for a moment, he was going to run like hell, but by the time he reached the threshold, Bear was snoring reliably again.

Chance gave Maggie the keys and whispered for her to put the pickup in neutral. She got in and gave him a thumbs-up through the window. Putting his back into it, he pushed the pickup like he was guiding a boat away from a dock. Thankfully they were on an incline, so once Chance got the pickup moving, gravity got interested in the goings-on. The pickup's wheels began to roll without him. He grimaced at the noise they made in the gravel, which sounded like gunfire to his sensitive ears. He glanced back over his shoulder, but Bear hadn't stirred.

As they gained speed, Maggie steered the backward-facing pickup down the hill, while Chance jogged alongside until he couldn't keep up and jumped on the running board. She stopped at the bottom. Chance got in.

"Which way?" she asked, starting the pickup.

"Away."

They had other things to figure out before he would give her more specific directions.

———

Maggie drove south, keeping the sun to their left. Chance guessed they must be somewhere north of Los Angeles, judging by the terrain, but he couldn't be sure since they didn't have their LFDs, and the GPS screen of the pickup was cracked and broken. A sign announcing they were entering the town of Lancaster confirmed his suspicions that they were heading back the way they'd come. Navigating a warren of boarded-up shops and FOR SALE signs while following directions to the 138, he could see it had probably been a decent place to live back before the fight over water rights had turned vicious. When he saw the entrance ramp to the highway, Chance told Maggie to pull over. She didn't ask why; she knew.

"Ask your question," she said.

"How do you know Bear Conway? Or his brother, or that guy Paul? How do you know any of them?" Technically that was four questions, but he was afraid to start with the big one. He needed to work up the nerve.

"From *Redwood Code*," she answered, staring straight ahead at the sign for the freeway. It was the Anton Brätt movie for which Maggie had received her Oscar nomination.

"Wait, that's the Anton Paul meant?"

"Yeah," she confirmed. "Paul and Bear both worked on it. They worked on all of Anton's movies before he became persona non grata in the industry. Bear was his cinematographer, if you can believe that. Paul is a production designer."

He realized now why Lee Conway looked familiar. They'd never met, but he was in one of the photographs at Maggie's bungalow. It had been there the whole time.

"And Lee Conway? Did you know him too?"

"Little bit. He was more of a hanger-on," Maggie said. "Bear brought him on set once, and Anton liked having him around because Lee was such a groupie and did anything he asked. When I told Marley that I was still close to Anton, he wouldn't let it go until I introduced them. You know how your brother was about movies."

"It was going to be his life," Chance agreed. *Copperfield Avenue*, Brätt's second movie, was one of Marley's all-time favorites. His brother would have lain down in traffic for the chance to meet him.

"Marley was starstruck. Anton went into his misunderstood-genius act, jacked up the charisma. Marley never had a prayer. And Anton had this script. *The* script. His masterpiece, according to the gospel of himself. Except, of course, no one would bankroll him after all the scandals. Marley started talking a big game that he could produce it. They spent weeks planning Anton's triumphant return. But when your dad wouldn't front Marley the money . . ." She trailed off.

"They kidnapped me and Marley instead," he finished for her.

She nodded.

"And Anton Brätt is behind all of it. He's the one you asked to talk to back in the stable?"

She nodded again.

"And you've known, all this time, and never said anything."

"I knew."

"How?" It felt like the most dangerous question he'd ever asked. The wrong answer would rewrite everything he thought he knew about his life.

"Because I was involved."

"Involved with what? The kidnapping?" He needed her to be explicit, because he wouldn't believe it otherwise, and maybe not even then.

She unbuckled her seat belt and pivoted in her seat to face him with eyes filled with shame and self-loathing. "The kidnapping. Yes. I was part of it."

His head dropped. He should have been angry. He should have been screaming in rage. But all Chance felt was a creeping numbness spreading through him like he'd been hooked up to an IV of ice water. Up until now, he'd thought the word *heartbroken* was only a figure of speech, an ancient misunderstanding of human anatomy. One that had hung on through the ages through stubborn poetic license—the human heart pumped blood, not feelings. That was just science. Then why could he feel the outline of where his had once been inside the bars of his chest? When he looked up, there was someone else sitting in Maggie's place. She had Maggie's nose, Maggie's mouth, Maggie's hair, but she didn't look anything like the Maggie he'd known. This person was a stranger.

"What was your part?" he asked, surprised at how casual and conversational his voice sounded.

"Stay close to your family. Keep an eye on your dad. Report in if I saw anything out of the ordinary."

Chance laughed as he started putting this new piece into the puzzle. "So the morning of the kidnapping, when you went out shopping with my mom, you knew what was going to happen?"

"What do you want me to say? That I have no excuse for myself? I don't. Anton had been spoon-feeding me his bullshit since I was eleven. I believed in him. He made everything sound straightforward. A simple transaction. No one would get hurt; he'd get the money, and then we could make his movie. He said I'd be an actor again."

"Oh, you never stopped being an actor. You deserve awards for your performance."

"It wasn't an act."

"You let me fall in love with you."

"I fell in love with you too."

"Fucking don't, Maggie. Just don't." He didn't want to hear that. "So are you still on the job? Is that what this is? Have you been keeping an eye on me for them all this time?"

"No. Absolutely not. I haven't seen any of them since before the kidnapping. No one was supposed to get hurt," she said with a searching hopelessness.

"People definitely got hurt, Maggie. So what happened?"

"I don't know."

"Stop. Stop lying to me."

"I'm not lying. I wasn't there. I was at your parents' house the whole time. No one was supposed to get hurt," she repeated, as if it would ward off evil spirits.

"And they didn't tell you after, when you split the ransom?"

"I didn't take any money. I told you. I never saw any of them again. When things went bad . . . when they shot you . . . I told them I was out. I made a deal with Anton. If they left me alone, I'd keep my mouth shut."

"Was that the truce Bear Conway talked about?"

She nodded morosely. "I look back. I don't even recognize that girl who went along with any of it."

For the first time, his voice spiked with anger. "I haven't recognized myself in five years. Five years, Maggie. You've been watching me come apart for five years from not knowing the truth. But you did, didn't you? All this time you knew."

If there was any blood left in Maggie's body, none was in her face. She was trembling, her eyes red, but she didn't cry. He was glad of that. He thought he might lose it if she did.

"Can I ask you something?" she said, quiet as a cemetery wind.

"Yeah, ask your question."

"Is what Bear and Paul said true? Is Marley really alive?"

Chance took a long time answering. He didn't know why he felt guilty for keeping it from her, especially now. "Yeah, he's alive."

"Oh," she said, as if someone had had to explain a joke to her that she still didn't find funny.

"What? You think I should have told you? Is that what you think?" he said, his voice rising.

She shook her head, then said quietly, "No. We have to warn him."

His brain kept toggling between the two Maggies it knew, and for a moment he was looking at the Maggie he'd loved enough to run away with. "What do they want with him?"

"I don't know. I swear. But it won't be friendly."

He didn't know if she was telling the truth or not. It didn't matter. He wouldn't believe her now, no matter what she said. He'd sworn so many times that if he ever found his kidnappers, he'd kill them. Well, here one was, in the flesh. The last person he would have ever suspected. How would revenge fix any of that?

"Get out," he said instead.

"No. Please."

He reached across her for the handle and opened the door. When she still wouldn't get out, he tried to force her, but she fought him in a panic, like they were at thirty thousand feet in the middle of one of Chance's stunts. She kept saying no over and over through gritted teeth.

"Get the fuck out!" he bellowed, but she still wouldn't budge.

"Please. Let me help you. You need me."

"What do I need you for?"

"Because I know these people. Please. Once we're sure Marley is safe, I'll go to the police. I'll confess. Tell them what I know. Anything you want. But let me do this first. I'm begging you."

"I don't have time for your penance, Maggie."

"Then let's go. I'll drive. Just tell me where."

Chance looked at her and just for a moment saw the two Maggies simultaneously—the one he loved and the one who had betrayed him. Could they be the same person? Was that possible? Before he could answer, she split apart, and all that was left was the stranger he'd only just met. That was fine. She was right. He did need her help.

"South," he said. "Marley is south."

"Thank you," she said gratefully, and then started the engine.

CHAPTER TWENTY-TWO

The drive out to the Slabs was a grim affair: two lost souls in a funeral procession of one. It was the first time Chance hadn't made the journey alone, and it felt wrong not to be behind the wheel. Would Charon let his passenger steer the ferryboat? Chance rolled his eyes at himself, although his mother would have applauded his pretention. He didn't envy the reunion awaiting Maggie, though. Not that it was likely to go well for him either. He wondered if Marley would ever forgive him for giving away his secret. Even if his brother was in danger, Chance wasn't sure Marley valued his life above his solitude.

It was a good five-hour drive from Lancaster, and the pair didn't speak until they reached the Salton Sea. Maggie covered her nose and mouth with her hand.

"What's that smell?"

"The lake where they shot Marley." That stopped her asking any more questions, and they drove in sanctified, uneasy silence punctuated only by Chance's terse directions.

It was late in the day when they passed through the Slabs. Maggie stared out the windows openmouthed. Living in LA, you heard stories about life out in the desert and figured it had to be an exaggeration. She looked at him, and he could see the bewilderment on her face. It was impossible to imagine Marley Harker living out here. He understood and could've explained that the Marley Harker she knew was gone. But for what? She would see for herself soon enough. Why ruin the surprise?

Up ahead, the yellow roof of the school bus caught the sun, guiding them like an ancient lighthouse. At the turnoff from the main road, he told Maggie to stop the pickup and opened his door to stand on the running board for a better look. There was no sign of Marley, but that didn't mean anything one way or another. More crucial, he didn't see any vehicles. Either he and Maggie had gotten here first, or the kidnappers had already come and gone. For all he knew, they'd passed each other on the road. Had he seen a panel van going the other direction? He'd been so intent on ignoring Maggie that it hadn't occurred to him to watch the other side of the road. He kicked himself for being so careless.

He got back in and pointed at the way ahead. The pickup bumped its way up to the bus and stopped, throwing up a cloud of dirt that glittered in the air like phosphorus. Nothing stirred. Maggie opened her door, but Chance gestured to wait. Just wait. He leaned over and honked the horn, listened, then honked once more.

"Stay here," he said, then repeated himself when she began to protest. "I'm serious. Stay in the truck."

He went and checked in the bus, but no Marley. He climbed up on the roof and yelled Marley's name, which echoed across the desert floor. No one answered. Either Marley had gone scavenging or he'd already been taken. The third option was that he'd seen the pickup and was hiding somewhere out in the desert, watching and waiting. If he was, Chance might never see him again. He looked down at Maggie, who was staring through the windshield like a child in a reptile house who couldn't quite believe her eyes.

"This is really where he lives?"

"Home sweet home," he answered, and then beckoned that it was okay for her to join him.

"Jesus," she said, summoning the courage to get out of the pickup. "How long has he been here?"

"Couple years."

"And you let him?" she said sharply, then caught herself. "I'm sorry. Not my place."

"Really isn't."

"So where is he?"

Chance held out his hands at the obviousness of the answer. "Not here."

"When will he be back?"

"Marley doesn't exactly keep a regular schedule. He'll be back when he's back."

"Or they already got him," Maggie said. "I mean, look at this place."

He understood why she'd think that. To the untrained eye, the camp looked like a cyclone had hit it. But he didn't think so. Call it a hunch or just wishful thinking, but sneaking up on his brother's camp was next to impossible.

"No, that's how it always looks."

"Unreal." She nodded vacantly and walked away toward the field of sculptures. Chance came down from the bus and jogged after her, slowing to a walk as he came alongside her.

"How long have you known where he was?" she asked without looking at him.

"He reached out about two years after he disappeared."

She took that in as if someone had just described the size of the universe—understanding in theory, but unable to grasp the actual scope. "Where was he before?"

"He moved around a lot at the beginning," he answered vaguely, bracing for her to ask him where, but she didn't, instead stopping at the first pair of sculptures to study them as if they were strolling through the Getty. In all his visits to Marley, he'd never been this near his brother's . . . his what? His art? His masterpiece? His life's work? Whatever the hell all this was supposed to be. And now that he was up close, he wish he'd stayed away. From a distance, the sculptures looked like ordinary silhouettes of two boys. Up close, he saw them for what they were—a patchwork of scrap metal that had been welded together like an army of Dr. Frankenstein's children.

Maggie seemed to understand immediately. "These are all you and Marley. How many pairs are there?"

Chance didn't know.

"Has to be over a hundred of them," she said in awe. "It's beautiful."

"What are you talking about, Maggie? It's ugly as hell."

"No, that's the point, don't you get it?" she said, touching one of the statues delicately. "From far away, they just look like two ordinary brothers standing side by side. But then when you get up close—"

"We're broken," Chance finished. Now that she'd pointed it out, it was so obvious he wondered how he'd never noticed.

"But there's more to it," she said, pointing out differences between each pair. Chance looked closer and saw what she meant. The larger sculptures, representing Marley, were all crudely assembled with ugly, brutal seams. That had to be intentional. His brother was a virtuoso with an arc welder; the modifications and additions he'd made to the school bus were seamless, much like the smaller sculptures of his kid brother. It was almost impossible to tell where one piece of scrap ended and the next began. "He's saying he's the one who's broken, but you've put yourself back together. Don't you see? He's proud of you."

"Don't know why," Chance said, pressing the heel of his hand into the corner of his eye. "Doesn't feel like anything's changed."

"Never does when you're in the middle of it. But you have. You were going to leave all this behind. You'd decided," she said, and for a brief moment it was as if the last twelve hours hadn't happened. He reached out for her, and they joined hands. They stood like that for a long time.

"Did I know about you?" he said, pulling his hand away.

He could see her wrestling over how to answer him. "Yeah, you knew. Lee told you everything."

He wondered if Maggie was the reason he'd gone home that night and pulled the trigger. Had knowing the truth about her pushed him too far? An ignorance-is-bliss type of deal.

No. It was a horrible thing to know, and he wished like hell it weren't true, but he just didn't buy that as the reason. He'd been obsessed with learning the truth about his kidnapping for five years. There was no way he would've sacrificed what he'd learned from Lee Conway just to forget Maggie had been involved. He knew now, didn't he? Her betrayal hurt, but he didn't want to forget it. Not ever. So what had been different the night Lee Conway died? There had to be more. Something worse. It was a scary thought.

"What about now? Do I know everything, Maggie?"

"You know enough, don't you think?"

"That's a bullshit answer," he said, but part of him wondered if maybe she was right. Maybe he knew as much as was safe to know. If there were things he'd made her promise not to tell him, then maybe there was a good reason. Maybe the way things had turned out the last time ought to have been a cautionary tale.

Down by the road, a plume of orange dirt exploded. The cloud moved toward them silently. A vehicle was coming. Maggie followed his eyes and walked a few steps past him to get a better look. It was the gray panel van. They watched it rumble up the dirt track like a broken-down horse of the apocalypse. The kidnappers had arrived.

Chance's first thought was to make a run for the pickup. It could cover this terrain a lot easier than a van. He'd been out here enough times that he felt reasonably confident that he wouldn't get them too lost out there. Maggie pulled him down behind the nearest pair of sculptures before he could do anything stupid. There was no way the van wouldn't be first. The only option was on foot: take refuge in the desert, find somewhere to hide, and with luck find their way back to the Slabs at first light.

The van skidded to a stop broadside to the pickup, showering it with rocks. The back doors of the van swung open, and Bear Conway hopped down holding a rifle. Even from a hundred yards away, Chance could see the grin on his face.

"Come on out!" he yelled.

Maggie shook her head at Chance, though it was hard to tell whether at Bear's demand or the hopelessness of their situation. A hole appeared in the forehead of one sculpture less than a foot from Maggie. The rifle's report followed after like a bad rumor. For a man who'd drunk a bottle of whiskey, his aim was really good.

"I'm not as good a shot as my brother. Sooner or later, I'm liable to miss. I know it don't matter to you, King Clone, but why don't you come on out before I accidentally put a hole in your girl?"

"She's not my girl," Chance yelled back, then said to Maggie, "We can still make a run for it."

As if rebutting the idea, Bear notched two more holes in the sculpture, each one an inch closer to Maggie. Lee Conway must have been one hell of a shot.

"You really want to bet he can't hit a moving target?" she said.

It was a good point.

"Alright, alright," Chance called out. "We're coming out."

"Good boy," Bear said. "Nice and slow."

They stood, hands in the air.

From behind, a voice said not to do anything stupid. While Bear was keeping them occupied, Paul Lin had circled around. He tossed plastic handcuffs to them and told them to put them on. Once their wrists were secured, the pistol in his hand flicked in the direction of the van. "Lead the way."

The trio trudged back to the camp. When it wasn't fast enough for Bear's liking, he slung the rifle over his shoulder and strode out to meet them. He took them by the necks and steered them toward the bus.

"Where is he?" Bear demanded, giving them each a shake like he was trying to loosen the last ketchup in a bottle.

A figure emerged from the bus, nearly as tall as Bear, but thin and willowy like secondhand smoke. He held a scarf over his mouth and nose like he was touring a quarantine zone.

"Anything?" Bear called to him.

"No, our lad appears to have flown the coop," he said in an English accent bordering on self-parody that Chance recognized from interviews. Anton Brätt, legendary bad boy and alleged auteur, had joined their little party.

"Maybe this isn't the right place?" Bear suggested before forcing Chance and Maggie to their knees by the firepit. They'd driven five hours, only to end up where they'd started.

"Oh no," Anton said, gesturing to the bus. "This is definitely the place. Can't you feel it? And what a location. Like something out of a George Miller movie. You did a magnificent job, might I add, Bear. Top notch. I've seen Academy Award winners who can't play drunk as convincingly as that. I should write a part for you."

"Thanks, boss. Helps when you have a couple of idiots for an audience," Bear said, and then gave Chance a wink. "For such a scrawny kid, you make a hell of a lot of noise when you're trying to be sneaky. I almost lost it when you took my keys."

Chance dropped his head, realizing how completely he'd been played. The whole thing had been carefully staged from the moment they'd arrived at the ranch, all so he could lead them right to Marley. Paul Lin had probably only driven a little ways off and then circled back to pick up Bear after they'd left. What an idiot he was. He'd kept his brother's secret for two and a half years, only to give it up in a matter of hours.

He glared at Maggie. Had she been in on this too? Confessing to one betrayal so she could commit another. Was she still in thrall to Anton Brätt? So much so that she'd let Bear shoot at her? But even as he was trying to decide, he realized it didn't matter. He could never trust her again, so what difference did it make?

"Maybe they warned him and he took off?" Paul suggested.

"No, we have their LFDs and were only a few minutes behind," Anton mused. "Where would he have gone?"

"Into the desert?"

"With the pickup right here? I don't think so."

"He wasn't here," Maggie said.

Anton looked at her as though she'd appeared out of nowhere. "Hello, little girl. Look at you. What's it been? Five years?"

"Anton," Maggie replied as if identifying a rare phylum of poisonous insects.

"We had an understanding, you and I."

"Yeah, and then Lee showed up with a gun. Take it up with him."

"It is likely unwise, this early in the grieving process, to mention Lee," Anton said, giving Bear a cautioning look. He then turned his attention to Chance, regarding him with interest. "I must say it's strange seeing you again, Chance Harker."

"Why? Because you killed me?"

"Yes, but there's so much more. Think about it. We have an entire history, you and I. Our lives, intertwined in a way that is singularly unique. And yet you have no memory of me at all. It's positively gothic. I have an idea for a screenplay. Memory and forgetting. Cloning is such a brilliant, untapped metaphor."

"Maybe we can collaborate."

"What do you think we're doing?" Anton smiled, then added, "Where is your brother?"

"What do you want with him?"

"A few questions, nothing more."

"My father didn't give it to you, did he? The ransom. That's why you're back from Mexico," Chance said, finally seeing the angle. Anton Brätt and his lackies had gotten away clean. Why else risk coming back and sticking their necks out like this if they'd gotten the fifty million?

"As I said, we have questions," Anton replied.

"Why not just ask my father?"

"We'll get to your father in due time. First, I wish to talk to your brother."

"What happens after you do?" Chance asked.

"If you cooperate, I'll tell you everything. Answers to all those questions that have obsessed you these past five years. Your candor in the Highsmith article was so endearing."

"Maggie already told me."

"But not everything, did she? I can tell. And besides, there are parts she doesn't even know herself. I'm sure she clutched her pearls and told you that no one was supposed to get hurt. I can see from your face that she has. That was her big line five years ago too. I'll tell you the parts she missed."

"And you won't hurt anyone?"

"Not if I get exactly what I want," Anton said.

Chance didn't believe a word from this man, but playing along was a better option than calling him a liar.

"I don't know where Marley is."

Anton sighed theatrically. "This is disappointing. And I thought we'd reached an understanding."

"We have," Chance assured him. "But that doesn't mean I know where he is right this second. Sometimes he's just not here when I arrive."

"When do you imagine he'll be back?"

"The hell if I know. My brother isn't exactly punching a clock out here. Could be an hour. Could be a couple of days."

"Then we wait a couple of days," Bear said.

Anton frowned at the interruption, and Chance saw his opening. "You can do that, but better odds of Marley showing himself if it's just me. He sees two cars and a bunch of strangers around his fire, good chance we never see him again. He's done it before."

"The boy has a point," Anton said. "But I'm not leaving you here unchaperoned."

"We should all wait together," Paul countered.

"Suit yourself," Chance said. "But if everyone's staying, then someone should think about making a fire. It's going to get dark soon, and then it gets cold. There's no toilet, so just go wherever you want. Marley pisses against the side of the bus, so he won't mind. No electricity, no running water. Definitely no cell service."

"It's the twenty-first century," Anton said, as if a dinosaur had just tap-danced into view.

"I don't think the desert cares much about the year. And you're really going to love the menu."

Anton reached an abrupt decision. "Paul. You'll stay."

To say the least, Paul looked supremely unenthusiastic at the prospect. "Why not Bear?"

"Yeah, I'll stay," Bear agreed.

"No," Anton said. "I don't think that's a good idea. Too much history there."

"Dammit, Anton," Paul said. "I didn't sign up for desert patrol."

"But," Anton said, "Maggie will accompany us. If we don't hear from Paul with good news in forty-eight hours, she dies."

"So? She's one of you. What do I care what happens to her?" Chance said, really wanting to believe that he meant it.

Anton leaned toward him as if studying an audition reel from some acting hopeful. "Mmm, no. The thing is, you're just not selling it. But if you really mean that, well, I guess there's no reason to keep her around. Is there? Bear? Be a good lad and put Maggie out of her misery."

"Happy to, boss," Bear said as if he'd been asked to make a simple coffee run. Shouldering the rifle, he ambled over to Maggie, who'd begun to shake.

"Stop!" Chance shouted. "Just stop."

From her knees, Maggie glanced toward him, her expression unreadable.

Anton motioned for Bear to wait. "Forty-eight hours?"

"Forty-eight hours," Chance agreed miserably. He didn't know why he still gave a damn. He'd been dreaming of revenge for five years, but it was Maggie. He didn't know how he could be this angry and still want nothing bad to happen to her.

"The human heart," Anton said almost pityingly. "Ineffable, isn't it?"

CHAPTER TWENTY-THREE

Chance was half-asleep when, for a brief moment, the desert floor cracked open. He lifted his head to get a better look, but there was nothing to see. It was well past midnight, and the squinting eye of the moon wasn't offering much in the way of illumination. He assumed the fire had just been playing tricks on his eyes. Given how little sleep he'd had, he was surprised he wasn't hallucinating more. Not thinking he'd be gone this long, he'd left his Palingenesis meds back at the apartment. Plus he doubted the can of pork and beans scavenged from the bus had the eleven essential vitamins and minerals a growing clone needed. He was arriving at the dangerous stage where he knew objectively he was outside his right mind, even as that same mind was assuring him that everything was hunky-dory.

Anton and Bear had left with Maggie hours ago. If his brother didn't turn up in the next forty-something hours, Chance was going to need one hell of a plan B, not to mention the higher brain function to carry it out. That required sleep. Sleep, however, was challenging while being tied to a clubfooted lounge chair. Every time he shifted positions trying to get comfortable, the chair wobbled and threatened to collapse beneath him: Paul's punishment for talking too much and asking that his handcuffs be removed.

His captor was sitting sullenly on a bald tire across the fire from him, poking at the embers with a stick. Chance didn't get the impression the accommodations were to his liking. Paul definitely hadn't been pleased to get this shit detail (his words) while everyone else had left in the van and returned to civilization (also his words).

Chance had just about gotten situated again when, on the far side of the fire, the desert floor lifted up again. A perfect four-by-four square. Chance squinted through the flames, trying to make it out clearly. Through the slender gap, a pair of eyes blinked, reflecting amber light from the fire like a demon that had climbed up from hell to find out what all the commotion was about.

The demon put a finger to its lips.

Paul coughed, and the trapdoor eased shut again. The tire was only a few feet away. If Paul turned his head six inches to the left, he and the demon could have had a staring contest.

"I have a question," Chance said. They hadn't spoken to each other in hours. What did bait say to the fisherman?

"I'm not uncuffing you," Paul replied without looking up from the fire.

"Who cut the biometric chip out of our necks? Was it you?" It was an honest question, and he badly wanted the answer. That wasn't why he was asking, though. Right now, he just needed to keep Paul's attention on him.

"What?" Paul said, glaring across the fire at Chance.

Marley slithered out and lay on his belly, waiting to see if he'd been heard.

"You heard me. Five years ago. Was it you who stuck the knife in my neck and dug out the chip? The police found a lot of blood at the scene. Did you get a lot on you?"

This was clearly a topic that Paul didn't care to think too much about. "I didn't have the knife."

"But you were there, yeah? So what, you just held me down? Was I screaming? Was it your job to keep us quiet?"

Marley slowly stood, unfurling against the night sky. Picking up a length of pipe from the ground, he took a careful step toward Paul, who was busy defending his honor.

"I was the driver. I drove. That's it. That other stuff? That was all the Conway brothers. They've got no problem with shit like that."

"I was sixteen. I was a kid," Chance said, not letting up. "You're just as guilty as they are."

"Shut up, alright? I can make you less comfortable."

Marley took another step.

"Sixteen," Chance repeated. "So who shot me and dumped my body? The Conways again? Were you just 'driving' that time too?"

Marley was right behind Paul now. His boots must have scuffed in the dirt as he raised the pipe, because Paul turned his head and screamed. Chance couldn't blame him. It must have been an awful sight, Marley lit by fire from below like some vengeful desert spirit. The pipe whistled down and cut the scream short. Paul didn't get his hands up in time, and it caught him flush across the temple. His body rag-dolled and went sprawling into the dirt, where he lay unmoving. The fight was over before it began, but that wasn't good enough for Marley, not nearly good enough, and he stepped over the body and swung again. Paul didn't move or make a sound, so Marley hit him a third time.

"Stop!" Chance yelled.

But Marley didn't stop. The pipe danced mercilessly in the firelight.

Chance strained against the plastic handcuffs. "Marley, stop! Don't kill him."

Marley took his brother's advice under advisement and brought the pipe down again, on the verge of losing all control. Five years of rage and pain and loss finally unleashed on one of those responsible. Chance felt like a hypocrite for telling him to stop. He'd fantasized about revenge for years, in graphic terms that he would never admit to a living soul. Who was he to tell Marley to show mercy?

"They have Maggie!" Chance had been given forty-eight hours, but Anton had told Paul to stay in regular contact. They needed Paul Lin alive, at least for now. At the mention of her name, Marley paused, the pipe suspended over Paul's head like the rusting Sword of Damocles. "Please, Marley. Think. You kill him, she's dead."

The pipe fell from Marley's hand.

"You're a lucky, lucky man," his brother told Paul's unconscious form and then stalked around the fire hunting for an outlet for his unquenched fury. He came to a halt at the body, then doubled over and let out an awful, inchoate roar. Spent, he sat down heavily in the dirt and stared into the fire, panting.

After a few minutes of waiting patiently, Chance cleared his throat and shook his wrists at his brother. Marley looked up as if surprised to discover that he wasn't alone. With a grunt, he disappeared into the bus and returned with a wickedly sharp hunting knife. Once Chance was free, he took the knife out of his brother's hand, just in case Marley changed his mind and decided to carve Paul Lin into steaks.

Chance went over and checked on him. Lin wasn't dead, but he'd been beaten halfway there. Even if he did regain consciousness, Chance had his doubts about what would be left.

"He needs a hospital," Chance said.

"He needs someone who gives a shit. Ain't no hospitals around here."

His brother might be crazy, but he wasn't wrong. One of the trade-offs for all this freedom and nature was a total absence of anything remotely resembling emergency services. The nearest hospital was in Indio. Theoretically, Chance could stop on the way back to Los Angeles, but even if he wanted to, he wasn't sure that was a good idea. Hospitals would have questions that Chance had neither the time nor the inclination to answer. But doing nothing would make him an accomplice to murder.

"You have any bandages?" Chance asked, hoping for a tolerable third option.

Marley pulled off one of his filthy T-shirts, tore it into long strips, and wrapped it around Paul's head. "There," he said, stepping back to admire his work as though he'd just successfully completed a revolutionary heart transplant. "Good as new."

"Wait. Where's his gun?" Chance asked, realizing they'd forgotten to disarm him.

There it was, still on Paul's hip. Chance took the holster and clipped it to his own belt. They'd gotten lucky: a reminder that he wasn't any good at this sort of thing and needed to be more careful.

A search of Paul's pockets turned up the key to the pickup. In the glove compartment, he found two LFDs. One was his; the other, he assumed, belonged to Paul. Both were useless out here, but Chance would need to keep an eye on Lin's once he made it back to civilization. If Anton Brätt called, and Lin didn't answer, then Maggie's remaining time would be cut even shorter.

Curious, Chance went over and lifted up the cleverly camouflaged trapdoor that Marley had crawled out of. Even though he knew it was there, he had to look close to see the handle. He didn't know what he'd expected, maybe a ladder down to a survival shelter or the land that time forgot. But no, it was only a crude foxhole.

"What the hell is this?" Chance asked.

Marley was squatting in the dirt next to Paul Lin, studying the man's face. "Sometimes I'm gone for a while. Don't want anyone stealing my valuables."

"Your valuables?"

"Value is all perspective, brother. Out here, things are priceless that you wouldn't pay five cents for on Rodeo Drive."

Chance felt quite sure that was true. "And you were just down there the whole time?"

"I've been in worse places for longer."

"Were you ever coming out?"

"I did come out."

Chance thought about explaining that he meant back when he'd first arrived at the camp, but from the look on his brother's face, he knew there was no point in getting into it. He hadn't had a satisfying conversation with Marley in two and a half years. That wasn't about to change tonight.

"Did you remember the bourbon?" Marley asked.

Chance rolled his eyes. "No, Marl. I didn't have time to stop for bourbon."

"You said you would. You said next visit."

"It isn't that kind of visit. We were kind of in a hurry to warn you."

"Warn me about what? That you were leading them right to me? Good looking out."

Chance started to defend himself, but his brother had already turned away. "I'm hungry," Marley said. "I'm going to make some grub."

Chance threw a log on the fire. Paul was still breathing, although it was a shallow, wheezing pull. The man was sweating like it was a hundred degrees out. Even an optimist would admit it didn't look good for him, and Chance was no optimist. He sat on the couch, intending to figure out what to do if Paul didn't wake up soon. It was his second time underestimating a couch, and he was asleep by the count of three. When he woke, the fire had long since burned out. Marley had covered him with a blanket, and a tattered umbrella had been wedged between two couch cushions, shading him from the sun just beginning its morning ascent in the eastern sky.

Paul Lin was gone. Chance threw off the blanket and sat up, cursing. He yelled his brother's name. There was no answer. If Paul had gotten away . . . but no, the pickup was still there. So where had he gone? He yelled for Marley again.

"I'm back here," came the reply from the far side of the bus.

Chance found his brother standing in a rectangular hole. Marley stopped his work and leaned on his shovel.

"What are you doing?" Chance asked.

"Digging a hole," Marley answered, as if that should be self-evident.

"What kind of hole?"

Marley gestured at Paul Lin, who lay in the shadow of the bus.

"Is he?" Chance asked.

"Not yet. But he don't smell too fresh, you know? Thought I should get him out of the sun before he turned."

"And what are you doing?"

"Just being prepared," Marley said with a practical shrug. "Either he wakes up or he don't. Better odds than he gave us. Worst case, I got an extra hole."

Chance wondered if he'd slept an hour more, whether Paul Lin would already be at the bottom of that hole choking on dirt. Digging a man's grave before he was dead felt like a dangerous precedent to set. "How about you take a break? I'm starving. Any chance of that food?"

"I already made it. But no, you needed to go and fall asleep on me. Hard. I couldn't've woken you with a bulldozer. Dinner has come and gone," Marley said like a famous chef who'd been mortally insulted by a renowned food critic. But then he sighed, relenting, and held out a hand. "Alright, fine. Help me up and I'll make you something."

Chance heaved him up and out of the hole, but Marley didn't let go of his hand.

"What the hell's that?" Marley asked, staring at the ring on Chance's finger. Chance pulled his hand away, embarrassed as if he'd been caught trying on someone else's underwear. He always took the ring off before he drove out here, but with everything else going on, he'd forgotten all about it.

"Your graduation ring," Chance said, not knowing how to explain that the ring was a way of reminding himself of what life had been like before. "I'm sorry. I kind of took to wearing it."

"What are you talking about? That's not my ring."

"What are *you* talking about?" Chance replied.

Marley reached into his shirt and drew out a chain that hung around his neck. At the end of it was a ring.

"*This* is my ring."

———

Chance sat on the couch holding the two rings in the palm of his hand. In the sun, they were identical, right down to the inscription on the inside of the band. If not for the chain, he wouldn't have been able to tell one from the other.

"Why are there two?" Marley asked, giving voice to the million-dollar question.

"I don't know. Maybe Mom and Dad had an extra one made?" Chance suggested, although the theory sounded absurd as soon as it came out of his mouth. "Where did you get this one?"

"When they brought me home from Palingenesis, everything was just wrong. I felt out of place. Unwanted. Like they'd had a painting commissioned to remember their dead son, only the painting could walk and talk, and no one was ever going to want to look at it."

"I felt the same way," Chance blurted out. The two brothers had been dancing around this subject for years, afraid to address it head-on. At least Chance had been; he didn't know what Marley thought or felt. To hear him describe how the first revival had felt, and for it to be nearly identical to his own recollection of those days, was overwhelming. To have one person in the world understand what you'd been through, and for that person to be your brother? Well, it was everything. "Exactly the same."

"When I decided to disappear, I knew I couldn't take much with me. But I wanted something to remember everyone. So I took the ring."

"Where was it?"

"In my room at the house. This little coin tray on my chest of drawers. You know the one I mean?"

Chance did. Until the fire, it had been part of his family-history museum at the house on Blue Jay Way.

"The ring was just in there," Marley continued. "Nothing special about it. Where'd you get yours?"

"The police. They dragged their heels forever, but eventually they returned your things. It was among your personal effects."

"So I was wearing your ring when I died? Then what's this?" Marley asked, lifting up the ring on the chain. "I don't understand."

"Neither do I. What—"

Out of nowhere, Marley took off running like he'd remembered he'd left the gas on. It was so unexpected that Marley had disappeared around the side of the bus before Chance realized where his brother was headed. He sprinted after him, yelling for Marley to stop. Rounding the bus, he saw Marley dragging Paul Lin by the heels toward the freshly dug grave. Lin's head bumped sickeningly along the uneven ground.

"Marley!" Chance yelled, but his brother, almost to the edge of the hole, paid no attention. He was locked in a furious argument with Paul Lin. No matter that Lin was in no shape to respond: Marley looked more than happy to carry both sides of the conversation, how he could tell Lin was faking and that Marley was going to bury him alive unless he started talking.

Marley leapt down into the hole, intent on dragging Lin in after him. Chance grabbed Lin under the arms and pulled him back from the edge. Determined, Marley braced his leg against the side of the hole and heaved with all his might like he was trying to land a marlin. Both Lin and Chance slid back toward the hole. Chance pleaded with him, but Marley was in a world of his own, teeth clenched in a rictus of determination, tears pouring down his face. Chance knew Marley was profoundly damaged, but it wasn't until he saw the anguish and heartbreak in his eyes that Chance fully understood the cruel depth of the injury. Was this what people saw when they looked at him?

With a cry, Marley let go of Lin and pointed an accusatory finger at Chance. "He killed us."

"We're still here. We're still alive."

"You call this alive?" Marley asked, echoing Chance's own words to their father. "You call this living?"

Marley slumped down at the bottom of the grave and let out a wretched sob. Chance jumped in and threw his arms around him. He expected Marley to push him away, but instead his brother crawled into his embrace like a child frightened by a violent storm. The two brothers clung to each other a long time. Chance put his head back, looked up at the rectangle of blue sky overhead, and lied to his brother that everything would be alright.

Eventually Marley calmed down and pushed himself away. "So you and Maggie?" The words weren't an accusation, but it didn't need to be.

"Yeah," Chance admitted. There was no point in denying it. Marley had been down in the hole for the entire conversation with Anton Brätt. "Not at first, but yeah. Eventually."

"That makes sense, I guess."

"Why?"

"Because you were always in love with her. Can't really blame you for that. Everyone was."

"I still should have told you."

"Why? It's not like I ever asked about her. Anyway, I'm kind of relieved."

"Relieved?"

"You have absolutely zero game. I just assumed you were some lonely incel."

"Look who's talking," Chance said.

"Hey, I'm not lonely."

Chance chuckled, even though it felt like an opportunity was slipping through their fingers. It was a day of miracles: he finally knew the names of his kidnappers, and Marley Harker had made a joke to avoid an awkward conversation. Just two regular-type brothers talking trash at the bottom of a freshly dug grave. Nothing to see here.

"Anyway, it was all a lie," Chance said. "She was part of it. All this time."

"I don't believe that."

"She admitted it, Marley."

"I don't care. No. It's Maggie we're talking about. There's no way. They had to be pressuring her. Something."

Chance put his hands up in surrender. He'd heard the confession from her own lips and still didn't want to believe it. There was no good reason to try and persuade his brother if he couldn't accept the truth.

"Marley, I have to go."

Anton had given him only forty-eight hours, so as much as he wanted to stay here and keep talking to his brother, the clock was ticking. Then there was the LAPD. According to Wolinski, the charges against him would be reinstated anytime now. He couldn't find the truth from a jail cell.

"Let me get my things. I'll go with you," Marley said, but Chance's expression must have given away more than he'd meant. Marley slumped back down. "I can't go with you, can I?"

"You think that's a good idea?" Chance said as gently as he could.

"I've been out here too long, haven't I?" Marley said. "I'm sorry."

"For what?"

"For being such a fuckup. You shouldn't have to do this alone. I'm your big brother."

Chance took Marley by the hand. "I'll find out what happened to us. I promise."

"Chance?" Marley said. "Why do they want to talk to me so bad?"

It was a question that Chance had been circling ever since Anton had set out the terms of their deal. "It must have something to do with Dad and the night of the exchange."

"But I don't have memories of any of that. What could I tell them?"

Chance didn't know that any more than he knew why there were two rings, but he meant to find out. Maybe it was nothing . . . a prank, an oversight. Hell, Marley had two and a half months of lag before the kidnapping. Maybe he'd lost the original ring and had a duplicate made, but Chance had a feeling there was more to the mystery.

"Promise me something?" Marley asked.

"I promise," Chance said automatically without waiting to hear what he was promising.

"No matter what, you come back and tell me the truth. No matter what it is."

"I will."

"I have to know," Marley said.

Chance understood that. Nothing else mattered anymore.

"What about him?" Marley asked.

Chance glanced up at Paul Lin, who lay by the edge of the hole. "Help me put him in the back of the truck," he said finally.

"You're taking him?" The disappointment in Marley's voice let Chance know that this was the right call. If he left him with his brother, Lin would end up at the bottom of the grave before Chance had made it back to Niland.

To his surprise, that wasn't something he found he could live with.

CHAPTER TWENTY-FOUR

Normally, Chance looked forward to the drive back to Los Angeles. He imagined it was how the astronauts must have felt on those old Apollo missions when returning from the moon. Visiting Marley in his alien, inhospitable world always put his life in perspective. It made him feel weightless, and as he hurtled toward home in his primitive spaceship, he could almost see how all the broken pieces of his life might fit back together. It didn't feel that way this morning, even though he knew so much more than he had just a day ago. The last twenty-four hours had taken the largest, most dependable pieces of his world and smashed them into indecipherable fragments.

Maggie remained first among those fragments. She had already admitted her involvement in the kidnapping, but it was obvious she wasn't telling him everything. She almost seemed like she was trying to protect him. But from what? He knew the answer lay with his father, and the two identical rings. Chance wished the old truck had a working auto-drive so he could sit back and think things through. First, though, he had to decide what to do about Paul Lin, who was lying unconscious in the bed of the pickup. They'd tied a tarp down over him to hide him from prying eyes, but he could feel Lin back there, waiting for Chance to pass sentence. It was on him to decide whether the man lived or died.

The simplest solution would be to leave Lin somewhere in the desert and let nature take its course. That wouldn't quite meet the definition of murder, would it? But if he was going to let the man die, then why hadn't he just left him with Marley? Turned out revenge was much easier to contemplate in the abstract. He'd daydreamed of killing a thousand faceless kidnappers. Now that he knew their names, though, they had become real people. Maggie Soto was one of those people. Try as he might, the only feeling he could conjure where she was concerned was a profound sadness at the scope of her betrayal. But he didn't want to kill her—her or anyone else.

No, that wasn't entirely true. He still might make one exception.

At Indio, he pulled off and found the hospital. He left the engine running and fireman-carried Lin inside. The nurse behind the plexiglass divider at the reception desk was locked in a heated argument with a woman who'd been waiting for five hours and wanted to talk to a supervisor. Chance wished her luck with that and deposited Lin in a seat directly across from reception. If and when the fight ended, the nurse would hopefully notice Lin and do something about his condition. Hanging around to ensure this happened would lead to questions that he couldn't afford to answer at the moment. The drop-off would have to be the extent of Chance's good deed. He would keep Lin's LFD, though. If the man did regain consciousness, Chance didn't want him warning Anton Brätt.

Back in the pickup, Chance put a dozen miles between himself and the hospital before pulling over to the side of the road. He sat there a long time studying the rings in the palm of his hand. One of them had no business existing, but he'd be damned if he could tell them apart.

He powered on his LFD to make the call, but the moment it reconnected to the network, a tidal wave of information began to roll in. A lot had happened in his absence, most of it grim. The curfew hadn't been much of a deterrent. Protesters had clashed with police again last night, with more unrest anticipated. Video of the Los Angeles skyline showed a city on fire. Arson, looting, six deaths, dozens missing, and over a thousand arrests. Citywide damage was already predicted to dwarf the '92 and '29 riots, and the end was nowhere in sight.

The mayor had declared a state of emergency, and the governor had responded by deploying the National Guard. To assist, she said, with "peacekeeping operations," an unfortunate choice of words that protesters seized on as overtly militaristic. Whatever words you chose, however, peace had not been achieved. Late yesterday afternoon, a massive rally at the Federal Building in Westwood had drawn an estimated crowd of over two hundred thousand.

Franklin Butler, the head of the Children of Adam and never one to miss the opportunity to grandstand, had delivered a fire-and-brimstone speech accusing the state of California of once again siding with the wealthy over the hardworking people of California: "If they will not listen to our words, then it is our duty to make a sound so terrible that even these jaded billionaires in their gated mansions cannot ignore us."

Many in the media had been quick to condemn his words as an incitement to yet more violence, but others cast him as a true patriot, speaking truth to power. Butler, for his part, was unrepentant and dared the police to arrest him. Rumors were circulating that musician and clone activist Con D'Arcy was organizing a concert amid calls for calm. Butler, who had been sparring in the media with D'Arcy for the past two years, was already threatening to disrupt it.

What was strange was that Chance was barely mentioned. Then again, perhaps it made perfect sense. This had never really been about the murder of Lee Conway. The protests were less about what Chance had done and more about what he was and represented. He was a symbol. He'd served his purpose, and having ignited this inferno, the world largely seemed to have forgotten about the match.

His messages were the usual assortment of nothing, with a thick frosting of crazies who'd tracked down his number to leave threats and dire warnings. The only real surprise was the message from his mother.

She'd called from LAX to announce she was back in California. News of his predicament had finally penetrated her bubble, and she'd flown home to support him. He should have found it moving. It was the type of gesture he longed for from his parents, but time and experience had made him a cynic where they were concerned. Was she really here for him, or did she have business in town, now that one of her houses had burned to the ground?

His LFD rang with a call from Detective Wolinski. Maybe Los Angeles hadn't entirely forgotten about him after all. Looked like it was her fourth call this morning, and she'd left two messages. Against his better judgment, he answered.

Wolinski began talking as though they were already midconversation. "The DA has refiled the charges against you. Where are you right now?"

"Running an errand. I'm not in LA at the moment."

"You left town?"

"What's it to you? Aren't you suspended?"

"I am, but I want to make you an offer. If you surrender to me, I'll bring you in myself."

That sounded more like he was doing her a favor. "Why would I do that?"

"Because the current thinking is to make the arrest as public and unpleasant as possible. Your perp walk will have more cameras than the Oscars."

"Why do you care? I thought you hated me."

"Because I do my job. My feelings about you aren't relevant. And because I like my police work like I like my coffee. No politics added."

He paused long enough for it to seem like he was considering her words. "I appreciate the offer, but I've died on camera four times. There isn't anything they can do to me I haven't done to myself. Oh, and I don't know if you care, but I found the rest of my kidnappers."

Wolinski took the news in stride. "I want to hear more. I really do. But right now I don't think anyone has time to worry about a five-year-old case. If you give me the names, I'll run it down when they let me come back to work."

Disappointing, but not exactly surprising. Anyway, he didn't have all the answers he wanted yet and wasn't ready to hand things off to the police. "How long do I have?"

"Let me bring you in."

"How long?" he asked again.

"I'd be thinking in terms of hours rather than days."

He thanked her and hung up the call before Wolinski could pitch him again on turning himself in to her. She called right back. He declined the call and set an instruction for his LFD to forward her calls straight to voice mail.

Wolinski wasn't the only one eager to have a word. There were also a half dozen calls from Mary. No messages, but after the last call she had texted him once: We had a deal. It wasn't a threat, not exactly, but it still gave him an unpleasant chill. He tried consoling himself that she was only a strange kid. It didn't help. She had him good and spooked for reasons he couldn't quite articulate. It didn't matter, though. She'd have to wait like everyone else until he had some answers from dear old Dad.

Their last meeting hadn't been pleasant, but he had a feeling it was only an overture to what was to come. He had let his emotions get the better of him; he couldn't afford to be outmaneuvered that way again. But keeping his composure would be only half the battle. If he hoped to get the truth this time around, then he would need to know the right questions to ask. He needed more information about these rings. Knowledge was power, right? Wasn't that how the cliché went? He knew one person who might be able to help arm him with just that.

CHAPTER
TWENTY-FIVE

Darsh did not seem overly thrilled to hear from him. The trademark bounce was notably absent from his voice, and he sounded very much like a man who'd answered the phone too quickly and was now stuck talking to a bill collector. Chance offered him a thousand dollars; Darsh tripled it. It was a relief that was all Darsh had done. There was enough in his account to cover it, but he couldn't afford much more of this.

"What's your address?" Chance asked, realizing he had no idea where Darsh lived. They'd never had that kind of relationship.

"Payment first."

Maybe they didn't have any kind of relationship at all. "Really?"

"Don't make this awkward."

Too late. But, out of options, Chance transferred the money and then waited in silence for it to appear in Darsh's account.

"Address?" Chance asked again.

"Are you alone? Anyone following you?"

Chance assured him it was safe, although spotting a tail wasn't exactly a part of his skill set. Reluctantly, Darsh gave him an address in Koreatown before hanging up.

When Chance arrived, the streets were mostly deserted. The neighborhood had a hushed *High Noon* vibe, as if everyone had hunkered down inside, waiting for the showdown. He parked across from Darsh's nondescript, low-rise apartment complex and hustled over to the front entrance. In the outer vestibule, he rang up to the apartment from an antiquated call box that might have been fifty years old. He waited impatiently for Darsh to answer, with the creeping suspicion that he'd been given a bad address. Finally, though, Darsh deigned to buzz him in.

"Thought you'd ghosted me," Chance said after he'd climbed the three flights of stairs to Darsh's front door.

Darsh grinned uneasily, as if the thought had never crossed his mind.

"You alright?"

"I was out taking pictures all last night. Shit is out of control out there. You shouldn't be here." Darsh looked nervously past him down the empty hallway. "You sure you weren't followed?"

"I'm sure." He wasn't.

"So what do you want?"

Chance put the two identical rings in Darsh's hand. "What's different about these?"

"How the hell should I know?"

"Because your parents own a jewelry store. You worked there growing up."

"Yeah, so? I was a sales assistant, not a gemologist."

"Well, these rings don't have gems. I just figured you'd know how to tell. Like, is one older than the other?"

"What do you want me to do? Carbon-date them? They're rings, not dinosaur bones."

"Please," Chance said. "I need this. I'm begging here."

Darsh relented and held the rings up for a closer look. "Why is this one on a chain?"

"So I can tell them apart," Chance said, not mentioning it had recently hung around his brother's neck.

"I'll have to take it off," Darsh said as he did so.

"Just don't mix them up."

Darsh flashed him an irritated look at the mere suggestion. "And what makes you think there's anything different about them?"

"Because there are two of them," Chance said. "And there shouldn't be." He expected that to invite more questions, but Darsh seemed satisfied and opened the door just wide enough for Chance to slip inside.

Darsh's apartment was less a home than a series of work spaces dedicated to his varying interests, hobbies, and side hustles. It would be easy to look around and assume Darsh was a slob, but everything had its place—cluttered wasn't the same as messy. One area was piled high with film equipment, another with camera gear that he used as a freelance paparazzo. Next to a desk with schoolwork laid out neatly were rows of carefully tended plants under grow lights. Darsh beelined for a broad worktable and flicked on an adjustable lamp clamped to the edge of it. Perched on a stool, he studied each ring under the light, lips pursed in concentration.

"They look the same," Darsh said.

"I know. That's why I'm here."

"Hmm," Darsh said to himself, slipping on a magnifying visor and reaching for a digital scale. "Give me a few minutes."

There was a small couch, but Chance didn't have a good track record staying awake on furniture lately. He put his back against an uncomfortable-looking wall and slid down to the floor. He checked Paul's LFD for what felt like the hundredth time, but there were still no missed calls. That felt like a lucky break, but he knew he shouldn't count on it to last. With little more than twenty-four hours to go, Anton would be wanting an update soon.

A few minutes turned out to be half an hour. Darsh pulled off the visor, set down his tools, and stared up at the ceiling.

Chance couldn't take the suspense. "Well? Are they the same?"

"Short answer? No. The one on the chain is ten millimeters wide and weighs fifteen grams," Darsh said. "The other one is 10.13 millimeters wide and weighs thirteen grams."

"So it's bigger but weighs less? How is that possible?"

"Lots of reasons. Might not be the same metals, for starters. Or . . . ," Darsh said, trailing off.

"Or what?"

"Let me check something," Darsh said, slipping his LFD back behind his ear before typing commands against his chest. He frowned. "Are you carrying any air-charging electronics?"

"Just an LFD. Why?"

"Because the firewall for my electricity logs all connectable devices in the vicinity. I see your LFD trying to connect, but another device also tried to connect when you arrived. The weird part was it only tried once."

"So?" Chance said, feeling like a freshman asking a question he would have known the answer to if he'd only done the reading.

"Usually devices keep pinging away, hoping for access, but not this one. When it got blocked by the firewall, it went dormant and didn't try again. Sneaky sneaky."

"You think it's one of the rings."

"There's one way to find out," Darsh said. "I'm granting it access now."

Nothing visible happened, but Darsh was nodding encouragingly at whatever he saw on his screen. "That was fast. All charged. Whatever it is must have a very small battery," Darsh said, studying the rings with renewed interest. "I have an idea."

They relocated to a desk that was barely visible beneath all the computer parts. Darsh flipped on a massive tower desktop computer. The case looked ancient and had been set to one side, revealing a motherboard that had been heavily modified and upgraded. Darsh placed the two rings on a scanner and typed away at the keyboard with the enthusiasm of someone who loved solving a riddle. After punching the "Enter" key, he sat back in satisfaction as information spilled down the gigantic monitor.

"It's a parasitic flash drive," Darsh said. "Designed for hyperfast data transfer. Once it establishes a secure umbilical with its target, it can copy and delete a gigabyte of data every two seconds."

"How does it do that?"

"Physical contact. One tap is usually enough. Never seen one built into a ring before. A little dated now, but it was state of the art in its day."

"Which one is it?" Chance had already lost track. He would have been terrible at three-card monte.

"Not the one from the chain," Darsh said, handing him one of the rings.

Chance stared at the one in his hand, the ring Marley had been wearing when he'd been kidnapped. Chance had been wearing it for five years, never suspecting it was anything but a ring.

"Is it large enough to hold fifty million in crypto?" Chance asked.

"Oh, easily. Why? You think that's what's on it?" Darsh asked with newfound interest.

"It's possible. Can you check?" Chance gave him back the ring, but took the other one and put it back on Marley's chain.

Darsh put it back on the scanner and frowned. "This thing is encrypted out the butt."

"Can you crack it?"

"Yeah, it's just a matter of time with the right gear."

"Which you have."

"Which I have. And like I said, this thing is a little past its prime. I'm happy to crack it open for you, for another five. Up front. Figure you're good for it, if there's fifty mil on this thing."

Chance didn't waste his breath arguing. He transferred the money from his rapidly diminishing bank account. If Darsh found an excuse to demand an additional two thousand, Chance would be down to the lint in his pockets.

Negotiations concluded, Darsh got down to work.

Chance sat back down on the floor and tried to reconcile what he'd learned with what he knew. He knew Marley had been shot at the exchange, but that seemed to be the only universally agreed-upon fact. His father insisted the kidnappers had been covering their tracks by killing Chance and then Marley—the brothers could hardly identify kidnappers they had no memories of. That had actually made a lot of sense. What didn't add up was his father's story that he'd given them the ransom. If they'd gotten their money, then why were they back, looking to talk to Marley and his father?

Because they hadn't.

The fifty million was on this parasitic flash drive made to look like Marley's graduation ring. That gave him the leverage to get Maggie back without involving Marley. What it didn't give him was an explanation for who'd made the ring, and why.

Chance called his father. They had a chicken-and-the-egg question to discuss—at gunpoint, if necessary. Chance was past the point of asking nicely. The call went straight to voice mail. That wasn't unusual in and of itself. Back in his Palingenesis days, Brett Harker had been surgically attached to his phone. But now in his new life as a man of leisure, his father took great pride in being disconnected from it all. But given everything that was happening, it felt purposeful and pointed. Chance called back and got dumped to voice mail again. This time he left a curt, defiant message for his father to call him.

"Done," Darsh called out.

"Already? That's it?" Chance was happy but somehow didn't feel like he'd gotten his money's worth. For five thousand dollars, breaking the encryption should have been a little harder.

"Physical possession is ninety-nine percent of the battle," Darsh said.

"How much is on it?" Chance climbed excitedly to his feet.

"Nothing. No money. Just documents."

Chance felt a huge sense of disappointment. He'd been so sure the ring would have the missing fifty million. But no. Just when he thought he had this thing figured out, he was back to square one. "Documents of what?"

"Beats me, man. Way above my pay grade. Whatever this is, it's insanely technical. And there're reams and reams, like tens of thousands of pages."

Chance leaned in over Darsh's shoulder to watch him flip slowly through the documents. "What the hell is all this?" Chance asked, mostly to himself.

"No clue. This would take me months to read, much less understand. But I could start digging through it if you wanted," Darsh suggested.

"Thanks, but I don't have another two grand."

"This I'll do for free," Darsh said, curiosity apparently getting the better of him.

"What's that?" Chance asked, pointing to a watermark on the screen.

Darsh stopped and enlarged the image. It was the Palingenesis logo, a modification of the Gemini Roman numeral II. Darsh scrolled through the next fifty pages. They all had the same watermark. Chance massaged his temples. Where was the fifty million? And why did his brother have a library of Palingenesis documents on his finger when he'd died? Chance was beginning to worry that all his assumptions were wrong.

"I've got to go," he said, taking both rings back, much to Darsh's evident disappointment. Darsh followed him as far as the door, trying to convince him to leave a copy of the documents for him to study. Chance thanked him and said he'd bring the ring back later, knowing even then that he never would. He didn't know why his father was ducking his calls, but he intended to find out, even if he had to drive up to the vineyard and shake the truth out of him.

"Thanks for your help," Chance said, and then held out his hand.

"No hard feelings?" Darsh asked, shaking it.

Chance shook his head. "I wish we'd been real friends."

"Me too."

A call came in as Chance got back to the pickup. He dared get his hopes up that it might be his father doing the right thing, but it was only a 703 number that his LFD didn't recognize. He sent the call to voice mail, but they hung up and called back. He had no idea where 703 was, only that it wasn't Southern California. A quick search revealed the numbers were a Virginia area code. That piqued his interest enough to answer.

"Chance Harker?" a woman asked when he answered. He couldn't quite place her accent, but she sounded like a high school friend who was Israeli.

"Every day. Who's this?"

"My name is Yael Lavi. I'm Con D'Arcy's assistant."

"Oh." It was a dumb thing to say but adequately summed up his surprise.

"She wonders if you're free to meet."

"Now?" It made him curious what they'd talked about backstage at the Troubadour that night. "I don't know if you've been following the news, but it's not a great time for me."

"She wouldn't ask if it wasn't urgent. Are you free?"

"I'm sorry. I really can't."

An icon appeared on his screen indicating that Yael wanted to send him a file. He accepted, curiosity getting the better of him. An old photograph opened: a woman and a girl, both very pale of complexion, posed on the front porch of a clapboard house. One was a teenager, while the second was perhaps ten years older. They looked enough alike to be sisters but not close ones. Although they stood side by side, the chasm separating them was plain. Neither sister smiled. The older of the two wore jeans and a casual shirt, hair in tight braided cables, arms folded impatiently across her chest. The other wore an ankle-length skirt that might have been stylish in the 1880s. Her fingers were interlocked primly in front of her as if in midprayer, but judging from her expression, Chance didn't think it was for peace on earth.

The younger sister looked oddly familiar. Chance zoomed in on her face and felt a chill in the hot Los Angeles sun. The hair was different; the clothes were very, very different; but there was no mistaking her. It was Mary. He couldn't explain why the picture looked so last century. Someone must have used filters to age it, although he couldn't guess as to why.

"Now are you free?" Yael asked.

"What is this picture?"

"Do you know where Cherokee Studios is?"

"Near Santa Monica Boulevard?" He knew the name of the historic recording studio, but that was all.

"Close. Corner of North Van Ness and Melrose. I can send a car."

"No, I've got a ride," he said. Checking his watch, he calculated how long it would take him to get to the vineyard and how much time that left Maggie. Every minute counted at this point, but he rationalized that the studio was more or less on his way. Something told him this was a stop he had to make.

CHAPTER TWENTY-SIX

The front entrance of Cherokee Studios was under siege by about twenty Children of Adam protesters, recognizable by their trademark black umbrellas and ghoulish chants. Maybe while they were in LA, they could spring for a songwriter to come up with something catchier than "No birth, no soul."

A woman emerged from the glass double doors of the studio flanked by two men in off-the-rack suits from wherever it was bodyguards shopped. Neither was the biggest man Chance had ever seen, but both gave off the unmistakable calm of highly competent men whom it would be wise to listen to the first time. The protesters did exactly that when the bodyguards waded into the crowd, parting obediently while simultaneously hectoring the men with threats and taunts. Each taking a shoulder, the bodyguards shepherded Chance inside as the protesters rushed forward and hammered at the doors with their palms.

Inside, Yael formally introduced herself with professional if not genuine warmth. In LA, "assistant" generally meant ambitious twenty-something looking to trade up at the earliest opportunity. Yael looked to be twice that old, with a battering-ram chin, a flatline frown permanently stitched to her face, and an evident distaste for small talk. She announced that the bodyguards would search him now. When he didn't jump for joy at the prospect, she identified the bodyguards as Dominic and Marcus. As if being on a first-name basis made being frisked any friendlier.

To hurry things along, Chance put his hands out and let them pat him down. Satisfied he wasn't a threat, they gave Yael a nod and fell in behind as she led Chance back to the studio. They went down a long hallway lined with photographs of legendary musicians dating back seventy years: Michael Jackson, Frank Sinatra, Barbra Streisand, Van Halen, Guns N' Roses, Tom Petty. It went on and on, a mausoleum of American music. His dad would have loved this place.

Yael paused when they reached the door to the control room. "Con receives constant death threats, so we have to be careful. Doubly so now."

Chance bristled. "Doubly so now" sounded accusatory, and his instincts for starting shit kicked into gear. He was sorry for all the commotion but wasn't quite ready to take personal responsibility for the decline of Western civilization. But then he caught himself, and he bit his tongue in two places. What exactly was that going to accomplish? For once, maybe he should try not pissing everyone off the moment he walked into a place. See how that worked out for him.

"I'm sorry for the precautions, but I'll also need your LFD," Yael said. "I'll return it afterward."

"No," he said with a finality that surprised him. He was the guest here, and he wasn't in the mood.

"I beg your pardon?" Yael said.

Dominic and Marcus seemed to glide toward him, twin icebergs that had spotted a wayward cruise liner. Yael stopped them with one raised finger. An impressive trick.

"She asked to see me," Chance said. "So I'm here. I even let you search me. That's all fine. But you're not taking my stuff. And if that's a problem, I can go."

"Would you compromise and turn it off?"

That was more diplomatic than he'd expected. Con D'Arcy must really want to talk to him. In the spirit of cooperation, he agreed and held out his LFD so Yael could see it power down. She thanked him as if he'd done her a personal favor (another nice trick) before opening the door to the control room. Inside, two sound engineers were working intently at the massive console making constant, minute adjustments to the mix. Through the glass that separated the control room from the live room, Chance saw a woman playing at a grand piano. A drummer, guitarist, and bassist sat motionless and ready. He couldn't see Con D'Arcy, but her voice, gravelly and raw, filled the studio, singing about being out of time, out of place.

Yael guided Chance to a leather couch against the back wall and pressed a finger to her lips. Chance nodded and sat on the arm to listen. The song, which had begun almost ethereally, pivoted hard, the rest of the band then picking up the thread and driving it forward. It was the same melody, but what had begun sad and wistful turned inexplicably hopeful and longing. It felt like a song he'd heard a million times, an old favorite familiar down to his DNA, and yet entirely new and unexpected and therefore thrilling. And Maggie hadn't been lying—her voice was magic.

It wasn't as if he had never heard any of Con D'Arcy's music. He'd have to have been living under a soundproof rock for the last twelve months to miss it entirely. She'd been everywhere, to the point of oversaturation. That was why he hadn't given her a chance. She just came off as so damned passionate about everything, her earnestness ringing false to him, although that probably said more about him than her. Wasn't it the nature of a cynic to assume everyone around them must be one too? And maybe he didn't like that everyone expected him to be a huge Con D'Arcy fan just because they were both clones.

By the time the song ended, he was a convert.

The engineers and musicians began discussing tweaks for the next take. Con emerged from an isolation booth out in the live room. She was smaller than Chance thought she'd be. Frail. She took a few steps and sank into a waiting wheelchair. Chance had read that she was in poor health, but they'd done one hell of a job concealing how serious it really was. There'd never been any mention of a wheelchair, and in all the concert footage he'd seen of her, she'd been animated and vibrant. Now he wondered how she'd made it through an entire tour. How could she sing like this?

Yael brought her a bottle of water, which Con took gratefully. Even pushed to exhaustion, she was beautiful. From a profile piece, Chance knew that she was originally from Texas and that her mother was white and her father was biracial. Her hair fell in a striking scarlet wave across one side of her face, and her left arm was a swirling sleeve of tattoos. Yael leaned down to whisper in her ear. Con looked over her shoulder, spotted Chance, and beckoned him over.

"Let's take five, everyone. May I have the room?" Con asked.

The musicians murmured agreement, set their instruments carefully aside, and filed out for a well-earned break.

Only the pianist, a white woman in her twenties, lingered behind. She squatted down beside Con and put a concerned hand on her arm. "How are you feeling?"

"Like a rock star," Con said with a weak laugh.

"I'm serious. You promised you'd take a break after the tour. Does this seem like a break to you?"

"'I'll sleep when I'm dead,'" Con sang.

"And how did that work out for Warren Zevon?"

Con looked the woman in the eyes for the first time, turning serious. "Same as it works out for all of us. But before the cancer killed him, he finished *The Wind*. A masterpiece. You understand what I'm saying?"

The woman nodded reluctantly.

"Stephie, I'm fine. I swear," Con said, taking her hand.

"You're not fine. It's time to go home. You've done enough," Stephie said, catching Chance's eye.

"Just let me talk to him, okay?"

Exasperated, Stephie put up her hands as if surrendering to a relentless sheriff. "Alright, I'm going to take the band out and get them fed and watered. But we're talking about this when I get back."

"Deal."

"I'm serious."

"And I said deal," Con replied.

Stephie left the studio without looking back before closing the door behind her. When they were alone, Con told Chance to pull up a chair. "Sorry about that. Stephie can be a little overprotective. She's not wrong, though. Everyone needs a best friend slash den mother slash voice of reason."

He couldn't have agreed more. "How long have you known her?"

"Stephie? Since forever. We were in a band in college."

"Awaken the Ghosts?" He remembered the name from the same profile. Their band had been in a terrible car accident late at night after a show while leaving Washington, DC. Three of them had been killed. Or maybe two. The third had been in a coma or something. It had all sounded pretty grim.

"That's the one," Con said. "I promised her we'd go back to Charlottesville right after the tour. But then this studio became available, and I always dreamed about recording here."

"What's so special about it?"

"David Bowie recorded *Station to Station* here," she said, transforming into a giddy fan, excited at the mere mention of the name. "Legend goes he hated LA and fled to Berlin after the album was finished. Said the city should be wiped off the face of the earth."

"Might be getting his wish."

She laughed wearily. "Ain't that the truth. Not a safe place to be for the likes of us right now, but *Station to Station* was a masterpiece. 'TVC 15'? 'Stay'? 'Wild Is the Wind'? Come on, how could I pass up the opportunity?"

Chance didn't know any of those songs but nodded along as if he did, irritated by how much he already liked her and by his need to impress. "So what you're saying is you're a little into Bowie?"

"Little bit," she said, smiling for the first time. He guessed it wasn't something that came naturally or easily to her, but it was a warm, infectious grin that made him wish she had more reason to use it. "Wasn't easy growing up where I did, feeling like an outcast. Let's just say Bowie was pretty formative."

"I liked your song, by the way. It's beautiful."

She probably heard compliments like that all the time but still looked genuinely touched. "Thank you. Work in progress. It'll get there." Her right hand began to spasm, and she clasped it with the other, holding it against her chest.

"Are you okay?" he asked, looking around for Yael.

"I'm dying," she answered matter-of-factly.

"You're what?" he said, feeling like he'd walked through a door that should have been locked.

"Dying. But not this minute or anything. I'm fine. You don't need to get anyone."

"But you have another clone, right?"

"I can't," she said, waving her fingers at the side of her own head. "Everything is screwed up in here. Too much lag from the last time. Eighteen glorious months' worth. I'm the all-time world champ."

"How's that possible?" All the media covering Con D'Arcy was either noticeably vague or outright contradictory on the subject of her clone. "What about Palingenesis's three-month lockout? I thought downloads beyond three months were impossible and dangerous."

"Did I mention the part about me dying?" she said, seeming to gauge how much she wanted to say before settling for frustratingly vague. "This clone was activated despite the lockout protocols, so my consciousness never properly meshed with my body. Which is now in the painful process of rejecting it. Medication manages it to a point, slows the inevitable, but it's a when, not an if. Funny, you know, I grew up pretty dirt poor. Now with my aunt's inheritance, I can afford the best doctors on the planet, but all they can do is prop me up and make me comfortable." She rolled up the ankles of her loose-fitting sweatpants. Underneath, her legs were sheathed in a latticework exoskeleton. She slipped her fingers in between the braces and massaged her skin. "My legs stopped working about a year ago. This thing has been a lifesaver. Lets me get around on my own. But man, after a concert? I feel like I've been cooked on a waffle iron."

Chance said he was sorry. It wasn't much, but it was the sort of thing he wished someone would have said to him more often. "I had no idea."

"No one does, really, except for Stephie and her family. Yael, obviously. Beyond that it's not something I broadcast."

"So why tell me?"

"You must have a trustworthy face or something, Chance Harker, because I told you the last time we talked too," she said, and then smiled for the second time. "Trust me, I know how unsettling this is for you. That feeling that someone knows you, but you don't remember them. You catch yourself questioning whether you can really be you."

He found himself nodding in agreement. It felt good, really good, to be acknowledged by someone who knew what being a clone was like from personal experience. He didn't know any clones in real life besides his brother, and it wasn't a topic open for discussion between them. "Can I ask what we talked about that night at the Troubadour?"

"The same thing we're going to talk about now. This." She handed him a worn and creased photograph. The two mismatched sisters stared out somberly from the porch. He could feel Con watching him.

"So I've seen this picture before?" he asked.

Con nodded. "I asked if you'd ever seen either of them. You said no. I believed you. I warned you how dangerous they were and to let me know if you did. You found that part funny."

That might have been true then, but he didn't think so now. "Then what happened?"

"Then you went to meet a man who'd promised to tell you about your kidnapping."

"Lee Conway," Chance said, inserting another piece into his reconstruction of that night.

"You didn't say, but that's what I assume. And whatever he told you was enough for you to put a gun to your head. I hadn't counted on that. But it's the reason we're having this conversation a second time. And it's why I need to ask again if you've seen either of these girls. Although we both know your answer is different this time."

"Why do you say that?" Chance asked.

"Because you weren't going to come until Yael showed you the picture. My guess is you were approached. So, which one was it? Which one do you know?"

"Her," he said, tapping his finger on the teenage girl. "Who is she?"

"What did she want?" Con asked, dodging his question.

"A conversation with my kidnappers, if I found them."

"Which you have now, I'm guessing. Has she talked to them?"

"Not yet."

"Thank God," Con said. "I can't tell you how important it is that she doesn't."

"Who is she?" Chance asked again. He had an armful of questions, but this seemed like a good place to start.

Con sat forward in the wheelchair and took the picture, looking at it soberly. "It's a picture of my mother. The other woman is my aunt, Abigail Stickling."

Chance frowned and looked at the picture again. "When was this taken?"

"2011."

"That's thirty years. So you mean she looks like your mom? The spitting image or something like that? Do you have a little sister?"

"I'm an only child," she answered a little too cryptically for his liking. But before he could point that out to her, Yael chose that moment to return, bursting through the door to the studio with a pistol in her hand. The soundproofing had done its job, because the unmistakable sounds of rage and fury arrived with her. A steady concussive pounding echoed through the studio.

"What the hell is that?" Con said.

"Protesters. They're trying to force their way inside," Yael said.

"How many?"

"Maybe a hundred. More than enough. They've been arriving steadily ever since Chance got here. Dom and Marcus are reinforcing the entrance, but it won't hold."

"Did you call the police?" Con said.

"911 is overwhelmed and isn't answering, so don't expect the cavalry. We need to think about getting you out of here," Yael said, turning to Chance. "Where's your vehicle?"

"Around the corner from the studio."

"Good. The emergency exit opens on the back side of the building. We'll keep the protesters focused on the front entrance until you're gone."

The sound of shattering glass from the direction of the lobby froze them all momentarily in place. They listened to the chaos of gunshots and screams that followed: a bloodthirsty roar and a noise like medieval hand-to-hand combat. Yael started back at a run toward the lobby, barking at Chance to get Con out of there.

"Go back to the hotel. We'll meet you there," she ordered as she disappeared from view.

Con protested furiously that she wouldn't leave Yael behind and reached to power on her exoskeleton. Chance pulled her hand away, and she snapped around to stare razor blades at him.

"Get your hands off me."

"Stop. Think. We'll only be in her way. She can handle herself." He'd known Yael for all of five minutes and saw that to be true.

Con relented and slumped back in the wheelchair, which Chance was already wheeling toward the emergency exit. It led to a service corridor and finally out to a street that thankfully looked mostly deserted.

It took a second to orient himself, but then he spotted the pickup parked at the end of the block. He jogged them down the sidewalk, and they made it without incident. Chance thought that was pretty impressive for two of the most despised clones in the country during the middle of an anti-clone protest. Con was still too livid with him for abandoning Yael to appreciate the miracle of their escape, but she grudgingly activated her exoskeleton and helped him lift the wheelchair up onto the tailgate. It was about then that their luck, however short lived, decided to take a smoke break. He heard someone yell his name, and not in a good-to-see-you kind of way.

They scrambled into the pickup truck, and Chance floored it. They were fifteen blocks away before he took his foot off the accelerator. At a red light, they stopped and looked around to see if they'd been followed. A woman wearing a black cocktail dress and Joan Didion sunglasses strolled past walking her dog, an old dachshund with its mind set on sniffing each and every lamppost, street sign, and fire hydrant. Neither dog nor owner seemed in any kind of hurry, nor did they acknowledge the wail of sirens that had become the city's ambient soundtrack.

"Now that's Los Angeles," Con said as if she'd lived here her entire life.

Chance couldn't argue with her there.

CHAPTER TWENTY-SEVEN

Con was staying at the Hollywood Roosevelt. Built in the early years of the previous century, it was one of those Los Angeles relics that still drew tourists looking to soak up the nostalgia of old Hollywood. In its 120-year history, the hotel had survived earthquakes, fires, and some said the ghost of Marilyn Monroe, who'd lived at the hotel for two years early in her career. Turned out Con D'Arcy was a bit of a tourist. Ordinarily, he found that annoying, but with her it was inexplicably charming.

As they pulled up out front, his LFD announced an incoming call. A blast from his recent past, Chelsea Klos. As resignations went, his longtime manager's had been relatively unambiguous. So for her to pick up the phone and call him, someone must have offered her seven figures for his life story. Maybe it was worth more, now that he was responsible for reducing Los Angeles to rubble. Curious, he took a breath and tamped down on his cynicism. No reason to set the bridge she might be building on fire while she was still on it.

"Chance?" she said when he picked up.

Who else would it be? "Yeah," he said instead with Herculean effort, managing to feel proud of himself for it.

"Your father needs to talk to you."

Setting aside for a moment that Chelsea had quit, he didn't know what to make of that. His dad had always been a fairly straightforward sort of man. If he had something to say, he said it to your face. Also, his father loathed Chelsea Klos on general principle for encouraging Chance's quote-unquote unsavory behavior.

"Why isn't he telling me this?"

"I don't know. He said it wasn't safe for him to call you directly."

Chance felt himself frown. "Where's my father, Chelsea?"

"I don't know that either. He just asked me to give you a message," she said. "Do you remember watching fireworks the first time? He said he'll be there waiting."

Chance knew immediately where she meant.

"I'll meet him," he said, wanting to say more, wanting to apologize but unable to find the words.

Before he could summon them, Chelsea said, "Please let him know I don't work for you anymore. I'll be changing this number." The line went dead.

Con had been watching him intently this whole time. She put a hand on his arm. "Can I come with you?"

"To meet my father? Why?"

"I really need to talk to him."

If it was that important, then this seemed an opportune time to press Con for some answers. "You do? Okay, sure. Who's the girl in the photograph? Because she sure as hell isn't your mother."

Con winced at the question. "It's complicated. The less you know, the safer you'll be."

"Oh, come on. That's so patronizing," he said.

"Maybe, but it's true."

"Tell me what's going on."

She was shaking her head rapidly from side to side. "It's just not a good idea."

Chance snapped. He'd about hit his limit of people not giving him straight answers. Apparently the entire world had gotten together and pledged to dance around any question he might ask. If he stopped at a deli and ordered a sandwich, he wouldn't be surprised if the guy behind the counter was noncommittal on the existence of bread.

"Then get out of my truck," he told her.

This wasn't technically his truck, but it sounded more authoritative that way. Or not, because Con didn't move.

"Fine," he said, and then opened his own door, meaning to go around and escort her to the curb.

"Wait," Con said.

He paused, door half-open. They sat there like that until he started to wonder if she'd even been talking to him.

"Anytime now," he nudged her. "What's the story with the picture?"

Con nodded to let him know she was thinking. "It's an old family photograph of my mother and my aunt. It was taken the summer after Abigail finished her MD/PhD program at Harvard. There aren't very many. They were sisters, but they had nothing in common except blood. It was one of the last times she came home."

"So who's Mary? Why does she look exactly like your mom? Because she looks spectacular for a woman in her fifties."

Con took a deep breath as if preparing to dive deep into the ocean. "It's Abigail Stickling."

Chance frowned and reached across her to open the passenger door. "Get out."

"Wait. Just wait," she pleaded.

"Abigail Stickling is dead."

Con began nodding at the same time as he was shaking his head. "She died. She's not dead."

"Stop it," Chance said. "Stop playing me. Abigail Stickling died. She jumped off the roof of a hotel on Christmas Day." When that didn't seem to sway Con, he felt compelled to state the obvious. "Your aunt couldn't have a clone. She had Wilson's disease."

She stared at him patiently, as if he were a small child trying to work out a simple algebra problem on his own. He understood what she was driving at, but it was impossible. Wasn't it?

"What? You're saying Abigail Stickling cloned herself into the body of her seventeen-year-old sister. Your mother. Is that the fairy tale you're telling me?" He was insulted that she thought he would believe such an absurd story.

Con sighed. "My best guess is she thought it would help her slip back into the country undetected. But I was ready for that move. Two days after Imani Highsmith's article was published, my aunt flew into Seattle from Malaysia."

"Wait, wait, wait," Chance said. "*Wait*. No. That's not what I meant. A person's consciousness can only be cloned into their own body. And the body has to be the same age as the consciousness." Those were the rules. It was gospel. Abigail Stickling had driven herself crazy trying to overcome that barrier. That failure had ultimately led to her suicide on Christmas night four years ago. She'd leapt off the roof of a hotel in DC in front of a hundred people. Everyone knew the story.

"My aunt is a very clever woman," Con said.

"You're saying she solved it? Then why did she kill herself? Why isn't Palingenesis selling it? You know how much eighty-year-olds in this town would give to be sixteen again?"

"Anything," Con said. "They'd give anything. But my aunt didn't feel the urge to share it with them. That was Vernon's dream, not hers. She hates the commercialization of her work and doesn't trust it being a lifestyle perk for the one percent. The potential for abuse is too great, in her opinion."

"Case in point," he said, tapping his own chest.

"Case in point," she agreed. "And if Vernon found out and got his hands on it, her breakthrough would mean—"

"Immortality," Chance finished as the implications dawned on him. "It would mean immortality."

"But only for the obscenely wealthy."

"'Meet the new gods,'" Chance said, quoting Imani Highsmith's article.

Con nodded gravely in agreement. "That's why she made a spectacle of killing herself. She meant to disappear."

"So why didn't she?" he asked. "Why isn't she off forming her own dystopian paradise? What's she doing in LA?"

"Because she did all her research at the Palingenesis labs in Washington, DC. She was able to reconstruct some of her work on the outside, but only partially. Her version of the technology is incomplete, flawed. In time, my mother's body will reject Abigail's consciousness and will die. The problem was that stealing her research without raising suspicion was virtually impossible. She tried two years ago and failed."

"How?" he asked.

"She hid it in my upload. Then she had my original killed so my clone would waltz unsuspectingly out the front door with her immortality research stashed in my head. Didn't go exactly as planned. That's the real reason I'm dying, actually. Apparently you can't just jam terabytes of research into someone's consciousness without irreparably corrupting the host."

"I'm sorry," he said.

"Truth is, I'm not still in LA because of David Bowie. I'm here for her. She and I have unfinished business."

"So what does she want with me?" he asked, although he was starting to have suspicions. He glanced down at his ring to make sure it was still there. How much data had Darsh said was stored on it? Terabytes, he'd said. Tens of thousands of documents. Highly technical research data all bearing a Palingenesis watermark.

"I'm not one hundred percent sure. There isn't much that would tempt my aunt to stick her neck out. Coming home like this is a huge gamble. Whatever it is would have to be damn near irresistible. But one of the perks of my aunt's inheritance was that I became a significant shareholder in Palingenesis. It gave me access to internal records. That includes documents surrounding your father's exit from the company in '37."

"Dad resigned after the kidnapping. He retired."

"I believe that was just the story Palingenesis created to cover up the scandal of a senior executive caught stealing intellectual property. That's what I need to talk to your dad about."

Chance's hand curled into a fist around the ring so tight his knuckles burned. Con's story sounded absurdly far-fetched, but despite only knowing her for a few hours, he found himself believing her. It would explain why his mother's forensic accountant hadn't been able to find any trace of a $50 million ransom. The ransom had never existed. The whole twisted enterprise had never been about money; the kidnappers were after a far more valuable prize—the secret of human cloning. If Con was right, then his father had stolen it from Palingenesis and tried to trade it for Marley. But the handoff had all gone wrong somehow. Marley had ended up dead, and the Palingenesis IP had been stored on this ring. Chance couldn't see how, but his father had a lot to answer for.

"Why is this so important to you?" he asked. "No offense, but you're not exactly in any kind of shape to be messing with this."

"I'm willing to die to make sure what my aunt hid in my head never gets out into the world," Con replied. "I still am. If there's another copy out there somewhere, I need to know. This technology? I don't believe it's safe for anyone to have. Vernon already has his suspicions that Abigail betrayed him. I have to find my aunt before he finds out she's in Los Angeles."

"He's here," Chance said, remembering his conversation with the lawyer at Palingenesis.

"What do you mean he's here?" she said.

"He flew out to LA after Sy Berger got my charges dropped."

"Vernon Gaddis got on an airplane?" she said, eyes widening.

"That's what I was told."

"Damn," she said.

"What?"

"He already knows. Vernon knows about Abigail. The man is deathly afraid of flying. No way he gets on a plane for anything less," Con said, taking his hand and squeezing it tightly. "Please let me come with you. I know you don't know me, but I promise I won't interfere with what you have to do."

"You really think my father stole Palingenesis IP?" Chance asked the question rhetorically to himself, trying to wrap his head around it, but Con answered him.

"I don't know," she said. "But I'm going to find out. I'll play the martyr and take this secret to my grave, but I need to know that I'm not dying for nothing."

CHAPTER TWENTY-EIGHT

Chelsea had asked him whether he remembered seeing fireworks for the first time. How could he forget? He'd been terrified of them as a little kid. There was no good reason for it. He'd never actually seen fireworks at that age, but the idea of something exploding overhead freaked him out. Marley, like any responsible older brother, had teased him mercilessly for being a chicken. His favorite game was to sneak up behind Chance and scream "Boom!" mimicking a firework with his hands. By the time the Fourth of July rolled around again, Chance had been inconsolable, convinced the holiday signaled the end of days.

That morning his father had announced they were going out for a little father-son time, just the two of them. They'd driven to the zoo, Chance's favorite place in the world at that age. He loved penguins the best, and they'd spent an hour at the enclosure watching them play and swim. It had been magic. The Harker brothers were usually a package deal, and it was rare Chance spent time alone with his father. He'd been so happy that he'd forgotten all about the festive apocalypse scheduled that night. He hadn't even realized it was getting late until the zoo announced over the intercom that it was closing.

They went for tacos. Chance still ate his the way his father had taught him that day. Then, instead of going home, his dad had brought them to the house in the Bird Streets, which had been vacant at the time. They'd watched the fireworks together out back by the pool, with Chance sitting on his father's lap. Turned out, he loved fireworks, and to this day couldn't remember what he'd been so afraid of. It was still one of his best days.

The pickup made a slow pass of the house on Blue Jay Way. It was little more than a burned-out shell now. A halo of yellow caution tape stretched around the perimeter to warn off the curious. Chance thought he'd feel sadder, but it had only ever been a house, never a home. A place to mark the passing of time as he hid away from the world. Even if it hadn't burned down, he wasn't sure he would want to live there anymore. That time in his life was over, but it looked like the house had one final part to play. He didn't see any cars on the street that didn't belong there, but he parked a few blocks away to be safe. There was no reason to advertise their presence.

After killing the engine, he checked Paul Lin's LFD again. There was still nothing from Anton Brätt, which had been encouraging at first but was beginning to make Chance nervous. Had he made a huge mistake in taking Lin to a hospital? What if he'd regained consciousness and somehow alerted his accomplices? Why else would Anton go radio silent on him? Chance didn't like to think about what they might do to Maggie then. He needed to make this quick. There was no time for his dad's usual stall tactics.

Con seemed to pick up on his nervousness. "Are you okay to do this?"

"Were you ever able to let it go? All your lag?"

She snorted at the question. "Only if you call nearly getting myself killed letting it go. You wouldn't believe the risks I took."

"Sometimes I'm scared of how far I'll go to know what happened."

"Preaching to the choir. I don't think anyone who hasn't been through this can understand the . . . craving to feel whole," Con said, and then looked uneasy at her choice of words. "You know, you asked me the same question at the Troubadour."

"I did?"

"Yeah, someone had approached you with information about your kidnapping. You seemed to want my permission."

"To talk to him?"

"No, to let it go," she said gently, as if knowing it wasn't the answer he expected. She was right. "You were with a woman, an actress. You said you were going to go away with her, but first you needed answers. You seemed frightened by what you might do to find out. What you might do if you did."

"I guess I wasn't frightened enough."

"Doesn't look that way, if whatever Lee Conway told you was enough for you to put a bullet in your own head. Have to admit that's a pretty radical approach to forgetting."

"Did the trick, though."

"Except it didn't, did it? Because you're all fired up to dig it all up again, aren't you?"

"Wouldn't you be?"

Con looked at him seriously. "No one could talk me out of it. I'd even try if you asked me, but we both know that'd be a waste of both our times. And that's probably why my aunt approached you."

"Meaning what?"

"Meaning she knows, better than anyone, what a clone will give up to feel complete. So I need you to listen to me. Whatever she offered you, whatever deal you two made, I'm telling you from experience . . . her price is too high."

———

After Con got out of the truck, Chance hesitated long enough to slip Paul Lin's gun out of the glove box, telling himself it was only a last resort. They backtracked down the hill and ducked under the caution tape. As they worked their way around the side of the house, the smell of fire hung heavily in the air. Maybe it was his imagination, but he could still feel a faint heat emanating from the ruin. There were no fireworks tonight, but a constellation of helicopters and drones made tumbling circles above the city, while down below, massive plumes of smoke trailed skyward.

Con followed behind. Her exoskeleton worked well on flat ground but was struggling to negotiate the debris from the fire. She said for him to go ahead without her, so he scrambled up and over the remains of the privacy fence and into the backyard. His father was sitting on the lone surviving patio chair, miraculously undamaged in the wild stampede to exit the inferno. Chance had made a racket coming over the fence, but his father didn't seem to register it. Brett Harker stared absently into the pool, filled with water for the first time in years, the runoff from the fire department's activities turned black with soot.

"Well? I'm here," Chance said, his heart pounding. His father didn't acknowledge the question. Chance had been psyching himself up on the way like a prizefighter before a championship bout. He hadn't anticipated his opponent not answering the starting bell.

"Look what they did to the old place. Your mother and I fell in love by this pool," his father said without looking up from the filthy water.

"Where the hell have you been?" Chance asked, circling around to stand in his father's eyeline. He was in no mood for nostalgia. It felt like a ploy. "I've been trying to reach you."

"I thought our lives would go differently." His father went on as though Chance hadn't spoken. "Sitting here with your mother, everything seemed possible. I suppose everyone feels that way when they're just starting out. You don't see all the ways life is going to fill your pockets with rocks and drop you in the deep end. We thought we knew how to swim. We really did."

"Am I supposed to be the rock in this story?"

His father looked aghast. "No, Lord no. You boys were the deep end."

The pain in his father's voice was unfamiliar. If he ever had fears or regrets, he wasn't a man to share them with his children. As much as Chance had needed to find a crack in the wall his father had built between them, it was hard to hear. He didn't want to feel empathy or pity, but wasn't that how it went with parents? They could beat the hell out of their kids for years, but show them a glimpse of humanity, and didn't children buy it every time? Not so much unconditional love as an unconditional *need* for love. It made Chance angry that he was still susceptible after all this time.

"Cut the crap, Dad," he snapped in an effort to cauterize any empathy for his father. "You've been lying to us for five years."

"I never lied," his father said.

Over his father's shoulder, Chance saw Con appear, having finally negotiated the broken fence. She kept her distance and said nothing. Chance had hoped for more time alone with his father, but it was what it was.

Chance could feel the gun against the small of his back, but he left it there for now. "You invented a fifty-million-dollar ransom. What do you call that? Creative bookkeeping?"

His father looked stricken. "It's complicated."

"You stood by while they killed me and Marley."

"I did everything I could!" his father said, voice rising in personal affront.

"I know you stole intellectual property from Palingenesis," Chance countered bluntly, hoping to catch his father off guard and pry an honest, unguarded reaction out of Brett Harker for once.

Instead of denying it, his father looked almost relieved. "You always were a very clever boy. Remember those models you built of carbon-capture plants? I thought you were going to help save the world."

Chance wasn't letting himself get sidetracked, instead driving forward to the question at the center of his paranoia. "Were you a part of it? My kidnapping?"

His dad blinked and sat forward as if waking from a long, not entirely pleasant, dream. "Is that what you think?"

"I don't know what to think. Why the fake ransom, Dad? Just tell me the truth."

Brett Harker sighed and looked past his son at the skyline. "Because if I'd involved your mother, then she would have been *involved*. Criminally. Do you understand? I have my strengths, but corporate espionage isn't one of them. Telling her would've made her an accomplice, and there was no chance I wouldn't be caught. I tried to convince those sons of bitches that it wasn't an *if* but a *when*. I offered them fifty million as an alternative, but my money didn't interest them. Why would it? My entire net worth couldn't touch the value of that technology on the open market. Instead, they killed you as a warning.

"I thought I'd lose my mind that day. Your mother didn't really sleep for weeks after you boys were taken. And then you came home to us, the same but different. Between trying to help you cope with being a clone and tearing her hair out over what might happen to Marley, she was a wreck. She blamed me, but by then the police knew I was stonewalling them. All I could do was keep up the fiction that I was negotiating a cash ransom. I was sure the company was onto me. It was an act of God that I actually succeeded . . ."

His father trailed off. Chance couldn't interpret his expression. If it had been anyone else, he'd have said Brett Harker looked close to tears, but that was inconceivable. In Chance's mind, his father had always been a rock: a stylish, fit, impeccably poised rock. Cool, calm, and collected when everyone around him was losing their composure. During the divorce, his father had never once raised his voice, never said anything cruel, never fought back, even as his wife went to extraordinary lengths to provoke him. He'd just taken whatever she'd dished out. It gave the impression that he was above it all, that he didn't care, and was watching his life unfold from a disinterested remove.

Chance realized it was a perception of his father that he'd never shaken or even taken the time to question. Brett Harker had auditioned for and won the role of villain in the family's mythology. He'd played the scapegoat when there'd been nowhere else for the family to place its anger.

"Why didn't you tell us afterward?" Chance asked, feeling a complicated mixture of guilt and anger. "I don't get it."

"Because I was right. The company *was* onto me. Three days after the kidnappers murdered your brother, Palingenesis dropped an army of lawyers on me like I was a beach in Normandy. They had me dead to rights. I'd left digital fingerprints everywhere. The only question was how long I'd go to prison."

"Why didn't you?"

"Because the last thing Vernon or Abigail wanted was word to get out that Palingenesis had been breached, that their precious IP was out in the wild. They offered me a deal. In the wake of my personal tragedy, I would resign to focus on my family. It's a clichéd cover story that politicians have been using for a hundred years, but under the circumstances, no one questioned it. I left Palingenesis a hero of the company. Vernon even gave a touching speech at my send-off. But an hour earlier, I'd been in a conference room signing a nondisclosure agreement thicker than a Tolstoy novel. It was complex, but it boiled down to this: if I ever told a soul, they would destroy me and my family."

"Jesus, Dad. You still could have said something."

"Maybe I should have," his father said, but Chance knew he was only being kind. What were the odds that either he or his mother could have kept that secret for five minutes, let alone five years? His father had done what he did best—carried the weight alone and let his family hate him for it.

"It didn't have to be this way."

"Well, this is the way it is. I did what I did, and it made no damn difference in the end. We destroyed ourselves instead."

Neither father nor son spoke for a long time after that. They'd covered a lot of ground very quickly, and both needed time to acclimate to their new altitude. Chance saw Con step forward. He'd forgotten she was even there. She must have taken the silence as an invitation to make her presence known.

"Mr. Harker, may I ask a question?"

His dad leapt out of his chair as if someone had fired a starter's pistol next to his ear. "Who the hell are you?"

"Dad, this is Constance D'Arcy. The singer."

"Among other things," she acknowledged. "Hello, Mr. Harker."

His father didn't appear to be ready for formal introductions just yet. "She's also Abigail Stickling's niece and Palingenesis's second-largest shareholder. Are you out of your mind bringing her here?"

"She's a friend, Dad. I think she can help us," Chance said, glancing back at her and hoping that was true. "Why did you have Chelsea set this up? Why all the secrecy?"

His father glared from him to Con and back to his son. "Because they're back. Your kidnappers. And they have your mother."

Chance's head was shaking before he could get words out. "No, no, what? No, Mom just got back. She called me from the airport."

"Well, she never made it home. They sent me proof of life."

His father threw a photograph from his LFD to Chance's: his mother tied to a worn wooden post on a sheet of all-too-familiar blue plastic. In it, she looked up at the camera defiantly, an expression Chance knew well. But also, layered in thickly like impasto oil paint, was fear.

Beside her, Maggie lay on her side, back to the camera. Chance couldn't tell if she was alive or dead, but the fact she was in the picture at all was hopeful. Wasn't it? He slipped down onto his haunches and put a hand out to steady himself. Was this retaliation for Paul Lin?

He'd been wondering why Anton Brätt hadn't made contact. Now he knew. They'd decided Maggie wasn't the leverage they needed and had upgraded to his mother.

"We have to get her back," his father said.

"Did they say what they wanted?" Chance asked, although he had a pretty good idea the answer was on his left hand.

"They said you'd know."

"I know who they are, Dad."

"Who?" his father said, not understanding.

"*Them.*" Something in his tone must have told his father exactly who Chance meant. "And I know this place. I know where they are."

CHAPTER TWENTY-NINE

They headed north on the 14 toward the ranch where Chance and Maggie had been taken after being snatched outside the Decameron. Chance just hoped he could find it again; he hadn't exactly been paying attention to landmarks when they'd made their escape. He was behind the wheel, not because it was his pickup, which it most definitely was not, but because Con seemed phobic about cars in general and his dad had grown accustomed to a chauffeur. They sat three across, with Con squeezed in the middle. It didn't seem right, but she insisted half her childhood had been spent in the middle seat of a pickup and she felt right at home there.

His father passed the time gazing out the window, lost in thought. Back at the pool, Chance had begun with Lee Conway and told him the whole story. He'd expected his father to ask a lot of questions, but he'd taken it all in without so much as a change of expression. It was unnerving. When he'd finished, all his father had to say was, "Let's go." He hadn't spoken since.

Chance glanced across Con at his father. That wasn't entirely true, was it? More accurate to say he'd told him almost the whole story. He'd left out a few minor details, if the whereabouts of Palingenesis's stolen

IP could be considered minor. Why leave it out? Well, for one thing, Chance still didn't trust him.

Maybe his father really had told the truth at last, but then again, maybe he hadn't. There was an art form to getting caught in a lie and replacing one falsehood with another. It looked like coming clean when really it was simply one more layer of dirt. In PR they called it *spin*, and his father had built his career on being a human centrifuge. The fact that his father had told him exactly what he'd needed to hear made him suspicious. Call him a cynic, but Chance would withhold judgment until after Maggie and his mother were safe. That was his only priority for now.

As for Con, he believed her. It wasn't her apparent sincerity; he'd grown up in a town that minted counterfeit sincerity like bad hundred-dollar bills. No, he believed her because they weren't after the same things, and she hadn't tried to make it sound like they were. Con wanted her crazy aunt and to prevent the Palingenesis IP from getting out into the world. He wanted the truth and his family back. If it came down to a choice between one or the other, would they still be on the same side?

Oh, and he hadn't told his father about Marley. There was no good excuse this time. It was cowardice, plain and simple. He knew he'd have to, sooner or later, but he just wasn't ready to look his father in the eyes and tell him his eldest son had been alive all this time.

"You," his father said, meaning Con. "What was your question?"

It had been so long since anyone had spoken that it took Chance a moment to realize what question his dad meant. But Con spoke up like she'd been waiting for an invitation.

"You said it was a miracle that you managed to steal the IP from Palingenesis," she said. "Did you mean that figuratively, like you were out of your element but with a little inspiration you figured it out? Or literally, like there was no way you should have been able to steal it, and then a miracle happened?"

"As a practicing atheist? It was a miracle. Abigail had that place locked up tighter than Fort Knox. Breaking into her network was like trying to dig a hole to China with a toothpick. It was impossible. Especially for someone like me. That's why I offered the kidnappers the fifty million instead."

"That's when they shot Chance," she said.

"Yeah, that's when they killed my boy," he said in a flat monotone. "So I went back to Palingenesis and tried again. And that time, somehow, I found a way in. Don't ask me how. I couldn't believe it. Still can't. How Abigail missed that vulnerability, I'll never know."

"It was too easy, wasn't it?" she asked.

"What are you thinking?" Chance asked, hearing the thoughtful shift in her tone.

"My aunt doesn't make mistakes. Not about things like this," Con said. "I think she caught your dad poking around and saw an opportunity. I think Abigail Stickling was your dad's miracle. She created a vulnerability that even he couldn't miss. No offense, Mr. Harker."

"None taken."

"She hid her new research inside the cloning IP," Con said.

"Why? Why not just take it herself?" Chance asked. "Why go to all these lengths?"

"Plausible deniability. She and Vernon had a falling-out over his commercialization of her work. After she made her breakthroughs enabling human cloning to achieve its full potential, she had no intention of sharing it with him or anyone else. Her endgame has always been to keep it for herself."

"Why?" Chance asked, feeling like a broken record.

"Because she thinks it's hers and hers alone. She has no interest in being one of the new gods. She wants to be the *only* god," Con explained. "Unfortunately, all of her research had been done at the Palingenesis labs. She became a victim of her own brilliance. Her own safety protocols made it nearly impossible to take anything out without being caught."

"But if she could pin the theft on someone else . . . ," Chance said.

"It would throw Vernon off the scent," Con finished. "But when things went sideways at the exchange five years ago and the kidnappers didn't get what they wanted, I became her plan B—"

"Excuse me," his father cut in angrily. "I gave those sons of bitches exactly what they wanted."

"Are you sure about that, Mr. Harker?"

"Damn right, I am. I wasn't about to get cute with them, not after what they did to Chance. I followed their instructions to the letter. I met them at the Salton Sea. They made me throw my LFD into the water. Then they sent Marley across to me. He was scared to death. I gave him the hard drive. He walked it back to them. They checked it out, confirmed it was all there. They seemed satisfied. Bastards let him get almost all the way back to me before they killed him. Then they shot out my tires and left me there."

Chance had never heard the story before. He only knew its outcome. Sounded like one of those Brothers Grimm fairy tales the way his father told it, the kind that never ended well for anyone. Disney rewrites need not apply. He hadn't known the part about Marley handling the hard drive. That could explain how Palingenesis's IP had ended up on Marley's ring. What it didn't explain was why Marley had the ring in the first place.

"So you gave them what they wanted. Then they shot your son anyway but left you alive," Con said. "Do I have that right?"

"Look, I know how it sounds, dammit, but that's what happened. Believe me. I've been replaying it in my mind for five years."

Con put her hands up as if offering a truce. "Mr. Harker, I'm not questioning your story. If you say you gave it to them, then you gave it to them. But what I do know is this: There's no indication that Palingenesis cloning technology has been reproduced. Anywhere in the world. By anyone. So either the kidnappers sold it to someone who never used it, or—"

"They never sold it at all," his father finished.

"Because they didn't have it to sell."

"I gave it to them," his father insisted.

"I believe you," she said. "But why else would they stick their necks out again? They got away clean the last time and should be set for life."

His father was nodding in agreement now. "So why aren't they living on a beach somewhere trying to decide which Maserati to drive to dinner?"

Chance, knowing the answer, kept his mouth shut and both hands on the wheel.

"So what is it you know?" his father asked him.

"What?" Chance said, playing for time. There was no avoiding it now; he had to give his father something. Either the truth about the ring or the truth about Marley. His foot eased off the accelerator. He didn't want to be going too fast when his father throttled him.

"These people said *you'd* know what they want."

"Marley, Dad. They want to talk to Marley."

"Marley's dead," his father said.

Chance didn't answer and kept on driving.

"Marley's dead," his father repeated, the certainty gone from his voice.

"No, he's not."

A long ten seconds passed as though his father were running a hundred-yard dash to catch up to the conversation. "How long have you known?"

Chance took a deep breath, not knowing when he might get another. "Two and a half years."

"Stop the truck," his father said, then slapped his hand on the dashboard when it didn't happen fast enough. "Stop this goddamned truck."

"I am," Chance said, crossing two lanes onto the shoulder.

His father opened his door and got out before the pickup rolled to a complete stop, storming away down the shoulder. Chance could hear him arguing with himself. With a sigh, he undid his seat belt and asked Con to wait in the truck.

She looked at him like he was crazy. "Oh, don't worry. I've got my own family drama. No way I'm getting in the middle of this."

That was fair. Chance got out and called after his father halfheartedly to stop. His father didn't, his mind seemingly set on hiking back to Los Angeles. Chance ran after him. There was no question a part of him felt guilty, the same part of him that had always felt bad for keeping Marley's secret. It hadn't been an easy decision. He hadn't made it lightly. But if he had it all to do over, he knew he wouldn't do anything differently. It had been Marley's condition for Chance being a part of his life again. He didn't regret honoring it.

That realization gave him an unexpected feeling of clarity and calm. He wasn't chasing his father, and he wasn't about to pick a fight with him either. Instead, he sat down on the concrete barrier lining the edge of the highway and stared out at the red Vasquez Rocks slanting up out of the ground like teeth grown in crooked.

Down the shoulder, his father ran out of steam and turned back. Seeing his son sitting patiently seemed to reinvigorate him, and he strode purposefully back like a man who'd just thought of the perfect comeback to an old insult. Chance stood and braced himself. For years all he'd wanted was open conflict with his father. Now the idea of fighting with him just made Chance depressed.

His father didn't stop until they were nose to nose. "You had no right. No right to keep this a secret from me. From your mother. He's our son."

"It's no different than what you did," Chance replied, fighting to keep his tone level even as his heart was pounding.

That seemed to unbalance his father momentarily, but he was quickly back on the offensive. "It isn't the same thing at all."

"It's exactly the same. Did you know what keeping your secret was doing to us? What the consequences were?"

"Chance, I—"

"Answer the question, Dad. Yes or no. Did you know?"

His father's head dropped an inch. "I knew."

"But you did it anyway because it had to be done, because it was the only way. You were in an awful situation with no right answers. I'm still angry, but I get that now. When Marley reached out a few years ago, he said if I told anyone, *anyone*, he would disappear for good."

"But we could have brought him home," his father said desperately. "We could have helped him."

"He doesn't want to come home, Dad." Seeing his father couldn't accept that, Chance described Marley, leaving nothing out. His father's face paled, but Chance didn't pull any punches. "He's broken, Dad. I mean we're all broken, but with Marley it's different. It's . . . Well, he isn't the same person you remember."

"Oh God," his father said, putting his hand to his mouth and stumbling away down the highway again. This time, Chance followed, taking his arm to steady him.

"But you help him?" his father asked.

"Best I can. I go out there about every six months. Bring him things I know he needs. I don't stay long. He doesn't do well with people."

His father turned toward him. Chance flinched and stepped back, but his father kept coming, reaching out a hand to pull him close. Chance tried to remember the last time his father had hugged him and came up blank.

They stood there like that a long time while traffic whistled by.

"Thank you," his father said.

Chance didn't answer, and when his father released him, it occurred to him he hadn't hugged him back. His arms had hung limply at his sides. Not out of cruelty—he'd simply been too startled to do more than just stand there.

"That woman isn't telling us everything," his father said, meaning Con.

Chance wiped his eyes. He'd been crying and not known it. "She thinks it's for our own protection."

"Pretty patronizing."

Chance let out an unexpected laugh. "That's what I said."

They both looked over at the pickup truck idling on the shoulder like a frigate waiting for a tailwind.

"The smart thing to do would be to call the police," his father said.

"They've reissued a warrant for my arrest, Dad," Chance said. "If we call the police, their first priority will be putting me behind bars and getting the riots under control. Afterward, if I have to go to jail, I go to jail. I'm okay with that. But only once this is over, and Mom is safe."

"Okay," his father said and then hugged him again. "But I promise we'll figure something out."

This time Chance remembered to hug him back.

CHAPTER THIRTY

Chance stopped the pickup at the top of the hill overlooking the old ranch. He put it in park, killed the headlights, and leaned forward, arms crossed over the steering wheel as he studied the property below. In the moonlight, the old ranch house looked like an Andrew Wyeth painting in search of its Christina. He didn't see the van or any signs of life. But that didn't mean no one was home. He could feel it.

"You didn't say anything about it being a farm," Con said.

"Technically it's a ranch."

She didn't appear to take much comfort in the distinction. "I have a bad history with farms."

She didn't elaborate, but he suspected that whatever was waiting for them wouldn't improve her opinion. He suggested leaving the pickup here and walking the rest of the way. His father didn't like that idea at all. What if they needed to retreat in a hurry? Did a quarter-mile uphill walk sound like the stuff of fast getaways?

"Suddenly you're an expert on getaways? You don't even drive, Dad."

"It's just common sense."

"What if one of us goes on foot?" Chance suggested. "And circles around."

"Let me out here," Con said, powering up her exoskeleton. "I'll do it."

"Why you?" Anyone who didn't know his father well would have heard old-fashioned sexism, but Chance had heard the same uncertainty a thousand times. His father always needed a reason for doing anything.

"Because they're not expecting me."

Neither father nor son could fault her logic. His father got out and held the door for her.

"How's the charge on your legs?" Chance asked.

"Should be fine."

They both recognized that *should* was doing a lot of heavy lifting and then smiled when they saw the other recognized it too. It was strangely good for morale to know that everyone acknowledged the long odds against them. Chance pulled out the pistol. It didn't feel good resting against the small of his back, and he'd be happy to be rid of it. His father stared at the weapon like Chance had produced an armor-plated rabbit from a hat.

"Where the hell did you get a gun?"

"Been a long couple of days, Dad," he said before handing the gun to Con. When she asked if the weapon was loaded, he was forced to admit he had no idea. It had never occurred to him to check, and even if it had, he wasn't sure he'd know how. She gave him a curious look before popping the clip, inventorying her ammunition, and slapping it back into place. *Was it a clip or a mag?* he wondered. He was fairly certain one was wrong and got the impression she would know. Asking didn't feel confidence-inspiring, though, so instead he asked, "How do you know guns? Is that a Texas thing?"

She shook her head. "A Yael thing."

"Your assistant?"

"She was a sniper in the IDF."

"The what now?" he asked.

"Israeli Defense Force," his father said as though such things should be common knowledge.

"A condition of her working for me was that I become competent with firearms," Con said. "She's a very good teacher."

"Maybe we should call *her*?" Chance suggested. "This seems like an IDF kind of deal."

Con smiled grimly. "That's not a bad idea."

"So is firearms training like a standard part of the assistant package these days?"

"I'm far from a standard client," Con said as she handed him back the pistol. "Keep it. I won't need one."

"I don't like guns."

"If I thought you liked guns, I wouldn't give it back to you," she said, and then seemingly anticipated his next question. "Seventeen, by the way. You have seventeen shots. If it comes to that."

That seemed like a lot, but if it actually came to hitting something, he might need at least that many.

His father appeared to be having second thoughts. "Should we maybe call the police? Is this a bad idea? This is a bad idea, isn't it?"

"This *is* a bad idea," Con agreed. "But if it's any consolation, the police would only get in the way."

"In the way of what?" his father asked.

"Just be prepared for anything. Even if it gets weird."

"Define *weird*," Chance said.

"You'll know it when you see it," Con replied before slipping away into the dark.

Once she was out of sight, his father got back in, and Chance shifted the pickup into neutral.

"Ready?" Chance asked, not at all sure he was himself.

It reassured him when his father answered with an honest no. Chance eased his foot off the brake anyway. From experience, he knew overthinking a dangerous decision only led to catastrophe. Maggie and his mother were down there somewhere in the dark. There was nothing to overthink. After a moment, gravity saw an opening and gave the truck a gentle nudge.

"Here we go," his father announced, and then reached over to pat his son's leg.

Gradually, the vehicle began to roll down the hill, silently gathering speed. It felt like a metaphor, as though Chance's entire life had been leading him to this moment. His father must have sensed something, because he patted him on the leg again.

"Why are you doing this?" Chance asked. "She's not even your wife anymore."

"I don't believe in ex-wives."

"She kind of hates you, Dad."

"It's family. What does that have to do with anything?"

Chance couldn't think of a single thing off the top of his head.

At the bottom of the hill, he swung the pickup wide into the oncoming lane, out onto the shoulder, and made a sweeping turn up the driveway. Momentum carried them up to the top, where Chance shifted back into gear and made a slow lap around the gravel enclosure, getting the lay of the land. Despite spending several unpleasant hours here, he'd left too quickly for the guided tour, so it was his first real look at the ranch. He hadn't missed much. Whatever charm it might once have held had withered away when the water had been shut off. Even the moonlight couldn't hide the fact that this was a dead place.

The pistol rested on Chance's thigh just in case, but there was nothing to shoot at. Nothing stirred. No one appeared to greet them. Could he have been wrong about the picture of his mom? Had they taken her somewhere else?

Wait.

He braked and backed up two feet. There, poking out from behind the house, was the front bumper of the van. It had been parked where it wouldn't be seen from the road. He pointed it out to his father, who nodded, understanding the significance without having to be told. They sat there side by side, father and son, pondering the great mystery of the van. Chance hadn't pulled up and leaned on the horn but somehow doubted they'd gone completely unnoticed.

"Where the hell are they?" his father asked, reading his son's mind.

Chance didn't know, but he had the uneasy feeling they were being watched, which he was willing to dismiss as a side effect of idling outside a spooky, long-abandoned ranch house on a moonlit night. Of course there was the distinct possibility—no, call it a probability—that it was the other thing. So what were the kidnappers playing at? He'd already been fooled badly by them once and didn't want to run his record to zero for two. Unsure what to do, he continued on their circuit, finishing at the stable. He parked facing back down the hill, which earned him an approving nod from his father, newly anointed saint of fast getaways.

"Let's check the stable," Chance suggested. "That's where they kept me."

"Which one do you want?" His father held up a flashlight.

Chance traded the pistol for the flashlight.

"I'm not any better around guns than you," his father said.

"If this comes down to guns, I think we're out of luck."

That earned a weak chuckle from his father. "You're probably right. But what say we not let it?"

CHAPTER
THIRTY-ONE

They worked their way into the stable single file, Chance in the lead with the flashlight, his father trailing behind with the gun. It was funny the tricks the mind played. He remembered the stable being smaller, the ceiling lower, the whole vibe more claustrophobic and menacing. Even in the dark, the flashlight told a different story, and his memory struggled to reconcile how far back the stable went.

The last horse had long since been led away, but only fire would eradicate the saturated perfume of petrified hay and manure. There was something else in the air tonight, though. Something that hadn't been there last time: a violent, metallic aftertaste that grew stronger with each step. Chance heard the excited hum of insects. He played the flashlight across the stable, looking for the source. A swarm of flies hovered over one spot. He felt a sickening curiosity about what had drawn them. He panned down with the flashlight, and it caught the edge of the plastic sheeting still laid out on the ground, casting blue-green reflections against the walls like an incoming tide. On the plastic, back to the doorway, the unmoving outline of a figure slumped splay-legged against a wooden post.

With a cry fueled by adrenaline and fear, Chance scrambled over to the figure and fell to his knees. He tried to wave away the cloud of flies that flew hungrily around the figure's head, but the insects only pulsed angrily and re-formed. Who was it? He feared the worst: retribution for Paul Lin. Then his eyes focused and saw what was actually there, not just what he feared.

It was a man. It was a man, not a woman. Chance rocked back, sitting down hard and taking a breath he hadn't known he'd been holding. It was strange to feel both relief and horror simultaneously. Someone had died terribly here, but selfishly all he cared about was that it wasn't his mother and it wasn't Maggie. He studied the figure, trying to make sense of it.

The body (he could call it a body now) was naked, apart from filthy underwear. His arms were bound, drawn back painfully behind the post. He made no complaint, though, nor would he again, judging from the car-crash angle of his head. Despite Chance's unique relationship with death, he'd never seen a dead body before. Still, he didn't need to check for a pulse to know this was his first. Two fingers under the man's chin, he lifted the familiar face up to the flashlight. Lee Conway would have company in hell.

"Who is it?" his father asked, coming around the post to see for himself.

"Bear Conway."

The big man's expression was peaceful, but his passing had been anything but. His bare chest was crosshatched with cuts, some shallow, some deep down to the bone. There were cruel abrasions where someone had tried to polish the skin to a high sheen but had stripped it away instead. The body glistened unnaturally in the light and smelled of motor oil. Nearby, a scalpel and a fistful of bloody steel wool looked on like witnesses to a cruel prosecution. An overturned bottle of hydraulic fluid explained the sheen. It had been poured into the open wounds. Chance didn't know the reason why but suspected it hadn't been a friendly gesture.

His father rested a hand gently on his shoulder and reminded Chance that they weren't finished with their search. What else might be waiting for them? Chance found his answer at the back of the stable—laid out on a workbench was another body. It had been strapped down and given the same brutal treatment. Chance checked the stalls. All were empty, which was a relief. He wanted his mother and Maggie far, far from this horror.

"My God, that's Anton Brätt. The director," his father said.

Chance stumbled away and retched against the far wall. All those years of dreaming of revenge, but the distance between imagination and reality was the difference between looking up at the moon and standing on it. The worst part was knowing that he was never going to get an answer. It was like coming to the end of a long, long book, only to find someone had torn out the last page.

"I had dinner with him once," his father said.

"You did?" Chance said to keep his father talking for a minute. He just needed the sound of a familiar voice while he tried to think.

"Yes. Marley put it together. Your brother was trying to sell me on bankrolling Brätt's next masterpiece. He wanted to produce."

"What did you tell him?" Maggie had told him her side of this story, but he wanted to hear his father's version.

"I said if he wanted to get into film, he should get a job and learn the business. I wasn't giving a twenty-year-old millions of dollars to play Robert Evans."

That sounded like his father. "You never told me that."

"Well, I put him in an awkward situation. Marley inherited my gift for salesmanship, and he'd made promises to Brätt that he couldn't keep. I didn't see the need to embarrass him in front of the family as well. Once things calmed down, he knew that I was right," his father said, staring down at the dead man's face as if it were tea leaves at the bottom of an unwashed mug. "Never once crossed my mind that it might have been these parasites who took my boys. Over what? A movie?"

Chance played the beam of the flashlight around the stable. Finding the bodies this way had paralyzed him. It had also caused him to overlook far more immediate questions, like who had killed Anton Brätt and Bear Conway. It felt disloyal, but his first instinct was his brother. He couldn't forget the ferocity with which Marley had attacked Paul Lin. Could he honestly say this barbarism was beyond his brother? And if this was the handiwork of Marley Harker, then did that mean his mother and Maggie were in less danger or much more?

They backtracked out of the stable and emerged into the moonlight. Chance flicked off the flashlight and spat in the dirt, trying to get the taste of death and vomit out of his mouth.

"Where's your mother? Or Maggie?" his father asked, the shock of their discovery receding far enough to remember why they were there.

"How long do you think those two've been dead?" Chance asked.

"That's not really my area."

It wasn't Chance's either, but that wasn't going to stop him from speculating. "The blood was dry."

His father nodded, looking like he was trying to remember. "It was, wasn't it? But in this heat? How long would that take?"

"I think they've been dead a little while." Was this the reason he hadn't heard from Anton Brätt since leaving the Slabs? Had he been too dead to make a call? "When'd you get the picture of Mom?"

His father checked his LFD. "Five hours ago."

Had they been dead that long? Chance thought maybe they had. "I think whoever killed those two has Mom and Maggie."

"How do you know that?" his father asked, switching on his skeptical voice.

"We'd have heard from them by now if they got away."

"So who has them?"

"Chance Harker," a female voice called out from the direction of the house. Chance wasn't sure who jumped higher, father or son. It was pure luck his father's finger wasn't on the trigger, or one of them could have easily caught a bullet. When they landed, father and son went into a crouch, flattening themselves against the side of the stable.

"Who the hell is that? Is that D'Arcy?" his father asked, sounding more hopeful than anything else. It didn't sound like any of the women they were looking for.

"May I have a word with you?" the voice asked almost cordially.

"Who's there?" Chance yelled back, although through process of elimination he knew now it was Mary. Or Abigail, depending on how you looked at things. This meant that it wasn't Marley's handiwork in the barn. That should have been more of a comfort than it was. Con had tried to warn him of the danger her aunt represented, but he hadn't taken her seriously. He was now.

"You're a difficult man to reach. You haven't been answering any of my calls."

"I've kind of had my hands full," he countered.

"We had a deal. I thought I made that clear," she said, "that I would talk to your kidnappers before anything befell them."

"I didn't break it."

"Paul Lin begs to differ."

He would have liked to know how she knew about that but wasn't about to ask. "Well, he was alive last I saw him. And I wasn't the one who killed Brätt or Conway."

"No, that was me. And you're welcome."

"Thank you?" he said, although gratitude wasn't his prevailing emotion in the moment.

"Why don't you come out now so we can talk face-to-face." It was framed as a question but wasn't one.

"Where's my mom?" Chance asked. "Where's Maggie?"

"They're quite safe. For the moment."

Why didn't that fill him with confidence? "I want to see them."

"Then come out here," she said, beginning to sound peevish and impatient. When they didn't immediately show themselves, she added, "So you know, I'm not out of steel wool."

That was all there was to that. Having seen her handiwork in the stable, Chance knew he had no choice. He looked over at his father, who was already looking at him.

"She wants me," Chance said. "You should go."

In lieu of an answer, his father stood up, dusted himself off, and walked away toward the ranch house. Chance scrambled to follow. It was time to see what the night had in store.

CHAPTER THIRTY-TWO

Chance had to remind himself that although it might be the body of a teenage girl waiting for them on the porch of the abandoned farmhouse, it was an insane fifty-eight-year-old woman staring out at them through those eyes like a ghost. A shiver of superstitious dread ran through him. It had taken twenty-first-century science to make demonic possession a reality. He didn't know what else to call it. The sadistic deaths of Bear Conway and Anton Brätt made a compelling case that whatever lurked inside this teenage girl wasn't human. Not anymore. Con had tried to warn him; he couldn't say she hadn't. Only his mother's and Maggie's lives kept his feet moving toward her.

As they approached, a buzzing erupted that rose into the air like angry hornets. With a flash, night became day. Chance and his father shaded their eyes and stumbled forward. Four illumination drones had formed a hovering rectangle overhead that bathed the compound in light. His mother and Maggie lay on the porch at their captor's feet. His father started toward them, but Abigail held up a cautioning hand.

"That's close enough for now."

"Are they alive?" his father demanded. Neither woman had stirred, which made it a fair question, considering the bodies in the stable.

The girl frowned. "I'd be a pretty lousy negotiator if they weren't."

"Then why aren't they moving or saying anything?" Chance said. "Mom, are you okay?"

"Because of the explosive, vibration-sensitive collars around their necks. It's a little theatrical, but I thought it fitting for Los Angeles. They're fundamentally unharmed and will remain that way so long as I get what I want."

Chance took a deep, steadying breath, fighting his body's strong urge to freak the hell out. Under the circumstances, he hoped it would be forgiven, but that would only get his mom and Maggie killed. "You had your . . . conversation . . . with Brätt and Conway. Isn't that what you wanted?"

"What I want is answers. If they'd had any, believe me, they would've given them," she said with a gleam in her eyes made twice as horrible in such a young face.

"What makes you think I know anything?"

"Because your brother is alive. My guess is you saw him after those idiots left you alone with Paul Lin, who's coincidentally clinging to life in an ICU in Palm Springs."

"So?" Chance said.

She scowled at him. "When we met, I gave you credit for not being as stupid as you appeared. But if you're committed to playing the part, I should mention these collars are also remote controlled and that my patience is running very short."

"Okay, okay," Chance said, showing his palms in surrender. "Ask your questions."

"Let's start with an easy one. Where have you been since delivering Paul Lin to the hospital. Why did it take you so long to rendezvous with your father?"

Chance didn't know much, but he didn't think mentioning Con would go over well. "I pulled off the highway and slept in the truck."

She squinted down at him. "With Maggie's life hanging in the balance? How gallant of you."

"I was exhausted. New-clone fatigue. It wasn't safe for me to drive."

"Sure," she said. "So would you like to pick which one dies first, or should I?"

"You don't want to do that," he said. "Abigail."

"What did you say?" she asked, her expression changing from arrogance to momentary uncertainty. It was a hell of a risk admitting he knew her real identity. Con had warned him explicitly against exactly that. But he needed to rattle her, get her off script, because he had a pretty good idea how her draft of the script ended, whether or not she believed her secret was safe.

"You heard me. *Abigail.*"

Behind her eyes, he could see turning wheels that—if the stories about her fearsome intellect held water—were massive and unrelenting. His father, who didn't know the Abigail Stickling piece, just looked confused.

"Constance," she said finally. "You talked to Constance. She's been filling your head with tall tales."

"Well, they're really good tall tales."

"Did she make you an offer?" She paused for his answer, but when Chance didn't, she added, "Well, I hope for your sake that you didn't accept. After all, I have items of value to offer in trade." Abigail gestured down to the women at her feet as though they were spoils of war.

"Let them go, and we can talk."

"That's not how this is going to work."

Chance felt himself becoming impatient. He held out a hand. "Dad, let me see the gun for a minute."

His father, who was still playing catch-up, casually passed him the pistol as if Chance had asked for the salt at dinner.

Abigail sighed. "Don't grandstand with me, boy. Let's not forget the explosive collars. If you shoot me, they die."

"Who said anything about shooting *you*?" Chance asked, and then put the gun to his head.

"What are you doing?" Abigail and his father asked in unison, although their concerns couldn't have been more different.

"Offering you a deal," Chance said. "I can tell you what you want to know, or I pull the trigger."

"You don't have the nerve," Abigail said, but her tone wasn't as confident as her words.

"Look who you're talking to. This isn't my first rodeo, Abigail."

She stood there staring down at him, calculating, scheming. He could practically see those big wheels turning behind her eyes. "So what is it you think you know?"

"I know what my kidnappers really wanted. What my father stole for them five years ago."

Abigail cast a pitying look toward his father. "So you finally violated your NDA? Vernon will be so disappointed."

"What is going on here?" his father asked, clearly baffled by the conversation. "Who is this girl?"

Chance ignored the question. He might not have inherited his father's salesmanship like Marley had, but he knew Abigail was on the hook, and he meant to keep her there. "No, he didn't. I worked it out on my own."

"Constance," Abigail said with a knowing frown. "Another of her tall tales."

"Maybe, maybe not. But I do know the kidnappers never got their hands on it. And that you want it more than anything in the world."

"Do you know where this item is now?" Abigail asked, unable to mask her eagerness.

"I do," Chance said, pausing for effect. "But it's like this. Everything I know, I learned since my last upload. So if I die? It dies with me. And then what happens? I wake up at Palingenesis good as new, but you? You never find what you're looking for." He could tell from the sideways glance his father gave him that Palingenesis had notified him that his son had been cut off. If Abigail still had sources inside the company, then he was dead in the water, but Chance was gambling that she didn't.

"Well, you'll have a lot of funerals to attend," she said, but without her previous bravado.

"Maybe, but that still won't get you your research back. And it was a total fluke I figured it out once. There's no way I'd be able to do it again," he said, adjusting his grip on the pistol. It felt strangely weightless in his hand, and an unfamiliar calm settled over him. He had no desire to pull the trigger but knew that he could. That was important. For her to believe his ultimatum, he had to believe it even more.

They stared each other down like two poker players over the biggest pot of their lives. One had just gone all in, the other left to calculate whether it was a bluff.

"Why should I believe you?" she finally asked.

"Because I just want my family. I don't care about the rest. You can have it," Chance said, then added, "once they're safe."

She thought it over. "They go. You stay."

"I stay. They go," he agreed.

"Quickly, before I come to my senses."

Abigail toggled the locks remotely from her LFD. The collars fell open with an audible click, and Maggie and his mother yanked the collars off and helped each other to their feet. They hurried down the porch steps, giving Abigail a radioactive berth. His mother threw her arms around Chance. She was ashen faced and trembling. Aware that he might not have another chance, he badly wanted to say something significant to her, something meaningful. But in the hot chaos of the moment, the best he could manage was a pro forma "I love you." He couldn't remember the last time he'd said the words and meant them.

Reluctantly, he pried himself free of her embrace. "You have to get out of here."

"Are you sure about this?" his father asked.

"I'll see you soon," Chance assured him. He wasn't sure either of them believed that, but he pressed the pickup key into his hand. "Just get them far away from here."

His father put a hand behind Chance's neck, pulled him close, and whispered in his ear, "The cavalry's coming. Just hold tight."

When they parted, Chance tried to catch his eye, trying to understand what that meant, but his father had already taken Emelia's arm and was guiding her toward the pickup. True to form, his mother shook herself free and then followed him anyway.

"I'm staying," Maggie said.

Caught up in the moment with his mother, Chance had forgotten Maggie was even there. He looked at her now and felt muddled, like a man lost in an enormous foreign airport trying to figure out which way to go to get to where he needed to be. He hadn't wanted anything to happen to Maggie, but now that she was safe, he didn't know what to do with how he felt about her.

"This isn't going to end well, Maggie."

"So? You think there's a happy ending in my future?"

Maybe it was the way she said it or the absurdity of the situation, but he began to laugh. Maggie didn't join in and only smiled sadly, crossing her arms as if she'd caught a chill.

"I don't know about the future, Maggie. I only know I don't want yours to end today," he said, taking her hand. "So would you please get the fuck out of here? Please?"

She nodded and started to say something but thought better of it and stopped herself. He was grateful for that, grateful, too, that she didn't look back as she walked way.

He watched the pickup drive away. His mom waved from the passenger seat, and he held up a hand in return. The pickup made a left at the bottom of the driveway and accelerated away. Chance watched until the taillights had crested the hill and disappeared. He smiled, happy that they were safe but also aware that this was the first time his parents had been in close quarters in years. It probably wouldn't go well, but he'd have given just about anything to be sitting between them now.

"Well, that had to feel good," Abigail said. "Took a stand. Saved your parents. Even the girl who betrayed you. I'll admit I don't understand that impulse. You'd have thought nature would've culled the instinct for forgiveness generations ago. Not exactly evolutionarily advantageous for the wildebeest to give the lion a free pass. I swear I don't understand people, but here we are."

"Here we are," Chance agreed, realizing they'd been waiting like children who'd called time-out to renegotiate the rules of their game. The time-out was over, though, and the game was back on. He could tell that from the gun that had magically appeared in Abigail's hand. From the way she held it, he could also tell she didn't share any of his discomfort with firearms.

"Unload your gun," she said. "Toss the clip in one direction, the gun in the other."

"I don't actually know how to do that," he admitted.

Abigail leveled him with the withering gaze of an elementary school teacher catching the class dunce disrupting her lesson. "You have to be kidding me. Fine. Just throw it as far as you can. You can throw, can't you?"

In another time, that would have demanded a smartass response. Now Chance didn't even need to bite his tongue. He turned and threw the gun as hard as he could. It arced high up into the sky, beyond the light of the drones, and disappeared into the night. He was happy to be rid of it; guns had never brought him anything but misery. Besides, whatever came next wouldn't be solved with a bullet.

CHAPTER THIRTY-THREE

"Where's my property?" Abigail demanded, cutting to the chase. The gun in her hand was pointed at the ground, but Chance could feel it itching for something to do.

"It's not far."

"Not far?" Abigail said suspiciously. "You understand that if you're lying, I'll make what happened in the stable look like a spa day?"

"It's not far," Chance repeated, and then held up his hand so she could see the ring.

The effect was immediate and profound. Abigail fell silent and came down the porch steps as if hypnotized. She took his hand, studying the ring like a jeweler making an appraisal.

"And this is it? It's all here?" Abigail asked in wary disbelief.

"I have no idea about *all*, but there's over a terabyte of Palingenesis documents and files here. I couldn't tell you what any of it means, but I'm guessing it's what you came for."

"Clever boy. I'll have to verify it first," she said, trying and failing to keep the anticipation from her voice.

Abigail connected her LFD to the ring and stood gathered around his outstretched hand like he was the captain of a losing team trying to psych itself up for the fourth quarter. No one was giving any inspirational speeches, though. Chance was afraid to move and had the morbid impression that once she was satisfied, Abigail would take his hand as a souvenir. Actually, he'd consider himself lucky if that was all she took.

"I've waited so long for this. What I sacrificed. No one understands," Abigail murmured, although whether to Chance or to herself it was impossible to say.

"I think I do," Chance replied.

Her eyes refocused from her LFD to the outside world, and she regarded him pityingly. "Yes, I suppose you might. It's quite a little odyssey you've been on. I should thank you for the boon your escapades provided my research. It's one thing to simulate it, but to have the opportunity to study the long-term effects of multiple revivals in an actual subject? It was a godsend to the work."

"That's why Palingenesis never canceled the policy? So you could study me?"

"If you wanted to play guinea pig, who was I to stop you?"

He had sometimes wondered about that and didn't enjoy having his suspicions confirmed. His rebellion had been a sham. Far from bothering Palingenesis, he'd been helping them all along. It was demoralizing but deserved, he supposed. It made him wonder what else Abigail Stickling had been behind. "Did you organize my kidnapping?"

"Please." She sounded almost offended at the suggestion. "I would never have been so sloppy. But when I realized what had been set in motion, I found your abductors sniffing around on the dark web for a buyer even before they had my research in hand. We struck a deal, but after the exchange, they vanished. I always feared they'd gotten a better offer, but since I never knew their identities, there was no way to know for certain. That's why I needed you to draw them out for me. You were the ideal bait after you gave that absurd interview to Imani Highsmith."

Guinea pig and bait—that was some résumé. He wondered if he would add *sacrificial lamb* before the night was through.

Abigail's attention returned to her LFD. Her head began to bob approvingly. "Unbelievable. It's here. It's all here." It was the first time he'd seen her smile. He didn't care for it much. There was no joy behind her eyes, only smug satisfaction. "And so our time together ends."

"What happens now?"

"You give me the ring. When you wake up, you'll have no memory of any of this. Or of me. And won't that be nice?"

Chance took a half step backward.

"Don't be difficult," she said. "Just get on your knees. I'll make it quick." She frowned when he kept backing up and then followed after him. "You're being ridiculous. How many times have you done this now? It's just like riding a bike."

"Doesn't feel that way," he said, playing for time. There was no point wasting time telling her Palingenesis had canceled his contract. After what he'd seen in the stable, he had a hunch it wouldn't make any difference to her.

"Just give me the ring," she said, snapping her fingers impatiently.

Nodding compliantly, he twisted off the ring and held it out in the palm of his hand so she could see. The way Abigail leaned in hungrily would have done Gollum proud. Chance took a quick step and flung the ring in the same direction as the gun. As eager as she was to get her hands on it, he counted on her reflexes to follow the ring. And that's exactly what happened. Abigail's head snapped to the right, trying to follow the ring's trajectory. The gun followed obediently.

Chance lunged for the weapon, hoping he had his geometry right. Abigail's expression changed. The gun swung back his way, but he got there first, one hand on top of the gun, the other around her wrist. He twisted down and away, using his leverage and strength so that if it went off, the only victim would be the gravel at their feet. He was so focused on the gun that he completely missed the stun gun in Abigail's other hand, which didn't miss him. His body went rigid, his legs went out from under him, and his grip on her gun slipped. The ring, which he had palmed, slipped out of the other. It fell in the gravel between them.

Abigail squatted down to pluck it off the ground. "Or we can do it your way."

He blinked and looked up at the gun aimed at the bridge of his nose. Maybe it was all his practice paying off, but he felt strangely calm in the face of death. He had done his best. He'd saved his parents, saved Maggie. He'd even shielded Marley from all this. That would have to be enough.

"Abigail!" a woman yelled out from the dark stable. It was Con, arriving like an explorer returning after years at sea. He'd almost forgotten about her and really wished she'd kept the gun. Now she was unarmed. What could she do except get herself killed alongside him?

"You," Abigail snarled. "Am I never going to be rid of you?"

Con stepped out into the light. "Maybe try not stealing the bodies of my family. That might do the trick."

"I thought perhaps I'd be able to sneak into the country without drawing unwanted attention," Abigail admitted. "But I see you anticipated that. You've gotten smarter since I saw you last."

"Well, when your aunt is a murdering sociopath, it pays to think like her."

"You betrayed me," Abigail said flatly.

"I betrayed you? You killed me and scrambled my brain. I'll be dead for good within the year."

"I would have made it right. You know that."

"The price was too high," Con said, walking toward them. "Now drop the gun and step away from him."

Abigail cast an amused eye around her. "That's bold, considering I am the one holding the gun."

"I'm not going to tell you again," Con said, continuing to close the distance between them.

Abigail brought the gun up to greet Con. Her arm never made it. Instead Abigail was driven off her feet as if hit by an invisible truck. She landed awkwardly on the porch steps and lay still. Chance was still wondering what the hell had happened when a single gunshot echoed down from the hills. He started, laughing to himself. He'd been used as bait again.

Con offered a hand to help him up, but he waved her away and climbed unsteadily to his feet.

"Where is she?" he asked.

"Yael? About a half a mile that way on a ridge." Con aimed a vague hand westward.

"How'd she get here so fast?"

"She's been tailing us ever since we left your house," Con said, gingerly kneeling to pick up Abigail's pistol and the ring.

She stayed there on one knee, turning the ring over and over between her fingers. Chance watched her, wondering what came next. Had Con beaten her aunt to the prize so she could have it for herself? Was that what this had all been about?

Abigail moaned but didn't open her eyes.

"She's not dead?" Chance said, confused even as he realized there was no blood.

"Non-lethal round. Packs a hell of a punch, though," Con said. "I'm sorry for not telling you I was bringing backup."

"What for? I think I said you should call her."

"Yeah, she was already here. I'm sorry. I wasn't sure who I could trust," she said, and then handed him the ring.

He slipped it gratefully back onto his finger. "Did you know I had it?"

She shook her head. "No, but I figured if you did, you'd keep the only leverage you had to yourself."

"I wasn't sure who I could trust either."

"It's alright. I'd have done the same for the people I love."

"I don't love them."

"Sure," she said agreeably. "You have a funny way of showing it."

"I don't," Chance said, perhaps too heatedly, as though she'd insulted his honor by suggesting he cared about his parents.

"Chance, remember I'm still on the board at Palingenesis. I know. That was a hell of a bluff."

Before he could argue the point, a set of headlights appeared on the road at the top of the hill, then another and another. The three vehicles were really moving, and from the way they were bunched together in tight formation, Chance just knew they'd turn off at the stable.

He wasn't wrong.

His first thought as the convoy sped up the driveway was that the police had finally tracked him down. But there were no sirens, no flashing lights.

"Are they with you?" he asked hopefully.

"They are definitely *not* with me," Con answered in a tone that told Chance that she knew exactly who it was.

CHAPTER THIRTY-FOUR

The two lead vehicles, large black SUVs, plowed to a halt side by side, scattering gravel like shrapnel. Doors snapped open with choreographed precision. Heavily armed figures in tactical gear fanned out. But no one yelled out announcing it was the police, nor did he see any official-looking logos or badges.

"Drop the gun," a no-nonsense voice called out. "Hands on your heads."

Chance did as he was told. In the light of the drones, he caught sight of the third vehicle, the old pickup. Whoever it was had brought his parents back, but willingly or otherwise?

Con tossed Abigail's weapon a few feet toward the vehicles but didn't put her hands on her head, not even when they told her a second and third time. Instead she fixed them with the ancient and unmistakable look of *I'm too tired for this shit.*

"Let's get this over with," she finally yelled.

The passenger door of one of the SUVs opened. A tall Black man in a suit stepped out and buttoned his jacket as though he were arriving for a film premiere. Vernon Gaddis had aged far more than the nine years it had been since Chance had met him. His hair and beard were white as springtime clouds, and stress had cut deep lines into his forehead and the corners of his eyes.

"Hello, Constance."

"Vernon," she replied.

"I'm disappointed to find you here."

"I could say the same about you."

"Is she dead?" he asked.

As if in answer, Abigail groaned. She tried and failed to sit up, instead rolling onto her side and throwing up over the edge of the stairs.

"No," Con said, stating the obvious. "She's not dead."

"Good," Vernon said, and then held out a hand like a man accustomed to being given what he wanted without asking. One of his men handed him a pistol. Vernon tested its weight and strode into the rectangle of light toward Abigail.

"Vernon," Con said sternly, "don't do it. Don't even think about it."

"I think of little else," he said, standing over Abigail.

"Hello, Vernon. What an unexpected surprise," Abigail wheezed, gingerly touching a hand to her chest. "This is so flattering. You getting on an airplane for me. I thought you didn't fly anymore. Since the accident, I mean."

Con's breath hissed sharply, as though Abigail had stepped on a land mine that any movement might set off.

"That was no accident," Vernon said.

Abigail nodded, conceding the point. "Well, no, it wasn't. But I was sorry about Cynthia. Such a terrifying way to die, I'd imagine, plummeting helplessly into the ocean like that. She wasn't supposed to be on the plane, just you. I always liked her."

"Don't talk about my wife," Vernon said, pointing the gun squarely at her head.

Abigail continued as though she hadn't a care in the world. "I've always wondered, in her last moments, did she regret her choices? Her decision not to have a clone herself. I guess neither of us will ever know."

Con put a hand on Vernon's arm, gently, insistently, trying to pull him away. He didn't budge.

"And how are your children?" Abigail asked. "I read that some of them are even speaking to you again. Learning to accept their clone father. Very inspirational."

"That's enough," Con snapped.

"Stay out of this, child," Abigail said. "Let the grown-ups talk."

Con tugged at his arm. "Vernon, listen to me. She's baiting you. She wants you to kill her."

"Well, she needs to die," Vernon said.

"But she won't. Think about it. Please. If you kill her, she just downloads to another clone. And this all just starts again."

Vernon blinked as the truth of what Con said seeped down through the bedrock of his anger.

"This has to end," she said. "Don't you see that?"

Grudgingly, Vernon nodded, and his gun hand dropped to his side. "What did you have in mind?"

"Leave her to me. I'll give her the last thing in the world she wants."

"What's that?"

"A long, comfortable life with no way to end it."

"No!" Abigail shrieked, and then lunged for Vernon's gun, but her injuries had hobbled her. Vernon stepped back, easily avoiding the attack. Abigail slipped down the stairs and lay in a heap on the gravel.

"You can have her. But I take the ring," he said.

"How do you know about that?"

Vernon pointed to the sky.

"You always did love your drones," Con said. "You were watching the whole time?"

"I find it pays to keep an eye on what belongs to me," Vernon confirmed. "Which reminds me. I brought a sniper of my own. Should yours interfere, or even scratch her ass, mine will put a bullet through her head. Are we clear?"

"The ring should be destroyed."

"We've been over this, Constance. I didn't agree with you then, and I don't agree now. It's not for you to decide what technologies the human race deserves."

"But you're not going to give it to the human race, just the ones who can afford it."

Vernon pursed his lips in evident frustration. "As ever, your arrogance is staggering. And I say that having been partners with your aunt." He turned to acknowledge Chance for the first time. "Hello, son. Good to see you again. Do you remember me?"

Chance nodded warily.

"Good. That's good. You're very fortunate that your father loves you so much. He's negotiated safe passage for all of you."

Chance glared at the pickup, realizing this was the cavalry his father had promised. He'd sold them out to Vernon Gaddis. "What else did he get?"

"Let's just say any lingering unpleasantness from five years ago is ancient history. Once I have what he stole back in my possession."

"He always was a hell of a businessman."

"And this is business. Give me the ring, and I'll be on my way. I have a plane to catch."

"Or?"

"Let's not think in terms of *or*. You were willing to give it to Abigail to protect your family. I think that should also be a good enough reason to give it to me."

Gaddis's smug confidence made Chance want to argue, but it was a good reason. Twisting the ring off his finger, Chance glanced over at Con. To her credit, she didn't try to talk him out of it. Her cards had all been played. There was no other way for this to end now. He held the ring out in the palm of his hand, the same as he had to Abigail in the very recent past. Vernon took the ring between his thumb and forefinger and held it up reverentially. Chance saw the same look in his eye that he'd seen in Abigail only a few minutes before, one of bottomless greed and anticipation.

Vernon patted him on the shoulder. "We're going to change the world."

"I like the world the way it is," Chance said.

"You've been spending too much time around this one. This is a good thing. The future is bright. I promise. Wait and see," Vernon said with an amicable smile, gracious in victory. "Oh, and one more thing: your policy with Palingenesis has been restored. In perpetuity."

"Keep it. I don't want it," he said defiantly, but then, after a moment, he realized that he meant it.

"You'll regret your decision one day."

"But not for long," he said.

Vernon looked at him quizzically but then must have seen what Chance meant, because he nodded seriously. "As you wish."

With that, Vernon left with a flourish of his hand, like a monarch waving farewell to his loyal subjects. Con started to follow him, seemingly unwilling to surrender, but the sound of a shotgun being racked brought her to a halt. She called after him, sounding hopeful but resigned. He got back in the vehicle without looking back, and after a moment both SUVs peeled out of the yard. The taillights hadn't even disappeared over the hilltop when Abigail, still lying in a ball on the ground, began hectoring Con.

"You stupid, stupid girl. Bravo. All I would have done was kept it for myself. I wanted to live long enough to see the future. I think I deserved that, since it's my invention. Instead you've delivered the secret of immortality into the hands of a man who will commercialize it and make all of your fears come true. So just tremendous work."

Con didn't respond or turn around, but Chance saw her shoulders slump in defeat. He gestured in Abigail's direction, encouraging her to shut the hell up for once. The suggestion fell on deaf ears.

"And you," Abigail sneered, sounding for the first time like the teenager she appeared to be. "I'd have thought you'd be down on your knees begging me to tell you what Anton Brätt confessed before he died."

Maggie appeared at his shoulder and took hold of his arm like a parent cautioning a child not to cross the street.

"About my kidnapping?" he asked.

Abigail sneered. "They were quite anxious to unburden themselves to me. I know the entire sordid story. Anton Brätt, for all his ego, didn't instigate your kidnapping," she said. "Although I can't decide which would be worse, leaving you to wonder or telling you the truth."

"No," Maggie said, snatching up the gun off the ground where Con had dropped it. She pointed it at Abigail. "Don't you do it."

"Why on earth not? The boy's not entirely stupid. He can probably guess. I would just be confirming what he already suspects in his joints," Abigail said with an earnest curiosity. "Why don't we leave it up to him?"

"Chance, I know you don't owe me anything. But please walk away. Just until she's gone," Maggie said, tears filling her eyes.

Even when he'd trusted her with his life, he probably couldn't have done what she asked. Now, if anything, it had the opposite effect on him.

"Oh, he's not going anywhere. Are you, Chance? And besides, deep down he already knows the answer. Don't you, boy?"

"My brother," he whispered. Although he couldn't make sense of it, he knew it was the truth. If he had any lingering doubt, Maggie's reaction had erased it. She swore at no one in particular, perhaps the universe and its monumental indifference to human suffering, threw down the gun, and strode away until she'd left the yard and was swallowed up by the night.

Abigail was watching him intently from the ground. "I said when we met that you weren't as stupid as you pretend."

"And what do you think now?" he asked, sinking down onto his haunches. The jangling cacophony building in his ears made keeping his balance a challenge, but he never once took his eyes off the gun.

Abigail only smiled. "Oh, the jury's out, wouldn't you say?"

CHAPTER
THIRTY-FIVE

Con sat at the top of the porch steps, staring off into the middle distance. She reminded Chance of a coach who'd just lost the big game and couldn't stop studying the court until she'd pinpointed where it had all gone wrong. Yael and her team were busy loading a hooded and shackled Abigail into their vehicle. They'd arrived a few minutes after Vernon departed in triumph and were anxious to get on the road themselves. No one wanted to spend any more time here than was necessary. It was a cursed place, and not even the bright glare of the drones could disguise the suffocating gloom. Even Yael, who'd doubtlessly seen her share of horrors, kept a superstitious distance from the stable.

His parents were yelling in the pickup. He could hear them from here, arguing over Marley. It was heartbreaking to listen to. Chance didn't know what was next for them, now the truth was finally out in the open. He wasn't so naïve to believe that they could forgive one another. But if the war could be over between them, it would feel like a step in the right direction. Chance's contribution to the cease-fire was letting go of his father's deal with Vernon Gaddis. It would have been easy to pick a fight over it. Chance could feel the routine of his animosity striking the match. With an effort, he blew it back out. The truth was, he understood why his father had done what he'd done. He wasn't the real enemy.

Maggie was nowhere in sight. That was fine by him, for now. She wasn't the real enemy either, although he didn't know what that made her. Whatever the case, he was in no frame of mind to go chasing after her. He'd had his suspicions about his brother, but having them confirmed? That was a whole other thing and had done a real number on him. Knowing the truth and admitting it to yourself were two very different things.

The gun was still lying in the gravel waiting for someone to pick it up. He was happy to oblige and tucked it into his belt.

He pointed at the step next to Con, who nodded wearily for him to sit. Yael called out to her that they were ready to go. Con gave a thumbs-up in return but didn't move to stand.

"Are you okay?" he asked.

"So close," she answered. "I was so close."

Chance had nothing to say and for once said nothing.

"Well, at least my aunt can't do any more harm," she said, hunting for a silver lining.

"What will you do with her?"

"Take her back to Virginia. Track down her base of operations in Asia. See if there are any other duplicates of her out there. Wouldn't put it past her. But the real danger now just left in a hurry. There's no limit to the damage he'll do with that tech."

"You really think it's that bad?"

She looked at him sadly. "Did you know that the more money a person has, the harder it is for them to identify facial expressions in others?"

"Is that true?"

"They've done studies on exactly that. Really, the only time the wealthy display any empathy is at the end of their lives. Then they're all charitable giving and boundless generosity. Anything to save their souls and polish up those tarnished legacies. But what do you think happens if the ends of their lives never come? Wealth and power just continue to accrue to a handful of individuals like black holes, swallowing all the surrounding light. Imani Highsmith called clones the *new gods.* She hasn't seen anything yet. Vernon is all set to become a modern-day Zeus."

"I wouldn't be so sure about that."

"How do you figure?"

Chance held up the ring with a magician's flourish. He was proud of himself for only saying *Ta-da!* in his head.

Brow furrowed, Con took it from him and turned it over and over in her fingers. "How? I don't understand. What did you give Vernon?"

"My brother's high school graduation present."

Con grinned at him. "There were two? But Abigail scanned it. When did you switch them?"

"You and Vern were a little distracted fighting over Abigail," Chance said.

Con leaned into his shoulder and laughed with relief. "I would pay good money to see his face when he realizes."

"He didn't strike me as a responsible party," Chance said with a shrug.

"Good luck finding one of those," she said, and then held the ring out for him to take back.

Chance pulled his hands away. It surprised him to realize how much he trusted her. "Keep it. Maybe it can save your life."

"No," she said. "That's not a good idea."

"Why not?"

"Because I don't trust myself with it any more than I trust them. Say I'm able to use it. Say it saves my life. Then what? What about the next time? Or the time after that? Even Pandora would know better."

"So why trust me with it?" he asked.

"Because you tried to give it to me," she said. "You just passed the audition. Anyway, who knows how easily this technology can be abused better than you?"

"Yes, because I abused it."

"But you're not going to, are you?"

He shook his head. Those days felt behind him now. "What should I do with it?"

"Where are you headed next?" she asked. "Back to the city or out to the desert?"

"The desert. I have a stop to make."

"Yeah, I imagine you do. Maybe lose it while you're out there," she said, and then held the ring out to him again. This time he took it, slipping it back onto his finger for safekeeping.

Yael whistled from the vehicle and pointed at the back of her wrist. They stood. Con brushed herself off.

"I'm glad I got to meet you," he said.

She grinned up at him. "Thank you for what you did. My family has a lot to answer for, but I'm happy knowing this won't be a piece of our legacy. I owe you one."

"Write us a song," he suggested.

She laughed. "I just might."

Chance watched her limp over to the vehicle, where Yael helped her into the back. As it began to pull away, the vehicle slowed. Con rolled down her window and called out to him. "Good luck out there. I'll be alive and kicking a little while yet, if you need to talk. We all have to look out for each other now."

———

Maybe it was because Abigail was out of range or maybe the batteries had simply run down, but about the time Con's vehicle crested the hilltop, the drones dimmed and fluttered gently to the ground. Whatever the cause, it felt deeply metaphoric, although Chance couldn't decide of what. He stood in the light of the faint moon, thinking about his brother and what to do now.

"Chance?" a tentative voice called.

It was Maggie. She was standing beside the gray van. He suddenly became very aware of the gun resting against the small of his back.

"I'm sorry," she said as he neared, but he wasn't interested in all that.

"The night we met Lee Conway. How much did he tell me?"

"Everything."

"So I knew about my brother? About you?"

"Everything," she repeated.

Everything. That was a big word. Did it explain why he'd gone home and played Russian roulette that night? He'd even warned himself to leave well enough alone and not go digging it all up again. But he had, of course he had, and so here he was again shouldering the burden that had been put on him and trying to decide what to do, now that he knew.

"And you've been trying to protect me from finding out again," he said. "Was that the deal we made that night? What I made you promise?"

She thought about how to answer before finally nodding. "I swore I'd stay away from you, but that if you found me, I'd do my best to stop you from finding out again. That was the deal."

"But I found out anyway."

"Yeah, I told you that you would. It felt inevitable. Like fate."

"I need you to do something for me," he said.

"Anything."

Even though he knew, he could still feel himself fighting the truth. He didn't know why, but he would believe it, coming from her. "I need you to tell me, so I can hear it out loud. Whose idea was the kidnapping?"

Maggie liked to joke that people were allotted tears at birth. She claimed that after everything she'd been through, hers were all used up. She was all cried out. Chance had never seen her cry. She was now. Not hard, but tears were running down her cheeks. She made no effort to hide them.

"Marley's idea," she said.

"All of it?"

"Please don't make me say that," she begged.

"You owe me this much."

"All of it," she confirmed. "I swear I tried to talk him out of it, but he was convinced no one would get hurt. You know how Marley was. Everything always sounded so simple the way he described it."

"So what happened to make it not simple?"

"I'd been wondering that myself for years. Didn't find out until Lee told us that night. Apparently it was just a stupid mistake. You overheard Marley talking to Anton after they thought you were asleep. The way Anton figured it, killing you was the simplest way to keep their secret. And since you had a clone, what difference did it make? Marley was against it, obviously. That's the moment the kidnapping stopped being a performance and became real. Anton realized he didn't need Marley either. It was the perfect double cross, when you think about it."

"Why?" Chance asked even as he did the math. "When did Marley first think of the kidnapping?"

"Only about six weeks before Thanksgiving."

Six weeks. His brother hadn't refreshed his upload for nearly two and a half months leading up to the kidnapping. Nothing about the kidnapping was in his download. The Marley out in the desert predated his betrayal. "Marley doesn't know what he did."

"No, I don't think he does."

"So what happened afterward, Maggie?"

"Anton was furious. He assumed your dad had pulled a fast one at the exchange. There was talk of payback, but it was just talk. There was too much heat on them to risk it."

"And you and Anton?"

"We agreed to a truce. I swore that if they tried anything, I'd go to the police. Anton made it very clear that I might not have been there when the triggers were pulled, but I was a coconspirator and would go to jail all the same. So I promised to keep my mouth shut, as long as they stayed away from your family."

"How noble of you."

She ignored his barb and finished her story. "I didn't see any of them again after that. Anton and Bear went to Mexico. Paul washed his hands of it all. Lee just kept on being Lee."

"And what about you? Was I just your penance?" he asked, then thought better. "Don't answer that."

"Please? I'd like to try and explain."

"It doesn't matter now."

"No," she said. "I guess not. So what will you do now?"

"Go see my brother."

She looked alarmed. "What are you going to tell him?"

He didn't know the answer to that yet. Part of him didn't have anything to say. Marley had dug a grave for Paul Lin out behind the school bus. It would be a shame to let all that work go to waste. But no sooner had he thought it than he cringed at the mindless bravado. *What good would killing Marley do?* he wondered. But then again, perhaps doing good wasn't in this particular deck of cards. Shouldn't someone have to pay?

"What about you?" he asked.

"I'm staying here," she answered. "When you're gone I'll call the police."

"And tell them what?"

"That I killed Lee Conway."

"I shot him," he said, and then registered her expression. "Didn't I?"

"It was me."

"No. What about the bloody T-shirt?"

"You really think you bought a Con D'Arcy concert T-shirt?" she asked. "We traded shirts."

"You shot Lee Conway?" he said, trying to wrap his mind around it. "Why?"

"Because," she said as if the answer were self-evident, "he was going to kill you."

"So we swapped shirts?"

"He fell on me after I shot him. I was covered in his blood. In shock. You said you had a plan to make it all go away, but we had to switch shirts," she said. "Then you called a paparazzi to come photograph you leaving the scene. I waited at the top of the culvert until you were gone."

"Then you went home, packed a few things, and went to stay with Nan," he said, finally stitching together the two halves of the story into one. "Where I found you."

"That night. You said you had a plan to make killing Lee go away. Didn't quite work out that way, so now it's my turn. I'm going to set the record straight about the kidnapping. Everything."

"Maggie," he said, but didn't know what to say next.

"It's okay. It's time. Who knows? Maybe it'll even stop the city from tearing itself apart."

Chance gave her Val Wolinski's number and said to call her. "She's a hard-ass, but she's fair."

"Wish we'd gone to Alaska," she said.

Chance wished a lot of things. Like that he knew what to say. Most of the time he didn't recognize the pivotal moments in his life until they'd passed. For once, though, he knew one as it was happening. A difficult chapter in his life was coming to an end. Right here, right now, in the dark of this godforsaken ranch. He could feel it in his bones. Didn't that demand the last word? Something profound to match the moment. But then he realized that it didn't matter what he said. The page would turn with or without him.

CHAPTER
THIRTY-SIX

Chance left the ranch, chasing the rising sun. He doglegged his way along the eastern rim of a Los Angeles scarred by fire and rage. After days and nights of protests, the city had fallen into an uneasy cease-fire, at least for the morning. Radio reports described it as a medieval army that had withdrawn from the battlefield to regroup before rejoining the battle. He wondered if the city would believe Maggie's confession and accept that the murder of Lee Conway had been done in self-defense. Was it even about that anymore? Had it ever been? The murder might have given the protesters a cause to rally around, but the death of Lee Conway had only ever been a symptom. As for the disease, well, Chance knew that wouldn't be cured so easily.

Windows down, the wind whipped through the gray panel van. He glanced down at the pistol in the passenger seat. It wasn't much of a conversationalist, more the strong, silent type, and it steadfastly refused to answer his questions. Like what was he driving out here to do, and why did he need a gun to do it? Back at the ranch, his parents had begged him to let Marley be. To leave him alone out there on the edge of the world to make his nickel sculptures and wonder why.

"Why tell him?" his father had implored.

"I promised him I would."

"But what good does it do? He's not even the same person who did it."

That was the same argument Sy Berger had made when Chance had been arrested for Lee Conway's murder: that he couldn't be held responsible because it hadn't been him who'd pulled the trigger. At the time, he'd thought it was a damn clever defense. So why did it sound so flimsy now? He thought about all his father had sacrificed by withholding the truth: his family, his career, his reputation. No, if Chance had to know, then so did his brother. Maybe it would even do him some good.

But just as soon as he'd made a decision, he began arguing the other side again. Maybe the agony of not knowing for certain was punishment enough. A lifetime of wondering what he might have done. And always there was the question of the gun. Around and around Chance went as the miles ticked by.

The overpowering stench of dead fish greeted him before the Salton Sea appeared on the horizon. On a whim, Chance pulled the van over onto the shoulder and bumped to a stop. He rested his chin on the steering wheel and looked out across the dead water, strangely tranquil and beautiful this morning. He took the gun and walked down the embankment. Over the years, the lake had receded, leaving rings of dried salt etched in the earth, so it took a few minutes to get to the water's edge.

The gun felt heavy in his hand. He held it up, sighting it along his arm at a lone pelican floating a ways offshore. The bird watched him with disinterest. He aimed the gun down and fired six times into the lake, curious to know how it would feel. It made a hell of a noise but surprisingly little impression on the water, which rippled as if slightly annoyed at the disturbance and then was still again. When he looked up, the pelican was gone.

He flipped the gun in his hand and heaved it out over the water toward where the bird had been. It landed with a dull splash and disappeared. He twisted the ring off his finger, looked at it one last time, and sent it skipping across the water. He wondered how many years it would take the water to recede enough to reveal either one. By then the poisoned water would have corroded both to the point of uselessness.

But nothing stayed hidden forever, did it?

About the Author

Photo © 2017 Douglas Sonders

Matthew FitzSimmons is the author of the Constance series and the *Wall Street Journal* bestselling Gibson Vaughn series, which includes *Origami Man*, *Debris Line*, *Cold Harbor*, *Poisonfeather*, and *The Short Drop*. Born in Illinois and raised in London, he now lives in Washington, DC, where he taught English literature and theater at a private high school for more than a decade. For more information, visit him at www.matthewfitzsimmons.com.

Printed in Great Britain
by Amazon

19619291R00181